BY NICHOLAS SPARKS

Counting Miracles
Dreamland
The Wish
The Return
Every Breath
Two by Two
See Me
The Longest Ride
The Best of Me
Safe Haven
The Last Song
The Lucky One
The Choice
Dear John
At First Sight
True Believer
Three Weeks with My Brother
The Wedding
The Guardian
Nights in Rodanthe
A Bend in the Road
The Rescue
A Walk to Remember
Message in a Bottle
The Notebook

COUNTING
MIRACLES

COUNTING
MIRACLES

 A NOVEL

NICHOLAS SPARKS

RANDOM HOUSE

NEW YORK

Published in the United States by Random House, an imprint and division of Penguin Random House LLC, New York.

RANDOM HOUSE and the HOUSE colophon are registered trademarks of Penguin Random House LLC.

LIBRARY OF CONGRESS CATALOGING-IN-PUBLICATION DATA
Names: Sparks, Nicholas, author.
Title: Counting miracles: a novel / Nicholas Sparks.
Description: First edition. | New York: Random House, 2024.
Identifiers: LCCN 2024017682 (print) | LCCN 2024017683 (ebook) |
ISBN 9780593449592 (hardcover) | ISBN 9780593449608 (ebook)
Subjects: LCSH: North Carolina—Fiction. |
LCGFT: Romance fiction. | Novels.
Classification: LCC PS3569.P363 C68 2024 (print) |
LCC PS3569.P363 (ebook) | DDC 813/.54—dc23/eng/20240422
LC record available at https://lccn.loc.gov/2024017682
LC ebook record available at https://lccn.loc.gov/2024017683

International ISBN 978-0-593-87472-1

Printed in Canada on acid-free paper

randomhousebooks.com

2 4 6 8 9 7 5 3 1

First Edition

Book design by Caroline Cunningham

For Dr. Eric Collins

He performs wonders that cannot be fathomed, miracles

that cannot be counted.

JOB 9:10

COUNTING
MIRACLES

CHAPTER ONE

I

March 2023

TANNER HUGHES STEPPED onto the porch of the cottage that had once belonged to his grandparents and locked the door behind him. In one hand, he held a duffel bag, in the other a garment bag protecting the suit he'd worn to his grandmother's funeral five weeks earlier.

He looked up, noting a single cloud glowing brilliant white in the morning sunshine. It would be another postcard-perfect Florida day and he thought again that his grandparents had chosen a nice place to settle down for good. Pensacola had always been a military town and many veterans moved to the area to retire; he suspected that his grandparents, especially his former army mechanic grandpa, had fit right in.

He left the key beneath a flowerpot for the realtor, who planned to come by later. The furniture had already been moved out, painters had been scheduled, and the realtor had hinted that the place would sell quickly. Tanner had spent much of the last month sorting through his grandparents' things and processing the final months he'd spent with his grandma.

He glanced over his shoulder one last time, missing her, missing his grandpa. His grandparents were the only parents he'd ever known, his single mother having died minutes after Tanner had been delivered. It felt strange to know they were no longer around, and the word *orphaned* felt apt. After all, his mother had existed for him only in photographs, and until recently, he'd known nothing about his biological father at all. In their taciturn way, his grandparents had implied they hadn't known his father's identity, and Tanner had long ago convinced himself that it didn't really matter. Sure, sometimes he wished he'd known his parents, but he'd been raised in a loving home, and that was all that really mattered.

Pushing his thoughts aside, he started toward his car, thinking it looked *fast* even while parked in the driveway. A reproduction 1968 Shelby GT500KR from Revology Cars, it was candy-apple red with Wimbledon white stripes; even though it was brand-new, it looked identical to the ones that rolled off the line more than half a century earlier. It was the most extravagant thing Tanner had ever purchased for himself, and when it had arrived, he'd wished his grandpa had been alive to see it. They'd both loved American muscle cars, and while this wasn't an original, it was made to be driven, not stored in a collector's garage, which suited him just fine.

Yet, come summertime, it was going to end up in a garage anyway.

Tanner squeezed the bags into the trunk next to a box of keepsakes from the cottage. His backpack was already on the passenger seat. The engine started with a throaty roar, and he headed through town, toward the interstate, passing chain stores and fast-food restaurants, thinking that aside from the beach, Pensacola didn't strike him as all that different from other places in other states he'd visited recently. He was still getting used to the sameness in much of the United States and he wondered whether he'd ever stop feeling like a stranger in the country.

As he drove, he felt his mind drifting through the highlights of his life: a youth spent on a dozen different military bases in Germany and Italy, basic training at Fort Benning in Georgia, nearly a decade and a half in the army. The numerous deployments to the Middle East and after he left the service, his security work with USAID—the U.S. Agency for International Development—all of it spent overseas.

And since then?

He'd pretty much stayed on the move, if only because it was all he knew. Much of the last couple of years had been spent on the road, his travels taking him from one side of the country to the other. He'd filled his phone with photos of national parks and various monuments as he'd reconnected with friends and, more important, visited the families of other friends he'd known in the service who'd passed away. In all, he'd been able to name twenty-three friends who'd been killed or died by their own hand after they'd left the service. Talking with their widows or parents felt right somehow, as though he was getting closer to an answer he needed, even if he still wasn't sure what the question might be.

Though there were a few more families on his list he intended to see, the road trip had been cut short last October, when he learned that his grandma's time was running out. Somehow, despite their regular calls and texts, she'd neglected to mention that she'd been diagnosed with a terminal lung condition a few months earlier. He'd rushed to Pensacola, where he found her propped up in bed and attended by a caregiver. His first thought was that she seemed smaller than he remembered and her breathing was labored despite the oxygen tank, making speech slow and abbreviated. The visible reality of her condition made his stomach clench, and for the next few months, he rarely left her side. He took over much of her feeding and grooming, and often slept on a cot he'd set up in her bedroom. He made calorie-dense milkshakes and mashed her food until it was soft enough to be eaten by a baby; he tenderly brushed her thinning hair and applied balm to her cracked lips. In the afternoons, when she wasn't sleeping, he often read to her from a poetry collection by Emily Dickinson while she focused on the view outside her window.

Because speech became more difficult for her as the weeks went on, he did most of the talking. He told her about the Grand Canyon, Graceland, an ice hotel in northern Wisconsin, and a dozen other places, hoping she'd share in his enthusiasm, but instead, the concern in her expression spoke volumes. *I'm worried about leaving you behind,* she seemed to be saying, *your life is unsettled.* When he tried to explain again that his recent travels had been a way for him to honor the friends that he'd lost, she shook her head. "You need a . . . home," she rasped out, before succumbing to a prolonged coughing spasm. When she recovered, she motioned for him to hand her the pad of paper and pen on her nightstand. *Find where you belong and make that place your own,* she scrawled.

Knowing she'd be disappointed that he seemed no closer to settling down, he didn't tell her that Vince Thomas, an old friend of his from USAID, had reached out to him in January. Vince was leaving for a new gig in Africa. They'd worked together in Cameroon before, and he'd told Tanner that he needed a deputy head of security who was familiar with the country and its politics. Tanner could remember accepting the offer, thinking at the time that it felt like as good a next step as any.

Now, back on the interstate for the first time in months, the flat countryside of northern Florida passed in a lazy blur. After a quick visit with his best friend, Glen Edwards, and his family, Tanner planned to travel to Asheboro, North Carolina, wondering what, if anything, he would find.

Asheboro.

His grandma had written the name of that small town on a notepad, not long before she lapsed into a coma.

II

LIKE PENSACOLA, EASTERN North Carolina was a favorite retirement destination for veterans, and after leaving Delta—army special forces—Glen had landed on his feet. He ran a tactical outfit there that trained police and SWAT teams from around the country, owned a home with his wife, Molly, in Pine Knoll Shores overlooking Bogue Sound, and was raising two kids, both approaching middle school age. Tanner wasn't surprised when Glen met him on the front porch with a bottle of beer as soon as Tanner had stepped out of the car; they'd been through so much together in the service that it almost seemed as though they could read each other's minds.

The house boasted high ceilings and gorgeous views and had the messy, lived-in look of a family, with backpacks piled in the corners and athletic gear stacked near the door. When the kids weren't demanding Glen's attention, they craved Tanner's, showing him videogames or asking if he'd watch a movie with them. He loved it—he'd always liked kids—and Molly, with her easy smile and air of patience, was the kind of woman who brought out the best in Glen.

He spent three days with them, sharing meals and visiting the family. They went to the beach and the North Carolina Aquarium, and in the evenings, they'd chat on the back porch beneath a canopy of stars. Molly would usually head off to bed first, and then Tanner and Glen would have long talks, one-on-one.

The first night, Tanner caught Glen up on his travels and the sights he'd seen before describing his visits to the families of friends he'd lost. Glen sat quietly through that part—he'd known many of them as well—and finally admitted that he wouldn't have been able to do it.

"I'm not sure what I would have even said to them."

Tanner knew what he meant—it hadn't always been easy for Tanner, either, especially when suicide was involved—and the conversation eventually shifted to easier topics. He told Glen about his upcoming job in Cameroon and toward the end, he spoke about his last few months in Pensacola, including the surprising revelation his grandma had finally offered, which explained his upcoming trip to Asheboro.

"Wait," Glen said, once he seemed to fully process the information. "She just shared that information with you now?"

"At first, I thought she was confused, but when she wrote it down, I knew she was serious."

"How'd that make you feel?"

"Shocked, I guess. Maybe even a little angry. At the same time, I knew she believed she'd done the right thing for me by withholding it. Like maybe she thought she was protecting me somehow. And . . . I still love her. To me, they were my parents."

Glen brought his lips together and said nothing, but later, on their last night together, Glen returned to the subject. "I've been thinking about what you told me the other night, and I've got to admit that I'm a little worried about you, Tan."

"Because you think I'm making a mistake by heading to Asheboro?"

"No," Glen answered. "Your curiosity about your past makes perfect sense to me. Hell, if someone dropped that sort of bombshell on me, I'd probably do the same thing. But I'm concerned about the way you've been living since you quit your last job. I mean, I can understand taking a little time to travel around and visit friends or whatever, and I get that you had to take care of your grandma when she was sick. But returning to Cameroon? I don't get that part. It strikes me that you're postponing your life instead of actually living it. Or even moving backward. I mean, you've never even owned a home, right? Hasn't life on the move gotten tiring for you yet?"

You sound like my grandma, Tanner thought, but he kept that to himself. Instead, he shrugged. "I liked it there."

"I understand that." Glen sighed. "Just know that if you ever decide to settle down, you have a job waiting for you with my company. You can live wherever, set your own schedule, and have a chance to work with some of the Delta guys again. Molly even has a sister who's single." He waggled his eyebrows, at which Tanner had to laugh.

"Thanks," he said, taking a swig of beer.

"And about your search . . ."

"I thought you just said you understood my curiosity."

"I do. I was just wondering whether you tried using 23andMe or one of those other DNA sites?"

"I tried all of them, but other than a couple of very distant relatives in Ohio and California—as in many, many times removed—there wasn't anyone. It must have been a small family. But if you have any suggestions that might cut the legwork, I'm open to ideas."

"I don't," he said, "and your plan is definitely old-school, but who knows? It's the way people used to search, right? You just might get lucky."

Tanner nodded, but wondered again what the odds were of locating someone from more than forty years ago, especially when the first and last names were so common as to be almost meaningless. In the United States alone, there were almost two million people with the same last name—he'd googled it—and more than a hundred of them lived in Asheboro.

Assuming, of course, his grandmother's memory could even

be trusted by that point. In her shaky, almost illegible scrawl, all
she'd managed was

Your dad
Dave Johnson
Asheboro NC
I'm sorry

III

FROM PINE KNOLL Shores, the drive to Asheboro took four
hours, and after pulling into town, Tanner swung by a Walmart
for a map, notebook, and pens before finding his way to the library. With help from a nice lady at the checkout counter, he
learned that while the library didn't have phone books dating
back to the 1970s or 1980s, she'd been able to scrounge up one
from 1992. It would have to do.

Next step, finding his father, a man he'd never met.

At one of the library tables, he unfolded the map and divided
the town into four quadrants. Then, using the old phone book, he
jotted down the name and address of everyone named Johnson
and roughly pinpointed their locations on the map; using his
iPhone, he cross-referenced the Johnsons in the recent online
white pages with the older ones from the phone book, circling on
the map those that matched. He figured that if he was going to
start knocking on doors, he might as well try to do it as efficiently
as possible.

He hadn't been able to finish before the library closed, which
meant he'd have to return on Monday. He considered visiting the
county offices as well; property records might aid in his search,
but that, too, would have to wait until after the weekend.

After dropping his things at a Hampton Inn and feeling the need to stretch his legs, he explored the downtown area. He strolled past an antiques store, a florist, and a handful of boutiques occupying the ground floors of buildings constructed early in the previous century. There was a lovely park in the center of town and, despite the thickening clouds in the sky, the sidewalks bustled with people walking their dogs and pushing baby strollers. The scene struck him as a throwback to another era and Tanner tried to picture what it must have been like to grow up here. Had his father somehow met his mother here? he wondered. As far as he knew, his grandparents had never lived here, so how would his mom and dad have crossed paths? More questions his grandma would never be able to answer, he knew, wishing he'd had just a bit more time with her.

He made it back to the hotel not long before the first drops of rain began to fall. He read until dinnertime, immersing himself in a book about the Pacific theater during World War II, thinking about the ways that modern warfare had evolved since then, even if some of the devastating effects on combatants remained the same.

When his stomach started to grumble, he found a sports bar on his phone where he figured he'd get some dinner. When he arrived at Coach's, he was surprised to find the parking lot full. He had to circle the area twice before finding a spot. He walked toward the entrance and after pushing through the door, he was deluged with the sound of multiple TV screens broadcasting a college basketball game on high volume and a packed house of cheering fans. He vaguely remembered Glen mentioning something about March Madness, the NCAA men's basketball tournament.

Tanner maneuvered through the crowd, automatically scanning the faces and body language around him, pegging anyone who was drunk or might be spoiling for a fight. Not far from the bar, clustered around a high-top table, he noted three men who were likely carrying weapons. Each of them had the telltale bulge at the small of his back, but judging by their haircuts and postures, he suspected they were off-duty police officers or sheriff's deputies, unwinding after a day at work. Nonetheless, he chose a spot at the bar where he could keep an eye on them, as well as most of the other patrons. Old habits died hard.

When the bartender finally noticed him, he ordered a burger and a craft beer, something made locally, and enjoyed both. After the bartender came by to scoop up his empty plate, he absently watched the game while finishing his beer. As he sipped, the crowd suddenly roared, making Tanner instinctively freeze. The televisions showed a replay of a point guard sinking a three-point shot. He exhaled, even as he picked up on another sound, one that didn't seem to belong.

A voice. A female voice.

"I said LET GO!"

He turned and saw a young woman with dark brown hair. She was standing next to a booth, struggling to free her arm from the grasp of a young man wearing a backward baseball cap. Tanner counted what appeared to be five teenagers—three guys and two girls, including the brunette—and watched as she was finally able to tear her arm free. While he wasn't eager to get involved, he was wary of men using their physical strength to intimidate women. If the guy grabbed her again, he decided, he'd feel compelled to do something.

Fortunately, the girl stormed off toward the front door. Her blond friend quickly slid out of the booth and followed while the guys at the table began to laugh and shout after the departing girls.

Idiots.

Tanner turned his attention back to the television and when there were only a couple of swallows of his beer left, he set it aside, ready to go. As he gathered his jacket, his gaze traveled to the booth he'd been watching earlier, and he realized that the guy with the backward baseball hat—the one who'd grabbed the girl—was no longer at the table, though his two friends had stayed behind.

Damn.

He hustled through the crowd toward the door. As he emerged from the bar, he scanned the parking lot and spotted Baseball Cap and the two girls near a black SUV. Even from a distance, it was plain that another argument was in progress. Baseball Cap had taken hold of the girl's arm again, but this time her efforts to free herself were futile. Tanner started toward them.

"Is there a problem?" he called out.

Their collective gaze swung in his direction.

"Who the hell are you?" Baseball Cap snarled, without letting go.

Tanner closed the gap between them until he was only a few feet away. "Let her go."

When Baseball Cap didn't react, Tanner stepped even closer. He felt his Delta training kick in, every nerve ending on high alert. "I'm not asking," he said, keeping his voice even and steady.

The young man hesitated another beat before finally releasing the girl's arm. "I was just trying to talk to my girlfriend."

"I'm NOT your girlfriend," the brunette suddenly shrilled. "We went out one time! I don't even know why you're here!"

Tanner turned toward her, noting that she was rubbing her arm as though it still hurt. "Do you want to talk to him?"

She let go of her arm. "No," she said quietly. "I just want to go home."

Tanner met the young man's eyes again. "Seems clear enough," he said. "Why don't you go back inside before you get into trouble?"

Baseball Cap opened his mouth to say something before thinking better of it. He took a step backward and then finally turned to leave. Tanner watched him go. Once Baseball Cap was back inside, Tanner directed his attention to the young woman again.

"Are you okay?"

"I guess," she murmured, not quite meeting his eyes.

"She'll be fine," her friend chimed in. "You didn't need to scare him, though."

Maybe, Tanner thought, *maybe not.* He'd learned that bruising an ego was often better than the alternative. But it was done now. "Have a good night, then." He nodded. "Drive safe."

He headed for the far end of the lot and found his car. Once behind the wheel, he maneuvered down an aisle of the lot to get to the exit. When he passed the spot where he'd encountered the three teens, the girls were gone.

Realizing he needed his phone for directions, he stopped the car and leaned sideways to fish it out of his back pocket. Just then, the large black SUV on the passenger side of his car suddenly reversed into the aisle at full speed. Before Tanner could react, he felt the rear of his car lurch sideways, his head whipped, and he registered the sound of crunching metal. And then all at once, it was over.

Reverting to training, he automatically surveyed himself for injury; his arms and legs were fine, he wasn't bleeding, and though his neck and back might be sore in the morning, he hadn't been seriously hurt.

But his car . . .

He drew a deep breath as he opened his door, hoping it hadn't been as bad as it felt or sounded, but already suspecting the worst. He went first around the front, then to the back, and saw that the rear quarter panel of the Shelby had been mangled to the point that it pressed into the tire. The taillight had been shattered and the impact had also popped open the trunk. When he tried to close it, the latch wouldn't catch.

My car, he lamented. *My new car . . .*

Caught up in a surge of rising anger, Tanner needed a moment to realize that the other driver had yet to emerge from the SUV. It was one of the bigger ones—a Suburban—and he steadied himself by drawing a few long breaths. When he was finally confident that he could deal with the guy without losing his temper, he started toward the driver's side, which seemed unharmed. As he reached it, the door swung open and a pair of thin, shaky legs emerged. Tanner came up short, realizing he was face-to-face with the brunette again. She was pale, her eyes wide, and she made a choking sound before bringing her hands to her face and beginning to cry.

Christ, Tanner muttered under his breath. *That's what I get for trying to be a nice guy.*

He gave her a minute, then another. Her age, coupled with the reaction, made him suspect it was her first accident, always a traumatic experience. Finally, when the waterworks began to subside, she swiped at her nose with her sleeve. Tanner pressed his lips together. He suspected that raising his voice might trigger another burst of tears, which was the last thing he wanted.

"Hey, listen to me," he said, using the same no-nonsense tone he'd used earlier with Baseball Cap. "Before anything else, can you tell me your name?"

It seemed to take a moment for his words to register. She looked up, as though trying to focus. "My mom's going to kill me," she offered.

God help me, Tanner thought. While she hadn't answered his question, he took her statement as a sign she was thinking straight. "I need to make sure you're not physically hurt. Can you turn your head from side to side, like this? And then, see if you can nod, okay?"

Tanner demonstrated, and after a brief delay, the girl slowly mimicked him.

"Does your head or neck hurt?" Tanner asked. "Even a little?"

"No," she said with a sniffle.

"How about your arms and legs, or your back? Do you feel any tingling or stinging or pain or numbness of any kind? Can you twist?"

She frowned briefly before rolling her shoulders and twisting at the waist. "It feels okay."

"I've had some experience with first aid, but I'm not a physician. While you seem uninjured to me, you might want to get checked out just to be safe."

"My mom's a doctor," she said, sounding distracted.

Noticing that her hands were still trembling, he continued to keep his voice reasonable. "The parking lot is private property so I doubt we need to call the police, but can you get your license, registration, and insurance card?"

"The police?" she asked, her voice rising in panic.

"I just said we won't have to call them—"

"She's never going to get me my own car now," she interrupted.

Tanner raised his eyes to the heavens before trying again. "Can you please find the things we need? Registration, license, insurance information."

She blinked. "It's my mom's car," she said, her voice almost a whisper. "I don't know where the registration is. Or the insurance stuff."

"You might try the glove compartment or the center console."

The girl turned, looking off-balance, and slowly crawled up into the SUV. Meanwhile, Tanner used his phone to take photographs of the accident from various angles. When she finally emerged, she handed over the registration and her license.

"I can't find the insurance card, but my mom probably knows where it is."

Tanner flipped the registration over; on the back was the name of the insurance company along with the policy number. "It's right here." He snapped photos before handing the license and registration back to her. Because she obviously had no idea what to do, he retrieved his own documents.

"Do you have a phone?"

She was staring at the damage to the vehicles. "What?"

"Use your phone to take pics of my license, registration, and insurance card."

"My cellphone battery died."

Of course it had. Using his phone, he took pictures of his own cards. "You said it's your mom's SUV, right? I'll text the photos of my info to you and her." He pulled up the dial pad on his phone. "Can I have your numbers?"

"Can't you just text them to me? So I can explain what happened before she starts getting photos from a number she doesn't recognize?"

He considered it. "Okay," he agreed, "I'll send them to you, but can I have her number, too? Just in case?"

She offered her cell number first, then her mom's. He stored the numbers and texted the photos to her; when he glanced at her again, he saw her biting her lip.

"You should probably call your mom to come pick you up," he suggested, offering his phone to her. "Your hands are shaking, you're in shock, and you're in no condition to drive."

She stared at the phone without taking it. "It's our only car."

"How about your friend, then? Is she still here?"

"She left already."

"How about someone else, then? Do you have another friend you can call?"

"I don't know their numbers."

"How can you not know their numbers?"

She stared at him as though he was daft. "They're in my phone and I just told you the battery's dead."

Tanner closed his eyes and tried to visualize himself as a Buddha. "All right . . . How far away do you live? Maybe I could drive you home in your SUV?"

She stared at him as though trying to gauge whether he was trustworthy.

"I guess that would be okay," she finally agreed. "It's not that far."

"Can you pull back into your spot? To separate the cars?"

"Me?"

"Better yet, I'll do it," he said. "Are the keys inside?"

Sniffling, she waved a hand at the car, which Tanner took as a yes. Luckily, the engine started right up, and he inched forward into the space. Next, he checked the rear bumper of the Suburban, but aside from a few scratches, it seemed fine.

"The good news is that yours has hardly any damage," he said, pointing. "Wait here, okay? I'm going to park my car and be right back."

Tanner hopped into his car and found an empty space in the next aisle, driving slowly and wincing at the sickening sound of metal scraping against the tire. In the rearview mirror, the cock-eyed trunk blocked part of his view.

He wondered if he'd have to get the car shipped back to Florida or whether the repairs could be done locally, but figured he'd find out soon enough. For now, he'd drive the girl home and hope he could find a way not to be too irritated to fall asleep later.

Returning to the SUV, he found the girl leaning against the side, morose but dry-eyed. She walked around to the passenger side, leaving Tanner to climb into the driver's seat. Once he got behind the wheel, Tanner pulled up the photo of her license on his phone.

"Do you still live on Dogwood Lane?"

She nodded.

"With your parents?"

"Just my mom," she mumbled. "They're divorced."

He entered the address into his phone, which showed that her house was only eight minutes away.

"Make sure you buckle up," he said before pointing the Suburban toward the exit. Once they reached the main road, he glanced over at her. She had the demeanor of a prisoner being led to an execution.

"You're Casey, right? Casey Cooper?" he asked. "I saw it on your license." When she nodded, Tanner went on. "I'm Tanner Hughes."

"Hi," she managed, her eyes flicking to his. "I'm sorry you have to drive me home."

"It's okay."

"And I'm really, really, *really* sorry about hitting your car."

You and me both. He tried to channel his grandmother's voice. "Accidents happen."

"Why are you being so nice about all this?"

He thought about it. "I guess I just remember that I was young once, too."

She was quiet for a moment before she looked at him again. "My friend said that you have cool eyes. Camille, I mean. The girl that was with me."

He'd been told they were an unusual color—hazel that appeared green or gold depending on the light. "Thanks," he said.

"She said your tats were cool, too."

At this he merely smiled.

She paused, staring out into the night. Then, shaking her head, she spoke in a low voice. "My mom is going to be so mad. Just, like, *beyond.*"

"It might take a little time, but she'll get over it," Tanner said. "She'll be happy you weren't hurt."

She seemed to think about that as they turned into a leafy subdivision, and she directed him through the appropriate turns. Most of the homes were two stories, with brick façades and vinyl siding, fronted by neatly trimmed hedges.

"It's that one," Casey finally said, pointing to one of the brightly lit homes. It had a small front porch complete with a pair of rocking chairs, and as he pulled into the driveway, he saw a flash of movement in the kitchen window.

Tanner shut off the engine, but Casey didn't appear to be in any rush to get out.

"Do you want me to wait here? While you tell your mom what happened?"

"Would you?" she asked. "In case she needs to talk to you?"

"Sure."

With that, she finally seemed to summon her courage. As Casey entered the front door, Tanner stepped out of the SUV and leaned against the door to wait.

About five minutes later, a woman emerged from the house, Casey trailing. *Her mom*, Tanner thought, but as she hesitated for a moment under the glow of the porch light, he found himself looking closer.

She was dressed in faded jeans and a simple white peasant blouse, her long brown hair pulled back into a messy ponytail; at first glance she looked too young to be Casey's mother. Her loose clothes couldn't hide the generous curves of her body, but as she raised a hand to tame a stray lock of her dark hair, he thought he saw an uncertainty there, a tentativeness that hinted at past disappointment, or perhaps regret. *For what?* he wondered.

It was just a gut feeling, an instinctual flash, but as he watched her gather herself and step off the porch, her bare feet with red nails flashing below the cuffs of her jeans, he found himself thinking, *This woman has a story to tell, and I want to know what it is.*

CHAPTER TWO

I

AFTER TRYING AND failing to reach her daughter yet again, Kaitlyn Cooper had set the phone on the counter and stared out the window above the kitchen sink. A half disk of a moon was sandwiched between clouds, casting a silver glow over the front lawn, and she wondered idly whether the storm had passed, or whether it was simply taking a breather.

It didn't really matter, she supposed. With the car gone, she was pretty much stranded at the house regardless of the weather. Surveying the kitchen, she felt the familiar dread of having to clean up from dinner. Instead of diving in, she reached for her wineglass. There was still a little wine left in it and she took a sip.

She supposed she could ask Mitch to help—at nine, he was old enough. But she could see him in the living room, assembling the Lego Star Wars X-Wing Starfighter that she'd picked up earlier from Walmart, and she decided not to interrupt him. It had been an impulse buy—the last thing he needed was more Legos, but since buying things for the kids seemed to work for her ex, she'd figured she might as well earn some brownie points instead of always having to be the bad guy. Besides, Mitch deserved a nice surprise now and then. He was doing well in school and was consistently cheerful at home, and Lord knows, she needed that, if only because she doubted it would last. His older sister, Casey, had been delightful—if strong-willed—when she was young, too. And though she was still a good kid, her teenage years had transformed Casey from a bright, pleasant little girl into a young woman Kaitlyn sometimes found insufferable. Even if, obviously, Kaitlyn loved her.

But those *moods* . . . those *tones* . . .

Kaitlyn knew she wasn't alone in navigating the challenges of raising a teenager, but that didn't make life with Casey any easier. In the past two years, the harder Kaitlyn had tried to be an understanding parent, the more Casey had seemed to challenge her. Like tonight, for instance.

Was it so hard to join the family for dinner one night a week? Between school and homework and Casey's cheerleading practice—and Kaitlyn's hours at the office—having a regular sitdown meal together during the workweek was all but impossible. Because Kaitlyn also saw patients on Sunday evenings, Saturday was the only remaining option. Kaitlyn understood that wasn't always convenient, but it wasn't as though she expected Casey to hang around afterward. All she'd wanted was an hour, from six to seven, or even five to six, and then Casey could have gone her merry way.

But what had she done?

She'd taken the old Suburban without asking, and then spent the next few hours ignoring phone calls and texts from her mother. Most likely she was with her friend Camille, but there was always the chance that she'd snuck out to see Josh Littleton, a young man who'd set off little alarm bells in Kaitlyn's mind. When he'd come to the house to pick Casey up a few weeks back, Kaitlyn sensed something *off* about him, for lack of a better word, and she'd secretly breathed a sigh of relief when Casey later insisted that she wasn't interested in him. In the past week, however, Kaitlyn gleaned that Josh had continued to text Casey, and knowing that Casey might react to her mother's disapproval by provoking it further, Kaitlyn had been careful not to comment.

Watching Mitch peruse the Lego instructions, the lenses of his glasses pressed close to the sheet of paper, made her heart contract just a little. She knew that he'd been bothered by his sister's no-show. He'd had a good day, spending part of the afternoon with Jasper—a nice old man who was teaching Mitch how to carve—and he was excited about going to the North Carolina Zoo tomorrow. But he adored his older sister and he'd asked more than once whether they should postpone dinner until Casey got home. Once he'd realized she wasn't coming, he'd barely spoken at all. Kaitlyn tried to soften his disappointment by joking that she hadn't liked hanging out with her mother when she'd been a teenager, either, but when he merely shrugged in response, she could tell he felt rejected.

She sometimes wondered whether Casey's attitude had been affected by the divorce. Casey had been twelve when they separated, and the following years hadn't been easy for any of them. Casey missed her father; and Mitch viewed George as something akin to a superhero. Kaitlyn, too, had once believed herself lucky in her choice of spouse. George was intelligent and hardworking, and as an interventional cardiologist, he had the ability to remain calm in the most volatile of situations. He saved lives daily, and he was successful enough to allow Kaitlyn to work part-time when the children were young, for which Kaitlyn would always be appreciative.

Moreover, he'd fit perfectly into Kaitlyn's life plan, the one she'd devised even before she started high school, and that now seemed painfully naïve: *Get good grades, go to college and then medical school. Date but don't get serious until the mid- to late twenties;*

after that, meet an intelligent, stable man, fall in love, and be married by thirty. Have two kids, buy a nice home, maintain a rewarding private practice while also treating underserved communities, and live happily ever after.

So much for that, especially the last part. While she was thankful that the sharp, often overwhelming emotions associated with the divorce had waned—and she'd definitely put George behind her—there were moments when she missed the intimacy and quiet moments associated with being a couple. These days, her life revolved around work and the kids, with no time left for anything else—tonight being a prime example—and she reached for her phone again. She tried Casey, listening as her call went straight to voicemail, and disconnected, feeling frustrated. She took a final sip of wine and dumped the remainder into the sink before beginning to clean the kitchen. She'd just finished when she noticed a flash of headlights through the window; a moment later, they swung into the driveway. She heard the familiar rumble of the Suburban's motor and drew a long breath, thinking, *Finally!*

As she left the kitchen, she debated how to handle Casey's infraction. Her daughter was the queen of excuses, but Kaitlyn knew that yelling, or even raising her voice, generally made Casey respond in kind, which would then escalate to the point where Casey screamed that she *hated it here!* before storming off to her bedroom. At the same time, rules were rules, and to Kaitlyn's mind, the young woman had some serious explaining to do.

"Casey's home!" Mitch called out. He was standing in the front window, looking through the curtains. "She's not driving, though. She's with someone."

"Excuse me?" Casey wasn't supposed to let anyone else drive the Suburban. That was perhaps the only rule she'd never broken; the girl loved to drive and would never hand over the keys, unless . . .

Kaitlyn felt a surge of anger course through her.

Unless, of course, she'd been drinking.

Kaitlyn was marching toward the front door when it suddenly swung open. Casey stepped inside, and a single glance at her splotchy face and wild eyes told her that her daughter was really upset.

Before Kaitlyn could utter a word, Casey closed the front door and burst into tears, her shoulders heaving. Kaitlyn wrapped her in a hug, her anger draining away as Casey sobbed, her frame trembling. Somehow in the cloudburst of emotion Kaitlyn noticed that Casey did not, in fact, smell of alcohol. That was good, she mused, even though it was obvious that something else was very, very wrong.

II

IT TOOK A few minutes for Casey to stop crying and sputter out the basics of what had happened: that she'd hit a man's car in the parking lot and that she was sorry and that she didn't know how it happened. Kaitlyn led her to the sofa and forced her to take a few deep breaths. With bloodshot eyes and mascara trailing down her cheek, Casey looked a wreck. Kaitlyn forced herself to tamp down the irritation she felt.

"Let me make sure I have this right," she finally said. "You were at Coach's with Camille, and when you were backing out in the parking lot, you hit a guy's car."

Casey nodded. "I didn't see him behind me. I don't know why."

"Are you hurt? Can you nod your head?"

"I already did all this with him."

"Did what?"

"This medical stuff. He checked me out."

"He checked you out?"

"You know what I mean." Casey waved a hand impatiently. "For God's sake, Mom. It's not like he touched me or anything. And I'm *fine*. He said the Suburban wasn't even damaged."

"You know that for sure?"

"I looked, Mom. But you can go look, too, if you don't believe me."

"It's not that I don't believe you. I'm still trying to understand what happened, all right?"

"I've already told you." Casey sniffed. "Weren't you listening?"

You were a little hard to understand, honey, and I still don't have the full story. But she didn't say that. Instead, "Who's with you now? Is it Camille?"

"No, it's the other driver. The guy I hit. The one with tattoos. He told me his name, but I forgot it."

Tattoos? Kaitlyn blinked. "You let a tattooed guy you don't know drive you home?"

"Nothing bad happened." Casey ran a hand through her hair, then searched her pockets for an elastic to tie it back.

"Why is he here?"

"He didn't think I should drive because I was upset." Gathering her hair into a loose ponytail, she squinted at her mother.

"You do understand you shouldn't have done that. Got in the car with him, I mean."

"What's the big deal?"

With getting into a vehicle with a male stranger? Oh, gee, what could possibly go wrong?

"It's dangerous. You don't know him."

She shrugged. "He seemed nice."

Nice? "I guess I should go speak with him, then."

As Kaitlyn stood and made for the front door, Mitch piped up. "I want to come, too."

"Just stay inside with your sister for now, okay?"

"Oh, no," Casey said firmly. "I'm going out with you."

"Why?"

"To make sure you don't freak out."

Lord help me, Kaitlyn thought, and it was all she could do not to roll her eyes.

She turned on the porch light, then the others over the garage, before stepping out the door with Casey at her heels. She hesitated, taking a few seconds to compose herself before spotting a man leaning against the Suburban, his arms covered with colorful sleeves of tattoos. He must have heard them, and when he stood to face her, their eyes locked. For what felt like a very long moment he simply stared, as though trying to read her. But when he flashed a quick smile, she felt something in her startle. She wasn't sure what she had been expecting, but his appearance somehow surprised her.

He was a little taller than average and clearly fit, his broad shoulders evident under a simple black T-shirt. Even in the glare of the garage lights, she noted the unusual color of his eyes. High cheekbones and a defined jaw created dramatic shadows. The dense waves of his dark hair were cut short, in almost military fashion, and she noticed a flash of silver in the hair near his ears. His faded jeans and loafers looked expensive to her eye, and his smile radiated an easy confidence. Even with the tattoos, he might be a tech guy or consultant or even a doctor like herself, and it wouldn't have surprised her. And yet . . .

She knew that he was none of those things. There was a *readiness* in the way he stood, an almost coiled intensity. No, this wasn't a man who sat behind a desk at work, or crunched numbers or assembled PowerPoint presentations; the sheer physicality of his presence told a different story.

"Mom!" Casey urged. "Why are you just standing here?"

The sound of her daughter's voice broke the spell, and Kaitlyn finally stepped off the porch. As she approached him, his eyes remained locked on hers.

"Good evening," he said, offering his hand. "I'm Tanner Hughes."

She stared at it for a beat, before deciding she might as well be polite.

"Kaitlyn Cooper," she said, keeping her voice cool. "Casey said that the two of you were in an accident?"

"She backed into my car in a parking lot."

"And you thought it was a good idea to drive her home? Alone? Even though she's a minor?"

"Mom!" Casey groaned, and Kaitlyn watched his gaze flick to Casey before coming back to her.

"I get it," he said, his tone understanding, if unapologetic, "and if I were in your shoes, it would probably concern me as well. But I meant no harm. I didn't think it was safe for her to get behind the wheel and her friend had already left. We drove straight here."

"I already told you all this!" Casey bit out, the mortification in her voice evident.

"Then I suppose a thank-you is in order," Kaitlyn said.

"You're welcome. And the good news for you—aside from the fact that Casey wasn't hurt—is that there was hardly any damage. Come take a look."

He walked toward the rear of the Suburban, and by the time she reached the hatch, he was already using the flashlight on his phone to shine it on her bumper.

"Aside from a few scratches, it's fine. There were no issues with the way it drove either."

She had to peer closely to see the scratches, though she figured there might be unseen damage. She made a mental note to drop it off at the service center if she noticed anything amiss.

"How is your car?" she asked.

"That's another story," he admitted. He pulled up the photos on his phone and offered it to her. "There's a few there, so go ahead and scroll through."

Kaitlyn felt their fingers brush as she took the phone from him. She swiped in the wrong direction and found herself staring at a photo of Tanner seated with a well-dressed couple about the same age, on what appeared to be someone's back deck overlooking the water. She found herself thinking, *He has nice-looking friends with kind smiles, so he's probably normal.*

Chastising herself for being nosy, she swiped in the other direction, her eyes suddenly widening. His car looked to be a very expensive classic muscle car from the sixties and would likely cost a small fortune to repair. When she handed back the phone, she had the strange feeling that he'd been studying her with interest.

"I'll let my insurance company know what happened. Did you get all the information you need?"

"I did," he confirmed. "You daughter was very helpful."

"Oh . . . well . . . good," she said, surprised Casey had known what to do. "I'm sorry about your car. I know Casey's sorry, too."

He tucked the phone into his back pocket. "I appreciate it." Again, their eyes met and held for a long moment before she finally glanced away, breaking the connection. "I guess that's it, then," he went on. "It was nice meeting you. You, too, Casey."

"Thanks for driving me home," Casey said with a wave.

"No problem." He turned, starting for the sidewalk.

"Wait!" Kaitlyn called out, caught off guard by the sudden end of the discussion. "Where are you going?"

He spun to face her, though he continued walking backward. "Back to my hotel. I'll call an Uber. If there aren't any around, I'll just walk back."

Casey suddenly poked her in the ribs. Turning, Kaitlyn saw

Casey glaring at her as though asking, *Are you really going to make him wait out here for God knows how long? Or let him walk?* It took a second for Kaitlyn to grasp her meaning, but when she did, she recognized that Casey was right.

"Where are you staying?" she called out.

"The Hampton Inn."

"Can I give you a ride back?" She raised her voice to make sure he heard her.

He paused before answering. "You sure it's no trouble?" he asked.

"It's the least I can do." Though she meant it, she realized that the idea of being alone with him made her a little nervous. "Just give me a minute to put on some shoes and grab the keys."

"The keys are still in the cup holder," Tanner said.

Of course, she thought, *that makes sense.* "Casey, honey, grab my flip-flops from inside the doorway, would you?" As Casey trotted back into the house, Kaitlyn watched Tanner walk back to the passenger side of the car.

When Casey returned, Kaitlyn slid on the flip-flops and murmured, "I'll be back in a few. Will you keep an eye on Mitch for me?"

"He'll be fine," Casey answered. Kaitlyn resisted the impulse to repeat her request. Instead, she found herself absently wondering when she'd last been in a car with a handsome guy she barely knew. College, maybe? High school? Ever?

Kaitlyn tried to clear her head as she got behind the wheel. Starting the engine, she listened for clanking or grinding or scraping as she reversed, but didn't hear anything. Tanner was looking out the passenger-side window.

"Are you in town on business?" she finally asked.

"Personal business," he said, glancing toward her. When he smiled, she noticed that his teeth were white and even. "You wouldn't happen to know anyone named Dave Johnson, would you? I'm guessing he'd be in his late fifties or early sixties?"

She considered it. "I don't think so," she said. "Sorry."

"It's okay. I didn't think finding him would be that easy."

"You don't know where he is?"

"Not yet."

She swept her gaze over him briefly. "Is he in trouble? I mean, are you a bounty hunter or something? Or does he owe you money?"

He laughed. "No, it's nothing like that. I'm not a bounty hunter, I'm not with law enforcement, and he doesn't owe me anything. If I do manage to find him, I just want to speak with him about something that happened a long time ago that involved my family. That's all."

The mysteriousness of his answer was tantalizing, but she knew it wasn't her business. "Good luck finding him, then."

"Thank you." He half-turned in his seat. "Casey mentioned you're a doctor?"

"I'm an internist here in Asheboro."

"Do you enjoy it?"

"What? Being a doctor?" When he nodded, she tilted her head for a moment, as if sincerely considering his question. "I do," she said. "I've wanted to be a doctor ever since I was a little girl." She raised an eyebrow at him. "How about you? What do you do?"

"Not much these days. I sort of walked away from everything three years ago."

"Okay," she said, unsure how to respond to a statement like that. "What did you do before then?"

"I was in the army for fourteen years, the last decade with Delta. Then, after I left the service, I worked for USAID for a bit more than six years."

"Oh," she said, the time line of his life quickly coming together. The military explained the tattoos and the way he carried himself, but she suspected he wouldn't go into further detail about his time in the service. Not with a stranger, not yet anyway, so she asked the obvious. "What's USAID?"

"It's the federal government agency that provides humanitarian and development assistance to foreign countries. It offers support for agriculture, education, infrastructure, public health, and a bunch of other things."

"So you worked in Washington, DC?"

"No. That's where the headquarters are, but the agency has missions all around the world. I worked overseas with the Office of Security."

She digested that. "Can I ask where, or is it classified?"

"It's not classified. There are field offices in a hundred countries, but as for me, I was stationed in Cameroon, Côte d'Ivoire, and then finally Haiti."

"How does a person even get that kind of job? Did you major in international relations or . . ."

"No, nothing like that," he said. "After my discharge, I worked with my TAP counselor to figure out what I wanted to do next. I didn't want to go the military-contracting route, so he suggested USAID instead."

"What's a TAP counselor?"

"Sorry. Transition Assistance Program. It's for vets returning to civilian life. The military likes acronyms."

She nodded, still thinking about what he'd told her earlier. "Aren't you kind of young to be able to stop working for three years?"

"Maybe," he acknowledged. "At the time, it felt like the right thing to do."

"And now?"

"It didn't stick. I'm leaving for Cameroon again in June."

"With USAID?"

"No. It's with IRC this time." Then, as though anticipating her next question, he added, "International Rescue Committee."

She supposed that made sense; he was still young and expenses were never-ending, which meant all breaks eventually came to an end.

"Can I ask how long you were planning to stay in Asheboro?"

"I was thinking that I'd stay until I either find the guy I'm looking for or I don't find him. Now, with my car needing to be fixed, my schedule is a little up in the air."

Kaitlyn looked chagrined. "I really am sorry about your car. From the photos, it looks like it belongs in a museum. Or it did before tonight, I mean."

"It's not a classic," he assured her. "It's a reproduction, only a couple of months old." He told her about Revology Cars.

"I don't know which is worse. My daughter smashing a classic car or smashing a new car."

"I can vouch for the fact that the latter isn't much fun."

The easy way he said it made her smile, and she felt herself beginning to relax for the first time.

"So, are you married?" she asked.

"No. I never took the plunge."

"Kids?"

"None that I know about."

She laughed, a little giddy for some reason. "So where are you from? Originally, I mean."

"Europe, I guess."

She glanced at him, curious.

"Military brat," he said, before offering a quick overview of his youth.

"And where's home now?"

He shrugged, almost in apology. "I'm not really sure how to answer that question."

"You don't have an apartment somewhere? Or a house?"

"I've never had one," he said. "In the army, I either lived in the barracks on base or I was deployed overseas; with USAID, I lived in official, albeit temporary, housing. My friends would likely tell you that I'm not wired to settle down."

She smiled, her mind flashing to the photo of the couple she'd seen on his phone, which triggered another thought.

"Before I drop you off, do you think you could show me your car so I can get more photos? In case my insurance company needs them?"

"Sure," he said immediately. "We were at Coach's. Do you know where that is?"

"I do," she said, rerouting the car in the direction of the bar.

A few minutes later they were searching for a parking spot in an overflowing lot, Kaitlyn wondering why everyone in Asheboro seemed to have descended on this one location.

"The basketball tournament," Tanner explained, as though reading her mind.

They reached the Shelby, but once she took in the damage it suddenly struck her what she'd forgotten.

"You're not going to believe this, but I just realized I don't have my phone with me," Kaitlyn said, flustered.

Tanner's eyes lit up in mirth. "Or your purse, which likely means you forgot your license, too."

Her mouth formed a small O of surprise when she realized he was right. "Ummm . . . I'm not normally so scatterbrained."

"I haven't the slightest doubt about that."

The certainty in his tone—and the directness of his gaze when he said it—made her flush and she turned toward the car, hoping he didn't notice.

"It looks worse in person than it did in the photos."

"It was a pretty good ding, that's for sure."

She watched as Tanner pulled his phone from his pocket; he snapped a series of photos from one angle, then another. Soon she heard the familiar *swoosh*, indicating that the photos had been sent.

"Where did you send those?"

"To you, I'm pretty sure," he said, holding up the phone. "This is your number, right?" She nodded, surprised. "Casey gave it to me. They should be on your phone by now. I texted the ones I took earlier, too."

"Thanks," she said. "I'm a little surprised at Casey—she's usually a very safe driver."

"I think she was upset before she got in the car."

"What do you mean?"

"I saw her arguing with a young man and he had a pretty good hold of her arm. I didn't catch the name, but he had brown hair and was a bit on the tall side."

Kaitlyn's lips formed a tight line as she realized right away that it must have been Josh.

"Thanks for letting me know," she said before shaking off the thought. It wasn't the time or place to go into it, and she forced a smile. "I guess I should probably get you back to the hotel."

They drove largely in silence, but as they approached his hotel, she heard his voice again. "Actually, could you drop me here?" he asked, flicking a thumb toward the passenger window. Her eyes flashed to the rearview mirror as he went on. "I think I spotted a brewpub, and I could use a beer after all this."

She nodded before pulling to a stop.

He reached for the handle and swung the door open before looking back at her. "I know it might sound odd considering how our paths crossed tonight, but any chance you want to join me?"

She opened her mouth in surprise, unsure what to say at first. "Oh," she finally offered. "I'm not really dressed . . ."

"You look beautiful," he said, "which is why I wouldn't forgive myself if I didn't ask."

She stared at him, feeling a tinge of amazement that he'd just called her beautiful. "The kids are probably waiting for me at home," she hedged.

"I understand," he said. "Thank you for the ride, Kaitlyn. It was a pleasure meeting you."

When he hopped out of the Suburban, she thought again about what he'd said to her, and the next words came out before she was even conscious that she'd changed her mind.

"Hold on," she said. "I guess one beer couldn't hurt."

She parked the Suburban on the street before walking beside him, strangely conscious of his proximity. Inside, the pub was only half full, and at the bar they ordered their beers. Kaitlyn couldn't believe she was doing this, even as they found an unoccupied table and took their seats. Staring across the table at him, she took a sip and thought about something he'd said earlier.

"You mentioned that you walked away from everything three years ago, but I'm not sure what you meant by that."

"Oh," he said, leaning back. "Covid left me marooned in Hawaii for a while, and after that, I guess you could say I've been on a road trip of sorts." He went on, telling her about it.

"And you came to Asheboro to look for someone?" she asked.

"Yes."

Because he added nothing else, she again stifled her curiosity, opting for something easier for him to answer. "And you arrived from?"

"I drove in from Pine Knoll Shores this morning. I just spent a few days with a friend there. Before that, I was in Pensacola for a few months."

"What's in Pensacola?"

"My grandma. She was sick."

"How's she doing now?"

"She passed away five weeks ago."

"Oh my God," she said. "I'm so sorry . . ."

"Me, too," he said. "She was a great lady. My mom died when I was born, so my grandparents raised me."

"And your grandfather? Was he with you while you were taking care of your grandmother?"

"He died eight years ago. Heart attack."

She absorbed the information, watching him as he stacked the coasters on the table before spreading them out like a deck of playing cards. He looked up at her, going on. "We've talked a lot about me, so it's your turn now. Did you grow up here in Asheboro?"

"No," she answered. "I moved here in my thirties. I was born and raised in Lexington, Kentucky. I went to college and medical school at the University of Kentucky. Go Wildcats."

He smiled. "What brought you here?"

"George," she said, "my ex. He's an interventional cardiologist and we moved here after he finished his fellowships. He practices in Greensboro."

"How long were you married?"

"Thirteen years," she said. "We've been divorced four years now."

As she answered, she hoped that he wouldn't ask more—the last thing she wanted to do was talk about George—and Tanner seemed to pick up on that.

"Is your family still in Lexington?"

"My parents are. But my older brother lives near Chicago now and my younger sister moved to Louisville six years ago. We all still try to get together as a family back home a couple of times a year, but it's harder now that the kids are older. Well, harder for Casey anyway. Mitch still likes to go."

"Mitch?"

She nodded. "My son. He's nine."

"That's quite an age gap," he observed.

"Casey was a surprise," she conceded. "As for Mitch, once we were ready for another, it took a while to get pregnant. Maybe it was stress, but I don't really know. I was busy back then."

"I'm guessing you're still busy," he said.

She appreciated that he got it, what it was like to be a single working mom. "So no kids, huh? Any regrets?"

"Sometimes," he admitted. "What are your kids like? Tell me about them."

Kaitlyn was mildly touched by his interest, if only because it seemed genuine. "You've already met Casey, so you can probably guess she's seventeen going on twenty-five. She's always been headstrong and smart as a whip, but her teenage years have been trying. Mitch is still in his easy phase."

"And?"

She took a sip of beer before sharing more details about each of them. That Casey was an excellent student with hopes of attending Duke or Wake Forest, popular with friends, and adored her little brother. She spoke about Mitch's love of soccer, even though he wasn't very good, and that he was learning to whittle. She described his obsession with Lego and animals of all types, but especially those that could be found at the zoo.

Tanner tilted his glass toward her in acknowledgment.

"They sound like great kids," he remarked. "And you sound like a great mom."

"I've been lucky," she said. Then, suddenly, she remembered something he had said before. "Earlier you mentioned that you saw a guy grabbing Casey's arm?"

Tanner recounted what he'd seen in more detail.

"No wonder she wasn't paying attention when she started backing out," Kaitlyn reflected.

"Do you know who the guy was?"

"I can guess," she said, frowning. "It was probably Josh. I'm not fond of him."

"I gathered that."

She laughed, before shaking her head. "Sometimes I just wish I could take everything I've learned, all my accumulated wisdom, and just dump it in her head. Instead, she's regularly being forced to learn from own her mistakes, and that's hard for a parent to watch."

He smiled in sympathy. "I'm guessing between work and your kids, you don't get lots of time to just hang out and have a beer. But I can't tell you how happy I am that you did."

Kaitlyn felt the beginnings of a flush creeping up her neck again. *He's flirting with me,* she realized. She hadn't even brushed her hair before leaving the house, she thought with wonder. Yet as he asked her questions about her education and medical training, her hobbies and interests, she found herself responding freely, sharing stories she hadn't thought about in years. The sensation was comfortable and warm, as if she were basking on a sunlit porch.

A little later, though, with her glass still half full, she knew it was time to go. Casey and Mitch were no doubt wondering where she was, but she'd be lying if she said she didn't want to stay at least a little while longer.

Maybe she was imagining it, but he, too, seemed conflicted about calling it a night, even as they rose from the table and strolled back to the Suburban. On the short ride to the Hampton Inn, he was strangely quiet, and when she pulled up in front, he hesitated before getting out of the car.

"I enjoyed that," he said, sounding sincere. "Thank you for joining me."

"I had fun," she agreed.

Tanner seemed to be wrestling with something before saying, "Can I see you again? Since I'll have to stay in Asheboro at least until I get my car sorted out?"

Kaitlyn hesitated. This was the moment to shut this down—whatever this was—and the rational part of her knew it was the right thing to do. Her life was busy enough and she knew he'd be leaving soon, so why risk forming an attachment? Logically, she knew exactly what to do, but she couldn't quite make herself tell him no.

"Sure. Why not?"

If he had sensed her hesitation, he didn't show it. "What are you doing tomorrow? If you're not busy, maybe we could grab lunch."

"Oh, well, I promised to bring Mitch to the zoo," she said, stumbling over her words. "And tomorrow night, I have house calls . . ."

He raised an eyebrow. "You do house calls? I didn't know that doctors still did that."

"It isn't common, but it's important to me and it helps to prevent hospitalizations. There are some people out there who just won't go to a doctor. Maybe they're in the country illegally, or they don't have transportation, or they're agoraphobic, or they're afraid of the cost, or whatever. So I go see them."

"How many are there?"

"Thirty or forty? I don't see them all every Sunday, of course. I rotate through them, but it'll still take me two or three hours."

"I'm impressed. Even more than I was already, and that's saying something. And I understand tomorrow night's a no-go, but how about the three of us have lunch at the zoo?"

"You want to go to the zoo?"

"Why not? It would beat being stuck at the hotel all day."

Again, she reminded herself that there were countless reasons to just say no, and yet, as she returned the curious warmth of his gaze, she realized that something inside her—the part of her so reluctant to take chances—had shifted in the last hour.

"Okay," she said. "How about I pick you up at half past eleven?"

III

ON THE DRIVE back to the house, Kaitlyn found herself thinking about Tanner, and trying to process the last couple of hours. Had someone told her that morning how she was about to spend her Saturday evening, she would have laughed aloud and sworn that the very notion was ludicrous. Drinks with a guy she just happened to meet? Flirting? Agreeing to see him again tomorrow? In her real life, things like this just didn't happen and she drew a long breath, feeling a bit lightheaded.

She drove home on autopilot. When she turned onto her street, it took her a moment to recognize there was a newish black pickup truck slowly backing out of her driveway. Confused, she slowed the Suburban, watching as the truck reversed to a stop in front of her house, then began rolling forward, its headlights making the asphalt look as though it was glowing.

She frowned in confusion, realizing that someone had been at her house. As the truck began to accelerate, it rolled past her and she recognized both the truck and the driver.

Josh, she realized, and all at once, thoughts of Tanner seemed very far away.

Trying to stifle her irritation, Kaitlyn parked in the driveway and pushed through the front door, surprised to see that that the living room was empty, and the television had already been turned off. The kitchen, too, looked deserted, and heading upstairs, she peeked into Mitch's room. He'd already taken his bath and was pulling on his pajama top, his hair still wet and poking in all directions.

"Hey, Mom," he said, wiggling into the sleeves.

She smiled. "I'm surprised that you're already getting ready for bed."

"We're going to the zoo tomorrow and I don't want to be tired."

"About that," she said. "Would you care if someone joins us tomorrow?"

"Who?"

For a moment, she was at a loss for how to describe Tanner. *A man I just met? A stranger? The guy Casey crashed into?* "A friend," she finally offered, knowing that while it wasn't exactly true, it was better than the alternatives.

"Fine with me," he said with a shrug. Then, after a moment, he lifted his gaze. "Are you going to go yell at Casey now? For wrecking that guy's car?"

"I'm not going to yell at Casey," she said. "I just need to talk to her."

"You two always yell when you say you're going to talk."

Not wanting to debate him, she offered a quick kiss on his head. "I'll see you in the morning, okay? Love you."

After turning off the overhead light, she left the door cracked—Mitch liked it that way—before heading to Casey's room. She knocked a couple of times without hearing an answer. Finally poking her head in, she saw Casey lying in bed on her stomach, a textbook propped open before her. From the doorway, Kaitlyn could hear the faint strains of music coming through Casey's headphones, which explained why there'd been no answer. Casey's eyes rose to meet her mom's as she slid the head-phones off.

"It took you long enough to get home," she said, her expression already wary.

Kaitlyn was amazed at Casey's knack for putting her mom immediately on the defensive. "Tanner and I stopped for beers before I dropped him off, and we ended up talking longer than I thought we would."

"You two went out for drinks?"

"One beer and I didn't even finish it," Kaitlyn said, then changed the subject. "I came to ask if you had a few minutes to talk."

"I guess," Casey finally answered, theatrically closing the text-book.

Kaitlyn crossed the room and took a seat on the bed. Figuring it was best to come straight out with it, she asked, "Was Josh at the house just a few minutes ago? I thought I saw him pulling out of the driveway."

"He came by to apologize," Casey said.

"Casey . . ."

Casey rolled her eyes. "I already know what you're thinking, Mom. No, I didn't invite him. No, I didn't know he was coming. No, I didn't want him here, and no, I didn't let him in the house. I already know that you don't like him, okay? And I already told you that I don't like him either."

"But you saw him earlier when you were at Coach's, didn't you?"

Casey's eyes flashed. "I didn't plan on seeing him! I met Camille there, okay? She wanted to talk to me about Steven because they'd just gotten in this massive fight, and then Josh and his brother and Carl suddenly showed up and sat down at our booth. What was I supposed to do?"

Steven was Camille's on-and-off boyfriend, and their

relationship—as far as Kaitlyn could deduce—included endless drama and one crisis after another. Which likely explained why Casey had taken the Suburban without asking.

"You also missed dinner, and when I tried calling you . . ."

"I'm sorry about dinner, but Camille was sobbing, and I already explained that my phone battery died," Casey shot back. "When I first got home, remember?"

Kaitlyn wasn't sure she recalled that part, but then again, Casey had been largely incomprehensible.

"About the accident . . ."

Casey rolled her eyes. "For the millionth time, I'm very, very, *very* sorry about the accident. It was a stupid mistake, and I didn't mean to do it, and I wish it never happened, and I'll never do it again. You can ground me or whatever you're planning to do."

Kaitlyn ignored the martyrdom in her tone and tried to keep her voice steady. "Like I said, I wanted to talk to you about Josh."

"We already did."

"Did he get physical with you earlier? In the parking lot? And is that why you weren't paying attention when you were backing out?"

Her eyes narrowed. "I guess that guy told you Josh grabbed my arm, huh? Is that what you two were talking about all this time? While you were out for drinks?"

Kaitlyn ignored both the questions and the accusatory tone. "You do understand that no one should ever grab you, right?"

"Don't you think I know that?" Casey snapped. "That's why I was upset! I'm not dumb, Mom."

"I know you're not dumb—"

"Then stop acting like I am!" Casey shouted, cutting her off. "I don't even know what you want from me anymore. I've already apologized for everything, over and over, and oh, by the way, in the meantime, I ace every test, I babysit Mitch whenever you need it, and I'm always in by my curfew. It's Saturday night and instead of going to a party, I'm studying for midterms. I don't drink or do drugs, but you seem to act like I'm this awful person . . ."

"I don't think you're awful," Kaitlyn said, surprised, wondering where all this was coming from. "I'm not sure where you get that idea . . ."

"You're always trying to tell me what to do, like I'm not measuring up somehow! I get that I'll never be perfect like you, but at least I haven't forgotten how to be happy."

Kaitlyn blinked at the comment, stung to the point that she wasn't sure how to respond. She said a quick good night, and then, flustered, wandered back down the stairs.

She sat on the couch, her mind spinning with all that had happened that night, from the accident, to meeting Tanner, to agreeing to see him again the following day. In any other situation, she knew it would be all she'd be thinking about, but now . . .

Did Casey really think her mom had forgotten how to be happy?

And, more important, had she?

CHAPTER THREE

I

EARLIER THAT DAY, the old man and the boy had sat in a gazebo. It had started to rain after they arrived, and water sluiced off the roof on all sides, forming puddles beneath the nearby swing set and slide. It was a soft, steady rain that followed more than a week of warmer than normal spring days, and Jasper smiled to himself, knowing exactly what that presaged.

They were whittling basswood with pocketknives, as they did every Saturday afternoon. The gazebo and the grassy play area were about a quarter of a mile from Jasper's cabin but within sight of Mitch's house. It allowed the boy's mom to keep an eye on them, which bothered the old man not in the slightest. Instead, he continued to work the pocketknife, putting the finishing touches on a lion with a flowing mane. The boy, he knew, had a fondness for zoo animals, and he was working on something that resembled a turtle, though on closer inspection, Jasper concluded it might be a spider. A small pile of shavings accumulated at their feet, the flecks sometimes landing on Arlo.

The dog was a part Labrador, part mystery mutt who'd darted, shaking and quivering, into the old man's cabin during a thunderstorm more than twelve years ago, when the Jasper had opened the door to peer out at the sky. At the time, Arlo wasn't much past the puppy stage, and the old man had given the dog an egg sandwich and some water, waiting for the storm to pass. The following day, Jasper had tacked up flyers and visited the veterinarians in town to find the owner, but no one ever claimed the dog. Jasper figured that Arlo, in his panic and fear, had jumped from the back of a pickup truck, his original owners none the wiser until they'd reached their distant destination, wherever that might be.

As for choosing the name Arlo, the dog had reminded Jasper of the young Arlo Guthrie, with his long shaggy locks and serious gaze; Jasper had been a fan of Guthrie's, back in the day. Now, with the dog's black muzzle that had turned largely white, and jowls that resembled the singer's droopy mustache, the name seemed even more appropriate. These days, Arlo was content to spend most of his time lying at Jasper's feet and snoring, or aimlessly wandering to his food bowl on the off chance something extra had been added.

For more than a decade, it had been just the two of them; in the decades before that, Jasper had lived alone. But the boy was nice company, and Jasper liked the kid's mother, too. Not in that way, mind you. Jasper had loved his wife, Audrey, and though she'd been gone for more years than they'd been married, her absence still left hollow places in him that he knew he'd never fill again. But Jasper had come to trust the boy's mother with all matters related to his health, which probably could have filled a small medical encyclopedia. His immune system was endlessly wonky, his heart prone to fibrillation, and both his blood pressure and cholesterol were high. Bulging disks in his lower back often led to painful spasms and numbness in his feet. Throw in mild tinnitus, slow-motion prostate cancer, and joints so arthritic that

they crackled and popped and ached whenever he moved, and it
was clear his body was slowly giving up the ghost. It was his skin,
though, that most concerned her. It was a horror show, and
though she hadn't been able to fix the problems, she'd largely
kept it from getting worse, which he considered a blessing.

It was her nature, though, that he most appreciated. She didn't
fuss at him about his diet, which mostly consisted of canned
soup, canned chili, or sandwiches, or lecture him about the importance of eating even when he wasn't hungry, since he'd been
losing weight the last couple of years. She never complained that
Jasper brought Arlo with him to his appointments. And, most
notably, she hadn't dropped her gaze when he first took a seat on
her examination table three years earlier. Dr. Jenkins had retired,
his patients were assigned to other physicians, and Jasper had
expected the lady doctor to reflexively look away. Most people
did, after all, and Jasper didn't blame them. Burn and grafting
scars covered more than half his body and had robbed him of his
hair; other patches of skin, including the parts of his neck and
face that hadn't been burned, were plagued by chronic psoriasis.
In that first meeting with her, he'd joked that on Halloween, he
could scare all the kids without even wearing a mask. Responding in a gentle but firm voice, she said she doubted that, since his
eyes were so kind. A lie, obviously, but he accepted it because her
eyes were kind as well.

Jasper had recognized the boy from a photo on her desk. Small
talk revealed that they didn't live too far apart. The doctor's house
was in a subdivision near Jasper's property. His land was bordered on three sides by the Uwharrie National Forest, and from
the subdivision, the quickest way to get to the forest was to cut
across the old man's property. Jasper had posted No Trespassing
signs and painted half a dozen of his tree trunks purple; nonetheless, some folks were perfectly content to traipse across his
land. Including the boy.

He'd seen the kid for the first time last summer; he'd been sitting on his porch, and the boy cut through his yard alone. He was slight and sported thick black-framed glasses and overalls; he carried a slingshot and a handful of paper targets. He reminded Jasper of his sons when they'd set out on quests for boyhood adventures, so Jasper kept quiet and merely continued to whittle.

A few days later, when the boy walked past his cabin a second time, Jasper recognized him as the kid in the photo on his doctor's desk. He'd set some of the animal carvings he'd whittled over the years on the ancient porch rail, and when the boy walked past on the way out of the forest, he slowed and then stopped to get a closer look. He asked Jasper what he was doing.

"I'm whittling an owl," Jasper responded, his head bowed. He knew from experience how the boy would react as soon as he revealed his face.

"Is whittling the same as carving?"

"It is," Jasper said, before finally raising his head. The boy took an involuntary step back. The lenses on his glasses were as thick as jelly jars, magnifying the size of his eyes.

"You're him," the young boy stammered. "The man in the cabin."

"I suppose I am," Jasper growled, already anticipating what would come next.

The boy swallowed. "Do you really eat children?"

Jasper had heard the rumor before but wasn't sure where such ideas spawned. Teenagers, probably, who wanted to scare their younger siblings, or maybe people with evil hearts.

"No," he said. "I'd rather have tomato soup or chili."

"I didn't think so. My mom told me it was a lie and that you were actually a nice man."

"She's a kind lady, your mom. Good doctor, too."

"What happened to your face?" the boy ventured.

"Life," Jasper answered, the way he always did. Then, because he was finished with the figurine he was whittling, he tossed it toward the boy. The boy scooped it up from the dirt and turned it over and over, inspecting it closely. "You made this? From a piece of wood?"

"I did."

"You made all of them?" he asked next, pointing to the railing.

"Yes."

The boy finally drew near, peering at them. "They look like they came from a store!"

Jasper knew it was meant as a compliment and he smiled, but because his smiles often looked like frightening grimaces, he quickly ducked his head again. He cleared his throat. "You can have the owl if you want. I have plenty of animals, as you can see."

Later that day, the boy returned with his mother, the doctor. She carried with her a covered plate, and as usual, she met his gaze directly. In addition to saying that she'd grounded her son for entering the forest without permission (*Because his sister said he could, even though she was supposed to be watching him, so she's grounded, too!*) she made the boy apologize for trespassing. And she made him apologize for the rude questions he'd asked.

Jasper accepted both apologies and said that her son could cross his property anytime he wanted. She then instructed the boy to return the carving, but Jasper insisted that he'd intended it as a gift and said again that the boy could keep it. It was then that she uncovered the plate and proffered it to him, revealing a mountain of homemade cookies. After biting into one, he was startled to hear the boy ask in a timid voice if the old man would teach him to whittle. Jasper chewed silently as he considered it. He was out of practice talking to people and hadn't spent time with children in decades, but in the end, maybe because he liked the doctor, he agreed. And he'd met the boy at the gazebo ever since.

It was a good thing, he came to learn. He enjoyed watching the way the boy puffed up with pride whenever the old man handed him a pocketknife. He liked the way the boy called him Mr. Jasper—using his first name as opposed to surname—like many southerners did. Best of all, the boy no longer refused to meet the old man's eyes or seemed perturbed by his appearance, which made it matter not at all that the boy still couldn't whittle worth a lick.

II

"Wow!" the boy had exclaimed that day. "Is that a lion?"

"Yup." Jasper nodded, making little grooves to highlight the mane, putting on the final touches. In his mind, he still sometimes liked to think of him as *the boy*, rather than Mitch.

"How's this?" the boy asked, holding out the turtle or spider or whatever it was supposed to be.

"Hmmm . . ." Jasper struggled with what to say.

"It's going to be Arlo when I'm finished."

"Hmmm," Jasper repeated.

"I did just what you said," the boy said. "I imagined it first, but I think I might have messed up the legs. Do you think you can fix it?"

Jasper set the lion aside and took the carving. "Let me see what I can do." He peered more closely at it before asking, "How's school?"

"It's fine." The boy shrugged. "Kinda boring, though."

"How's your mom?"

"She's fine. She works a lot."

"And your sister?"

The boy's sister was eight years older and the boy was crazy about her.

"Okay, I guess. She made popcorn and watched a movie with me when Mom had to work, but usually, she goes out with her friends. My mom says it's because she's a teenager."

"Hmmm."

"What else did you carve this week?"

"I didn't. My hands were hurting too much."

"Did you take a Tylenol?"

It was the same question he always asked when Jasper mentioned the pain.

"Sure did."

"Good," the boy said, sounding authoritative, like his mom. He even looked like her, come to think of it, something about the gentleness of his mouth, the way his slow smile spread across his face. They were alike, those two. Sensitive souls.

For a long moment, neither of them said anything else, but that wasn't unusual. Jasper began to work the pocketknife, and it took a few minutes for Arlo's legs to vanish, the dog's body eventually rounding into a curl of sleep. It was all Jasper could do to keep Arlo from looking like he'd been run over by a steamroller, starfished on the pavement.

"Did you hear about the white deer?" the boy asked.

"White deer?" Jasper paused his whittling.

"It was on the news. My mom showed me. There's a big white deer in the Uwharrie forest. There was even a blurry picture of it. Have you seen it?"

"No," Jasper said, a childhood memory rising unbidden, like the ghost of something from another life. His hand began moving again, continuing to sculpt the wood. "I've seen lots of deer, but never a white one."

"I don't think it's real. I mean, is there even such a thing as a white deer?"

"There is," Jasper answered. "It's an albino, which means that the deer doesn't have the usual pigment in its coat or nose. They're rare, though. Most of them die when they're young."

"Why? Are they born sick?"

"They don't blend in like other deer, so they can't hide as well. They tend to get killed."

"By bears?"

By hunters, Jasper thought. The kind of hunters who wanted to kill something rare and beautiful, simply because it was rare and beautiful. "Maybe bears," he said.

"Wow!" the boy suddenly piped up, leaping to another subject as he often did. "Arlo looks like he's sleeping!"

He was referring to the carving but could easily have been talking about the dog, who had begun to snore at their feet. Arlo's back leg was twitching, albeit slowly; he was no doubt lost in dreams of running through meadows or fleeing from the sound of thunder.

"Even if there isn't a white deer," Jasper confided, "there's another secret in the forest." Kids loved secrets; his had been the same when they were young.

"What secret?"

"Morels," Jasper announced. "It's a kind of mushroom. The weather's been cooperating lately, and they'll be ripe for picking tomorrow."

The boy crinkled his nose and looked at the old man as though he'd proposed eating worms. "Mushrooms?"

"Not just a mushroom. A *morel.* Which is why it's important to keep it secret."

"Why is it a secret?"

"Like white deer, they're special, the best-tasting mushrooms in the world. If word gets out, people will drive here from all over the state to hunt for them."

"How do you know where they are?"

"That's a secret, too. But I'll make sure to get enough for your mom. I'll even clean 'em for her, to get all the dirt and little bugs out."

The boy looked even more skeptical. "Bugs?"

"Like I said, you have to clean 'em first. And after that, you cook 'em in butter with a little salt and there's nothing better in the whole world."

The boy pondered this. "I think pizza is probably better," he finally declared.

"Hmmm."

When Jasper finally finished, he handed the carving back to the boy, who looked from it to Arlo and back again.

"Wow!" he exclaimed. "I'm going to put this with the others in my room."

Jasper nodded, amazed at how much he still missed his children. *If only he could do it all over again. Somehow make everything right.*

"Let's clean up the shavings and get you home, okay?" He sighed, handing the boy his jacket. "Your mama probably has supper going."

III

AFTER GRABBING HIS umbrella, Jasper removed his bandanna from his back pocket and wrapped it around his face like a mask. It was mainly for the benefit of others, especially little kids. For a couple of years there, when the world was going crazy with fears about Covid and everyone wore masks in town, he'd been able to shop for groceries while feeling almost normal. Though he wouldn't admit it to anyone, he sometimes missed those days.

They set out toward the boy's house, Arlo wandering along beside them. Years earlier, Jasper remembered, he'd tried to stop the developer from building the subdivision the boy's family lived in. The town of Asheboro had been creeping ever southward, getting closer and closer to his cabin, and he'd complained to the county commissioner at a public meeting about the revised zoning laws. But deals had been made and pockets had been lined and now there were tracts of identical homes where once there was nothing but virgin forest and farmland.

In his youth, there'd been trees to climb and caves to explore and forts to build and creeks to fish for miles in every direction outside the town limits. He was grateful for the Uwharrie National Forest, but even that had changed over the years. These days, he knew, the forest was *organized,* from official parking lots and camping areas to designated paths instructing people exactly where to walk and specific trails where Jeeps were allowed to bump over rocks. As though people couldn't be trusted to figure out what to do or where to hike or pitch a tent on their own. It was just another example of the world leaving him behind. These days, it was all computers and phones that took pictures and screens that hypnotized adults and children alike. Last week, he'd walked past a restaurant and seen four people eating lunch together without speaking, all of them lost in their phones.

Jasper knew the lady doctor worried that walking the boy home might be too strenuous for him, what with his arthritis and all, but walking was just about the only exercise he could still do. He hadn't even been able to chop wood for the potbellied stove in the kitchen the previous winter; he'd had to order it already split, which had been downright discouraging. Anyway, the boy seemed to understand that Jasper could only go so fast.

At the boy's house, the porch light was already on. Jasper closed the umbrella, remaining on the porch as the boy pushed through the front door. He removed the bandanna from his face—the doctor always insisted he take it off—but reminded himself to put it on again as soon as he left.

"Mom! I'm home," Mitch called out. "Look what I carved!" A moment later, the doctor was walking toward him, wiping her hands with a dish towel.

"Hi, Jasper," she said.

"Hi, Dr. Cooper."

That slow smile dawned on her face. "How many times do I have to tell you to call me Kaitlyn? Do you want to come in? I can make some coffee if you're interested."

"No thank you, but I appreciate the offer," he said.

"Can I convince you to stay for dinner?" she asked. "You're welcome to join us."

"Again, it's kind of you to offer, but I'll have to pass."

She'd asked him to join them multiple times and he'd always declined. By this point, he was pretty sure they were both going through the motions. Most evenings, he couldn't eat much at all without his stomach pitching a fit. "I do have a question, though, if you don't mind my asking," he went on.

Her expression took on a professional air and he could tell she assumed it was something medical. "Yes?"

"Mitch mentioned there's news about a white deer? And a picture of some sort?"

She blinked, looking momentarily confused. "Oh . . . yeah. It was on the news a couple of nights ago, and yesterday, one of my patients mentioned it. I guess it's been a long time since there's been a sighting around here."

So it's true, the old man thought to himself, feeling a twinge of amazement.

"Do you know where in the forest? I mean, was the photo taken nearby, or was it near Candor or Mount Gilead . . ."

The Uwharrie, after all, spanned more than fifty thousand acres.

"It was right off Scenic Road over there," she said, pointing vaguely in the general direction. "A woman took the photo from her car, which was why it was so blurry."

"Well, I'll be," he muttered, noting that it wasn't all that far from his cabin. Not far, in fact, from where he'd planned to begin his search for the morels.

IV

THE NEXT MORNING, before the sun had risen, Jasper sat at the wooden table in the small kitchen of his cabin, finishing his second cup of coffee. As he'd hoped, the rain had tapered off after midnight and the sky had cleared. With the temperature already rising, he knew the morning sun would work its magic.

He was placing the empty cup in the sink when he heard the shot ring out, the sound distant but unmistakable. He stepped out onto the porch, but it was still too dark to see much. He knew the Uwharrie was rich with game; hunters flocked to the forest from October through the end of December in search of deer, then returned in early April for wild turkeys. Young people could hunt with their parents for a week before the official season opened, but he'd had those dates marked on the calendar for months and was certain that the youth season wouldn't begin for another six days.

And why a rifle, not a shotgun? Despite the tinnitus, he could still tell the difference. The sounds of the two were as different as winter and spring, and a rifle didn't make sense. If someone was getting an early, albeit illegal, start to the turkey season, he should have heard a shotgun.

Rifles, on the other hand, were perfect for deer.

Standing on the porch, he thought about the white deer again and felt his stomach coil. In the distant past, he probably would have said a prayer for the deer's safety, but he was no longer that man. Still, he debated whether to head into the forest as planned. He had no desire to run into any poachers.

Deciding to play it safe, he took a seat in the rocker. He watched for lights in the forest—poachers often used spotlights to freeze deer—and listened for a second shot. But he heard nothing as the sky slowly began to brighten, bringing detail to the shadows. He heard a red-bellied woodpecker tapping on a tree and saw an eastern cottontail rabbit at the corner of the work shed. A low layer of mist hung just over the ground and began to sparkle as morning sunlight slanted through the trees.

Poachers generally avoided daylight, but there was no reason to take foolish risks. Rising from his seat, he entered the cabin, careful not to let the screen door slam. He walked through the living room, with the ancient TV and wood-plank walls and faded couch, passing into the back porch, where he kept gear. After reaching for a bright orange vest to wear over his jacket, he grabbed one for Arlo, too. Calling the dog over, he fastened the vest around Arlo's aging, barrel-chested torso.

Back in the kitchen, he stashed a thermos with more coffee in his backpack along with two bottles of water, a peanut butter and honey sandwich, and a bowl for Arlo. He grabbed a bandanna and finally slipped a few small Milk-Bone dog treats into his pocket. Arlo loved those things. He made sure to grab his nitroglycerin tablets in case his heart started acting up. Then, reaching for a five-gallon plastic bucket, he retraced his steps through the house and out the front door, Arlo at his side.

There was a joy in foraging for morels, which Audrey had introduced him to the first time he brought her here. Back then, she'd described it as a treasure hunt, but Jasper would always remember the day for another reason, if only because it had changed his life forever. It was a few days after his father's funeral and Jasper was so lost in his grief that he could barely think straight. He was seventeen years old and he'd been driving in downtown Asheboro when he stopped at a red light near her mother's clothing store. Audrey, who was putting out a Sidewalk Sale sign, had spotted him behind the wheel. Like many people, she'd heard what had happened to his father, and on the spot, she decided to hop into the truck with him, much to her mother's consternation and Jasper's astonishment.

He drove with her to the cabin, his eyes sometimes blurring with tears. The ache of his father's death was still too painful to discuss, something she seemed to intuit. Instead of pressing him to talk, she'd taken his hand and simply traced the outline of his thumb with hers. The unexpected gentleness of her touch was like a balm to his stricken soul.

He showed her the cabin that he and his father had built, before slowly wandering the rest of the property. Near the northern edge of it, a few steps from the Uwharrie, at the base of a cracked and toppled elm tree, she discovered the morels. There was another small patch less than thirty yards away, and after bringing them back to the cabin in the hem of her dress, she carefully cleaned them before cooking them with butter and a few pinches of salt on the potbellied stove. It was the first meal they'd ever shared together, and afterward Jasper was finally able to speak about the man who'd raised him.

As for the morels, they were like nothing he'd ever tasted, and it took some time for him to fully appreciate their earthy, almost nutty flavor. But she loved them, and when they were married, Jasper made a promise to always seek them out for her. He found the task easier said than done, however—the morels seemed to have disappeared—so he took it upon himself to learn everything he could about them. He even drove to Raleigh to meet with a professor at North Carolina State, coming away with a method that was said to help to cultivate the spores. It involved mixing distilled water, molasses, and salt, along with morels, all of it strained through cheesecloth, after steeping a couple of days. Jasper spread the mixture in the places he'd originally found the morels, then spread more around other nearby dead and decaying trees. Within a few years, the morels were back, this time in abundance. Since then, until about a decade ago, he'd spread the mixture annually.

In the beginning, there hadn't been enough decaying trees on his property. The morels only grew where a decomposing tree added nutrients to the soil, so he ended up venturing farther and farther into the Uwharrie, where anyone who stumbled across the morels could have harvested them. With God's grace—and because the section of the Uwharrie near his cabin wasn't easily accessible to the public—the secret had held, and for years, he and Audrey had feasted regularly in the spring. Even after she was gone, he had kept up those traditions, in honor of that first dinner at the cabin, but all their other dinners as well. It was a reminder of the good times, before the bad.

But so much had changed since then, and he was no longer the man he once was. Decades ago, he'd been young and strong, and he used to look in the mirror, concerned about combing his hair just right. He used to walk without fear of suddenly toppling. He'd owned a real home and the cabin and a successful business. He'd been a neighbor and a friend and a father and a husband. He'd read from the Bible every morning and evening, gone to church on Sundays, and sometimes prayed for more than an hour at a stretch.

Now, he was old and everything was different. And his prayers—if any—always came in the form of a single question.

Why?

V

IN THE UWHARRIE, Jasper and Arlo were on the hunt. Or rather, Jasper was foraging and Arlo was lumbering here and there, marking his territory and then returning to Jasper's side, where he'd stare at Jasper's pocket. How Arlo could smell the Milk-Bones amidst all the other scents in the forest and in the backpack was beyond Jasper.

He reached into his pocket and broke off a piece of a Milk-Bone, tossing it toward Arlo, who didn't even try to catch it. Instead, he ate it off the ground then looked up at Jasper as if to say, *That's it? I know you've got more in there.*

"Later," Jasper promised.

They'd been in the forest some hours by then, and though there'd been a little luck—a few stems he'd cut carefully—there were fewer morels than he'd hoped. Years ago, he'd wondered whether Arlo could be trained to hunt for morels, like those truffle dogs in Italy. When he was a boy, his father had told him that if something had a scent, a dog could be trained to track it. With that in mind, he'd set out morels and had Arlo sniff them; he even smeared some ground morels in a clean handkerchief and had Arlo sniff that, too. In the house, he'd hidden the handkerchief over and over, and rewarded Arlo with a Milk-Bone whenever the dog found it. After that, he and Arlo hit the Uwharrie, but Arlo promptly forgot everything he'd learned and seemed content to stare at Jasper's pocket instead. And now, Jasper was certain, Arlo was too old to be bothered with trying to learn anything new.

So Jasper had to use his eyes, which, aside from needing readers, were among the few parts of his body that had held up over time. He walked, noting the trees, looking for elms and oaks and poplars, keeping an eye out for decaying trees and patches of sunlight amidst the shade. He scanned near the roots, sometimes bending lower to brush the debris aside. It was slow going and hard on his back—morels could *hide*—and he was careful; he never cut any false morels, which were toxic. As he searched, he found his thoughts returning to Audrey.

Most people, including Jasper, had been puzzled by Audrey's sudden interest in him, which persisted after that first trip to the cabin. His feelings for Audrey, on the other hand, had taken root long before that day, when he'd seen her practically skipping into the classroom on their first day of kindergarten. With reddish blond hair and a light spray of freckles across her cheeks, she looked like a blue-eyed angel, and he had stared with wonder as she took her seat at the desk beside him. She said hello, but all he could do was nod, setting in motion a pattern that defined their relationship from one grade to the next. Even though they shared the same classroom year after year, Jasper remained too shy to ever strike up a conversation. Instead, he was content to steal the occasional glance from across the playground or marvel from afar at the elegance of her wrists and hands. Her fingers, unlike his, were long. She held a pencil with such delicacy that Jasper couldn't figure out how it never slipped from her grasp. When she turned the page of the book she was reading, she touched her finger to her tongue, a habit he found irresistibly seductive. Pretty much every boy in school was in love with her at one point or another, though Jasper did his best to keep his own feelings completely hidden.

They were nothing alike, after all. Unlike him, she was an excellent student; unlike him, she was popular, with a laugh that drew others into her orbit. She was also rich, especially compared to Jasper. Her father worked at the bank and her mother owned a successful clothing store; they lived in a two-story house with white columns gracing the front porch. Over the years, she was seen holding hands with various boys on the way to class, but in the end, everyone assumed that she'd marry Spencer, whose father owned the bank and had been one of the founding members of the country club. But a few days after Jasper had buried his father, she'd inexplicably climbed into his truck, and in that moment upended the expected course of both their lives.

After they'd married, Jasper lived his life wanting nothing more than to make her happy. Because she liked to read, Jasper built walls of bookshelves; because she wanted the cabin to feel like their home, Jasper helped her redecorate, moving furniture and placing colorful rugs and throw pillows until she was satisfied. In the evenings, she would sit beside him on the couch with a book in her lap, and Jasper would wonder again why she'd chosen him when she could have chosen someone like Spencer and spent her Saturday afternoons playing tennis instead of living in a ramshackle cabin on the outskirts of town.

"Don't be silly," she'd respond, rolling her eyes, whenever he said as much to her. "I knew exactly the kind of man I was marrying."

He'd wonder how she could sound so confident about such a thing, if only because he wasn't always sure he knew who he really was back then. He had few memories of his childhood, or of his mother, who'd died when he was a toddler. When asked, he'd say that his upbringing had been ordinary; he'd been neither particularly good or bad in school, nor particularly good or bad in sports, nor particularly good or bad in anything else for that matter. He lived in a small house in Asheboro that so closely resembled the neighbors' homes it wasn't uncommon for owners to accidentally enter the wrong house after a few hours at the local bar. He palled around with friends, but like a lot of kids in the late 1940s and early '50s, he was expected to help out the family, which meant working after school and in the summers at the peach orchard, of which his father was the foreman.

His father, Jasper sometimes thought, loved only five things in his life: his country, peaches, his only son, whittling, and our Lord and Savior Jesus Christ. On their porch hung an American flag, which his father raised in the morning and took down in the evening. Even before Jasper started school, he would spend days walking with his father through the rows of trees, absorbing everything his father told him. When it came to peaches, his father was one of the most knowledgeable men in the South. Jasper learned that there were roughly 150 peach trees in an acre, each of them needing space that measured roughly fourteen by twenty-two feet. He was taught that peaches grew best when the soil drained well. He was taught the importance of irrigation, regular pesticide application, and temperature's effects on crops. He listened closely to his father's lectures on treating infestations and diseases. By the age of ten, he was working in earnest at the orchard, where he cleared weeds, thinned the crop, or plucked peaches, loading basket after basket into trucks for delivery to canners.

At home, his father often read to him from the Bible. In the winter, they went hunting, filling their freezer with venison; sometimes they'd go fishing. His father taught him to whittle, their efforts eventually populating every surface of both the house and the cabin.

His father neither cursed nor drank, and Jasper couldn't remember ever seeing him angry. He often clarified quotes from the Bible, scribbling their meaning in his own words into the margins, and when Jasper had questions or shared something about his life, his father would often gaze at him over the top of his reading glasses and say something like "You might want to examine Luke 16:10." Opening the Bible, Jasper would read. *Un-*

less you are faithful in small matters, you will not be faithful in large ones. Even with the occasional rephrasing in the margins, half the time, he wasn't sure how the verses his father pointed out pertained to his questions in the first place.

Over time, he came to decipher his father's references with greater ease. Scripture was part of his heritage; after all, Jasper's grandfather had been one of the most prominent preachers in North Carolina and had supposedly briefly mentored Billy Graham. Jasper suspected that as much as his father wanted him to find meaning in his life, he ultimately wanted him to stay focused on the everlasting. Jasper might mention that he hadn't done well on a test at school and his father would say, "Second Corinthians 4:18." (*So we fix our eyes not on what is seen, but what is unseen. For what is seen is temporary and what is unseen is eternal.*) Or if Jasper boasted that he'd hit a home run to win a baseball game, his father would respond, "Romans 11:36." (*Everything comes from God alone. Everything lives by his power, and everything for his glory.*)

On Sundays, they would attend the church that Jasper's grandfather had founded. They prayed together in the mornings, before meals, and again before bed. They prayed for neighbors and friends who were struggling, and when they hunted, his father would say a prayer for the deer or turkey he'd killed. *Pray without ceasing* (1 Thessalonians 5:17). Often, his father would then deliver some of the meat, along with peaches, to folks who were worse off than they were. *Whoever is generous to the poor gives honor to the Lord* (Proverbs 19:17). He was kind to everyone he met. *Be kind one to another, tenderhearted, and forgiving* (Ephesians 4:32). Though Jasper's father was far from rich, his faith was radiant, and Jasper sensed that he had the respect of practically everyone in town. Jasper loved him, not only for his wisdom but for his demeanor and patience. Unlike many of the other boys in school, Jasper never showed up with bruises or welts inflicted by a father after an evening of drinking.

If his father had a single dream—aside from the caretaking of his son's soul—it was to one day build a cabin in the woods, where the two of them could spend their weekends surrounded by the beauty of nature, instead of being stuck in town. When Jasper turned fourteen, his father began scouring the newspaper for property listings. Jasper asked about it while they were loading crates of peaches in the bed of a pickup truck.

"But you'd never be able to afford it . . ."

"Matthew 19:26."

With God, all things are possible.

"But . . ."

"Mark 9:23."

All things are possible to him that believes.

"I don't believe miracles happen to folks like us," Jasper finally forced out with a touch of teenage defiance. "Not real miracles, anyway."

His father set his crate down and motioned for Jasper to do the same. "Did I ever tell you the story of how your grandfather became a pastor?"

Jasper shook his head as he set the crate in place.

"You should know that my father wasn't always a religious or righteous man. In his youth, he wasn't even a particularly good man. Before he met your grandmother, he was a gambler and even spent time in prison." His father paused, scanning the sky as if searching for the right words. "For a long time, he didn't learn the appropriate lessons, I guess you could say. Instead, he doubled down on the bad things he was doing, and though he was pretty good at poker, he got himself into debt with the wrong people. This was down in Texas, by the way." He took off his hat and wiped his forehead, then fixed Jasper with a serious gaze. "They took a knife to him and left him for dead."

Jasper remembered going silent as he waited for his father to go on.

"Anyway, he didn't die. Instead, met a nurse in the hospital. She read him stories from the New Testament that described Jesus's miracles. My father didn't care one way or the other about the stories or Jesus, but he came to care a great deal about the nurse who was reading them. He fell in love with her, but she wasn't blind to my father's flaws. After he was released, he found himself questioning the choices he'd made for the first time in his life. He started praying to God, even though he wasn't a believer, and he asked to witness a miracle. He wanted a sign from heaven, and if God would give him one, he promised to turn his life around."

His father paused, but Jasper knew there was more.

"Not too long after that, my father was out walking one morning, trying to loosen up the scar tissue where he'd been stabbed. He swears the weather was perfect, with clear skies as far as the eye could see, and when he reached the top of a hill overlooking the town, he decided to take a rest. He was sitting on a rock when a huge black thunderhead suddenly blew in from the east, the largest cloud he'd ever seen. One minute, it was blue skies, in the next minute, it was as if a curtain fell over the world. And all at once, it started raining, but it wasn't rain that fell from those clouds. What fell from those clouds were fish."

Jasper wasn't sure he'd heard him right. "Fish?"

"Fish," his father emphasized. "Most of them were still alive and they landed on the ground, twitching and flapping. Hundreds of them, thousands maybe. And all at once, he found himself thinking about one of the stories from the Bible that the nurse had read to him, the one where Jesus fed the whole crowd with bread and fish, even though there wasn't much to begin with. And in that moment, with fish still raining from the sky, he gave thanks to God for allowing him to witness a miracle, and he vowed to change his life. He became a traveling preacher, then a pastor, and eventually convinced the nurse to become his wife. In the end, he moved to Asheboro and founded the church where we still go on Sundays."

"Do you think it's true?" Jasper squinted at him, skeptical. "About the fish?"

His father nodded, and Jasper asked no more about miracles. But not long after that, his father found a notice for land near the Uwharrie that had been foreclosed upon by the bank and was about to be auctioned live to the public. The auction was to be held on site, and as fate would have it, the day dawned with a rainstorm heavy enough to wash out some of the roads leading to the property. Jasper's father ended up being the only bidder present at the auction, and he was able to buy the land at a shockingly low price, which meant he had enough remaining money for construction. Granted, the miracle might not have been as dramatic as fish falling from the sky, but to his father it was proof that the Lord had heard his prayers. And shortly after that, when Jasper was fifteen, he and his father built the cabin that Jasper now called home.

VI

IT WAS ARLO who found the dead deer.

Jasper had been searching in a thicket when he heard Arlo bark. It wasn't something Arlo usually did, not in recent years anyway, probably because it required a bit more effort than eating or sleeping. Curious, Jasper turned and watched as Arlo trotted toward him, then suddenly doubled back.

Jasper followed as Arlo continued tracking back and forth,

sick at the prospect of finding the carcass of the white deer. Instead, Jasper eventually found himself staring at a yearling, not much past the fawn stage, of ordinary color. Undersized, it probably weighed less than fifty pounds, and a single glance was enough to reveal that the shot had been a poor one. Instead of directly behind the front shoulder, the wound was about six inches back, closer to the belly. A blood trail led to the deer, and Jasper winced. The deer had been wounded and in pain, and it ran and crawled until it finally collapsed here.

The animal was cool, meaning it had died more than a few hours earlier. *The shot I heard this morning,* he surmised. Likelier than not, because it had been dark then, the poacher had used a spotlight to freeze the deer.

Jasper tensed, his anger rising. Regardless of how a person felt about hunting, there were *rules:* spotlights were illegal, hunting in the dark was illegal, hunting in the Uwharrie out of season was illegal. But no matter what, whoever had taken the shot should have done their best to track the deer afterward, to put an end to its suffering. The deer—undernourished and losing blood— couldn't have traveled more than a few hundred yards after it had been shot. It would have been easy to track. This was not merely poaching, it was target practice. It was killing simply for the sake of killing, and though it had been years since Jasper had opened a Bible, his mind suddenly flashed to Proverbs 12:10:

A righteous man regardeth the life of the beast: But the tender mercies of the wicked are cruel.

His mind held on to the words *wicked* and *cruel,* and as he continued to stare at the animal, his anger gave way to sudden fatigue. He'd long since given up trying to understand why a loving God would allow such suffering in the world, and it reminded him of the suffering that he himself had endured.

Arlo was nosing at the deer and Jasper nudged him back. He'd have to report the poaching. To mark the location, he removed the bandanna from his back pocket and tied it to a branch on the nearest tree.

With nothing more to be done, he left the deer in place.

Though his desire to find morels had waned, he'd promised Mitch that he'd bring some to the boy's mother, so that's what he was going to do.

VII

JASPER CONTINUED TO forage for another two hours, finally getting lucky near a fallen elm. By then, the sun had risen high enough to brighten much of the forest and he'd filled a quarter of the bucket, which was more than enough. It was time to head back, but he needed to rest first. He was in an area of rolling hills, and spying a good-sized rock near one of the crests, he made his way toward it.

He took a seat, knowing the tightness in his back was close to spasm, his hips and knees killing him. He tried his best to ignore the pain and concentrated on the sight of a hawk circling over-head. Arlo wandered over and plopped at his feet, panting. From the backpack, Jasper removed the bowl and filled it with water. As Arlo started drinking, Jasper poured himself some coffee from his thermos, then found the sandwich he'd packed earlier.

He unwrapped it, stuffing the cellophane into the backpack. He was taking his first bite when Arlo moved away from his bowl and began staring at his pocket. He tossed the dog a Milk-Bone and returned to his lunch.

Like most days, Jasper wasn't hungry in the slightest and he wondered where that feeling had gone. He recalled that in his youth, he had always been hungry; when Audrey made dinner, he often ate two platefuls. But after half of the sandwich, he felt as though he could force no more down and he tossed the remainder to Arlo.

On the gentle breeze, Jasper caught a foreign scent, something metallic, industrial. It took him a few seconds to identify the odor of gun oil, and by then, he heard voices and a snort of laughter before three figures finally emerged into view.

They were older teenagers, he guessed, dressed in camouflage jackets and pants. They wore sneakers rather than boots and hadn't bothered with orange reflective gear. The shortest one, who also looked the youngest, had a dimple on his chin and acne, and the boy next to him wore a T-shirt that read ASHEBORO HIGH SCHOOL WRESTLING beneath his jacket. The tall one, walking out front, was obviously the leader, and Jasper noticed that he carried a rifle slung over his shoulder, in addition to a large backpack.

Large enough to hide a spotlight?

No doubt about it.

Arlo raised his head as Jasper continued to study them. Even from a distance, he could see they were good-looking kids, with short, neatly trimmed hair, and straight, white teeth, like they'd all spent a lot of time at the orthodontist's office. Jasper suspected that their fancy sneakers cost hundreds of dollars a pair. When they finally spotted him, Jasper could read their puzzlement at his presence in this secluded part of the forest, but it quickly gave way to a swagger as they approached, almost as though they sensed a creature weaker than they were.

A low growl rose from Arlo, startling Jasper. It had been years since he'd heard Arlo growl; the dog seemed to unconditionally love everyone he met. Jasper reached down to pet him and felt the tenseness in the dog's muscles, the growl lowering to a steady rumble.

The teens stopped a few yards away.

"Damn!" the younger one suddenly called out. "Are you okay? What the hell happened to you?"

Jasper knew his appearance had finally registered.

"Oh wait, I know you," the boy in the wrestling T-shirt piped up. "I've heard of this guy."

"Yeah. He was in a fire," the tall one said. "Grow up." He offered an apologetic smile to Jasper, but Jasper sensed only emptiness behind it. Arlo must have sensed it as well; though he'd stopped rumbling, the dog's muscles remained bunched, the fur on the back of his neck bristling.

"What are you doing out here?" the tall one went on. "Are you lost?"

"I know where I am," Jasper answered.

"Out for a walk? Doing some bird-watching?"

Jasper didn't answer and the taller one's gaze flitted to his friends then back again.

"What do you have in the bucket?"

"Mushrooms," Jasper answered.

"From the forest? You gotta be careful with that. Mushrooms can kill you if you don't know what you're doing."

"I do."

"You mind if I take a look?"

"Feel free." Jasper nodded.

The tall one stepped closer and Arlo began growling again, this time loud enough for all of them to hear. Arlo's lips lifted, exposing his teeth, and the teen froze.

"What's up with your dog?"

"He's all right."

The teen, however, remained wary and moved no closer. Instead, he merely leaned forward, angling for a glimpse of the morels.

"That's a lot of mushrooms. How long have you been out here?"

"Some hours."

"You wouldn't have happened to have seen that white deer that people have been talking about, have you?"

No, but I found the one you shot earlier. "No. No turkeys either."

"We'll get those when the season opens." The tall boy smiled his empty smile again, as chilling as it was unconvincing.

"I hope you don't try hunting them with that rifle of yours. What is it? A .30-30?"

"Actually, a .30-06," he responded. "I just got it, in fact."

"You might want to clean the bore," Jasper remarked. "Get rid of any solvents or preservatives. I can smell the gun oil."

"I know how to take care of a rifle," the teen huffed, narrowing his eyes. "I've had guns since I was a kid."

Maybe so, but you're still a poor shot. "You wouldn't have been looking for that white deer yourself, would you? With that rifle?" Jasper nodded at the gun.

"Of course not. That would be illegal," the kid answered. "But you never know when you might come across an angry bear. It pays to be safe."

There were few, if any, bears in the Uwharrie, and the kid's tone made it clear he knew it. The kid was lying to his face, his insolence on full display. Around them, the forest seemed to have suddenly quieted.

"Let's get out of here," the younger one said, trying to dissipate the tension. Jasper caught a nasal whine in his tone. "I'm getting hungry."

"Me, too," said the one in the wrestling shirt. "I'm starved."

As they turned to leave, Jasper cleared his throat. "I heard a shot earlier this morning," he said. "Around six, maybe a few minutes later. It sounded like it came from a rifle like the one you're carrying."

They froze. The one in the wrestling shirt glanced at the kid who spoke with a whine. The tall one locked eyes with Jasper.

"It wasn't us," he said. "We just got here."

Jasper met his gaze. "I also found a dead deer just over yonder. Young one. Not much older than a baby. Shot through the belly."

At that, all three of them grew silent. When the tall kid stepped closer, Arlo began to snarl, his body thrumming with the sound.

"Are you accusing us of something, old man?"

"Not them," he rasped out. "Just you."

The tall one's eyes flashed, and he took another stride forward. Though Jasper might have been able to stop Arlo in his younger years, those days were long past. Before he could react, Arlo snarled and suddenly charged the kid, moving faster than he had in years and zeroing in on his leg. The tall one barely had time to react as Arlo latched onto his pants, causing the teen to stumble backward before toppling over, landing hard. He kicked furiously with both legs, somehow managing to twist the rifle free in the process. Grasping it by the barrel, he began swinging the stock at Arlo and connected hard a couple of times. Arlo yelped and backed away before trotting off toward a nearby thicket.

A good thing, Jasper suddenly thought. He wasn't sure what the kid would have done had the dog scurried back to his side. Anger and guns were a combustible mix, and when the tall one finally got to his feet, Jasper watched in horror as he quickly raised the rifle and took aim at Arlo's retreating figure. Jasper lunged forward and barely managed to flick the barrel upward as a shot went off.

The shattering sound made Jasper's ears ring, exacerbating the tinnitus, and the kid suddenly swung the barrel in his direction. Jasper felt his gut tighten.

Opening my mouth, he thought, *had been a bad, bad idea.*

Jasper raised his hands and took an immediate step backward.

"Your dog attacked me!" the teen screamed, spittle spraying Jasper's face.

Jasper slowly retreated another step, aware that saying anything might land him in even more trouble.

"What the hell's wrong with your dog?" he shouted again.

Jasper said nothing, waiting, hoping the sudden flood of adrenaline the teen was feeling would recede just as quickly. Whether it happened in time was the question.

"Aren't you going to say anything?"

Jasper remained silent and the tall one continued to glare at him. He wasn't hurt, probably not even bruised from the fall, but his eyes flashed with rage. His ego was wounded, and with his buddies looking on, he needed to show Jasper who was in control.

Jasper raised his hands higher. The barrel of the gun was still pointed in his direction. The sight of it made it difficult to see anything else.

"You need to have that dog of yours put down."

Jasper stayed quiet, inching back imperceptibly.

"C'mon! Knock it off! Stop pointing the gun at him!"

It was the short one. Perhaps it was the panic in his voice that broke through, but whatever it was, the tall kid finally lowered the gun barrel. Jasper flicked his eyes to the shorter one, noting for the first time a resemblance between the two. He wondered if they were brothers.

"Let's just go!" the other one pleaded, sounding equally panicked.

But the tall kid continued to glare at Jasper. Then, with a quick step, he kicked at the bucket, toppling it. He began crushing the morels beneath his sneakers, grinding them into the dirt. When he was finished, he spit on the remains.

"Next time, maybe keep your accusations to yourself. And make sure that psycho dog of yours is on a leash." His affect was oddly flat, but Jasper could sense the fury beneath his words. "If I see him again, I just might panic, and he could end up dead."

"Please!" the shorter one whined again. "We need to leave!"

"You got any money? For the pants your dog ripped?"

"No."

"Then how are you going to compensate me?"

"Jesus!" the one in the wrestling shirt cried out. "Quit screwing around! Just leave him, okay? Who cares about your pants! Seriously! Let's *go*."

After a few moments the tall one smirked, sensing Jasper's fear. Finally, he took a step back and turned around before motioning to the others.

"Let's get out of here."

Jasper watched them leave, his heart tripping unevenly in his chest. When they were out of sight, he turned, staggering back to the rock. He pulled out a nitroglycerin tablet and popped it under his tongue, allowing it to dissolve. His hands and legs were shaking.

Worried about Arlo, he listened for the sound of another shot. He knew the teen would kill his dog if he could: Jasper had not the slightest doubt of that. To his relief, he heard nothing. Only when his heartbeat regained some semblance of normalcy, and he was sure the boys had left the area, did he allow himself to stand. He felt frail and hollow, his skin a tight drum. Using his fingers, he whistled. When Arlo didn't appear, he whistled a second time, and after another minute, Arlo finally emerged, his head poking through some shrubbery. As he lumbered over, looking as worn-out as Jasper felt, Jasper spotted a gash on his muzzle and another on the top of the dog's head. Both had already begun to clot, so they probably weren't too deep. But he'd clean the wounds when he got back home.

From his pocket, he removed two Milk-Bones, watching as Arlo gobbled them up. He picked up the empty bucket, eyeing the remains of the scattered morels. Audrey, he knew, would have been brokenhearted.

CHAPTER FOUR

I

I N THE MORNING, not long after her eyes fluttered open, Kaitlyn found herself thinking, *I haven't forgotten how to be happy. Casey doesn't know what she's talking about.*

Yeah, her life was busy and yes, raising a teenage daughter could be occasionally wearying, but she loved her kids and her work. She volunteered for the community—something that had always been important to her—and made house calls. Add in the fact that she had a comfortable amount in savings, her health was good, she was close to her parents and siblings, and all in all, there was nothing to complain about. Casey had simply been trying to press her mother's buttons. Right?

Right.

Glancing at the clock, she was surprised that she'd slept later than usual, and slipping on a robe, she padded down the hall. Peeking in their rooms, she saw that both Mitch and Casey were still asleep. Downstairs, she enjoyed the quiet as she sipped coffee and had some fruit for breakfast.

Mitch appeared in the living room just as she was finishing. He was still in his pajamas and sat down in front of his Lego creation.

"Morning, sweetie. Want some cereal?" she called out.

"I'll get some in a little while," he answered.

She walked toward him and kissed his messy hair. "Can you let me know when Casey gets up? And we'll probably be leaving around eleven-fifteen."

As she went upstairs, she felt a flutter of nerves in her tummy, knowing that in just a little while, she'd see Tanner again.

II

AFTER HER SHOWER, Kaitlyn stood in front of the mirror in the master bathroom, trying to convince herself that technically, she wasn't going on a date. A *real* date would mean leaving Mitch at home. Today, she told herself, was more of an *outing*. And surely, her thoughts continued, Tanner didn't view it as a date either. What had he said? That it beat being stuck at the hotel all day?

It was settled, then. It definitely wasn't a date, but if that was the case, why had it taken twenty minutes for her to figure out what to wear? She'd finally decided on a pair of newish jeans and a top her sister had bought her for Christmas that she hadn't yet worn.

"Mom?"

It took Kaitlyn a moment to register Mitch's voice. He was standing in the bathroom doorway, his hair uncombed and his shirt wrinkled. "Yeah, sweetie?"

"When are we leaving again?"

She glanced at her watch. "We still have half an hour," she said. "C'mere. Let me fix your hair so it's not so messy."

Turning on the faucet, she wet his hair. "You should probably change your shirt, too."

"I like my shirt."

"I know, but you wore it yesterday. You should put on a clean one."

"Why?"

"Just do it for me?" she asked, bending over to kiss his forehead. "Do you know if Casey's awake yet?"

"Uh-huh," he answered. "But she left. Camille just picked her up."

"And you didn't tell me? I thought I asked you to let me know when she got up."

"I did. That's why I came upstairs to find you."

Casey had a knack for remaining one step ahead of her mother. Kaitlyn finished combing through Mitch's hair with her fingers and showed him his reflection in the mirror. "That's better, don't you think?"

Mitch shrugged. "I guess."

"Hey, listen," she began, squatting down to meet him at eye level, "I know I asked you last night, but I wanted to make sure it doesn't bother you that Mr. Hughes will be joining us at the zoo."

"Who's Mr. Hughes?"

"He was the one who drove Casey home last night. After she hit his car."

"I thought you said that a friend was coming with us."

"He's a new friend," she said, thinking Mitch was still young enough to likely accept that as an answer. "Now do me a favor and change your shirt?"

"Okay," he said. Looking up at her, he squinted. "Why are you so dressed up?"

"I'm not dressed up. I always dress like this."

"Not on the weekends."

"Well," she said, "we don't always go to the zoo, do we? Why not make it special?"

III

HALF AN HOUR later, with Mitch seated behind her playing on his Switch, Kaitlyn pulled up in front of the Hampton Inn and saw Tanner standing next to the entrance. When he raised a hand and sauntered toward the car with the same easy confidence he'd displayed the night before, she was struck by what an anomaly he was in a town like this. Most men's bodies were testimonies to their love of extra sausage gravy on their morning biscuits.

"Good morning," he said as he climbed into the passenger seat.

"Hi," she answered. He held her gaze for a moment before turning toward her son. "And you must be Mitch. My name's Tanner. Thanks for letting me tag along with you and your mom today."

Kaitlyn watched Mitch in the rearview mirror.

"You're welcome," Mitch said, studying Tanner. "Have you been to the zoo before?"

"No," Tanner answered. "I've been to other zoos, though. Which animals do you like to see?"

"I like the lions. And the giraffes."

"I like giraffes, too."

"Did you know they have the same number of neck bones that people do?"

"I didn't," Tanner said, sounding intrigued. "That's cool. What game are you playing?"

"Mario Kart Tour."

"I love Mario. I used to play it all the time."

"Do you want to try?"

"Maybe later." Tanner nodded.

Tanner turned to buckle up, and Kaitlyn smiled to herself, liking how relaxed he seemed with Mitch. Releasing the brake, she started toward the road.

"For some reason you didn't strike me as the videogame type."

"I was deployed for months on end in both Afghanistan and Iraq. You can only work out so much, and watching the same movies over and over gets boring. Everyone plays videogames."

"Were you any good?"

"Depends on the game," he said. "I was good at Mario, above average with Madden and FIFA, but if you ask me about Call of Duty, I'd have to say I'm an expert."

"Good to know."

He lowered his voice. "How's Casey this morning?" He stole a quick look at Mitch behind them. "I've been wondering . . ."

Mitch piped up from the backseat: "They had a fight in Casey's room last night."

Kaitlyn's eyes flashed to the rearview mirror. "We didn't fight, sweetie. We had a discussion."

"It sounded like a fight to me. And then Casey snuck off this morning."

Kaitlyn sent Tanner a long-suffering look. "Camille picked her up even before I knew she was awake. I'm pretty sure she did it to avoid talking to me again."

"Smart girl," he said, looking amused. "When my grandparents were angry with me, I'd stay at my friend's house all day."

"Changing the subject, how was your morning?"

"Great. I went for a run, explored the town a bit, and now I'm off to the zoo."

"I have to admit I'm impressed by your energy and enthusiasm."

"Why? I like animals."

"I don't know. I guess given all the exotic places you've been to around the world, I didn't think our little zoo would hold much appeal."

"You forget that I didn't grow up in the States, so pretty much everywhere I visit is new to me," he reasoned. "I was planning to go to the zoo anyway while I was here, so this worked out perfectly."

"Seriously?" Kaitlyn looked skeptical.

"According to Tripadvisor, it's the number one thing to do in Asheboro. I've become a big fan of Tripadvisor in the last few years."

She laughed, shaking her head.

IV

As soon as they reached the zoo, Mitch jumped out of the car, skipping ahead of them to the entrance.

Tanner nodded in his direction. "He looks like he knows where he's going."

"It's his happy place," she explained. "Well, here, and the Lego section at Walmart. And Chick-fil-A. And the gazebo, where our neighbor Jasper is teaching him how to carve."

She caught Tanner's fleeting smile as he followed Mitch's progress toward the entrance.

"How about I get the tickets and lunch?" Tanner offered. "It's my treat."

"You just need to get your own ticket," she said. "We have a family membership, so Mitch and I get in free."

While Tanner paid, Kaitlyn ran a hand through Mitch's hair.

"Are you hungry yet?" she asked. "Do you want to eat?"

"Not yet," he said. He pushed up his glasses. "I want to see the animals first."

Once inside, he veered to the left, toward an area of the zoo called the Cypress Swamp. Tanner and Kaitlyn followed at a desultory pace, just fast enough to keep an eye on Mitch, and as she walked beside him, she marveled at how ordinary this expedition felt. "Tell me more about Cameroon," she ventured. "I know it's in Africa, but that's about it."

"The country itself is stunning," he answered. "It's on the west coast and close to the equator, so it's generally warm year-round, but the landscape is hugely varied—desert, rainforest, and mountains."

"Where were you posted?"

"Yaoundé."

"Is that a village or a city?"

"It's the capital. It's almost three million people."

"Oh," she said, feeling foolish.

"Don't feel bad," he said, catching her reaction. "Until I learned I was being posted there, I hadn't heard of it either."

"What do you remember most?"

"The people," he said. "Even though it's a poor country compared to the U.S. or Europe, there's a lot of laughter there. People seem to have a knack for finding pleasure in everyday things, despite their hardships. The country has a refugee crisis because of the wars going on in neighboring countries, and there's definitely poverty and suffering, but I was always amazed at how much more resilient, and even happy, most people seemed there compared to folks living in America." Then he broke into a wide smile. "Oh, and I remember playing soccer. I played a lot of soccer."

"Yeah?"

"On my first day there, I met a guy named Vince Thomas. He'd been with USAID in Cameroon for a few years. He helped me settle in and we ended up becoming pretty good friends. He convinced me to join him in pickup soccer games after work. He had this crazy ability to locate a game we could jump into, anytime—games in empty lots, even on the streets. Some of my best memories are of chasing the ball, sweating like crazy and having the time of my life."

"Were you any good?"

"I think I could be categorized as . . . a slightly below-average player. But in my defense, people are absolutely obsessed with soccer in Cameroon. They have one of the better national teams in Africa, and *everyone* plays the sport growing up."

"Excuses . . ."

He laughed. "You asked."

"What did you do there? For work? You mentioned something about the Office of Security yesterday?"

He nodded. "USAID had a lot of different projects, with people working all over the country. It was my job to help keep them and the locals we were working with safe, sometimes by setting up procedures like traveling in caravans with the right emergency supplies; other times by guarding the perimeter of our camps. In the far north and southwest, there's ongoing violence from insurgencies and political instability, like the spillover effect of Boko Haram. Girls and women are at particular risk, so having an armed presence was critical, even when all we were doing was vaccinations."

She glanced over at him. "It sounds like you were able to change people's lives for the better."

"I hope so," he said with a nod, "and the longer I was there, the more I fell in love with Cameroon. I can't wait to visit some of the places I didn't get to the last time."

"Like where?"

"The Nki National Park, for one. It's one of the few places in Africa where you can see huge groups of elephants and chimpanzees together in their natural habitat. Usually, they live in different places."

"And you'll play soccer again."

"Knowing Vince, I'm sure that will be a big part of it."

By then, they'd reached the Cypress Swamp. Up ahead, Mitch was peering into one of the enclosures, looking for the mountain lion.

"If you enjoyed Cameroon so much, why did you leave?"

"That was Vince's fault. He promoted me, and then recommended me for what was essentially his position in the Côte d'Ivoire."

She smiled. "And you did the same thing in Côte d'Ivoire?"

"Kind of. Because I'd been promoted, I had people working under me, which meant more time in the field office and less time in the field. And unlike Cameroon, the country is growing fast economically. Côte d'Ivoire harvests a big chunk of the cocoa in the world, so a lot of our work there was about helping with governance or arranging for other business initiatives. Like . . . helping the cashew cooperative get commercial financing, things like that."

They caught up with Mitch. She put her hand on his shoulder, bending close to his ear. "Do you see the cougar?"

"He's lying in the rocks over there," Mitch said, pointing to a mountain lion. "In the shade. You can see part of his head, but I think he's taking a nap. He hasn't moved at all."

"Don't they sleep during the day?" asked Tanner.

"They do," Mitch answered with authority. "C'mon. Let's go check out the alligators." He turned and was off again, leaving them behind.

She nodded in his direction. "This is how the whole day will go. He runs ahead and gets there first. Then, as soon as I arrive, he's off to see the next one. We usually finish the entire zoo in about an hour and a half."

As they set off for the next enclosure, Kaitlyn said, "And Haiti was where you went next?"

He raised an eyebrow. "I'm impressed you remember. Yes, that ended up being the last place I worked."

"How was it?"

"Again, an amazing local population. But the field office there is huge, so it was much more bureaucratic. And then there's the work itself. It seems like the country gets hammered by hurricanes and earthquakes every other year. You finally think you're making progress on infrastructure or cholera or setting up polling stations or whatever, and then another disaster strikes and you're back to square one. There was a constant sense of being overwhelmed, with never enough time or money to make a lasting difference."

"Which I suppose made your efforts even more critical, no?"

"I guess," he said. "That's why I went. But I felt a bit burned-out by the end."

"So you took a break?"

"Between that and Covid making it impossible to get back there, yeah."

"Hey, Mom!"

Kaitlyn spotted Mitch sandwiched between a family and a woman taking photos.

"Coming!"

"He's got his mouth open!"

As they hurried to join Mitch, Kaitlyn reflected on the fact that she hadn't had such an interesting conversation in years, maybe ever. In her world, people didn't talk about soccer games in Cameroon, or cashew initiatives in the Côte d'Ivoire.

Sure enough, one of the alligators was lying in the sun with its mouth wide open.

"He's regulating his temperature," said Mitch. "I wonder if he could swallow me whole."

"Hmmm . . ." Kaitlyn said. "His mouth is big, but you've grown since the last the time you were here."

"They grab you and drag you in the water and spin you in circles until you drown. It's called a death roll."

"Good to know."

"C'mon. Let's go see the polar bears," he said.

A moment later, they were retracing their earlier steps.

"Sorry," she said to Tanner. "I warned you."

"Don't apologize. I'm having a great time, but I feel like I've been doing all the talking."

"My life's not all that interesting."

"I doubt that. You're a physician who also makes house calls, and a mom who's raised two amazing children."

She squinted at him skeptically. "That's not exactly in the same league as vaccinating kids in a war zone."

Tanner picked up a cup that had been discarded on the ground and dropped it in a nearby garbage can before returning to her side. "It wasn't me who vaccinated the kids. Nor did I set up the program or pay for it."

"I still think it's remarkable that you chose to do that kind of service work in the first place. I try to do that, too, but obviously on a much smaller scale." His expression encouraged her to go on. "In addition to my house calls, I volunteer once a week at a place that provides free meals to those who need them."

"That's great," he said. "Is it at a church, or . . . ?"

"No, it's a nonprofit called Our Daily Bread," she said. "They're only open at lunch, but I've been volunteering there on Mondays since I first moved to Asheboro. They've been around for a long time, and I think they serve something like twenty thousand meals a year."

"What made you decide to do something like that?"

"My dad," she said simply. "He always had this thing about Mondays. When we were little, we'd be at the breakfast table and he'd walk in to pour himself a cup of coffee, and say, *I was just thinking that Monday is the perfect day to start being the best version of yourself, since you've got six more days to practice.* Or, *Every week should begin with generosity, don't you think? Wouldn't the world be a better place?* My brother and sister and I would roll our eyes at each other. But over time, I guess his attitude sank in, at least with me. He always walked the walk. He's a dentist, and the first thing he did when he set up his practice was to reserve Monday mornings for patients who couldn't afford to pay. It's all his fault."

"It's a good thing."

"I know it is, and I love him for it," she said. "And I guess it makes sense, because he understands more than most people what it means to need help. He was born in the mountains of Kentucky, which is very rural and very poor, to a single, teenage mother with a sixth-grade education. He grew up in a decrepit mobile home. They lived on whatever his mom could trap or shoot along with food donations from the church, and in the winter, sometimes there was no heat at all. Not that my dad ever talks about his youth like that. He's the kind of guy who just shares the good stories in life, like how much fun he used to have catching lizards or swimming in the pond or whatever. My mom told me about it. She's a little more objective when it comes to my dad's past."

"Why do you think that is?"

"My dad's a natural optimist, but I also think it was important to him that his kids love and respect his mom as much as he did. And we did. I mean, my grandma was her own cup of tea, no doubt about it. She chewed tobacco and was addicted to soap operas, and spending time with her was like visiting a different planet. I remember once when I was little, we arrived at her house to find her in the backyard shooting squirrels with a pellet gun. Of course, my sister and I started to cry when we saw the little corpses all laid out on the picnic table, but she was excited about the squirrel stew she planned to make for us. I think my sister and I gagged on the spot."

Tanner grinned. "How was the stew?"

"Thank God my mom arrived in time to save us from having to eat it. But as out-there as my grandma seemed to us, she had a lot of love in her heart. I mean, look at how my dad turned out. He worked hard and had some caring teachers, but clearly his home life was somehow solid enough for him to earn a full scholarship to Eastern Kentucky University. And as soon as he could—even before he bought a house for himself and my mom—he moved my grandma to a small house in the suburbs of Lexington. She said it was the first place she'd ever lived with hot water that you didn't have to heat up yourself."

"That's quite an upbringing."

"No kidding. My dad is still practicing, by the way, though he's finally—just this year—begun to cut his hours. He *loves* what he does. Nonetheless, he always made us feel like we were the true passion of his life. He made it to every one of our games and dance recitals and never a missed a parent-teacher conference."

"And your mom?"

"She's probably even smarter than my dad."

"Yeah?"

"She went to fancy private schools and her family belonged to the country club. She majored in math and philosophy and was valedictorian in both high school and at the University of Kentucky. She started off teaching, but after she and my dad got married and had kids, she chose to be a stay-at-home mom. She was always available when one of her own kids needed her, even after we moved away. When I was pregnant with Mitch and on bed rest, she dropped everything and stayed with me for months."

"They sound like a great pair."

"They are," said Kaitlyn.

By then, they'd reached the polar bears. Because one of them was splashing in the water, Mitch had hung around longer than usual. Nearby were seals and sea lions, as well as arctic foxes, which captured his attention as well. When Kaitlyn asked him again if he was hungry, he shook his head and announced that it was time to check out the African animals, and again, he led the way.

"What do you do when you make house calls?" asked Tanner.

"The same things I do in the office. I'll check vitals and take blood samples and make sure people get the prescriptions they need. If there are children, I'll do vaccinations. Or I clean wounds and do stitches. It sort of depends on who I'm seeing. Officially, they're patients of the office, even though they've never set foot inside."

"What if they need an X-ray or something?"

"In that case, I try to convince them to go to the hospital."

"It seems like it would make for a long workweek, since you're probably on call as well, right?"

"Not really. Being on call is different than it was when I first started to practice. The hospital here now has its own clinicians, so you're not expected to go in. Instead, you might hear from a patient who didn't get their prescription or needs a prescription refilled. If they're having problems, you either tell them to come into the office in the morning or you send them to the emergency room. If you have your phone, you don't even have to leave the house."

As they reached the area of the zoo dedicated to elephants, giraffes, lions, rhinos, and chimpanzees, their conversation drifted back to Tanner's time overseas. He described puff-puff and beans, which he ate whenever he went to the market, and mentioned ndolé, a flavorful spinach stew that Vince had introduced him to on his first night in Cameroon. He described watching the African Nations Championship in 2016 in a bar so packed that the crowd spilled onto the streets; Cameroon beat DR Congo 3–1, and the jubilation lasted until almost dawn. He told her about the apes and monkeys he saw at Mefou National Park, and somewhere along the way she found herself thinking, *One day I'd like to go there, too.*

On their way back—as they viewed the exotic animals a second time—Mitch asked if Tanner had heard about the white deer that had been spotted in the woods.

"I haven't," he said. "I didn't even know there was such a thing as a white deer."

"There is," Mitch said solemnly. "It's been on the news."

When Tanner glanced at Kaitlyn, she nodded. "It's real."

"Maybe they'll catch it and put it in the zoo," Mitch speculated.

"I hope not," Kaitlyn interjected. "I want it to remain free in the wild."

"I want to see it," Mitch said, before skipping ahead again.

Over lunch at Junction Springs Cafe, Mitch was spellbound by Tanner's description of the wildlife in Cameroon. For his part, Mitch shared a stream of animal trivia he'd learned from a book—that an elephant has forty thousand muscles in its trunk, or that lions can get their hydration from plants. Through it all, Kaitlyn found her gaze drifting from Mitch to Tanner, relieved that Mitch seemed perfectly at ease. As they were leaving, somehow they started talking about Frisbee. In the end, Mitch convinced her to swing by a nearby Walmart, where Tanner hopped out of the car and vanished into the store, reappearing with a Frisbee a few minutes later.

They drove to Bicentennial Park and for half an hour, Kaitlyn, Tanner, and Mitch tossed the Frisbee back and forth. They started by standing close to one another, but as they gradually moved farther apart, Tanner and Kaitlyn found themselves chasing one errant throw after another while Mitch giggled and called out, "Sorry!" After twenty minutes, a thin sheen of sweat coated both their foreheads.

Kaitlyn tried to remember the last time, if ever, George had done something like this with Mitch, but nothing came to mind. It warmed her heart, but it was getting late.

Tanner made a final lunge to retrieve Mitch's wildly undirected throw. As he approached her, Frisbee in hand, he smiled.

"I know you're working tonight," he said, still catching his breath, "but I couldn't resist the Frisbee thing once Mitch said he wanted to try."

Mitch ran to join them.

"Do we have to go?" he said.

"It's time. But you had fun, right?"

"It was awesome!" Then, with his mind moving quickly, he furrowed his brow. "Is Casey going to be home tonight?"

"She should be. She knows the drill."

"Okay," he said. "Can we have hot dogs for dinner?"

"I was thinking tuna casserole."

"With potato chips on top?"

"Of course," she said. Satisfied, Mitch started toward the Suburban. As they followed, Kaitlyn glanced at Tanner. "I assume you'll want me to drop you at the hotel?"

"If you don't mind," he said. "After all this running around, I think I need a shower and some horizontal time before dinner."

The drive to the hotel took only a few minutes. After Tanner got out, he hovered in the open door.

"I had a great time, Mitch," he said with a playful salute. "And thanks for teaching me about the animals."

"No problem," Mitch said, sounding distracted; the engine noise of Mario Kart Tour drifted from the backseat.

"Thanks again for today, Kaitlyn," Tanner said. "And just so you know, I'm going to be thinking about your dad and his ideas about Mondays. I think it's a good goal for me."

"Thanks for coming with us."

With that, he started toward the hotel entrance. Part of her expected him to look back at her, but he didn't. Instead, he pulled open the glass door and stepped inside, quickly vanishing from sight.

Releasing the brake, she tried not to feel deflated that he hadn't suggested getting together again; at the same time, it was probably for the best. Wasn't it enough to simply enjoy the day they'd had?

Of course it was, she decided. She hadn't spent a day like today in forever—couldn't remember when she'd felt like just a woman—not simply a mother or a doctor—and Tanner made her realize how much she'd missed that feeling.

V

"WHERE WERE YOU?" Casey asked, as soon as Kaitlyn walked in. Mitch had already burst inside, making a beeline for the kitchen.

"We were at the zoo," she said. "You knew that." Catching sight of her son reaching for the cookie container, she called out, "Mitch! What do you think you're doing?"

"I'm getting some cookies."

"Only take one—"

"Mom," Casey interrupted. "I'm trying to talk to you. Why didn't you answer my texts earlier?"

"I'm sorry. I didn't check my phone."

"She was talking to Mr. Tanner," Mitch explained. "He's cool."

"Who's Mr. Tanner?" Casey asked.

"Tanner Hughes," Kaitlyn said. "The guy you hit last night?"

"Why were you at the zoo with *him*?"

"When he found out we were going, he asked if he could join us," she said, as if it were the most natural thing in the world. Then she quickly deflected. "Why were you texting?"

Casey stared at her, but miraculously she let it pass.

"I wanted to know when you were getting home because I need the Suburban to pick up supplies. We're decorating the lockers tonight, remember? Ahead of the baseball game? I told you last week."

Kaitlyn vaguely remembered Casey mentioning it, though she hadn't realized it would be on Sunday.

"You can't go to the school tonight. I'm working and you have to watch Mitch."

"It's only going to be an hour or two. He'll be fine by himself. Or we can ask Mrs. Simpson to watch him."

"Casey—"

"All right," she said, cutting her mother off. "What if I bring him?"

"To the high school? With your friends?"

"Why not? He'd have fun."

"What if he doesn't want to go?"

Casey turned toward the kitchen. "Hey, Mitch! You wanna come with me and my friends to the high school tonight? To decorate some lockers with streamers and stuff?"

"Yeah!" he cheered. "That sounds awesome! Can I help?"

"Of course." Casey turned a triumphant look on Kaitlyn. "See? No problem. He wants to come."

Kaitlyn felt cornered. "Fine. But you need to be home no later than eight."

"If Camille can give us a ride to school later, can I use the car to get supplies now?"

"I'm not sure it's a good idea," Kaitlyn said.

"Because of the accident?"

"You're making it sound like it's no big deal."

"I know it's a big deal! But just so *you know,* all of this is partly your fault, too. I shouldn't have had to drive the Suburban last night in the first place."

It took Kaitlyn a moment to catch up.

"Are you talking about having your own car? We've talked about this and decided that once you graduate . . ."

"No, *you* decided that. And if I lived with Dad, I'd already have a car."

"Are you sure about that?"

"I just talked to him, Mom. Right before you got home." She tossed her head in defiance. "He said"—she drew out the words deliberately—"that if I move in with him, he'd be happy get me a car."

Kaitlyn felt a chill go through her. *Of course he'd say that.* "You don't want to move right before your senior year. You'd leave all your friends behind."

"I'm going to leave them behind as soon as I start college any-way, so what's the big deal? And until then, I'd have a car."

Kaitlyn stared at her. From the corner of her eye, she saw Mitch in the kitchen and knew he'd heard his sister as well. "And you're considering it?"

Casey put her hands on her hips, a challenging light in her eyes. "Why shouldn't I?"

VI

WHILE CASEY HEADED out for supplies, Kaitlyn made dinner. She didn't want to think about Casey and what she'd threatened, but she couldn't help it. There'd been something in her tone this time that made Kaitlyn wonder if her daughter was serious.

The thought of Casey going to live with her dad made her feel ill; she couldn't imagine not having her around. The truth was, Casey was a good kid—what other teenager would invite her nine-year-old brother along when doing something with her friends? She really tried to make time for her brother in her busy life. She took him to the beach last summer, she regularly watched movies with him, and when he'd been sick last November, she'd let him sleep in her room. Mitch, Kaitlyn knew, would be heartbroken if Casey left.

Trying to push the worry aside, she went to her home office and opened her laptop. Uploading the accident photos from her phone, she dashed off an email to Dan Hendrix—her insurance broker and someone she'd known for years—explaining what had happened.

Then she organized the medical bag she used for house calls, checking the batteries in the oximeter and that the blood pressure cuff, thermometer, and portable EKG were working. She reviewed the list of patients to visit and their medical charts on her iPad, making a list of supplies to get from the office. Because one of her patients had a joint infection, she needed to prefill a syringe with lidocaine and triamcinolone; because one of the families had children in kindergarten, she would bring along DTaP, MMR, and IPV vaccines. Still another patient might need a cortisone injection in her knee. She reminded herself to pick up the prescriptions that had been delivered from the pharmacy, some of which she paid for herself when she knew her patients couldn't afford them.

Finally ready, she emerged from the office. Casey had returned and was sitting with Mitch watching one of the Transformers movies.

"I'm heading out," Kaitlyn announced. "The casserole is ready to put in the oven for dinner. Is there anything you need before I go?"

"How about a million dollars and a red Ferrari?" Casey said without looking up.

"And I'd like Bumblebee," Mitch added.

Kaitlyn felt proud of herself for remembering that Bumblebee was one of the characters in the Transformers movies. "Anyway, you'll be home by eight, right?"

"Yes, Mom," Casey drawled.

"I shouldn't be home much later than that, but I'll let you know if something comes up. See you in a bit."

Engrossed in the movie, neither replied, and a moment later, Kaitlyn was out the door.

VII

KAITLYN DROVE TO the office and collected everything on her checklist. As she was leaving, her phone rang. She was surprised to see that Dan, her insurance broker, was calling.

"I didn't expect to hear from you already," she said. "It's Sunday. Why are you working?"

"Lori went to her mom's this weekend with the kids," Dan replied, "so I was just getting a jump start on the week. Can you tell me what exactly happened?"

Kaitlyn told him what she knew, including the fact that the Suburban seemed fine and that neither Casey nor Tanner had been hurt.

"Okay," he said, before letting her know that the adjuster would contact Tanner in the morning and everything would be taken care of. For a few minutes they chatted about their families.

After hanging up, Kaitlyn was about to put the phone back

into her bag. Instead, she pulled up the text thread with Tanner and messaged him:

> I spoke to my insurance guy. You should hear from the adjuster in the morning. He also said not to worry—your car will be good as new by the end.

Her fingers hovered as she debated. Then, after drawing a breath, she added:

> I had a lot of fun today. Have a great night.

She waited for a moment, watching for the dots that signified he was responding, but none appeared. Sliding the phone back into her bag, she loaded the Suburban and hit the road, leaving Asheboro for the surrounding county. Her first stop was a mobile home park six or seven miles outside the town limits.

For the next hour and a half, she saw one patient after another. She injected one patient in the elbow and another in the knee. She took a dozen blood pressure and temperature readings; examined ears, noses, and throats; listened to hearts and lungs; and immunized a five-year-old. There were two new patients, both of whom had cuts that had become infected. She cleaned the wounds, provided them with antibiotics, and while she knew it made them nervous, nonetheless created medical records for them. She dropped off three prescriptions as well.

After finishing up at the trailer park, she visited three more homes. These patients were elderly, so all received an EKG, in addition to the more routine tests. She also took vials of blood to forward to the lab.

From there, she made two more visits to drop off prescriptions, arriving home at half past eight.

When she walked in, Mitch and Casey were sitting together on the couch again, this time with a bowl of popcorn between them.

"How did it go at the school?" she asked.

"It was awesome!" Mitch answered. "We put up balloons and everything!"

"I'm glad you had fun," she said. "But shouldn't you be getting ready for bed about now?"

Reluctantly, he rose from the couch.

"Good night, you bedbug," Casey said, tossing a piece of popcorn at him.

"Good night, you bubble butt," Mitch retorted, and Casey giggled.

For a moment, Kaitlyn wondered whether she should try to speak with Casey again but decided that it might be best to let things rest for now.

The last thing she wanted was another argument, if only because it might make Casey even more determined to go.

VIII

LATER, AFTER MITCH had bathed and put on his pajamas, she read him a chapter from the novel *Wonder*, by R. J. Palacio. Though Mitch was old enough to read on his own, it was something she'd done with him ever since he was a baby, and she wasn't willing to give it up just yet. She figured the day was coming soon enough; Mitch would bring an end to that tradition just as Casey eventually had.

After kissing him good night, she was about to turn out the light when Mitch spoke up.

"Mom?"

"Yeah, sweetie?"

"Casey isn't really going to move in with Dad, is she?"

"She just talks sometimes," Kaitlyn answered, hoping she was right. "You know how she is."

"I don't want her to leave."

Kaitlyn could hear the fear in his voice. "I know, honey."

She gave him an extra kiss and turned out the light before half-closing the door behind her. Peeking in on Casey, she saw her studying in bed and decided not to interrupt. It had been a long day—a long weekend, in fact—and she was tired.

And yet . . .

She wrapped her arms around herself, thinking again that, even if Casey's threat had definitely thrown her for a loop, today was one of the better days she'd had in a long time.

IX

KAITLYN TIDIED UP the living room and the kitchen downstairs before traipsing up the steps to the master bathroom and turning on the shower. As steam began to fill the room, she found herself reflecting on her time at the zoo with Tanner.

It was uncanny how comfortable she felt around him, almost as though they'd been friends for years. Their easy give-and-take underscored how much she missed her social life. She missed adult conversations. All in all, it was a reminder that she *was* more than simply a mother and a physician, and if nothing else, their afternoon at the zoo had reawakened that awareness of herself.

In the shower, she shampooed and lathered before rinsing her hair. After drying off, she wrapped herself in a towel and realized she'd left her phone in the bag downstairs in her office. Making sure her towel was secure, she padded from her bedroom to the office and retrieved it. When she pressed the side button, her heart skipped a beat as she saw that Tanner had answered her text.

> I appreciate you reaching out to the insurance company already. Thank you also for letting me tag along today. It was great getting to know you a little better, and meeting Mitch. Perhaps I'll see you around?

She smiled and debated sending a response. *I'd like that* sounded too eager, maybe even desperate; *We'll see* struck her as too coy. Unable to reach a decision, she decided to sleep on it.

> Perhaps I'll see you around?

He likes me, she thought, feeling slightly breathless. *And I like him.* But again, that wasn't the issue. *He's leaving,* she reminded herself.

On impulse, she crawled into bed naked for the first time in years. Luxuriating in the feel of the sheets against her skin, she waited for her mind to slow down. Instead, she kept visualizing Tanner as he walked beside her.

He likes me, she thought again, and it took her a long time to finally fall asleep.

X

MONDAY BEGAN WITH the rush typical of a weekday. Kaitlyn got the kids to school and went to the office, where she worked steadily until eleven. Then she replenished her medical bag and headed for Our Daily Bread.

As soon as she entered the nondescript building, she grabbed an apron from one of the hooks on the wall. She called out greetings to the regular volunteers. Entering the bustling kitchen, she did a double take when she noticed a man slicing tomatoes for a huge container of salad.

"Tanner?"

"Hi, Kaitlyn," he said with a friendly wave. "Happy Monday."

A few of the other volunteers exchanged glances but said nothing.

"What are you doing here?"

"Volunteering," he said. "I called earlier to see if they needed help today, and it turns out that Evelyn couldn't make it. So here I am."

"But why?"

"Because I had some free time, and it's a good thing to do," he explained in a matter-of-fact way. "And I wanted to see you again."

The other volunteers' eyes widened with what seemed to be delight. As for Kaitlyn, she wasn't exactly upset by his presence, but she wasn't sure what to think. All she knew for sure was that she didn't want an audience while she tried to figure it out.

"Oh, well . . . good for you," she responded. She swallowed. "I'm going to head out front since they'll be opening the doors in a minute."

"Do your thing," he said with a casual wave before turning his attention to the tomatoes again.

Kaitlyn walked to the serving line while trying to ignore the obvious fascination of those around her.

"Everything okay?" Linda asked her. She'd been volunteering here even longer than Kaitlyn had, and they had been friends for years.

"I'm fine," Kaitlyn answered.

"I'm glad," she commented. "Because, you know, Margaret's already nicknamed him Handsome Stranger."

All Kaitlyn could do was close her eyes and think, *I can't believe he's here.*

XI

THEY SERVED MORE than seventy meals over the next hour and a half, and toward the end, an older man with a bad cough asked if she had a few minutes to see him. She conducted an exam in the small administrative office and diagnosed bronchitis. Kaitlyn gave him antibiotics, the samples courtesy of the pharmaceutical rep who'd brought donuts earlier that morning.

Afterward, Kaitlyn returned to the kitchen, where the cleanup was in full swing. While most of the other volunteers were out front cleaning the tables, Kaitlyn wandered to Tanner's side as he was scrubbing down the cutting board in the sink.

"How did it go with the patient?" he asked. Though she had the sense that the few remaining workers were watching out of the corners of their eyes, she managed to maintain her composure.

"It was fine."

"You didn't mention that you treat patients here, too."

"It doesn't happen that much." She cleared her throat. "But . . . I must say that *your* presence here was a little unexpected."

"I told you that I'd be thinking about your dad," he said, "and it's Monday." He smiled, those green-gold eyes holding her captive. "It's good to see you again."

She felt the familiar flush creeping up her neck. "You, too. But I have to head back to the office."

"Did you even have time to eat?"

"No, but I usually skip lunch."

"That's not good for you, you know. I'll have to talk to your doctor about that."

She tried and failed to suppress a giggle.

"Can I walk you out? I'm guessing I'm going to be here for another hour or so."

"Sure," she answered, before falling in beside him. "Oh, before I forget," Kaitlyn went on, "did you hear from the insurance adjuster yet?"

Tanner nodded. "I spoke to him this morning. He's already had the car towed, and I'm supposed to meet him at Bill's Body Shop at three to go over everything. He also set up a rental for me."

When they reached the Suburban, he said, "I'm glad I came here today."

"If I'd known, I would have warned you that we wouldn't have a chance to talk."

"It's okay," he said with a lazy shrug. "But I was wondering if you'd like to have dinner with me tomorrow night?"

She felt her heart start to race in her chest. *Not a good idea,* a sensible voice inside her head scolded.

"I'll have to see what the kids are doing," she replied after a moment's hesitation. "Can I text you later? Once I talk to them?"

"Absolutely," he said. "And if tomorrow doesn't work, maybe another night?"

She expelled a sigh. "Sounds good."

CHAPTER FIVE

I

ON SUNDAY EVENING, after cleaning Arlo's wounds, Jasper whittled on the porch until dark, then wandered back inside the cabin. He opened a can of chili for dinner and split it with Arlo, but his mind continued to whirl, and his stomach remained too clenched to eat. He couldn't forget staring down the barrel of a rifle, or the empty smile of the young man gripping the gun. After forcing down only a few spoonfuls, he gave the rest to Arlo.

As he was rinsing out the bowl, his mind turned to the dead deer he'd found and he wondered how long the white deer would survive in a world where people prized the killing of beautiful things.

A lifetime ago, he remembered, a different white deer had been spotted in the Uwharrie. He was seventeen and the news had been just as exciting back then as it was now, so his father brought him to the forest in the hope of a sighting. It was the last time they'd spent a weekend together at the cabin before his father's heart had given out.

They'd spent hours in the forest trying to find it. His father was an excellent hunter; he could tell at a glance how recent a track might be, he knew that scat could indicate the health of an animal, and he had an instinctive feel for places where deer might have bedded overnight. In late afternoon, when they'd finally stopped to eat, his father began to speak. It was an odd conversation, for his father never mentioned peaches or even a single Bible verse. Instead, he related to Jasper some of the myths and stories associated with white deer. He said that King Arthur had tried and failed to trap one, and that the Kings and Queens of Narnia had chased one, only to tumble out of the wardrobe. He mentioned that the Ojibway—a tribe in the upper Midwest—regarded the white deer as a reminder of our own spirituality, before sharing with Jasper a legend from the Chickasaw.

In the legend, a young warrior named Blue Jay fell in love with Bright Moon, the daughter of the chief. The chief, who didn't believe Blue Jay was worthy of his daughter, decreed that the young couple could only be together if Blue Jay brought to the chief the hide of a white deer. Blue Jay spent lonely weeks in the forest in search of one. Finally, he found just such a deer and loosed an arrow, and though it struck home, the deer strangely didn't die. Instead, it fled, luring Blue Jay deeper into the forest, until he eventually became lost. Bright Moon, with a broken heart, never loved another man again. Instead, in the smoke of the evening campfires, she often saw the white deer fleeing through the forest while her Blue Jay chased after it; in the legend, she lived the rest of her life praying for the deer to die so Blue Jay could finally return to her.

As he listened, Jasper wondered whether his father had also been speaking about himself. Somehow, he had the sense that his father wanted him to know the depth of his longing for the wife he had lost, a woman Jasper never knew. He wanted his son to understand why he'd never remarried or even dated. Perhaps, Jasper reflected, his father saw himself in both Bright Moon and Blue Jay.

Struck by these insights, he sat in silence. His father moved on to another myth, this one from Europe, before they resumed their search once more.

But they were never able to catch sight of the white deer, much to his father's disappointment. A few weeks later, as Jasper stood over his father's grave, he found himself wondering whether his father had sensed his time on earth was coming to an end; he wondered whether his father saw in the deer a last chance to glimpse the woman he had loved and lost.

In Celtic mythology, after all, white deer were believed to be messengers from the otherworld.

II

AFTER BREAKFAST THE next morning, Jasper collected the keys to his truck and another bandanna. Arlo followed him out the front door and Jasper cautiously descended the steps to the dirt and gravel path out front.

The truck was more than half a century old, its paint faded and upholstery torn. When the engine was cold, it sometimes took three or more turns of the key before it coughed to life. Jasper often wondered whether he or the truck would give out first.

The tailgate groaned as he lowered it. Arlo wagged his tail but made no move to hop up. Instead, Jasper pulled out a set of plastic steps and Arlo walked up the steps as if he were royalty.

"You're welcome," Jasper said.

Closing the tailgate, he climbed behind the wheel and set off for town. When he reached the parking lot of the sheriff's office, he tied the bandanna over his face. At the tailgate, he set out the steps again and Arlo descended with dignity.

Inside, the deputy at the counter appeared discombobulated, her mouth forming the shape of an O before she quickly looked away. The bandanna, Jasper knew, helped only a little.

"Good morning," she said, sliding some papers off to the side. "Can I help you?"

"Is Charlie in?" he asked, referring to Sheriff Donley.

"He's on the phone right now," she answered, seemingly engrossed in the sheaf of paper on her desk. "Can I ask what this is in reference to?"

"Poaching," he said. "And more."

"Oh," she said, her gaze sliding to Arlo. "You know you're supposed to have your dog on a leash, right?"

"I don't have one with me. But he'll mind me."

"Uh-huh." She nodded, eyeing the gray in Arlo's muzzle and the old, scarred man standing in front of her. "I guess it's okay. Would you like to make a statement?"

"I'd prefer to speak to Charlie in private, if it's not a bother."

"And you are?"

"Name's Jasper. Charlie and I go way back."

Minutes later, he and Arlo were led back to the office, where he found Charlie behind his desk. Charlie stood, offering his hand as Jasper removed the bandanna.

"Jasper, my old friend," he said. The politician in him—sheriffs were elected officials—found it easier than most people to make eye contact with Jasper; then again, they had known each other for more than three decades, so Jasper's appearance no longer shocked him. Even so, he always smiled a bit too aggressively, overcompensating. "I haven't seen you around much lately. Still hiding out in that cabin of yours?"

"It's home." Jasper shrugged.

Charlie motioned to the chair in front of the desk. "You know, you should really have your dog on a leash."

"The lady out front said the same." Jasper took a seat while Arlo splayed out on the floor and promptly closed his eyes.

"What can I do for you?"

Jasper related the events of the day before. As he spoke, Charlie took notes on a yellow legal pad before finally looking up.

"And you said you found the deer yesterday? On Sunday?"

"Yes."

"Poaching violations should be reported to North Carolina Wildlife. Have you contacted them?"

"I came here instead."

"I can handle it for you," Charlie said, then confirmed he had the location correct.

"That's it." Jasper nodded. "Tell them to look for a red bandanna, too."

"I'll let them know." Charlie tapped his pencil against the pad. "And you don't know who the teenagers were?"

"No."

"Nor do you know for certain that they were the ones who killed the deer?"

"No, but who else could it be?"

Charlie leaned back in his chair. "I'm not saying that I don't believe you, but it's a bit of a quandary since you didn't witness the crime. I'm pretty sure that the wildlife officer is going to say the same thing. And because you don't know who the teens were, there's really nothing they can do anyway."

"Have you heard there might be a white deer out there?"

"Who hasn't? It's all the talk at the diner the last couple of days."

"I think those boys were out there looking for it."

"They might not be the only ones. Word's gotten out about the sighting and it's probably all over the internet by now. Those albino deer are only one in thirty thousand I've heard, so it's no wonder."

"Is there anything you can do?"

"It's not my jurisdiction," he demurred. "It's a national forest, meaning it's federal, and we both know there aren't enough wildlife officers to keep the forest completely safe from poachers. It's always been a problem, not just now."

"Maybe you should talk to the teens anyway. I told you that one wore an Asheboro High School wrestling shirt. That could be a start."

Charlie rubbed his chin, looking again like the politician he was. "The high school is in the city, not the county, so the Asheboro police would be the ones who'd have to look into it."

"The boy took a shot at my dog."

"I know it's upsetting, but what you're actually talking about in criminal terms is an illegal discharge of a weapon, which is just a minor misdemeanor. And frankly, you're in a bit of a gray area there, since the dog went after him first."

"What about the boy pointing the rifle at me?"

"That's also a misdemeanor. And again, there were extenuating circumstances because of the dog, so I doubt anything would come of it. I'm just glad you're okay. We both know it could have been worse."

Like it was for the fawn, Jasper thought. *And could be for the white deer.*

"Then how can we keep that deer safe?"

"Look, Jasper . . . do you still hunt?"

"Not in a long time."

"Still, like me, you've probably figured out that the white deer isn't from around here. More than likely, it wandered into the area temporarily in search of food or water or whatever. It's prob-

ably smart, if it's survived enough hunting seasons to reach adulthood. The point I'm trying to make is that this weekend, once
turkey season begins, there's going to be a lot of commotion.
Guns fired, hunters traipsing around—which means that the
deer will likely hightail it back to wherever it came from."

Jasper glanced toward the window, knowing he was right.
Still, the deer would be in danger until then.

"If I were you," Charlie added, "I'd try to put it out of your
mind. And I'd be careful in the Uwharrie for the next few days.
Remember what I said about the internet. You never know who
you might run into out there."

The meeting ended, and back at the truck, Jasper mulled
Charlie's words. Maybe he should try to put it out of his mind,
but he realized that he couldn't. The teens he'd encountered
needed to be held accountable. They were guilty of poaching and
given the chance, they'd do it again. Nor was it acceptable to
shoot at a man's dog or point a rifle in Jasper's direction.

On a deeper level, Jasper couldn't shake the feeling that he and
the white deer were connected somehow. He wasn't sure whether
it was an omen or a message, but as he sat in the truck, he felt
with a growing certainty that the white deer's appearance had
been meant specifically for him.

Like his father and grandfather, after all, Jasper had always
wanted to witness a miracle.

III

THERE HAD BEEN a time when Jasper didn't know whether he
would ever feel normal again. His father's death—so utterly
unexpected—left a hole that even Audrey's presence couldn't

fully fill. In the small home in town where he'd always lived, he was surrounded by the remnants of the life he'd shared with his father: photographs of the two of them on the mantel, fishing gear they'd used on lazy afternoons, carvings crowding the windowsills and every other surface. On the end table near the padded rocking chair in the living room was his father's Bible.

In the weeks that followed his father's death, Jasper would wander the silent house, hollowed out by grief. In those moments, he would turn to the Bible, trying to find solace in the words his father so often quoted or had scribbled in the margins.

Psalm 34:18 said: *The Lord is near to the brokenhearted and saves the crushed in spirit.* Matthew 5:4 said: *Blessed are those that mourn, for they shall be comforted.* He dropped to his knees and prayed not only for his father's soul, but for his own. Every now and then, Audrey would stop by after her classes with a casserole or a freshly baked pie. They would eat together, speaking quietly. She'd ask him how he was doing while every word and gesture radiated a deep sympathy, and as those terrible weeks and months wore on, Jasper grew to love Audrey with a devotion he hadn't thought possible. *Love is,* more than anything, *patient and kind* (1 Corinthians 13:4), and indeed, she seemed to understand that Jasper needed to grieve on his own time line before reentering the current of life.

Without his father to support him, Jasper dropped out of high school and began working full-time at the peach orchard. Though it meant he wouldn't see Audrey at school, he had no other choice. He paid the household bills, packed his father's lunch pail, and worked from dawn until dusk. A man named Richard Stope had taken over his father's former position. Stope was the owner's son-in-law, and he'd long been jealous of the trust that Jasper's father had earned from the owner. He was a hard man and he'd place the blame on others when anything went wrong. More than once, Jasper had seen him strike one of the seasonal workers. Years earlier, when asked by Jasper why Stope acted the way he did, his father responded with "Proverbs 24:2." That evening, Jasper read in his father's scribbled handwriting, *For their minds devise violence. And their lips speak of trouble.* In the past, Jasper knew that Stope had tried to get Jasper's father fired for one infraction or another. Now, Jasper kept his distance and focused on his job.

But Stope's jealousy found a new outlet in Jasper. If Jasper worked fifty hours, Stope would find reason to pay him for only forty; if one of the truck engines malfunctioned, Stope blamed Jasper. In time, other workers began to distance themselves from Jasper, knowing that Stope would make their lives miserable, too, if they associated with him. Instead of having lunch with the crew, Jasper would eat by himself. If he had to repair an engine or fix the irrigation pumps, others no longer would help him. Once the repair was completed, he'd be blamed because the job took too long.

Finally, after he'd been working full-time more than a year, two peach trees at the farthest end of the property were struck with brown rot. The fungus had spread from a neighboring grove, where an entire section of the peach crop had been affected. But Stope singled out Jasper for responsibility. While other workers watched from the corners of their eyes, Stope fired him. By that point, Jasper had expected as much, so he merely nodded.

It was 1958. He was eighteen and his father had been dead for a little more than a year. Audrey would soon be graduating from high school. Jasper had a small amount in savings, so he'd be okay. As he turned to leave, Stope called out, "You're a good-for-nothing country cracker, just like your father."

Jasper stopped, his shoulders suddenly tightening. In his mind he heard his father whisper, "Proverbs 29:11."

Fools give full vent to their rage, but the wise bring calm to the world.

He relaxed his shoulders and took another step toward the warehouse where he kept his father's lunch pail. Stope rushed forward and grabbed him by the arm.

"You'll leave the property now," he demanded.

Jasper could feel the eyes of the other workers on them. He deliberately shook off Stope's grip, and took another step to retrieve the pail. Stope closed the distance again, his face red and eyes flaring.

"Don't ignore me, boy!"

Wheeling Jasper around, Stope cocked his fist; as the blow connected, Jasper felt the edges of his vision go black and he collapsed in the dirt. Knowing what his father would have wanted him to do, Jasper rose. He looked Stope square in the eye then slowly turned his head. He pointed at his other cheek, just as Jesus had urged, in case Stope wanted to strike him a second time.

Stope's face flushed a dark purple. He clenched his fist again. But a sense of amazement, even awe, seemed to settle over the other workers like an indrawn breath. Stope must have felt it, because instead of striking Jasper a second time, he eventually lowered his gaze.

Jasper continued toward the warehouse and retrieved his lunch pail. Leaving the peach orchard, he walked to what had been his father's truck, knowing he'd never return.

IV

AFTER LEAVING THE sheriff's office, Jasper drove to Asheboro High School and pulled into the parking lot. He paused to rub Arlo's head.

"You have to stay this time," he said. "I can't be bringing you into the school with me."

As he approached the entrance, he marveled at how much larger the school was compared to the one he'd attended, and how many cars filled the parking lot. When he was young, no one he knew owned their own car, but these days, it seemed like practically every kid had one.

He attempted to enter the building, only to realize the front door was locked. He tried a second time before he heard a voice crackle through the intercom.

"Can I help you?"

He had no idea to whom he was speaking; he couldn't see beyond the reflective glass. "I was hoping to see if you had any yearbooks."

There was a pause. "The yearbooks won't be ready until May. Are you here to place an order? Do you have a student in school here?"

"No. I wanted to look through the yearbook from last year."

"I'm sorry . . . who did you say you were?"

Jasper offered his name.

"And you have a child at the school? Or a grandchild?"

"No. I just want to look at a yearbook. Doesn't the school keep copies of their own yearbooks?"

"I don't know. I'd have to check. But if you're not a parent or guardian, and you're not here on official business, I'm afraid I can't let you in."

"But it's a school—"

"Exactly," the woman said, cutting him off. "There are safety issues. I'm sure you understand."

"All I want is to look at a yearbook from last year—"

"Sir," she interrupted, "I can't let you in unless you're a parent or you have an appointment . . ."

Jasper shook his head and walked away.

V

BACK AT HOME, Jasper whittled on the porch, thinking. Around midafternoon, he drove to the doctor's house and knocked on the door.

It took about a minute before the boy unlocked and opened the door.

"Hi, Mr. Jasper," Mitch said, brightening. "What are you doing here?"

"I came by to see you."

He shuffled his feet. "My mom says I'm not supposed to let anyone into the house unless she's at home."

"I wouldn't want to upset your mother, so I'm happy to stay on the porch. I was just wondering if Casey has last year's yearbook from the high school."

"I think so," the boy said. "But she's not here now. Why do you want her yearbook?"

"I'm looking for someone who might go to her school."

"Why?"

"I'd rather not get into it, if it's all the same to you."

"Because it's a secret?"

"You could say that," Jasper equivocated. "I don't need to take it—I just want to look at it."

The boy went back toward the living room, where he grabbed a cellphone from the coffee table. "I'm not supposed to go into Casey's room without asking, but I'll text her, okay?"

Jasper nodded.

In a couple of minutes the boy looked up from his phone and smiled. "Hold on," he said, vanishing up the steps, then reappearing with a book under his arm.

"I told her that you said it was super important," Mitch said, handing it over. "And I'm supposed to put it right back after you're done. And she doesn't want you to read anything her friends wrote in it."

"I won't."

Jasper took a seat on the porch swing, the boy joining him with obvious curiosity. Opening the leather-bound volume, Jasper turned to the index, finding the appropriate page. Sure enough, there was a group photo of the wrestling team.

He quickly identified the teen in the wrestling shirt he'd encountered—Carl Melton. As he continued to scrutinize the team photo, he recognized a second face. One of the boys standing in the back row was the taller one—the one who'd been holding the gun.

Josh Littleton.

Jasper looked up, blinked, and took a breath.

Dear God, he thought.

The Littletons.

Following his hunch, he checked the index a second time. Directly above Josh's name was another entry, and Jasper flipped through the pages, finding it. Eric Littleton, Josh's younger brother, had been the final member of the trio. Jasper closed the book and handed it back to Mitch.

"That's it?" the boy asked.

"That's all I needed. Thank you. And make sure you thank your sister for me, too."

"I will."

Jasper stood a moment, lost in thought about the Littleton family, and Mitch shuffled his feet before him. Coming back to the conversation, Jasper asked, "How's your sister doing?"

Mitch glanced away and shuffled his feet. "She said that she wants to move in with my dad. Starting this summer."

"Doesn't he live in Greensboro?"

"I'd hate it if she left."

Knowing how much Casey meant to the boy, Jasper put a hand on his shoulder. "She might have been talking just to hear her head rattle."

"What does that mean?"

"Let's just hope she decides to stay, all right?"

Mitch nodded.

VI

MAYBE IT WAS because of his conversation with Mitch, but when Jasper returned to his cabin, he decided to visit his family.

They could be found at the foot of an ancient live oak with thick, low-slung limbs, some draped with Spanish moss. It was the perfect climbing tree, and Jasper could remember his children testing their balance and courage as they scampered and clawed their way up and around. For a few years, there'd even been a swing; Jasper could remember the day he'd hung it and how each of the children had begged him to push them higher and higher.

Now, the swing was gone and the tree hadn't been climbed in decades. It was here, though, where Jasper had buried his wife and four children, the small plot surrounded by a low brick wall. The pansies he'd planted last November still held their blooms, but next month, the spring flowers would emerge from the mulch—trillium, creeping phlox, dwarf crested iris, bloodroot, and trout lily. Audrey had always loved flowers.

The headstones were arranged in a semicircle, with Audrey in the center. He'd known she would have wanted that, for she'd always been the center in all their lives. She was the sun while her children were the planets. He had chiseled the names and dates into the headstones himself, along with a line of scripture for each.

Jasper carefully lowered himself and began pulling weeds that had sprouted amidst the pansies, his memory returning to 1958, not long after he'd been fired from the orchard. Though Audrey had been coming by his house and the cabin every so often for more than a year, Jasper had yet to kiss her, even if he already knew he wanted to spend the rest of his life with her. Whenever they spoke, he felt as though he could listen to the sound of her voice forever. She told him she wanted to be a teacher at a school outside of town, where she could work with rural students. She said she wanted to have at least four children and live in a two-story house with a porch and a kitchen large enough for the whole family to gather in. She wanted to spend her honeymoon on Sullivan's Island, near Charleston, where they could watch porpoises ride the breakers. That she was so clear about the specifics of her life was dizzying to him. Like his father, Jasper had never been much of a dreamer, and he made a silent promise to himself that he'd find a way to make all her wishes come true, even if he had no idea how to go about it.

But it was her eyes, not her dreams, that captivated him most. Whenever he stared into them, he was unable to look away, as though she'd cast a spell. A few weeks before she graduated high school, Jasper brought her a bouquet of freshly picked daisies. Her parents thought little of him as a prospect for their daughter, and when Audrey's mother saw Jasper standing on the porch with flowers in hand, her face contracted in a pinched expression. Audrey, though, had bounded down the steps and shooed her mother away while the two of them sat on the porch. Her mother reluctantly closed the door and Audrey buried her face in the bouquet.

"They're wonderful," she said, breathing in. Jasper finally whispered the words he'd been holding inside him since the moment she first climbed into his truck. "You're wonderful, too."

They visited for an hour and split a piece of pie. Crickets were chirping and from the woods, Jasper heard the hoot of an owl. Stars pricked the nighttime sky, and he knew it was time for him to go. Just as he was about to step down from the porch, however, he turned to face her. He placed a gentle hand on her waist and edged closer; a moment later, her lips met his for the very first time. He tasted remnants of apple and cinnamon on her breath, and on the way back to his house, his legs were so shaky, he nearly drove his truck into a tree.

Over the summer, their relationship blossomed quickly, like wildflowers in a meadow. They went for walks in the evenings, after the heat of the day had passed, and sometimes stopped for a soda downtown. They went on picnics and saw the occasional movie, mainly because she loved them. At the bookstore, she'd point out to him novels that had moved her most deeply—despite widespread suspicion of the Soviets, she gravitated to Russian writers like Tolstoy and Dostoyevsky. And on Independence Day, while fireworks exploded in the evening sky, he finally whispered to her that he loved her.

"Oh, Jasper," she said with a wide smile, "I love you, too."

That August, she left for college. The day was sweltering, and they'd spent their last morning together at her home, under the disapproving glares of her parents.

He asked to speak to Audrey's father alone. In his pocket was his mother's wedding band, and he formally asked for her father's permission to propose.

In controlled tones, her father explained the impossibility of such an event. They were too young, he clarified, but left unspoken the fact that Jasper hadn't graduated from high school and had no job, let alone prospects for any type of career.

Jasper left with the ring in his pocket and later, when Audrey climbed into the backseat of the family Cadillac for the drive to Sweet Briar College in Virginia, Jasper forced a brave smile. He waved despite the nausea he was feeling, and as he returned to his house, he wondered whether she would forget about him. But she didn't; instead, the distance seemed to draw them even closer together. He wrote to her twice a week and would read the letters she wrote in response again and again. Occasionally, he sent her small gifts in the mail—usually something he'd whittled, but he also sent a scarf and a small locket—and spent every possible minute with her during Thanksgiving and Christmas breaks. And always, whether he was with her or when she was away at college, he continued to ponder how to make all her dreams come true.

Now, a lifetime later, he rubbed the granite, feeling her engraved name beneath his finger. He did the same with each of his children, and despite the ache in his heart, he related all that had happened in the last couple of days. Toward the end, he found himself speculating again on whether the white deer had appeared because God knew that Jasper longed to witness a miracle. A rational voice inside dismissed the notion as ridiculous, but he'd lived long enough to know that hope and doubt could coexist, so Jasper raised his eyes to scan the forest. He looked left and right and then attuned himself to the sounds beyond, but there was nothing but birdcall, and the white deer did not appear. Shaking his head, he chided himself for his foolishness.

After a while, Jasper rose, his knees and hips and lower back emitting sharp twinges. His skin stretched painfully with every move, and as he stared one last moment at the headstones, he felt the dark weight of loneliness settle, suffocating him.

"I love and miss you all," he said aloud, before trudging back to the house.

VII

KNOWING HE STILL had time before Charlie called it quits for the day, Jasper phoned him at the sheriff's office. He let Charlie know that he'd identified the boys he'd seen in the forest.

"I'm not going to ask how you learned their identities, but are you sure?"

"I'm sure," Jasper answered, before reciting the names.

He heard Charlie draw a long breath, then pause before responding. "You're welcome to come in and file a complaint, but even putting aside jurisdiction issues, it's not going to do you any good."

"Why?"

Charlie's silence filled the telephone line. Finally: "You know the reason as well as I do."

In fact, Jasper did. After hanging up, he considered the situation over his dinner of tomato soup. Because Arlo wasn't a fan, Jasper spooned some Alpo into the dog dish before finally reaching for his keys. Arlo looked up from the dog dish and licked his lips, as though wondering where they were off to next.

"It's just me this time. You gotta stay."

Jasper patted the dog on the head and left to make the short drive back into town. Eventually he turned onto a street lined with stately homes, occupied by families whose wealth had passed from one generation to the next. In the driveways he noticed Mercedes and BMWs, even the occasional Bentley. Jasper slowed as he approached a brick colonial partly hidden by lush landscaping. This was the house, Jasper knew, where Josh and Eric Littleton lived; it was also in this house that their father, Clyde, had been born and raised alongside his brothers, Roger and Vernon.

As in Honorable Judge Roger Littleton.

As in District Attorney Vernon Littleton.

The Littletons had a long history in the area, one that dated back to before the Civil War, having built a fortune in railroads and land speculation before branching into law. They were still among the richest families in the state; even now, the family owned tens of thousands of acres, most of it leased to farmers. For as long as Jasper had been alive—and longer than that, he was pretty sure—there had always been a Judge Littleton in Asheboro. Roger, Vernon, and Clyde's father and grandfather had been judges; Vernon, meanwhile, had been serving as the district attorney for almost three decades. When their generous political donations, along with their having friends in high places, were added to all this, it went without saying that the Littletons had been, and still were, the law in the county.

But if Roger and Vernon Littleton were respected in the community—or perhaps, at times, feared—Clyde was merely tolerated. In his teens, one of Clyde's friends had overdosed while at the Littleton home, and there were rumors that Clyde had supplied the drugs. When he was in his twenties, word around town was that Clyde had beaten his girlfriend. Though no charges had been filed about either of those things, the whispers in the community were enough to prod Clyde into leaving town, at least for a while. In Raleigh, he supposedly cleaned up his act. He became a developer and met a woman named Anne, whom he eventually married. They had two sons, and fourteen years ago, after his misdeeds had faded from memory, Clyde and his family returned to Asheboro, where they moved into the original family home. One of his first projects in the area was the subdivision Jasper had tried unsuccessfully to stop.

Clyde also enjoyed hunting, or rather a particular kind of hunting. For Clyde, the more exotic the animal the better, and

Jasper had heard that many of his prizes had been mounted for display throughout his house. He'd killed a lion, a jaguar, and a panther. He'd shot and killed a rhinoceros in Namibia and had traveled to the Himalayas to kill a bharal, or blue sheep. Though not all the animals he'd hunted were endangered species, some of them were, and Clyde was notorious in certain corners of the hunting world thanks to his penchant for posting his exploits on social media. His argument was that he did things legally and with the government's full approval, but Jasper—like many— had no doubt that Clyde sometimes skirted the rules, bribing government officials to look the other way.

A few years ago, Clyde's social media post had been picked up by the local news station. In the first photo, Clyde was shown holding up the head of a giraffe he'd shot in South Africa; in the other picture, he was holding its heart and grinning. When he defended his actions—it was legal, the meat was donated to the locals, the bull had been an old one—animal rights activists from as far away as Florida had demonstrated outside his office in downtown Asheboro. There were signs and people chanting slogans through bullhorns, but the protests had been quietly dispersed by the police.

And now his sons were prowling the forest where a white deer, another exotic animal, had been spotted practically on their doorstep.

Sons chasing their father's approval? To Jasper it seemed obvious.

At the entrance to the driveway was an elaborate wrought-iron gate. On the keypad, Jasper hit the call button. It was answered by a woman announcing the Littleton residence.

"I'd like to speak with Anne or Clyde Littleton."

"Do you have an appointment?"

"I don't. But it's about their sons, Eric and Josh. It's important."

"And you are?"

Jasper offered his name before the speaker went silent. He expected that when he heard the woman again, she would tell him that neither of the Littletons was at home, or another excuse. Instead, the gates swung open.

Jasper pulled slowly up the long drive, bringing his truck to a stop behind a black pickup. He got out and walked to the door, remembering at the last minute to retrieve the bandanna from his pocket and wrap it around his face. He knocked and then stepped back from the entrance.

It was Anne who opened the door. She was a small, brittle-looking woman who wore her hair pulled back into a tight bun; he recognized her from photos in the newspaper. The Littletons were frequently profiled for their local charity work, and the new wing of the hospital had been named after the family.

"Good evening, Mrs. Littleton," Jasper greeted her. "Thank you for agreeing to see me."

Anne's eyes skittered away from his face. "I was told it had something to do with my sons?"

"Yes, ma'am."

Over her shoulder, Jasper saw Clyde descending the grand staircase into the marble-tiled foyer. As he approached, his eyebrows lifted in recognition.

"I remember you. I hope you're not here to complain about the Neely Ridge subdivision."

Jasper shook his head. "No, sir. It's about your sons."

Jasper was led into a library off the foyer, lined with mahogany shelves stretching to the ceiling. One wall featured the mounted head of a black panther; across from it was the bharal. Next to the fireplace stood a taxidermied grizzly bear, maybe nine or ten feet tall. Clyde gestured at a chair that looked like an antique and Jasper took a seat. Anne perched on the edge of the couch, while Clyde remained standing.

"What did you want to tell me about my sons?" Clyde asked.

Jasper recounted the events of the previous day, and by the time he finished, Anne's hands were clenched tight in her lap. Clyde, however, stood arms akimbo, his expression no longer friendly.

"Let me get this straight. You're accusing Josh and Eric of poaching, you're claiming that Josh took a shot at your dog, and you're also claiming that Josh pointed his rifle at you?"

"Yes, sir. And demanded money. And destroyed my morels. That's exactly what happened."

"My sons wouldn't do any of those things," he said. "They've been around guns their entire lives. They know not to point a gun at someone or shoot at someone's pet. And why on earth would they kill a young, worthless deer?"

"I believe they were hunting the white deer."

"That doesn't explain why they'd shoot a different deer, though, does it?"

"I suspect your son was testing the sights on the rifle," Jasper responded. What he didn't add was that maybe Josh wanted to kill it, simply because he could.

"Well, then, let's ask them about all this—shall we?"

Clyde left the room and shouted upstairs for Josh and Eric to come down. When the boys entered the room, they exchanged nervous looks before turning their gaze to their father.

"Jasper here has been telling us quite a story," Clyde began. "Were you boys in the Uwharrie yesterday morning?"

"Yes, sir," Josh said.

"Can I ask why?"

"Scouting," Josh replied, the word coming easily. "Turkey season is about to open, so we were out there to find where they might be."

"Did you see this man out there?"

"Yes, sir," Josh said. "We came across him right before we left. We were talking, and when I tried to look at the mushrooms he'd collected, this man's dog attacked me."

"This man here," Clyde said, motioning to Jasper, "also claims that you poached a young deer."

Josh shook his head. "No sir. He accused us of it, but we told him then that we didn't know anything about it."

"And his dog attacked you?"

"Yes, sir. Out of the blue. I stumbled when I was trying to fight off the dog, and that was when the gun went off. It was an accident."

"Did you then point your gun at him? And demand money? And destroy his morels?"

"No, sir. I mean, I don't think so. Like I said, I stumbled, and the bucket must have tipped over when I fell. I was on the ground trying to get the dog off, which is probably why the mushrooms were crushed. And when I was getting up, maybe the barrel might have swung in his direction, but if so, it was an accident. I was pretty shaken up, you know? And no, I didn't shoot at his dog or ask if he had any money."

Jasper listened, amazed at how easily the boy could lie. Clyde swung his gaze to Eric.

"Is that right, son? Is that what happened?"

Eric shifted from one foot to the other, looking frightened. "Yes, sir."

Clyde nodded before turning back to Jasper. "Is there anything you have to say about their recollection of events?"

Jasper met Clyde's gaze. Proverbs 14:5 had always been one of his father's favorites: *An honest witness does not deceive, but a false witness pours out lies.*

"Your boys aren't being truthful," he said.

Anne flinched, while Clyde's expression hardened. "My sons

aren't liars," he bit out. "Which makes me wonder what you really want. Did you come here for money?"

"I came because I thought that as parents, you'd want to know what your sons did, so you could hold them accountable."

No one said anything for a moment and Clyde brought a hand to his chin, pretending to search his memory.

"Funny you should offer parenting advice . . . I think I remember hearing something about your son. Didn't he end up in prison? It had something to do with a fire, didn't it?"

Jasper said nothing, but Clyde knew he'd hit the mark.

"Next time, look in the mirror before you start questioning the way I raise my sons," Clyde added. "As for your allegations, I'm confident that my sons didn't do anything wrong. I'm curious, though, as to whether you'll apologize to them for what your dog did to my older boy?"

Again, Jasper remained silent. After a few beats, Clyde took a step back and gestured toward the foyer. "Then I think it's best if you leave. My patience is at an end, and you're not welcome in my home."

With that, Jasper was shown the door.

VIII

JASPER HADN'T BEEN in the cabin for more than a few minutes before the phone rang. When he picked up, Charlie was on the other end.

His tone wasn't happy. Not only were the Littletons upset, they felt that they'd been threatened.

"I didn't threaten them," Jasper countered. "I told them what their sons had done."

"Did you call them liars?"

"I said that their sons weren't being truthful."

Charlie sighed and Jasper could hear his frustration. "Look, Jasper. Just let it go. We both know they're not the family you want on your bad side. Just stay away from them, okay? No more visits to the Littleton house."

After hanging up, Jasper stood in the kitchen. Beyond the windows, the world was dark, and he wondered where the white deer might be. Was it still in the area? Were hunters in the forest right now, trying to kill it? He wondered how long it would be until the Littleton boys tried their luck again, and whether the deer would end up stuffed and mounted as a trophy because of their desire to emulate their father.

In the darkness, there was no answer. All he really knew was that it was up to him to save it.

CHAPTER SIX

I

AFTER FINISHING UP at Our Daily Bread, Tanner went to Bill's Body Shop. Because it was only a mile and a half away, he decided to walk, even though one of the volunteers, Trudy, offered to drop him off. A bit of fresh air would do him good, and the day had warmed up nicely, bringing with it memories. One of the things he'd most enjoyed about his time in North Carolina at Fort Bragg had been the weather—months of blue skies and perfect temperatures during the spring and fall.

Tucking his phone back into his pocket, he started off, his pace neither hurried nor slow. Earlier in the day he'd spent half an hour on the phone with a woman who worked at Revology. As he'd anticipated, she had strongly recommended that the company provide the necessary parts, instead of having them procured through the aftermarket. Unfortunately, she couldn't make any promises as to how long it would take. Some might be in stock while others might have to be ordered. He wasn't thrilled that his car might take weeks to repair, but he reminded himself that his schedule was his own, at least for a while.

In any case, Asheboro was proving to be more interesting than expected. Or, rather, Kaitlyn interested him in a way that few other women had. The night before, he'd tossed and turned for nearly an hour because he hadn't been able to stop thinking about her. In the morning, as soon as he'd opened his eyes, images of her came back, and he knew with certainty that he wanted to see her again.

His decision to volunteer at Our Daily Bread had nonetheless been a tricky one. He'd wondered how Kaitlyn would feel about his showing up unannounced—was it presumptuous; was it even a bit creepy? Still, he'd decided to risk it. He hadn't been lying when he told Kaitlyn that her father's philosophy had inspired him, and he'd told himself beforehand that if he sensed that she was even slightly bothered by his presence, he'd simply keep his distance while volunteering, and afterward, back off entirely.

That was easier said than done, however, if only because the crew of regular volunteers—Trudy, Lisa, Margaret, and Linda, among others—peppered him with questions from the moment he arrived. While at first their inquiries betrayed nothing more than general curiosity, their interest became pronounced when they learned he'd heard about Our Daily Bread from Kaitlyn. One by one, it was as if little lightbulbs above their heads were illuminated and they began sharing knowing looks among themselves. Kaitlyn, he was certain, had noticed those looks as soon as she arrived. He'd forgotten how gossipy small towns could be.

To his relief, she hadn't struck him as angry or upset when she first spotted him in the kitchen. She did look a little thrown, however, and in that moment, he realized he should have—at the very least—alerted her ahead of time via text. *Why hadn't he?* he wondered in retrospect.

Because he hadn't wanted to risk her telling him not to come.

He shook his head, wondering what had gotten into him.

As he strolled the quiet streets of Asheboro, he pondered her response to his dinner invitation. It hadn't exactly been a no, but it hadn't been a yes either. He understood her reluctance, but even so, he couldn't stop thinking about her, calling to mind her startling beauty or the profound kindness she radiated. Or that her smile was so genuine and sunny it was difficult to imagine she'd ever shed a tear. It was clear that she was an outstanding mother—observing her interactions with Mitch made that obvious—and he flashed on his first impression of her standing on the porch the night of the accident. *This woman has a story to tell,* he remembered thinking, and he admitted that the last couple of days had only sharpened his desire to hear even more of it.

II

BY THE TIME Tanner reached Bill's Body Shop, the insurance adjuster was already taking more photos of the car while the owner and other employees gathered around, mumbling statements like "It's a damn shame, that's for sure."

Tanner introduced himself, and for the next twenty minutes, the adjuster and the owner went over the paperwork and discussed what needed to be done. Tanner provided contact information for Revology; the owner in turn promised to figure out the parts he'd need to order in a day or two. On the plus side, he said, the frame wasn't bent, which would make the repairs that much easier.

Toward the end, the insurance adjuster removed a set of keys he'd attached to his clipboard and motioned toward a relatively new silver Chevrolet Impala parked out front.

"I know it's not what you're used to," he said to Tanner, "but it'll get you from here to there."

Tanner completed the rental forms, signed on the dotted line.

Firing up the engine felt anticlimactic compared to his own car, but the Impala handled relatively well. Thinking he needed a bite to eat, he parked near the entrance of a local sub shop.

Bringing his sandwich and bottle of water to a table near the front window, he checked his phone. There wasn't a message from Kaitlyn yet. No matter. He unwrapped his sandwich and had taken a couple of bites when the door to the shop swung open. Three teenage girls strolled in, chattering loudly as they approached the counter. Recognition dawned a moment later.

One of them was Casey.

She looked different than she had on the night of the accident. Without mascara running down her face, she looked older and her resemblance to Kaitlyn was noticeable. She had the same dark hair and dark eyes and he was willing to bet that pretty much every guy at her high school thought she was beautiful.

He watched as she turned to one of her friends and whispered something; when the girl turned in his direction, her eyes widening, Tanner recognized her from the night of the accident as well. *The blond friend,* he thought, *the one who'd chastised him for scaring Josh.* He watched Casey as she mouthed the words *Give me a few minutes.*

Casey marched toward him; he watched with curiosity as she pulled out the chair across from him and sat down, resting her elbows on the table. Tanner slowly lowered his sandwich, smiled, and said, "Hey, there."

"So you decided to go out with my mom, huh?"

He was amused by her moxie. "We went to the zoo, if that's what you're asking." He leaned back in his chair, wiping his hands on a paper napkin.

"What's that all about?"

He fixed her with a quizzical look. "I'm not sure what you're asking me."

"I'm asking *why* you took my mom out."

He reached for his bottle of water and twisted open the cap. "Technically, I didn't take her out. She picked me up from the hotel. As to the why, spending time at the zoo seemed like a nice way to pass a few hours on a Sunday afternoon."

"It was all about the zoo, then? Is that what you're telling me?"

He raised an eyebrow, suddenly understanding why Kaitlyn often had her hands full with this one.

"Going to the zoo was something I planned to do, even before I arrived here. And when I heard your mom and Mitch were going, I asked to come along."

Her narrowed eyes remained focused on him. "Are you going to go out with her again?"

He admired her protectiveness toward Kaitlyn. "I don't know. I asked her to dinner, but she hasn't answered yet."

"I *knew* it," she said. He watched as she expelled a breath. "I could tell by the way you were looking at her after the accident that you thought she was pretty."

He took another long sip from his water bottle. "Am I allowed to ask a question now?"

"I guess."

"Does it bother you? Because I'm getting the sense you don't approve."

"I don't know you well enough to approve or not," she said. "So let's start with that. What's your story?"

He raised an eyebrow, realizing that he liked her. He gave her a quick rundown, similar to what he'd shared with Kaitlyn. When he finished, she reached for her soda. "You're one of those guys, huh?"

"What do you mean?"

"You've never been married. But you've dated, right?"

"I have."

"What's been your longest relationship?"

Oh my, he thought. But again, because she'd had the courage to ask, he answered.

"A year or so."

"That's what I thought," she said.

"You make it sound like it's a problem."

"Well is it? If you were me, and it was your mom? And some stranger, who's never had a long relationship and doesn't plan on sticking around, rolls into town?"

For the first time, he wasn't sure what to say. Finally: "It's not my intent to hurt your mom in any way," he said. "And I've enjoyed having the chance to get to know her a little better."

Casey nodded, staring out the window for a beat, then came back to him. "I know that none of this is really my business. It's just that she's my mom. And it's not like she goes on lots of dates. I think she's gone out with three guys since the divorce, and none of them lasted past the first date."

"I get it. And I think it's terrific that you're watching out for her."

She was quiet for a moment. "Did you ever get deployed when you were in the army? To Iraq?"

"Yes."

"Do you know a guy named Marshall Cullen?"

He searched his memory. "The name's not familiar."

"He's the father of one of my friends. He was in the army, too, and that's where he was sent."

"A lot of people were."

"My friend says he has nightmares. Really bad ones."

"Many veterans do."

She seemed about to ask him whether he, too, suffered nightmares, but instead she changed the subject. "Mitch told me that you taught him how to throw a Frisbee. He said you were cool."

"I like him. He's a great kid."

"He's my little buddy," she said. "I love him like crazy."

Tanner smiled but said nothing. After a beat, she went on. "Once you find this guy that you're looking for . . . what happens then?"

"I suppose that depends on how it goes."

"But no matter what, you're leaving, right? Back to Africa?"

When Tanner didn't answer, she glanced toward her friends. Then, rising from the table, she went on. "I should probably go. They're waiting for me."

"I understand," he said. "But you never answered my earlier question."

"What question?"

"Is it going to bother you if I take your mom to dinner?"

She stared at him. "I haven't decided yet."

III

AFTER FINISHING HIS sandwich, Tanner drove back to the hotel.

Kaitlyn still hadn't answered him and he found himself wondering what Casey was going to tell her. He believed Casey had been honest about being undecided about him, which mattered to him more than he wanted to admit. At the same time, he hadn't been lying when he said that he didn't want to hurt Kaitlyn either. Which left him where, exactly?

He wasn't sure, other than to accept that the next move was Kaitlyn's. No more showing up out of the blue at places like Our Daily Bread, for instance, and no more texting or calling either. She'd answer soon enough.

In any case, he should probably focus on the thing he came to Asheboro for in the first place. He gathered the information he'd assembled at the library on Saturday and began putting together a list of calls he could make to those Johnsons that had been in Asheboro in 1992 and were still here now. He jotted the phone numbers into the notebook, took a minute to think about what he was going to say, and then dialed the first number. It rang without an answer, and he proceeded to the second phone number on the list. Again, it rang without an answer.

Of the first ten calls, nine went unanswered. The one time he was able to speak with someone, he was informed that the name didn't ring a bell, and he crossed that entry off the list.

His lack of success wasn't baffling. Most people had mobile phones these days, and the only people who still called land-lines from unknown numbers were telemarketers or pollsters, or were wrong numbers. He'd never answered those kinds of calls either.

Not wanting to waste his time, he plugged his phone into the charger and propped himself on the bed, his hands clasped behind his head, making plans for the following day. He needed to return to the library so he could finish with his list. After that, he'd chart an efficient route and start knocking on doors. He estimated that quite a few of his knocks would go unanswered in the same way his phone calls had. In the middle of the day, many people would be at work. For them, an early-evening visit might be better, even if it meant interrupting their dinner.

Grabbing his iPad, he read his World War II book for the next few hours, then vegged in front of ESPN until after dark. When he turned out the light, he found his thoughts returning to his conversation with Casey. Her confidence had impressed him. It was hard to believe she was only seventeen; she was a lot more mature than he'd been at that age. He couldn't remember thinking much about his grandparents at all when he was a teenager, let alone feeling as though he had to watch out for them.

And Mitch . . .

He was also terrific, his enthusiasm contagious. We're going to the zoo? *Awesome!* The polar bear is making a ruckus? *This is great!* Would you like to try your hand at Frisbee? *Can we? Please?* It had been impossible not to smile as he'd chattered his way through lunch, and again, Tanner knew that he'd been far less charming at Mitch's age. Moving from base to base had meant leaving friends behind; it meant struggling to fit into constantly changing environments. It meant being slow to trust and even slower to open up to others, and way too many fights to remember. Mitch, on the other hand, was pretty much a happy, open book; Tanner couldn't imagine Mitch fighting with anyone.

In a way, Casey and Mitch reminded him of his friend Glen's kids. He remembered the older one was sharp and even a little pushy, while the younger was content and up for anything. Kaitlyn also reminded him a bit of Molly, he decided. And though it was a truth he kept hidden from others, Molly had always been his favorite of his friends' wives. She was, he thought, a class act in every way.

Just like Kaitlyn.

IV

THE FOLLOWING MORNING, Tanner went for his run and stopped for breakfast in the lobby before returning to his room to shower and change. He was at the library not long after it opened, and the librarian at the desk again retrieved the old phone book. Just as he'd done before, he cross-referenced the names with the newish white pages he pulled up on his phone. He then pinpointed the addresses and marked them on his map. Thinking that someone may have lived in Asheboro, moved away for a spell, and then returned to the town—or knew a family member who had—he decided to add everyone named Johnson from the newish white pages to his list and, again, pinpointed them on the map. In the end, there were more than ninety stops on his list, and he was out the door a few minutes before noon.

He decided to start on the western side of town. There were a lot of Johnsons in that area, and after reaching the first house, he approached the door and knocked. Though no one was home, a neighbor had emerged not long after he'd pulled into the drive. She was an older lady and dressed for gardening. He told her who he was looking for, but the woman shook her head.

"Henry and Ethel have daughters, not sons," she said. "They moved here from Fayetteville in 1990."

That would have been eleven or twelve years too late. "Are you sure about the date?"

"I am," she said, "because we'd just moved here the month before. I remember bringing them my famous peach pie. It placed third at the North Carolina State Fair."

Though he was itching to get to the next house, the neighbor kept talking. After describing the peach pie and sharing her secret—a pinch of nutmeg—she started asking about him, so she could tell Henry and Ethel who'd come by. He implied that the man he was looking for had been a friend he'd known in the army, which led her to another round of questions, because Henry had been in the army as well. Like Tanner, he'd been stationed at Fort Bragg.

It took nearly twenty minutes for Tanner to extricate himself, but at the second house, he got luckier. Or unluckier. The Johnsons had moved out three months earlier, and the new owners had no information at all.

Tanner hit three more houses without luck before stopping for a late-afternoon snack at Kickback Jack's. He ordered a salad and was poking at the lettuce when his phone vibrated with an incoming text. Kaitlyn. On the screen, he saw only the first part of it:

> I checked with the kids. Casey reminded me that she has midterms early this week, so I didn't want to ask her to . . .

He hesitated, thinking *I guess that's it, then,* before scrolling further.

> watch Mitch. She did suggest, however, that you come over for dinner on Wednesday night. She said she wanted to thank you again for driving her home after the accident. Does that work for you? Say around six-thirty?

Tanner raised an eyebrow, knowing that Casey hadn't made the suggestion because she wanted to thank him again. She wanted to act as a chaperone, no doubt so she could form her own opinion about her mother and the stranger who'd soon be leaving town. He typed a quick response.

> 6:30 on Wednesday sounds great. See you then.

Setting the phone aside, he smiled. Though he would rather have seen Kaitlyn sooner, he reminded himself that he had plenty of things to do until then.

V

HE SPENT THE rest of the afternoon traveling from one house to the next and crossed more names off the list. As for the ones who weren't home, he figured he'd try again in a few hours.

Finished for the time being in the western part of town, he focused next on the northern part, visiting seven more homes without luck. Once, he thought he got lucky; it was the correct name, but a single glance revealed that there was no way the man could have been his biological father. He was only a few years older than Tanner.

Finally, as dusk began to mute the brilliant colors of the spring day, he doubled back to the houses he'd visited earlier where his knocks had gone unanswered. A little more than half were now home, and with one response, he suddenly felt his heart begin to hammer in his chest. The name was right, and the man also looked to be the right age. But then he said he'd moved to Asheboro in 2001 from Pennsylvania, so again, the dates didn't work.

It was dark by the time he returned to the hotel. In all, the day had been relatively productive; he figured he'd knocked off more than a quarter of the list. At this rate, he'd be able to finish by the early part of the following week, or sooner, if he happened to get lucky.

For dinner, he went to an Italian restaurant he'd spotted a few days earlier; as he ate, he found himself wondering yet again what his biological father was like, even if he also accepted the idea that it was more than possible he was wasting his time and the man was long gone. Forty years was a long time for anyone to remain in a small town, but with his car in the shop for the foreseeable future, he had nothing better to do. More important, he knew any lingering uncertainty about the Asheboro connection to his father would plague him until he learned the truth one way or another.

Around 8:00 P.M., Tanner started making calls again. Three people answered, allowing him to cross more names off his list.

VI

ON WEDNESDAY MORNING, Tanner was back on the phone and four people answered. Again, his hopes were momentarily raised on one of those calls, but again, follow-up questions revealed that much of his day would be spent knocking on doors.

As usual, he went for a run before downing two cups of coffee, and he picked up his search where he'd left off the day before. He stopped at mobile homes and tract homes, farmhouses, and a cabin so old it looked as though it was about to fall down in the next big storm.

By late afternoon, he'd made more progress than he'd thought he might, though he still hadn't found the man he'd been looking for. His thoughts kept drifting to Kaitlyn and dinner at her house. He was looking forward to seeing her again.

VII

HE STOPPED BY the body shop on the way back to the hotel; the owner informed him that the necessary parts had been ordered. On the downside, it would take two weeks—maybe even three— for them to arrive. It made him wonder what he'd do if his search in Asheboro didn't pan out.

He supposed he could use the rental car to visit a few of the remaining widows and families he hadn't yet seen. One was in Virginia and another in Pennsylvania, both close enough to make the drive relatively easy, while the last family lived in the upper Midwest. But he decided to figure it out later. Right now, there were more important things to think about.

After showering at the hotel, he swung by a grocery store to buy wine and then Walmart to grab something else. He arrived at Kaitlyn's home a few minutes early, but Mitch opened the front door even before he'd reached the porch.

"Hi, Mr. Tanner!" Mitch had draped a small blanket over his shoulders and was holding a partially eaten apple. "My mom said to be on the lookout and answer the door when you got here. But guess what?"

"What?"

"I brought the Frisbee to school. For recess."

"Very cool," Tanner responded. "Did you have fun with it?"

"It still curves when I throw it. One time, it almost landed on the roof."

"It takes practice, but you'll get the hang of it."

Mitch let Tanner inside, where a quick glance revealed a tastefully decorated, family-friendly living room, with a soft leather recliner and a gray plush sectional that was large enough for the family to sprawl. On one wall, a flat-screen television was playing a Jurassic Park movie; a cabinet decorated with books and photos of the children and intricate pieces of glass art dominated another. Above the fireplace hung a striking photograph of clustered birch trees in winter, an austere scene of blacks and whites and grays that lent an aura of peacefulness to the room. Straight ahead, off the main hallway, was a set of stairs, and to the right he assumed were the kitchen and dining room. There was no sign of Casey.

"My mom's in the kitchen over there," Mitch said, pointing. "I'm watching a movie."

"It looks like a good one."

"I've seen it before. The raptors are pretty cool. Have you seen it?"

"I think so," he said. "I like the raptors, too. They hunt like a pack and work together."

"Exactly!" Mitch said. "You can watch with me if you want."

He smiled. "Let me say hi to your mom first, okay?"

Tanner set the bag from Walmart on the table near the door, retrieved the wine bottles, and made for the kitchen. As he rounded the breakfast bar, he noticed that the table in the dining room was already set, complete with a couple of wineglasses. Beyond the center island, Kaitlyn stood at the stove in front of a roasting pan with her back to him. She was basting a chicken nestled in a bed of carrots and onions, and a savory aroma filled the air. Her dark hair, loose and wild today, spilled over her shoulders.

"Hey," she said, glancing over her shoulder. "You made it. I wasn't sure you'd remember where I lived. I was about to text you the address."

"I remembered," he assured her, certain that she looked even more beautiful than she had just two days earlier. He set the bottles on the counter. "How was your day?"

"Typical," she said, returning her attention to basting the chicken. "How was yours? Did you start your search yet?"

"I did."

"Any luck?"

"Not yet," he answered. "On the plus side, I feel like I'm really getting to know my way around Asheboro."

"And?"

"I can see why you like living here. It's so pretty, but as I was driving around, I couldn't help wondering what people here do for a living."

"There are schools and government offices and the hospital, of course, but unless you're a doctor or lawyer or an accountant or you own your own business, you probably work in Greensboro. It's a commute, but it can be worth it. Life moves a little slower here, which is rare in this hectic world of ours."

"I get that," he said. "I like small towns, too."

"Really? A cosmopolitan, European-born-and-raised world traveler like you?"

"I'm less cosmopolitan than you think. And after the life I've lived, believe me when I tell you that a little peace and quiet is just what the doctor ordered."

"Did I? Order that, I mean?"

He laughed. "If you didn't, you should have. Whenever I returned from deployments, I'd visit my grandparents for a few days and then rent a cottage somewhere on the coast. I'd spend hours walking the beach and just listening to the sound of the waves. In the late afternoons, I'd grill on the back porch, and it was usually lights out as soon as the sun went down. And I'd do that day after day until I finally had to go back to Fort Bragg. Asheboro reminds me of those kinds of places."

"You know we don't have a beach here, right?"

"No, but you've got the national forest. If I lived here, I'm sure I'd be running the trails there every day. I've done a lot of that in the last couple years at various national parks, and I've come to believe that good mental health requires spending time in nature on a regular basis."

"And yet, you'll soon be moving back to a city of three million people," she observed before quickly shaking her head. "Sorry about that. When it comes to work, I understand that we can't always choose where we live."

She turned her attention back to the pan and started basting again. "I hope roasted chicken is okay. I found a recipe online a while back and I've always wanted to try it."

"It smells fantastic."

"It still needs to cook a little longer, so I hope you're not starving. I was late getting home."

"I'm in no rush." He reached for the bottles of wine. "I wasn't sure what you'd be making, so I bought a Sauvignon Blanc and a Pinot. If you're in the mood for wine, I mean."

"I'm always in the mood for wine," she said with a mischievous smile. "Shall we start with the white?"

"Sounds great. Do you have an opener?"

"It should be in the drawer near the sink. Right over there."

Tanner retrieved the wineglasses from the table and proceeded to fill them. He brought one to her just as she was sliding the roasting pan back into the oven. "Unfortunately, it's not chilled," he apologized.

"Would you care if I add an ice cube or two?"

"Why would I mind?"

"I don't know. Maybe you're a secret sommelier on the side and you'd be offended."

He laughed. "Actually, I think I'd like a couple of ice cubes, too."

From the freezer she scooped a handful of ice cubes and dropped them into their glasses. He watched as she took a sip.

"Oh, this is good," she said, brightening.

"I'll trust you. I don't usually drink wine."

"Because you're a fancy beer guy, right?" she asked with a wink. "By the way, I don't think you ever told me why you were looking for the guy in Asheboro . . ."

Tanner let the comment hang for a moment before shaking his head. "I didn't," he said. "It's kind of complicated."

"If you'd rather not talk about it, that's fine. It's none of my business."

"No, I don't mind," he said, flashing on the memory of his grandmother. "I think I mentioned that my mom died when she gave birth to me," he started, before filling her in on the rest. Through it all, Kaitlyn remained quiet, before she finally raised an eyebrow. "Why do you think your grandmother waited so long to share that information? And why did she reveal it then?"

Tanner shrugged. "I've wondered about that every day since she died," he said. "The best explanation seemed to be either that they didn't know much about him, or that it was too painful to talk about. Another, less generous option would be that they didn't want anyone—including me—to know anything about my bio dad because they wanted to raise me. And I get it. I was all that was left of their daughter after she died." He ran a hand over his hair. "As for the timing, I'm pretty sure it was one of those deathbed things. I think it bothered her knowing that I'd never put down roots and found a place to call home. Maybe she thought finding him would give me a family tie, or at least a sense of having come from somewhere."

He could feel her gaze on him. "Do you think it will?"

He turned back to her, spreading his palms on the kitchen island. "I don't know. It's hard for me to imagine that meeting a man I've never known will change who I am or how I live my life. But who can say?"

Kaitlyn was the first to look away. "I suppose the idea of putting down roots anywhere feels pretty alien to you."

"I've never felt the pull to stay somewhere forever," he admitted. "But then, maybe I've never had a good enough reason to."

Kaitlyn seemed to absorb this. "Well, I doubt that you'll be able to answer that question tonight," she said. "But did you think about how you'll respond if you do happen to find your father and it's not what you want?"

"What do you mean?"

He watched as she swirled the wine in her glass. "I've been around long enough to know that people don't always want the truth, especially if it's news they're not expecting. And something like this . . ."

When she trailed off, Tanner frowned. "Are you saying I shouldn't look for him?"

"I'm not saying that at all," she countered. "I'm just wondering if you've thought through all the possibilities."

"Like what?"

"What if he doesn't even remember your mom and has no interest in meeting you? Or what if he has a new family?"

When Tanner said nothing, she went on. "There's also the possibility that he wouldn't be someone you even want to know. Like . . . what if your mom and grandparents cut off ties because he's not a good person—he's been to prison or something?"

Tanner stared at her, knowing that while he'd considered some of those possibilities, hearing them aloud made them seem more serious.

"Listen," she finally added, "it's none of my business, but it's something to think about, isn't it?"

"You're right," Tanner admitted.

"I'm sorry—maybe I'm just being a pessimist."

"Don't be." He smiled, grateful not only for her wisdom, but for her honesty. "I knew that coming here would be a good idea."

"Yeah, well, how about I put you to work, getting dinner on the table?" she said with a playful nudge.

"Gladly." Tanner made a show of rolling up his sleeves and held up his hands. "I'm ready to sous-chef."

"I noticed you were pretty good at chopping tomatoes on Monday. Why don't you assemble the salad? There are cucumbers and tomatoes on the island next to the bowl of grapes, and I've already rinsed them. The knife and cutting board are there, too."

Tanner washed his hands in the kitchen sink. After drying them on a hand towel, he moved the cutting board to the counter near the stove, where she was starting to melt some butter in the saucepan. As he stood near her and began to chop, he caught a whiff of her lavender-scented perfume.

"Tell me about this chicken recipe you always wanted to try."

"It's pretty simple, actually. Butter, fennel, salt, pepper, along with lemon halves in the cavity."

"It doesn't sound that simple."

"There's not much prep and if it was too fancy, I doubt that Mitch would like it. He's a picky eater."

"Most kids are," he observed.

"On that note, it's Rice-A-Roni," she said, motioning to the box of rice on the counter. "I'm not making rice pilaf from scratch."

"I didn't know it was possible to make rice pilaf from scratch," he joked, and saw her smile. "Thanks again for the invitation tonight."

"It was Casey's idea, but I'm glad you could make it."

"I didn't see her when I came in."

"She's upstairs in her room," Kaitlyn said. "She just finished her midterms, so she's probably listening to music or watching TikTok videos to unwind. She mentioned something about going to the beach tomorrow."

"Doesn't she have school?"

"It's a teacher workday tomorrow. They have to enter grades."

"They cancel classes for that?"

"They cancel school for all sorts of reasons these days."

"I would have loved that growing up."

"Me, too, but it makes it challenging for working parents, since you have to find someone to watch the kids."

"How do you handle it?"

"When there's no school, my next-door neighbor watches Mitch. Mrs. Simpson. Super nice, retired teacher, about a dozen grandchildren."

"She sounds trustworthy."

"She is. I also have her check on Mitch after school when I'm at work if Casey isn't around. I don't want him to feel like a total latchkey kid."

"If it makes you feel better, when I was Mitch's age, my grandparents worked, and they had no idea what I was doing after school until they got home. And on weekends, I sometimes took off with my friends and spent all day doing whatever and they had no clue where I was."

"Times have changed." As he began to slice the cucumber, she said, "What was it like growing up in Italy and Germany? Did you have to learn the languages?"

He shook his head. "I went to American schools run by the Department of Defense, so the classes were all in English. But I picked up enough here and there to get by with the locals."

"Do you still speak Italian and German?"

"Just a little. If you don't use it regularly, it's amazing how fast it vanishes."

Spotting movement from the corner of his eye, Tanner saw Casey entering the living room. As she passed Mitch, she reached down to tickle him. He shrieked, giggling and squirming before she stopped just as quickly. As she approached the kitchen, she pointedly raised an eyebrow at him, as though reminding him that she would be watching him. Reaching toward the bowl of grapes, she popped one into her mouth before leaning against the counter next to Tanner.

"Hey," she chirped innocently. "I hope I'm not interrupting."

"Not at all," Kaitlyn said. She reached for a saucepan, added some butter and the Rice-A-Roni mix.

"There's wine?"

"Tanner brought it."

"Can I have a glass?"

"I don't think so."

Casey grinned. "It smells good in here. What's for dinner?"

"Roasted chicken and veggies, rice pilaf, and a salad."

"Wow. Fancy."

"Oh, stop. We have chicken all the time."

"Rotisserie chicken from the store, you mean."

"Unless you intend to start cooking, you're not allowed to complain about my meals, remember?"

"Do you need any help?"

"I think we've got it handled. It should be ready in about half an hour."

Casey casually turned her attention to Tanner. "I'm glad you could come by. I wanted to thank you again for what you did the other night."

"You're welcome," Tanner said, playing along.

"How's your car doing?"

"It'll be good as new in a little while."

"I'm glad to hear it," she said. "I like your car. It's badass."

"Language," Kaitlyn chimed in. She stirred the rice.

Tanner watched as Casey rolled her eyes. "Sorry. I should have said it's stylish."

"I like it."

"Can I drive it? Once it's repaired?"

"Casey!" Kaitlyn said in a stern voice. "What kind of question is that?"

"I'm just asking," Casey teased. "He can say no, just like you did when I asked if I could have a glass of wine."

Tanner could sense she enjoyed putting him on the spot. "Let me think about it."

"He can think about it as much as he wants, but I'm going to say no," Kaitlyn announced. She put the lid on the saucepan. "What if you wreck it again?"

"I won't wreck it," Casey protested. "I've already made my one mistake. But changing the subject, what were you two talking about just now?"

"Why, we were talking about you, of course," Kaitlyn joked.

"Seriously."

Kaitlyn shrugged. "Nothing, really. School, the challenges of being a working mother. Grown-up stuff. Are you still planning to go to the beach tomorrow?"

"No," Casey answered. "That's off. It's supposed to be cold and windy at the coast. I'll probably just hang out with Camille."

"Can you watch Mitch after he gets home from school?"

"He doesn't need me to watch him, Mom. Mrs. Simpson is next door."

"I know, but he'd love it."

"Fine." She sniffed. "Before I forget, I'm planning to spend the night at Camille's on Friday."

"Will her parents be home?"

"Of course," Casey answered.

"And you're not going to a party?"

"We're going to watch scary movies."

"You know I'm going to touch base with Camille's parents beforehand, just to make sure."

Casey sighed. "Fine. We're going to a party at Mark's first, then we're going to Camille's to watch scary movies."

"Will his parents be there?"

"Yes, Mom. I promise."

"Okay. But make sure you don't stay out too late."

"I never do," she sang. "Anyway, let me know when dinner's ready. I'm going to go bug Mitch until then. So you two can discuss grown-up things."

She pushed off the counter and left. By that time, Tanner had finished with both the cucumbers and the tomatoes and Kaitlyn shared a long-suffering look with him.

"Welcome to my world."

"You're great with her."

"I've learned to choose my battles carefully."

VIII

WHEN THE MEAL was on the table, Kaitlyn called out to the kids and reminded them to turn off the television; as they ambled toward the dining room, Mitch poked Casey in the ribs and took off running when she yelped. They chased each other around the table before finally taking their seats, panting and giggling.

Kaitlyn stood so she could more easily cut the chicken into portions. Both Mitch and Kaitlyn favored the legs and thighs, while Casey and Tanner preferred the white meat. Rice and salad were passed around while Mitch pestered Tanner about the contents of the Walmart bag he'd left near the door.

"I brought Jenga," he answered. "In case you wanted to play after dinner."

Casey shot him a skeptical look. "Jenga?"

"Do you know the game?"

"I know how to play," Casey said. "It's just that the last time I played, I was probably in third grade."

"It's not just for kids. My buddies and I played it overseas when we were deployed."

"Cool!" Mitch said.

Casey wrinkled her nose. "It's still a child's game."

"Then you should have no trouble beating me, right?"

Casey's eyes lit up, and as they began to eat, the conversation flowed easily. Kaitlyn asked for updates on school; Casey announced that the midterms were so easy as to almost be a joke, while Mitch said that he'd begun reading *Where the Red Fern Grows* during quiet time. He asked Tanner if they could play Frisbee again after dinner before adding that he also wanted to show Tanner all the carvings he'd made. Casey told a funny story about Camille—that she'd frantically searched her backpack looking for her phone and had begun to cry hysterically, only to realize that her phone was in her jacket pocket when it suddenly began to ring. When Tanner asked Kaitlyn about the craziest diagnosis she'd ever had to make, she thought for a moment before finally relating a story about a female patient whose initial symptoms were slight bruising on her stomach and a vivid hallucination where she imagined that spiders were crawling over her skin. Kaitlyn had learned during her exam that she traveled frequently to Mexico; she'd also noted that the patient looked twenty years younger than she actually was, with glowing skin and nary a wrinkle.

"I was a resident at the time," Kaitlyn went on. "First, we thought it was a B-twelve deficiency, but when she started to bleed from her nose and ears, we knew something else was causing it. We ran tests for everything from Huntington's to multiple sclerosis. In the end, the attending finally diagnosed her with leprosy."

Tanner blinked. "You mean like leprosy in the Bible leprosy?"

"Diffuse lepromatous leprosy, also known as pretty leprosy."

Casey wrinkled her nose. "How can leprosy be pretty? Doesn't it make body parts fall off?"

"Wait!" Mitch cut in. "Body parts fall off?"

"Only in serious cases, if left untreated. But pretty leprosy, in the early stages, smooths the skin and erases wrinkles."

"Maybe people should get that instead of Botox," Casey snarked.

"Ha ha," Kaitlyn said. "Anyway, the diagnosis was a big deal at the time. It's not like doctors in the U.S. see leprosy regularly. But in the end, we treated the patient, and she was fine."

"She kept all her body parts?" Mitch asked.

"All of them," Kaitlyn assured him. "On the downside, she got wrinkles. She wasn't happy about that part of it."

After dinner, Tanner threw the Frisbee with Mitch while Kaitlyn cleaned up. Casey followed them out and joined the game. Eventually Kaitlyn came out to the porch to watch, though when asked if she'd like to join them, she passed.

"I'll just sip my wine and watch you three have fun."

Eventually Tanner begged off and they all went back inside. Casey grabbed the Walmart bag near the door and had already opened the box before taking her seat at the kitchen table. She quickly reviewed the rules as a refresher, then stacked the blocks into a tower.

"Using one hand, take out any block that's not in the top row and stack it on top," she said to Mitch. "If the tower falls, you lose."

It was clear to Tanner that Casey was intent on winning. Whenever it was her turn, she took her time to gently poke various blocks before making her choice. Mitch was less selective, and in the first game, he was the one who toppled the tower. In the next game, Kaitlyn toppled it. Mitch lost the third game, and to Tanner's chagrin, he lost the fourth one. He would have blamed the wine—he'd finished nearly two glasses by then—but Kaitlyn had the same amount and her hands seemed to be growing steadier, most likely because she was a doctor. Or at least that's what Tanner told himself.

Through it all, there was good-natured trash talk as well as laughter, and when Tanner finally put the blocks back in the box, Kaitlyn looked at the clock before reminding Mitch that he had to take his bath and start getting ready for bed.

"But what about the carvings? I haven't showed Mr. Tanner yet."

"Just grab a few of them, okay? It's getting late."

Mitch vanished from the table and came trotting back down the steps less than a minute later with his arms full. On the kitchen table he set them upright: a cougar, a dog, a donkey, a duck, an elephant, and a giraffe, among others.

"Wow," Tanner said, impressed. "You've got your own zoo."

"I know, right?"

"Is this one you?" Casey asked, pointing to one of them.

"No," Mitch protested. "It's a dog!"

"It kind of looks like you."

"Mom . . ."

"Casey," Kaitlyn warned.

"I just said that because it was cute," Casey said. "Mitch might not be cute yet, but one day, he will be."

"You're not cute either. I think this one is you," he said, picking up one of them.

"Hmmm. That makes sense. I have been told I'm a bit of a unicorn."

"It's a donkey, not a unicorn!" Mitch cried. "See? There's no horn and it has big ears just like you."

"I think that's enough for now," Kaitlyn said. "Go take your bath."

Mitch nodded before scooping up the animals. "Good night, Bubble Butt," he sang over his shoulder as he disappeared up the stairs.

"I'm going upstairs, too," Casey said. "I mean, I enjoy pretending it's the 1950s as much as the next modern teenage girl, but the texts are piling up."

A minute later, Tanner and Kaitlyn were alone at the table.

"I had a good time tonight," he said in the sudden quiet.

"It was fun," she agreed. "It's easier when Casey is on her best behavior."

"Want to sit outside on the porch?" he asked. "It's a beautiful night."

"Is there any wine left in the bottle?"

He reached for it and topped off both of their glasses before they moved outside. Seated in rocking chairs on the porch, they could see the neighbors' homes illuminated from within, the moonlight bathing the yards in a silver glow. From one of the homes, he could hear the faint sound of music playing.

"Do you sit out here much?"

"Hardly ever," she admitted. "That's more my parents' thing. They used to sit on the front porch after work and on the weekends. In fact, these rockers were among their wedding gifts. But sitting on the front porch wasn't something that George liked to do, even in the rare moments he was around."

"You've got to admit, it's kind of nice."

"It is." She rested her head on the back of her rocker, gazing at him from beneath lowered lids. "I'm really glad you came tonight," she said softly.

"Me, too."

"The kids like you. Even Casey, which is kind of astounding."

"Why?"

"She didn't like any of the guys I dated after the divorce. Not that there were all that many."

"That's normal, isn't it? A lot of kids fantasize about their parents getting back together, so it makes sense that they wouldn't like anyone new."

"I guess." She took a sip of wine. "I want to ask you something, but I also want you to know that I'll understand if you don't want to talk about it."

"Ask whatever you'd like."

"It's about your time in the military," she began.

He nodded. "What do you want to know?"

"I don't know. Why you joined, what it was like. Why you left."

"And whether it messed me up, right?"

"I don't think it messed you up," she protested. Then: "Did it?"

He gave a wry smile. "I don't think so, but as you've already learned, my life choices haven't exactly been typical." He stared up at the sky, collecting his thoughts. "By the time I was thirteen or fourteen, I knew that college wasn't for me, and because of my granddad, the army seemed like a natural fit. I was young and cocky and believed I was bulletproof, so I enlisted. And I quickly figured out that the army, in some ways, is just like any other bureaucracy. Some of those who outrank you are great, others are idiots, but in the end, you're just a cog in the machine. Then came 9/11. I don't know if you remember what those first years were like after the towers fell, but there was a massive surge of patriotism, especially in the military, and it felt as though I suddenly understood my purpose. And for a long time, I did. Which was why I ended up going the Delta route, after the Rangers. The U.S. had been attacked, and I was tasked with eliminating the infrastructure and people that made the attack possible. So that's what I did, night after night. And I felt like I was doing the most important job in the world."

When he paused, she stopped rocking and turned in her seat to face him. "But?"

"The mission evolved," he said with a shrug. "After a few years, it wasn't just about the Taliban or Al Qaeda or Bin Laden, it was suddenly about Iraq. We were sent to find weapons of mass destruction, but there weren't any. Then we were supposed to get Iraq on track toward democracy, and that didn't work out so well either. Then we were supposed to help establish a stable government in Afghanistan, which meant breaking bread with tribal leaders and villagers who might have shot up your camp earlier that same morning. It got . . . confusing. The goalposts weren't just moving; they were continually being shifted into entirely different stadiums. With every new deployment, there were new ideas, and eventually, the whole thing sort of lost its luster. A lot of my friends began stepping away and eventually, I did the same."

"Do you regret leaving?"

He leaned his head back, pondering the best way to explain it. "When I got out, I knew I was making the right decision. I knew I was done. But the passage of time changes things. Now, I can't help thinking that those were some of the best years of my life. I wouldn't trade them for anything."

"Seriously?" Kaitlyn's expression was doubtful.

"Unless you've been there, I'm not sure you can ever really understand it. But the truth is, you feel very much *alive* when you're undertaking missions with people you trust. There's a deep camaraderie, absolute unity of purpose, and overwhelming intensity, with actual human lives on the line. Factor in massive adrenaline dumps, and . . . war becomes its own addictive drug. I know I'm not the first one to describe it that way, but it's true, even if you don't want to admit it to yourself. I think that's part of the reason a lot of veterans have trouble adjusting to life in the civilian world. There's just nothing comparable."

He paused to take a sip of wine, feeling her eyes on him.

"I'm not trying to make it seem romantic, because it wasn't. It was dirty and stressful and frequently boring, and when you're in the thick of it, all you want to do is get out of there. You dream about spending time with your grandparents or enjoying the simple things in life. Activities like mowing the lawn or kicking back to watch a ball game on TV with friends take on almost spiritual significance. But then, when you do get back from deployment, you realize that those things aren't enough to fill the void created by what you left behind."

"I think I understand," Kaitlyn said after a moment. "And it makes sense that part of you would miss it. Which I assume explains why you decided to work for USAID, too. Because suburban life in America wasn't for you?"

"That was part of it for sure, but the other part had to do with guilt. I lost a lot of friends, as I already told you, but by the end, I realized that nothing we'd done in Afghanistan had really mattered in the long run. Most of the clans and tribes still considered us invaders and infidels no matter how much we were trying to help them. To them, we were the bad guys, and I guess part of me wanted to make up for that by doing something good in the world."

"And now?"

"What do you mean?"

"How does suburban American life strike you now?"

"It's hard for me to say. I was on vacation in Lahaina when Covid hit, so I stayed there for a few months, but it never really felt like home. Later, when I was with my grandma in Pensacola, that was its own sad situation, and again, it never felt like home."

"I'm just glad you're not haunted by what you went through in the same way that some of your friends were."

"Maybe," he said, "but I'm not sure I'd consider myself normal either. What about you, though? Any battle scars you want to tell me about?"

"Like my divorce, you mean?"

"Do you want to tell me what happened?"

She was quiet for a moment. "It was one of those things that worked until it didn't," she finally said. "That's what I tell people

and there's a lot of truth to it—we were more like business partners by the end, as opposed to a couple—but the way it happened
left me feeling worthless for a long time." She closed her eyes
and sighed before glancing over at him. "He left me for a Pilates
instructor a few days before my fortieth birthday."

"You're kidding."

"Nope. I remember kind of disassociating when he told me. I
mean, the whole thing was such a cliché. Even her name. Amber.
He moved out that same night."

"Is that the one he married?"

"It is," she said. "I'll give it ten years at the most, but that's just
me being the occasionally vengeful ex-wife."

He smiled before she went on. "But that was just the start of
it. The divorce process was awful, too. He kept insisting on joint
custody, with the kids moving from my house to his house every
other week, but to my mind, he was using the kids as leverage to
lower his property settlement. It's not that I didn't want the kids
to see him or spend time with him, but his work meant that he
was out of the house every day by six-thirty in the morning,
and he usually didn't make it home until half past seven. Unlike
me, he's on call at the hospital and even works two or three Saturdays a month. Which meant the kids were with a nanny, not
him, and they were struggling, so in the end, I caved. He got
most of everything, while I got primary physical custody of the
kids. If there was anything positive at all about the experience, it
was that I lost respect for him, which made it easier to finally
move on."

"Sounds rough," he said. "I already don't like him."

"Thanks," she said. She was quiet for a moment. "As far as
other scars, I think it's the same one all working mothers develop.
This feeling that I'm failing, no matter what I do. When I'm at
work, I wish I could be there more for my kids; when I'm with

my kids, I feel like I'm wasting my education. And it's complicated by the fact that work fills a need inside me, one distinct from my life as a mom, and that sometimes makes me feel guilty, too."

"So lots of damage in your past."

She laughed. "At least I'm not living in Motel Sixes."

"Excuse me," he said. "I'm staying at the Hampton Inn."

"My mistake," she said, her voice teasing.

"And the kids. How are they doing with all of it now?"

"I think they've gotten used to it. In all fairness, he does well at keeping in touch. He calls them regularly, sends them money and gifts, and they spend every other holiday and a month in the summer with him. But . . ."

He raised an eyebrow before she went on. "Casey just threatened to go live with him next school year. He said he'd get her a car if she did."

"Do you think she was serious?"

"I don't know. But she's old enough to make the decision, so if she does want to go, I won't try to stop her."

"She'll stay," Tanner reassured her, but he could sense how powerless Kaitlyn felt. In time, she shook her head.

"Anyway, that's my story."

"Thank you for telling me," he said, meeting and holding her eyes.

Kaitlyn was the first to look away. "I should probably make sure Mitch is in bed," she said.

Tanner nodded and the two of them rose from their seats and went inside. While Kaitlyn went upstairs to check on Mitch, Tanner washed the wineglasses. By the time he'd dried them, she was coming back down the stairs.

"All good," she offered when she reached the kitchen. "Would you like some coffee before you go?" she asked.

"Decaf would be great, but only if you're having some."

Kaitlyn prepped the coffeemaker and then pulled out a pair of mugs from the cabinet.

It didn't take long to brew, and Kaitlyn brought the mugs to the table.

"What are you doing tomorrow night?" he asked.

"I have no idea," she responded, wrapping her hands around her mug. "Why?"

"Because I was hoping we could do dinner again. I would have suggested Friday, but I heard Casey say she's going to a party."

Kaitlyn waited for a moment before raising her eyes. "I'm not sure that would be a good idea," she said, her voice soft.

Tanner had a feeling he knew what she was going to say.

"I like you. Talking to you tonight, I realized how much I enjoy spending time with you, and if we go out again, I'll probably like you even more. And that scares me. Because you're going to be leaving town soon. And then, after that, you'll be leaving the country. I'm not sure that's what I need in my life right now."

He recognized the truth of what she was saying, even if it wasn't what he wanted to hear. "I understand."

"But just know that yes, if things were different, I'd have loved to see you again."

"I can't say that makes me feel any better," he said.

"I know," she said. "And I'm sorry."

He stared into his coffee mug, then drained it. "It's getting late, and you have work tomorrow. Which means I should probably get going."

She seemed relieved, even if he noted a shadow of regret in her eyes. "I'll walk you out."

Tanner brought his cup to the sink and rinsed it; she set hers on the counter. As they started for the door, she paused. "Don't forget to take your game," she reminded him.

"Oh, that's for the kids to keep," he said.

"Thank you."

They descended the porch steps, heading toward his rental car. As he walked beside her, it struck him that these might be the last moments they spent together, a reality that felt strangely weighted. And yet, as they finally reached his car, he found himself turning toward her. When she met his gaze, he took a small step toward her, his hand automatically reaching for her hip.

He expected her to stop him, expected her to retreat, but she continued to hold his gaze as he moved even closer. He tugged gently, feeling as she responded by leaning toward him, their bodies slowly coming together.

Her lips were soft and warm, and when his tongue briefly met hers, he felt an electric charge run through him. He succumbed then to the sensation, the urgent press of her body against his own. His hand went to her lower back, holding her even closer, and for a long time, they continued to kiss, Tanner losing himself completely in the glory of her scent and skin, the hollows of her neck and the ragged sound of her breath.

When they finally separated, he sensed both her longing and her sadness. "Tanner . . ." she whispered, and though he knew she meant it as a goodbye, he couldn't bring himself to end it like this. Instead, he breathed the words that had been inside him, from the moment he'd first seen her.

"You're beautiful, Kaitlyn."

She closed her eyes, and for a moment her face seemed to glow in the milky half-light of the moon. When her eyes drifted open, her pupils looked huge, hypnotic, casting a spell that he was powerless to resist.

"Okay," she said, her voice sounding almost dreamlike. "Let's go to dinner tomorrow."

CHAPTER SEVEN

I

JASPER SAW THE white deer, though not in the way he wanted.

It was on the morning news, something Jasper seldom watched. He'd long since grown bored by the television, but for whatever reason he'd felt an undeniable urge to tune in shortly after he awakened on Tuesday morning.

He saw the blurry photo taken from Scenic Road before the segment segued into a video that a hiker had supposedly taken the day before. Roughly ten seconds long, it showed the white deer standing near a rocky outcropping and seeming to be staring at the camera, its head held high. Because of the foliage around it—and the shakiness of the video—it was difficult to make out the antlers or even its size, and soon enough it turned and started walking away until it vanished into the forest. The newscasters, practically vibrating with excitement on the early-morning broadcast, noted that the video had already gone viral.

Jasper wasn't sure what *viral* meant, only that it probably wasn't good. He guessed that it meant that more people would learn about the white deer, possibly luring even more poachers to the area.

Jasper turned off the television and mulled what to do next. Trying to save the white deer meant finding it first, and fortunately there were now two locations where it had been spotted. Even more important, he recognized the area where the video had been taken. There had been a unique outcropping of boulders in the background; decades ago, his kids used to scramble and climb over them on weekend hikes. A few times, they'd even picnicked nearby.

Walking to the kitchen, Jasper opened one of the drawers, where he stored his maps. Most of them were worn and out of date, but near the bottom, he found the one he wanted. It was a county map representing the city of Asheboro along with portions of the Uwharrie National Forest.

At the table, he used a pen to mark where the photo had been taken off Scenic Road; another mark, near the boulders, indicated the video. He estimated the distance between the two places at a couple of miles, and he drew an oval between them. This was, he assumed, the white deer's current range, and it made sense to him. He knew there was food and water in the area, and as Charlie had said, the deer would likely remain there until either the food stores were depleted or it felt threatened.

Smart poachers, he suspected, would also be able to estimate the white deer's current range. Anyone could mark spots and draw an oval on a map, even if they didn't know the location of the boulders. A deer's range was a deer's range, so all they'd have to do was draw a circle out from the photograph on Scenic Road. At the same time, it was one thing to find and kill the deer; it was another thing entirely to transport a heavy carcass from the forest without being discovered, which meant they'd need access for their vehicles. They'd have to know the roads that led in and out of the forest and predict how busy they might be at various times of day; they'd also have to find or create their own off-road trails to lead them close to the white deer's range. They'd need to know the locations of the campgrounds and the ranger stations, if only to avoid them, not to mention steer clear of hikers and folks who showed up in Jeeps to go off-roading. It had been years since Jasper had driven through the forest, and because he suspected that there were more roads and trails now than in the past, his first step was to figure out how a poacher might approach the deer's range and then exit the forest without being caught.

Before he set out to do just that, Jasper brewed a pot of coffee and made an egg sandwich for breakfast. The egg was burned at the edges, but he'd never been much good at cooking. That had always been Audrey's passion, demonstrated in the dishes she used to bring him before she left for college.

When she had left for Sweet Briar, Jasper's savings had been nearly depleted. He was eighteen, and needing a job, he'd found work with a contractor named Ned Taylor, who was unlike Stope in nearly every way. Elderly and overweight, with a shock of unruly white hair, he puffed ceaselessly on a corncob pipe whenever he was at the site. Most gratifying of all, he praised the quality of Jasper's work from the very beginning.

Jasper had barely settled into his new job, however, when his life was upended again. In September, only a month after Audrey had left, Hurricane Helene unleashed massive rainfall and a nearby creek in Asheboro quickly rose to dangerous levels. Fortunately—or unfortunately, as the case may be—Jasper was at his house in town, not the cabin, when it began to flood. He pushed through water that soon reached his waist, gathering up photographs from the mantel, his father's Bible, and as many of the carvings they'd made together as he could carry, hauling it all to his truck, which he'd parked on higher ground, just in case. As the storm continued to rage, a loblolly in the yard snapped and crashed through the roof. Days later, after the water finally receded and hot weather returned, mold began growing on the walls and the floors, ruining pretty much everything in the house that the storm hadn't.

Like his neighbors and others in town, Jasper contacted his insurance company. He wasn't worried. Like the other bills, he'd continued to pay the premiums after his father had passed, but when he finally met with the claims adjuster, Jasper discovered that buried in that policy was an exclusion for damage caused by flooding. The adjuster pointed out the section and read the words aloud, emphasizing the point. The policy would, however, pay for the roof damage.

The claims adjuster slid a check across the table. It wasn't much and nowhere near the amount it would take to repair the house. In the silence that followed, Jasper heard his father's voice: "James 1:12." *Blessed is the man who remains steadfast under trial.*

He deposited the check, moved into the cabin, and continued working for Ned. In the evenings and on weekends, he removed sodden, moldy furniture from the house in Asheboro. He stripped off the roof, tore up the floors, ripped out the plaster walls and all the electrical wiring. He hauled the debris to the dump. In the end, only the framing and plumbing remained, and he sold the property to another contractor, someone Ned had known for years. That check went into his savings as well.

In November, Ned asked him to drive to Charlotte to pick up a bathtub that had been delayed in delivery. On the outskirts of town, he noticed two new subdivisions, right next to each other, with dozens of homes already built and others still under construction. Independent contractors like Ned were slowly giving way to developers who built hundreds of homes at a time, and on a whim, Jasper decided to tour one of those neighborhoods. He found himself awed by the organizational prowess necessitated by such developments, despite his certainty that he would never want to live in such a neighborhood. There was an almost desolate feel, even on those streets with completed homes. Staring at the tracts of sterile, cookie-cutter houses, he suddenly realized that what would help make the neighborhood more inviting were *trees*. Not the skeletal saplings that had been planted haphazardly by the new owners, but beautiful, leafy trees that grew quickly.

The idea wouldn't go away, and as more subdivisions were built over the next year, he toured them as well, growing ever more certain that he was right. In early 1960, he visited the local library in search of an ideal tree, but it was no help; nor was the library in Raleigh, though the woman at the main desk recommended he visit the school of agriculture at North Carolina State University. It took time and persistence to get a meeting, but the professor there—the same one who would later instruct him on how to cultivate morels—told him about a tree that the USDA was thinking of formally introducing to the United States.

The professor shared photographs and information, and Jasper took it all in. Originally from Korea and China, the tree grew quickly, bloomed with white flowers in the spring, had a lovely pyramidal shape, and showcased brilliant colors in the fall. Its scientific name was *Pyrus calleryana;* at the U.S. Department of Agriculture, they were thinking about calling it the Bradford pear, even though it would bear no edible fruit. The professor added that few people—outside of agricultural research universities and the USDA—seemed to be interested in the tree at the present time, but he predicted the market would eventually grow to be substantial.

Jasper worked with Garner's Nursery in town to procure the obscure seeds from Korea; Mack Garner had served in the Korean War, and his wife was originally from Seoul. Using the insurance money and the proceeds from the sale of the house, he leased some inexpensive land about twenty miles away and bought fertilizer. He took a week off work, tilled and fertilized the ground, and planted enough seeds for five thousand trees. He hand-watered them on evenings after work and on weekends, and surprising no one more than himself, the seeds sprouted and burst from the soil almost immediately.

He showed Audrey what he was doing when she came home for the summer. In the previous couple of years she'd grown even more beautiful in his eyes, and they'd continued to see each other whenever she was home. They took long walks and split choco-late sodas, and she'd regale him with stories about her classes or her professors or the friends she'd made. Sometimes, when he wondered aloud whether she wanted to leave her previous life—and him—behind, she'd laugh and dismiss his words as nonsense. He told her regularly that he loved her and she said the same to him, yet when he said goodbye to her in August for the third time, her parents looked on with the same grim expressions he'd long since grown used to.

Meanwhile, he'd continued working for Ned and had leased even more land. He planted tens of thousands more trees. He showed Audrey's parents what he'd been up to. It didn't fully change their mind about him—there were no sales yet, or even a market—but he liked to think that her mother's expression seemed less pinched after that, even if her disapproval was still plain.

After Audrey graduated, in May 1962, she wasn't ready to begin teaching. In her mind, she'd been in school for a long time and needed a break, so instead, she went to work at her mother's clothing store. Jasper was thrilled by her return to Asheboro, and they picked up right where they'd left off. Then, in the spring of 1963, the USDA formally introduced the Bradford pear to the U.S. market. By that point, with Jasper's trees flourishing, the first year's crop was large and mature enough for sale. He quit working for Ned to devote himself full-time to the trees. He dug them up—wrapping the soil in burlap—loaded them into his pickup truck, and began meeting with developers in Charlotte, Greensboro, and Winston-Salem. His sales pitch was simple; he showed them the information from the USDA, kept his prices reasonable, then offered to place the trees in the fronts and back-yards of the subdivisions so the developers could see for them-selves how much aesthetic value they conferred. He also visited nurseries, and—because he had pretty much a monopoly on the tree—in no time at all, orders began flooding in. He sold not only the entirety of the first year's crop, but much of the follow-ing year's as well.

Flush with cash for the first time in his life, he made his way to Audrey's house. Again, he asked to speak with her father; again, he had his mother's wedding ring in his pocket. This time, her father agreed, and he proposed to Audrey two days later.

They were married in October 1963, and spent their honey-moon on Sullivan's Island, just as she'd always wanted. She moved into the cabin, and though she was pregnant within a month, she insisted on making the place *their* home, not simply *his*. She bought new furniture and sewed curtains and spread rugs in the living room and bedrooms. She bought pots and pans and plates and utensils that matched. They set up the nursery in what had once been Jasper's room, and whenever she cooked, the cabin would fill with delicious aromas. They made love almost every night, and for Christmas that year, as a gift, he built and installed the bookshelves she wanted, because he knew it would make her happy. He also spread before her rough floor plans for a lovely white house with a porch and a kitchen large enough to allow the whole family to gather. Because he knew she wanted at least four children, he'd filled the second floor with bedrooms and bathrooms. Surveying Jasper's plans, her eyes brimmed with tears of joy.

He started construction the following year, after Audrey gave birth to their first child, and after yet another bumper crop of Bradford pears.

II

AFTER RINSING HIS cup and plate, Jasper made a few peanut butter and honey sandwiches for both himself and Arlo and filled a thermos with the remainder from the coffeepot. He fed Arlo a bit more than usual and stuffed a handful of Milk-Bones into the pocket of his jacket. It was going to be a long day.

He grabbed his binoculars on the way out the door, and thinking he might want company, he decided to let Arlo ride in the cab. He rolled down both windows, watching as the dog raised his nose to the wind. When he stopped at a nearby gas station, there was a young man behind the register with long hair and a pierced earring; on his neck was the tattoo of a spider. Jasper asked if they carried any recent maps of the Uwharrie National Forest, but Spider Tattoo shook his head.

"We don't sell maps."

"How can you not sell maps?"

He seemed baffled by the question. "Uh . . . most people just use their phones."

Jasper had no more luck at the next gas station, nor at the third one he visited, proving again that the modern world had left him far behind. Resolving to figure it out on his own, he started toward the main entrance of the forest. Beside the entrance he spotted a sign bearing a general map of the forest, including its main roads. Jasper stopped the truck. In his glove compartment, he found a broken pencil and an envelope with an ancient repair bill tucked inside. On the back, he copied the map as best he could.

Though his truck was old, it had four-wheel drive, which was helpful as he followed a road into the forest before turning at a fork that led toward the campground. He spent a short time there looking for suspicious vehicles or people before realizing he wasn't exactly sure what either might look like. Beyond the campground was a fire access road, and he followed that until reaching a junction that led to yet another fire road and then, finally, back to one of the main roads. Every now and then, he'd stop the truck and sketch the new roads onto his makeshift map; he also used his binoculars to scan the forest, even though he was nowhere near the area the white deer had been spotted. Just in case.

By midafternoon, Jasper had figured out the lay of the land. He'd covered all the main roads and fire roads, even a few of the off-road trails. He had a good sense of how a poacher might access the deer's range and, crucially, exit the forest without being seen.

Jasper stopped to have lunch, and as far as he could tell, Arlo enjoyed the sandwiches as much as he did. He finished two cups of coffee, then loaded Arlo back into the truck. Next up was what he knew would be the most important scouting of the day.

He followed a fire road in a southerly direction until it ended, then bumped along an off-road trail that angled even farther south. Anyone trying to get to this area of the forest with a vehicle would *have* to go the same way; his earlier exploration had revealed that the terrain on either side of the trail blocked other possible access. The truck squeaked and bounced, the elevation gradually increasing. Jasper stopped more frequently and scanned the area with binoculars. He saw nothing but birds and trees. Eventually, the off-road trail came to an end, but it was still too far away from the white deer's current range for a poacher. Hauling a heavy carcass all the way to this spot would be all but impossible.

Jasper reversed the truck fifty yards. He looked around but saw no evidence that a vehicle had left the off-road trail and entered the forest. He backed the truck up again, then a couple more times, until he finally spotted a small sapling, recently snapped near the base. Looking closer, he saw tire tracks on either side of it.

Gotcha.

He followed the tracks, this time into the virgin forest. He drove slowly, veering around trees and rocks and over the undulating terrain. He continued to head south, in the general direction of his cabin, and eventually came to an area thick with heavy underbrush. Off to one side was a large berm. Dusk, he assumed, was still a few hours away.

Jasper got out of the truck. The temperature was beginning to drop, and he looked around, thinking he knew exactly where he was. In one direction was Scenic Road; in the other was the spot where the white deer had been filmed. He estimated he was a half a mile away from the heart of the white deer's range, but a poacher would want to get his vehicle even closer. Newer trucks, unlike his, might be able to handle the dense undergrowth ahead, and sure enough, he was able to find the spot where a vehicle had continued south. Most likely, he thought, it had been a truck with oversized tires, like the kind he'd seen in the Littletons' driveway.

The teens, he had to admit, had done well in identifying the white deer's range on Sunday. After all, they'd only had the single photograph to go on at that point. He wondered how much farther south they'd taken the truck, but he'd have to proceed on foot to figure it out. It was getting late for that, though, so instead, he crawled back into the cab. He inched the truck toward the nearest berm, eventually pulling behind it and turning off the engine.

Then he walked back to the spot where he'd originally stopped, ignoring the tightness in his back, and nodded to himself, thinking the parking spot was a good one. Assuming the Littletons and Melton would use the same route the next time they came, his truck was out of sight. Good enough.

Crawling back into the cab, he glanced at Arlo.

"I think we should rest our eyes for a bit, don't you?"

Arlo yawned as though in agreement and Jasper slouched lower, making himself comfortable. Closing his eyes, he figured he had plenty of time.

Poachers, he knew, were more likely to commit their crimes in the hours after sundown, and again in the hours before the sun came up.

III

JASPER DOZED BUT didn't sleep. He kept the windows rolled down, listening with half an ear for the sounds of any approaching vehicle.

Dusk arrived, then, finally, darkness. Though his nighttime vision had faded over the years, Jasper figured it wouldn't matter. Approaching headlights, or a spotlight, would be impossible to miss in the forest.

He poured the last of the coffee from his thermos. He fed Arlo another sandwich. Every now and then, he got out of the truck and walked to the other side of the berm, but aside from the hoot of an occasional owl, the forest seemed empty.

He stayed until just half past ten, by which point he figured the white deer—and other deer—had bedded down for the night. It took a series of cranks to fire up the engine and he slowly inched his way back through the forest to the off-road trail, and then to the fire road and finally the exit. Once he was back at the cabin, he set his alarm clock for very early in the morning.

Tuesday turned into Wednesday as he lay in bed, and maybe it was the coffee, but he couldn't sleep. Instead, he stared at the ceiling, his thoughts wandering back to the early years of his marriage, after he and Audrey had become parents. They'd named their oldest son after King David, one of the writers of the Psalms, and he remembered the exhausted pride on Audrey's face as she'd held their son in her arms. When he bent lower to kiss her, she'd whispered, "Look what our love has made," and his eyes had filled with tears.

He remembered working with Ned as they began construction on the new house, and the way Audrey insisted on visiting the site every afternoon, so she could follow the daily progress. He recalled the almost casual way Audrey rolled over in bed one day, and let him know that she was pregnant again. Mary—named after Our Savior's mother—was born in June 1965, three days after they'd moved into the new house. Though Audrey should have been exhausted, she immediately threw herself into decorating, adding her personal touches and flourishes, even while taking care of two children who were still in diapers.

Through all of that, Jasper continued to expand his business, selling Bradford pear trees in states as far away as Tennessee. He leased more land and hired employees, eventually topping out at more than a dozen. He owed nothing on his house and had money in the bank. But because he worried about what he'd read in Matthew 19:24—that it was easier for a camel to pass through the eye of a needle than it was for a rich man to enter the kingdom of heaven—he donated the funds necessary to renovate the church and supported the local food bank. For the most part, he kept only what he needed to support his family, and though his generosity sometimes made Audrey nervous, Jasper assured her that they would never lack for anything that mattered.

So much from those early years, he thought with an ache, were mostly a blur. He could recall the occasionally messy house and how lovely Audrey looked whenever she smiled. He remembered the births of Deborah, named in honor of the judge and prophetess, and Paul, named in honor of the apostle and martyr. By 1969, they'd become a family of six, and Jasper could still bring to mind the feeling of pride he experienced as a husband and father whenever they sat together at church or when they clustered around the dinner table.

As for Audrey, motherhood came as naturally to her as breathing. From the very beginning, she knew intuitively whether a baby was crying because he or she was hungry or needed a diaper changed or whether the baby simply wanted to be held. She smiled and laughed even on days with little sleep and was unfazed by the challenge of dragging all of them to the grocery store or getting them dressed for church, even when they were running late. She brought them to the pediatrician regularly but not obsessively, and somehow found time to make a journal for each child, in which she not only kept track of their development but made notes about their delightful quirks and idiosyncrasies. She sometimes admitted to Jasper that she wished she could lose the baby weight—an extra twenty pounds that never went away—but to him, she was even more alluring than when she'd first jumped into his truck, so long ago.

As his thoughts continued to drift, a carousel of images rolled through his mind.

The wonder he felt as he held his firstborn in his arms, right after birth . . .

Listening to Mary giggle as she was learning to walk . . .

Little Deborah squatting next to a toad as it hopped through the grass . . .

Paul's exuberant joy at learning to ride a bike . . .

Audrey on her first day of work, after Paul started kindergarten, when she began to teach at a school in the county . . .

When he concentrated, it seemed as though he was able to recall most of their lives together. He remembered the way the children would crowd around him on the porch and watch with fascination as he whittled pirates and ballerinas or animals from their favorite picture books. He could see their gap-toothed smiles as they posed for school photos. He summoned up memories of the family reading the Bible together every Wednesday and Sunday evening, always his favorite nights of the week. He thought briefly about their teenage years, that turbulent period on the verge of adulthood. Rules were sometimes broken, bedrooms were often messy, and the boys ate so much that Jasper sometimes opened the cupboards only to find most of the food gone. He remembered first loves—David, who'd fallen for Monica at sleepaway camp in Pinehurst, only to have his heart broken; Deborah, who was crazy about a boy named Allen when she was a sophomore, whom she swore she would end up marrying. He recalled with fondness the hours he'd spent teaching Mary how to drive, the car jerking back and forth as she tried to master using the clutch. He recalled the night that he caught Deborah kissing Allen as they stood on the front porch, and the gentle way Audrey had reminded him that their daughter, like her older siblings, was also growing up. He thought about Paul's excitement and nervousness when he was selected to represent the high school in a statewide debate contest and how he'd practiced for hours in front of the mirror.

Still, it was their love for one another as family that Jasper always remembered most. While they struggled with challenges and disappointments just like everyone, there was joy and caring as well, and for more than two decades, Jasper believed that his family had been singled out for blessings by the good Lord Himself.

Until, of course, it wasn't.

IV

JASPER WAS FINALLY able to nod off for a couple of hours, then woke to his alarm long before the sun came up. The night had been a short one and his body thrummed with exhaustion and pain. His psoriasis itched and prickled as though he were being continually stung by wasps, but he forced himself out of bed. When he hobbled to the kitchen, he could feel the tightness in his back and soreness in his joints, thinking that all the driving and bumping over rocks had done a real number on him.

He wondered what the day might bring. Would the Littletons and Melton come back to finish what they started, even though it was a school day? He didn't know. And if they did show up before dawn this morning, what could he do to stop them? Again, he didn't know.

He dressed in dark clothes and though he wasn't hungry, he forced himself to eat something. He grabbed an old backpack from the mudroom before stepping outside. A blanket of mist hovered over the earth, and though the moon was only half full, it was enough to paint the treetops silver.

He helped Arlo into the truck. From the work shed—and following a hunch—Jasper fetched a leaf rake, along with some plastic garbage bags. He loaded them into the bed of the truck and drove beneath a star-filled sky to the spot in the Uwharrie where he'd parked the night before. Again, he waited, watching for approaching headlights and listening for vehicles; again, there was nothing.

Once the sun came up and burned off the mist, Jasper figured it was time to leave. The truck bounced and dipped in the forest and on the trail, sending flares of pain up his spine; eventually he reached the relative smoothness of the fire road and then asphalt. From there, he drove to the Lowe's in Asheboro to purchase a large jug of deer repellent, along with six ultrasonic devices that promised to keep deer away. Just in case. Then it was back to the southern Uwharrie again, where he parked once more behind the berm.

Grabbing his binoculars, he got out of the truck. Arlo walked beside him as he started the longish trek toward Scenic Road. Though his pace was measured—he didn't want his heart acting up—his back continued to tighten, and he was slowed even further by numerous ridges and hills that dotted this part of the landscape. In his youth, he would have scampered over them with ease. Now, however, he often found it necessary to stop and catch his breath. As he panted, he'd put his hands on his hips and lean back to stretch his back muscles, sometimes letting out a groan. In those moments, Arlo would gaze up at him as though wondering what was going on.

He eventually reached a point within sight of Scenic Road, near the spot where the original photo had been taken. Then, orienting himself in the direction of the boulder outcropping, he began to trek toward it, through what he assumed was the center of the deer's range.

Again, it was tough going in places. Ridges. Hills. Rocks and boulders. A small stream. Shrubs that seemed intent on grabbing at his ankles. His hips and knees joined his back in a chorus of pain; his skin continued to sting. He tried to tell himself he was on an adventure, albeit a painful one taking place in slow motion.

He thought about the dead deer he'd found last Sunday. Wildlife officials, he assumed, had already removed the carcass, and he wondered if the bandanna he'd tied as a marker was still in place. It wasn't important enough to retrieve it; he had lots of bandannas, and the detour was the last thing he needed. Instead, he trudged up and over another ridge, a little past the halfway point in the deer's likely range, and stopped when he came to a small clearing. When something unusual in the center caught his eye, he raised the binoculars and focused farther. It took him only an instant to identify dry corn kernels scattered on the ground. He felt a surge of disappointment and disgust, but no surprise at all. It was what he'd been expecting, his suspicions confirmed.

Deer bait.

All hunters knew that deer loved corn, and as he closed in, he noticed hoofprints around the piles. By the differing sizes of the prints, he knew it wasn't just one deer; there had to have been several. That also meant the corn couldn't have been here long or there would have been nothing left at all. As he stared, his mind flashed to last Saturday, when he'd been whittling with the boy. He remembered that it had been raining then. Putting together those clues meant that the corn had been placed here and eaten in the last few days. But when exactly?

By Melton and the Littleton brothers on Sunday?

Probably.

They'd put the bait out, assuming it might take a day or two for deer to locate it. Then, knowing the deer would return in search of more, he assumed they'd be back to dump more corn. And after that . . .

Jasper turned, surveying the area. Where there was bait, there was also a need for a place where the poachers could hide themselves. On the southern side of the clearing, the forest was thin; ahead and to the east, there was a small ridge fronted by boulders. It took a minute or so, but he finally spotted what he was looking for on the northern side of the clearing, in the general direction of where he'd parked his truck. The trees were thickest there, and he made his way toward a fallen tree covered by a pile of branches. Though it had been hastily constructed, he noticed a clear firing window among the piled branches. Behind it, in the dirt, he found numerous prints.

Not hoofprints, not boots. Sneakers.

Again, it wasn't proof, but it was pretty darn circumstantial.

Jasper made the agonizingly long walk back to his truck, this time using as direct a route as possible. From the bed of the truck, he retrieved the shovel and rake, along with a garbage bag. He put the jug of deer repellent and the ultrasonic devices into the backpack, loaded up, then started back the way he came. By the time he reached the corn, his legs were wobbly, and he felt as though he'd hiked all the way to Canada, but he still had work to do.

He raked the remaining kernels of corn into small piles and used his hands to scoop it into the garbage bag. He then opened the jug of deer repellent. The air filled with the smell of rotten eggs as he splashed it in a circle around the baited area. He splashed more repellent at the tree line surrounding the clearing. Then he set up the ultrasonic devices where he knew they'd get some sun, since they were powered with solar batteries. He didn't know how well the devices would work or how long the repellent would last—the batteries might not receive enough sun to charge; the next rain might dilute the repellent to nothing—but it was all he could think to do for now. Finally, he raked over the obvious signs of his own footprints.

Weary yet pleased, he limped back to the truck before finally heading home in the early afternoon. He ate canned tomato soup and lay down for a nap; this time, he fell asleep quickly and the alarm woke him right on time. He and Arlo were out again well before dusk. He drove the truck to the berm and parked behind it, settling in for another vigil. The corn, he knew, would have to be replenished.

Lowering the truck windows so he could hear better, he watched as the sun dipped below the tree line and the sky above began to wash out. Beside him, Arlo was already asleep. The earlier march through the forest must have worn him out, too, and Jasper reached over to give him a couple of gentle pats. Arlo's ear twitched, but that was it. He remembered Arlo when he'd been young and full of energy and the way he used to spin in circles whenever he realized he was about to ride in the truck.

"Old age has changed you," he mumbled. "Just like me."

Gray light gave way to twilight and then finally to darkness. The change was subtle, almost unnoticeable at first, much like the course of his own life. He thought back to the business he'd owned and the hundreds of acres of Bradford pears he'd once harvested annually. That, too, had eventually changed. Where he'd once had a monopoly, with every passing year, new competitors began to emerge. Finding new customers and markets became increasingly difficult. Sales eventually stagnated, then slowly began trending downward, even though he worked harder than ever. He stopped renewing leases on some of the land, and then more of it. When inflation soared during the late 1970s, mortgage rates rose to crushing levels, which meant fewer homes were built. The cost of fertilizer and diesel fuel went through the roof. Nurseries took less product. Like most people, he hoped the situation would right itself but in the meantime was forced to lay off one worker after another, a situation he found agonizing. Even their acceptance of a severance package did little to assuage the guilt that Jasper felt. When he looked into the eyes of those he'd had to let go, he saw husbands and wives, sons and daughters, parents. He saw God's children, and prayed for forgiveness, even though he knew there'd been no other choice.

By the mid-1980s, Jasper found himself left with a single grove of maturing Bradford pears. As he had more than twenty years earlier, Jasper now worked the fields alone. The palms of his hands grew thick with calluses, and for the first time in his marriage, he was grateful for the money that Audrey earned as a teacher.

In April 1986, Jasper was forty-six years old. His eldest son was twenty-one and about to graduate with a degree in theology from Wake Forest University, with plans to pursue his master's in divinity. He hoped to become a pastor. Both of his daughters were at the University of North Carolina, one majoring in biology, intending to become a veterinarian, and the other planning to major in elementary education. Paul was looking forward to starting his senior year in high school.

The weather that spring was fickle, until it began to rain, day after day, for nearly two weeks. The ground was fully saturated when warm, humid air from the Gulf of Mexico began colliding with colder, dry air from the north. Storm cells began to form in Georgia and South Carolina, then finally North Carolina. Near Asheboro, in an area mercifully devoid of people, one of those storm cells spawned a tornado—or at least that was the assumption. Because there'd been no witnesses, the only evidence of the tornado was reconstructed in the aftermath: two small outbuildings leveled and thousands of trees whose leaves had been stripped from the branches while being uprooted and tossed like straws.

Because the situation was so odd as to be almost unbelievable, a photographer from the newspaper traveled to the location to document it. Photos would show that on the surrounding farms, neither houses nor barns had been affected. Neighboring crops of corn and cotton and tobacco continued to stretch toward the sun, completely undamaged. Only in one relatively confined area was the destruction utterly complete.

Jasper remembered standing with the photographer and staring at the ruins of what had been his last remaining grove of Bradford pear trees. Though the trees had been insured, he had contracts yet to fulfill that summer, which meant that he'd have to buy the trees from other growers and sell them, likely at a loss. No doubt, he would be left with practically nothing.

Dizzy at the realization, Jasper continued to stare at the toppled trees. The ninth verse in the fourth chapter of Job came to him unbidden: *By the breath of God they perish, and by the blast of His anger they come to an end.*

For a moment, Jasper wondered what he had done to anger God, before quickly shaking his head. He reminded himself that he led a blessed life, and thought instead about another storm from his past, the hurricane that had destroyed his house but also enabled him to start his business in the first place. He reminded himself that the Lord works in mysterious ways and thought about 1 Corinthians 10:13, which promised that *God is faithful, and He will not let you be tested beyond your strength.*

Despite the assurances of his faith, he had difficulty sleeping at night for months. He worried about paying for his children's college educations, and he worried about supporting the local food bank, for he knew that other families faced struggles far worse than his own. He'd been correct about the insurance proceeds; there wasn't enough for him to fulfill his contracts. Though he could have declared bankruptcy and simply walked away from his obligations, he thought about Psalm 37:21, which said that *the wicked borrows and does not pay back.* So he and Audrey went to the bank.

They took out a mortgage on their home, the first one they'd ever needed. As they signed the papers, Jasper wondered how he was going to be able to rebuild his life, but as they walked out the door, Audrey took his hand in hers, and in that moment he was sure everything was going to be okay.

V

IT WAS JUST after nine in the evening, and the world was inky black when Jasper noticed flickers of lights to the north, blinking in and out of sight like distant fireflies.

"Looks like someone's coming," he muttered to Arlo.

Beside him, Arlo yawned and then sat up, looking around. A minute or so later, he cocked his ears, his head tilting to the side. Jasper rolled up his window, then reached across Arlo to do the same on the passenger side, on the off chance that Arlo decided to bark.

It was another few minutes before the world in front of him momentarily brightened; the sound of an engine was unmistakable. Poachers, with spotlights and rifles beside them in the cab, a bag of corn in the bed.

The Littletons and Melton?

Just the Littletons?

Someone else?

He'd stationed his truck here because he wanted to know with absolute certainty.

The world went dark again and the sound of the engine faded away. Jasper waited another ten minutes to make sure they were gone, then turned the key.

The engine cranked but wouldn't catch. Jasper took a deep breath and tried again while pumping on the accelerator. Again, it failed to spark.

He closed his eyes, feeling a sudden tightness in his chest. He let the engine sit for a moment before trying again. He turned the key and pumped the accelerator, heard the engine finally turn over in protest, then catch with the loud squeal associated with a loose fan belt.

Good God, he thought. The sound was loud enough to have awakened the dead and he hoped that whoever had passed was far enough away that they hadn't heard it.

He shifted into first but kept his lights off, slowly rolling around the berm. He could barely see his tracks beyond the windshield, and even at a crawl, he had to jerk the wheel at times to avoid trees and gullies. His eyes regularly flashed to the rear-view mirror as he looked for headlights. Even after reaching the off-road trail, he felt nervous—armed men with a disregard for the law could be dangerous. Still, Jasper fought the urge to drive faster. Arlo seemed to sense his tension and let out a whine, then another. He wondered how long it would take them to reach the clearing and get back to their truck.

Jasper couldn't be certain, but in time, he reached the fire road and let out a breath he hadn't known he'd been holding. He felt safe enough to turn on his lights and speed up, knowing it would lead to the main road. After a while, that road would reach a junction, and the poachers could turn left or right to use one of two exits that bypassed both the campground and the ranger station.

It was only when Jasper reached the junction that he realized his mistake. He hadn't thought to find a place to hide his truck *here,* that would allow him to see which direction the poachers went.

He headed a quarter mile in one direction, then turned the truck around and did the same in the opposite direction. Scrutinizing both sides of the road, he searched for a terrain feature large enough to obscure his truck but couldn't find anything.

Which meant he'd have to make a choice.

One direction led toward Asheboro, the other to county roads and eventually a highway.

Following his hunch, he decided on the exit that led toward Asheboro, and ten minutes later, he was out of the forest. He drove another few hundred yards and finally turned onto a side street. He turned the truck around and shut off the engine, hoping he was right.

He waited half an hour.

Then an hour.

Then more.

His mind wandered as fatigue settled in. Arlo began to snore.

Well into the second hour, it had become difficult for Jasper to keep his eyes open. Just then, he saw trees begin to brighten as though illuminated by headlights. He sat up straighter. He stared intently, until finally he spotted a black pickup emerging from the forest. The truck rolled onto the street without stopping, and a moment later, it passed by him, even as it continued to accelerate.

Jasper turned the key, and to his relief, the engine cranked on the first turn. He began to follow. In the distance, he could see the vehicle's taillights. If the truck's destination was a specific neighborhood in Asheboro, which he suspected, the truck was going to take a left at a stop sign ahead.

It did.

Jasper continued to drive without his headlights until he reached the stop sign. Right before he made the turn, he flipped on his lights. By then, the truck was nearly out of sight and Jasper pressed the accelerator, closing the distance slightly. The road was devoid of other traffic, and he didn't want to arouse suspicion, so he remained a reasonable distance behind.

They reached Asheboro and then the downtown area. The

truck ahead turned again. Jasper slowed, growing more confident in his suspicion; when he turned, he saw the flash of taillights as the truck turned onto yet another street, the same one that Jasper had visited two nights earlier.

Up ahead, he watched the black pickup pull into Clyde Little-ton's drive. He pulled over to the side of the road and waited a few minutes, then quietly got out of his truck, leaving Arlo behind. He approached on foot, heading toward the house, trying his best to keep in the shadows. He felt foolish; he wasn't a spy or a criminal and figured that if any of the neighbors were to look out their windows, he'd stand out like a neon sign. But no one seemed to be watching.

Finally, as he neared the Littleton house, he ducked into the neighbor's bushes. Though landscaping still blocked much of his view, he was able to confirm that no one was hauling a carcass from the bed of the truck. Nor did he hear voices, which meant the boys had already gone inside the house. He breathed a sigh of relief, knowing the deer was still safe. More than that, he'd learned what he'd suspected all along.

The Littleton boys were intent on bagging their trophy.

VI

BACK AT HOME, Jasper undressed and went to bed, aware that this night, too, would be a short one. He fell asleep quickly and woke to a blaring alarm on Thursday morning. He fed Arlo and ate an egg sandwich with his coffee, feeling old and tired and achy in every part of his body. His back, knees, and hips were so sore that moving was difficult; his skin felt as though it was being jabbed with a thousand needles and itched like crazy. But he had work to do to keep the deer safe now that the Littletons had replenished their bait. It was the reason, he suspected, they'd gone into the forest last night.

He drove into the Uwharrie again, headlights on, jolting and bouncing all the way back to the berm. This time, he'd brought a flashlight as well as the rake and an additional garbage bag. He picked his way slowly through the forest, watching his steps. The last thing he wanted was to twist an ankle. He checked his watch, feeling the pressure of time. He wished he could move faster and wondered whether he should have started earlier, though having done so would have meant he likely wouldn't have slept at all.

Even Arlo seemed to be dragging, content to stay at Jasper's side instead of wandering ahead with his nose to the ground.

When Jasper finally reached the clearing, he saw fresh corn dumped into numerous piles. He moved as quickly as he could, using the leaf rake and his hands to scoop all of it into the garbage bag. He also understood the fresh corn meant that the Littletons were planning to come back, either this morning or tomorrow, since the forest would be crowded with people once turkey season began. If he had to guess, he'd say they were probably on their way right now. They, like him, knew the deer would be waking soon and would begin looking for food.

Once he'd collected the corn, he slung the bag over his shoulder with a grunt and retrieved the rake and flashlight. By then, the moon had drifted below the horizon and the stars had begun to fade. He shined the light on his watch, knowing he was running out of time. He started back toward the truck, but his concern that the Littletons might be approaching meant he had to keep the flashlight off, slowing his progress.

At the northern edge of the clearing—just past the fallen tree where the Littletons had built the hide and planned to station themselves—he stumbled. As he caught himself, however, his back suddenly lit up with a spasm that paralyzed the rest of his muscles. He collapsed, his knee slamming into a rock and sending shock waves of pain up his leg. On the ground, he squeezed his eyes shut, trying to breathe while pain from the spasm crashed over him in full fury, making him nearly pass out. His knee felt as though he'd crushed the bone with a hammer.

Not now, he thought. *I've got to get out of here.*

Above him, the sky was beginning to lose its inky color, turning an indigo shade.

He knew he had to get back to the truck, but the back spasms, coming in steady waves, made it nearly impossible to breathe, let alone move. The pain in his knee radiated all the way to his hip, agony throbbing with every heartbeat. When Arlo nosed at his face, he couldn't summon the energy to shoo the dog away.

He concentrated, trying to think of anything else, but the pain triggered the memory of even more pain. All at once, he had a vivid recollection of a Fourth of July weekend in 1983, a little more than two years after his business had been destroyed. He was working in construction again and the kids—though all four were technically young adults by then—were spending the long holiday weekend at the house. They'd gone to church as a family, and afterward, Audrey had set out fried chicken, cole slaw, and potato salad on the picnic table in their backyard. For Jasper, it was a meal he would never forget, because it was the last time that all of them would ever eat together.

The following day, on Independence Day, the kids went their separate ways. Mary and Deborah went to the coast with friends, albeit in different groups. David went to a barbecue that a friend was throwing, and Paul went boating with a couple of buddies. Some but not all would watch the fireworks display in Asheboro later that night; Deborah planned to watch the ones in Wrightsville Beach and wouldn't return to the house until after midnight.

After the fireworks were over, Paul planned to host a bonfire behind the house with some friends, as he'd done a handful of times in the past. Later, Jasper would learn that some of the young men had brought liquor and that Paul had joined in the festivities.

Jasper and Audrey stayed up late, waiting for the kids to get home. Mary arrived first, then David, and finally Deborah. The five of them visited for a while as they sat at the kitchen table. Paul was still in the backyard with his friends, seated around the fire pit with flames leaping toward the sky. Glancing out the back window, Jasper had considered reminding Paul to be cautious, as the wind had begun to pick up. Coming up behind him and wrapping her arms around his waist, Audrey had kissed him on the cheek.

"Let him be," she urged, reading his mind. "You know he'll be careful and he's having fun with his friends. Let's go to bed."

Jasper and Audrey retreated to the bedroom. Audrey slipped into her nightgown and Jasper put on his pajamas. As always, they faced each other in those final moments before sleep. In the darkness, he could see a slight smile playing across Audrey's lips. She loved having all the children home.

The next thing Jasper could remember was waking up and coughing so hard that it felt as though his insides were being twisted. It took less than a second for his mind to process what was happening; he saw flames on the back wall and the ceiling, black smoke everywhere. The room was on fire, his house was on fire. Jasper bounded from the bed and tried to shake Audrey awake. Her body remained limp, and panic took root. He shouted at her and shook her harder, but still, she didn't stir. Jasper scooped her into his arms and started toward the bedroom door. As soon as he opened it, there was an explosion of light and energy, and he felt himself being hurled backward. For long minutes, there was nothing but unconsciousness until the pain finally woke him.

Flames were opening and closing like fists, hot orange tendrils dancing all around him. Jasper, himself, was on fire, and he felt the hellish fingers devouring the flesh on his arms and legs and torso. Although he couldn't see clearly, he realized his head, face, and neck were burning as well. With a scream, he instinctively batted at the flames and frantically began to roll. The smoke had become a blackened fog, so thick that he could barely see, and he smelled something that reminded him vaguely of cooked meat. Once the flames on his body had been extinguished, his next thought was of Audrey and the children. Their images blinked into his consciousness as though a switch had been thrown. *Audrey*, he thought, *David, Mary, Deborah, and Paul . . .*

I have to save my family—

Everything seemed to be on fire now. The walls and floors and ceiling were burning, as was the furniture. Somehow, Jasper found the crumpled shape of Audrey's body near the window, engulfed in flames. Her skin was blackened from head to foot. He beat out the flames and lifted her from the ground, watching in a stupor as his own skin peeled away. Somehow, he staggered down the steps and out the front door, where he placed her on the grass.

His neighbors' homes on either side of them were also on fire. A fire truck had already pulled to a stop out front, and he heard more sirens in the distance. From the corner of his eye, he saw Paul on the lawn, screaming hysterically while being restrained by a police officer. He saw his neighbors, standing amidst the small crowd that was already forming on the sidewalk. There was no sign of his other children and he wondered where they were.

Oh, God, please . . . No . . .

Already, two firemen were beginning to unwind a hose from

the truck. Another fireman rushed toward him, but Jasper turned and raced up onto the porch and back into the house.

The heat was a living thing, and the sound of the fire was like that of a jet engine; he felt the skin on his face instantly begin to blister. Flames were devouring the entire structure, as if swallowing it whole. He didn't care. He staggered toward the staircase, which had already become an inferno. He thought about his children and pressed forward, only to feel two sets of hands suddenly jerk him backward. Jasper struggled and screamed for his family, trying to fight the hands off, but both of the firemen were young and strong. A moment later, he was being dragged across the porch and onto the lawn.

The world descended into slow motion then, images forming and dissolving with dreamlike suspension.

Flames leaping toward the sky . . . neighbors huddling together across the street . . . water gushing from hoses . . . more police cars suddenly appearing, coming to a stop on the neighbor's lawn . . . Audrey's blackened body in the grass, surrounded by paramedics . . .

But most of all, it was his own screams that he would always remember—his own, and Paul's. Only when his throat gave out, hoarse and raw, did Jasper begin to feel the agony of his burns, so intense that the world around him shrank to nothing at all. Mercifully, he passed out.

VII

ARLO LICKED THE tears from Jasper's face.

He'd relived that night a thousand times and always cried when he did; even after the passage of decades the grief and shame and sense of failure had neither faded nor diminished. He hated himself for having been unable to save his family.

He moaned as his back spasmed again, and the world came into focus. He tried to remind himself that the Littletons were coming and that he was running out of time. In the distant past, he would have prayed to God for strength; would have prayed that He lessen his pain. Instead, Jasper simply closed his eyes, allowing himself to succumb to the memories. Once they began, he'd long since learned, they were almost impossible to stop.

Only later would Jasper learn what had happened to him: that he'd been rushed by ambulance to UNC Hospital in Chapel Hill, where he was placed in a clean room and put into a medically induced coma for more than eight weeks. He had second- and third-degree burns over more than 60 percent of his body. His wounds were methodically cleaned and debrided for weeks. He heard that the doctors even covered parts of his body with maggots to further remove dead tissue. He was treated with intravenous antibiotics and received skin grafts, both from his own body and from donors. For more than a month, no one knew whether Jasper was going to live or die. He suffered from arrhythmia, dehydration, and edema; twice, he caught pneumonia. There were a few days when his wounds bordered on becoming septic, which probably would have resulted in the amputation of both legs, but somehow each time the infection receded.

Eventually, he opened his eyes, emerging into a state of unimaginable agony. Tears leaked steadily from his eyes whenever he was conscious. The nurses wouldn't allow him to have a mirror, but he guessed by looking at his arms and legs and torso how his face must look. He was eventually transferred from a clean room to the ICU, then finally to a regular bed. It was around that time that a psychiatrist began to visit. Finally, after months in the hospital, he was moved to the North Carolina Jaycee Burn Center.

His stay there was even longer. Because the burns had damaged some of his nerves, he had to relearn how to stand and walk. He had to relearn how to hold a fork and spoon. He felt like a middle-aged toddler. Finally, more than a year after the fire, he was released from the burn center, but even then, his treatment was not finished. He had four additional skin graft surgeries over the next five years.

Two weeks after waking from the coma, he learned what had become of his family. The sheriff, along with a younger deputy named Charlie—who would eventually be elected sheriff—were in his room, as was a psychiatrist, a social worker, and the pastor from his church. They stood in a half-circle around his bed, their words spoken grimly, quietly. He was told that Audrey had died from her burns, while David, Mary, and Deborah had died of smoke inhalation. Jasper wasn't sure whether it was true, but he chose to believe that his three oldest children hadn't suffered in the flames because the alternative was too horrific to contemplate. He was also told there'd already been a small memorial and that his family had been buried in the local cemetery.

Paul hadn't passed away in the fire. Instead, because four people in his family had died and three houses had been destroyed, Paul had been arrested on felony charges, including negligent homicide. At the jail, in front of the officers who'd arrested him and their superiors, he waived the right to an attorney. He confessed to everything, things he'd done and maybe things he hadn't; that he drank for the first time in his life and had too much, that he had continued to feed the fire even after the wind picked up, until it was far too large for the conditions; that even after embers made their way to the roof, igniting flames, he hadn't called the fire department right away, instead attempting to put out the fire himself with the garden hose. In his panic, he hadn't rushed inside to awaken his family. In addition to being recorded on videotape by the police, he wrote out an account of the events. He'd wept through much of it, repeatedly asking how his father was, only to learn that Jasper had been taken to the hospital and was in critical condition. Because Paul couldn't stop crying, he had been placed on suicide watch in the county jail.

When his court-appointed attorney again showed up, hoping to reduce the charges to manslaughter, Paul had refused the offer of lesser charges. Instead, he demanded the earliest trial possible, one before a judge and without a jury. While Jasper hovered between life and death, his body fighting one crisis after another, Paul's request was granted. The legal process moved quickly, pushing through in weeks what might have otherwise taken months or even years. Standing dry-eyed and calm before the judge, Paul pleaded guilty. When his attorney began to argue for leniency at the sentencing, Paul fired him on the spot and demanded instead the maximum penalty allowable by law. The judge—the Honorable Roger Littleton—instead took pity. He refused to impose the maximum sentence, which could have kept Paul locked up for twenty years per offense. Instead, Paul received a sentence of six years, and was informed that he'd be eligible for parole in three.

On Paul's first night in prison, using the sheets from his bed, he hung himself.

That day in the hospital, after learning what had happened to his family, Jasper could remember turning away and asking to be left alone.

He didn't speak for weeks, even to the psychiatrist. There was nothing at all to say.

His livelihood had been destroyed, his body was in ruins, and his entire family had died.

In the weeks that followed, he dwelled on his fate, feeling that the pattern of it somehow was familiar. He finally realized that he indeed knew the story well; after all, he'd read it dozens of times in the Bible.

Jasper had somehow become Job.

VIII

ARLO WHINED, BRINGING Jasper back to the present. He drew a series of deep breaths, steeling himself, and slowly rolled onto his side. His back tightened but fortunately didn't spasm; his knee, however, made him wince. He wasn't sure how much time had passed, didn't know how much time was left, only that he didn't have much. Dawn was coming and the Littletons, with or without Melton, would be here soon.

He wasn't sure he could stand, let alone make it to the truck. But he knew he couldn't stay near the fallen tree either. Casting about for somewhere to hide, he remembered the ridge and boulders on the eastern side of the clearing. It would have to do.

Get up, he told himself.

But he couldn't. Struggling to stand made his back tighten again, and he realized he needed support, something to grab onto.

Or better yet, a stretcher, with three or four strong men to carry it.

He smiled at his own joke, until his knee throbbed again, making him wince. Scanning his immediate surroundings, he finally located a small tree. He pulled himself toward it, dragging his bad leg. In his peripheral vision, he saw Arlo staring with his head cocked, as though wondering what sort of game this was.

Jasper gritted his teeth and inched forward again. He reminded himself that he'd once struggled through a flooding house; he'd once run into an inferno. He caught his breath, covered a few more inches and rested, trying to keep the muscles in his back relaxed. Then he went through the process again. And again. And again.

He finally reached the small tree and slowly began to pull himself up. Though his back and knee seemed to be screaming at him, they held up enough to allow him to stand. Just then, he saw a pinprick of light in the distance and heard an engine.

They're almost here.

What would they do if they found him? If they knew he'd report them for poaching? If they knew he'd taken the corn and poured deer repellent and deployed those ultrasonic devices to keep the deer away?

He pictured Josh's flare of rage as he raised his rifle to kill Arlo . . . he remembered the ease with which the boy had swung the rifle in his direction. He saw again the empty smile, masking the fact that human emotion eluded him . . .

Josh wouldn't kill him, would he?

Of course not.

For the first time, Jasper realized he was frightened. He was foolish to have done all this, stupid to have believed it was his responsibility to keep the white buck safe from harm. He didn't want to test Josh's anger. Gritting his teeth, he limped a single step, then another, slowly and painfully making his way back to the rake, flashlight, and the bag of corn. He wondered if he'd be able to bend low enough to retrieve them without his back seizing up again.

Eyeing the forest to the north, he saw another pinprick of light, no doubt a flashlight sweeping the darkness.

They were closer now.

And soon enough, he knew, Josh was going to be very, very angry.

CHAPTER EIGHT

I

"WOW," CASEY ANNOUNCED as soon as Kaitlyn walked past the open door of her bedroom. "That was some kiss. I don't think I've ever been kissed like that."

Kaitlyn froze in the hallway. "You were watching us?"

"From my bedroom window."

She felt her neck begin to warm. "You shouldn't spy on people. And about what you saw, I should probably explain—"

Casey waved a hand, cutting her off. "It's no big deal, Mom. I like him."

Kaitlyn opened her mouth to say something, but nothing came to mind.

"Just let me know," Casey added.

"Let you know what?"

"When you need me to babysit," she answered, suddenly sounding as though she were the parent. "As long as it's not Friday night, I'm clear."

II

AFTER SHE'D SHOWERED, Kaitlyn stood in front of the mirror naked and took in her reflection. There were faint lines in her forehead and crow's-feet at the corners of her eyes; she also noticed a few gray hairs where the color had faded since the last time she'd had her hair done.

And the rest of her . . .

Pregnancy and nursing had done her no favors. Nor, frankly, had gravity. Her breasts, once firm, now seemed to droop, and the extra pounds around her midsection were all too evident. Her hips had expanded as well, and while she liked to think her legs still looked okay, she knew she wasn't the young woman she once had been.

And yet Tanner had called her beautiful.

Wrapping herself in a towel, she dried her hair and slathered on a dollop of face cream before turning out the bathroom light. Reliving the sensations of the kiss, she felt a dart of excitement at the thought that they'd be meeting again tomorrow. Depending on how she counted their interactions, this would be a third date of sorts, and as everyone knew, the third date was often . . . *significant.* As in, physical intimacy might be on the table.

She wasn't naïve, nor was she a prude when it came to sex. At the same time, more than five years had passed since she'd slept with anyone, and in the preceding fourteen years, it had been George and only George. In sum, it had been almost two decades since she'd slept with someone new, and the knowledge left her feeling strangely nervous. Moreover, she knew there was little prospect of her having a future with Tanner, so how would she feel about herself in the aftermath? she wondered.

Awash in anticipation and uncertainty, she again found herself slipping naked into bed.

III

KAITLYN TOLD CASEY the next morning that she'd be going out with Tanner that evening. The words were barely out of her mouth before Casey responded, "Yep, no problem," as though she happily and routinely agreed to her mother's requests to babysit. To Kaitlyn's relief, her daughter didn't grill her further, simply declaring in the next breath that she'd be heading to Camille's around ten, so they could go to the mall in Greensboro.

"But I'll be home by the time Mitch gets off the bus," she added.

At the office, Kaitlyn was grateful for the steady routine and regular flow of patients. When discussing a diagnosis or treatment options, she was able to avoid thinking about Tanner, but at half past ten she received a text from him, asking if he could pick her up at six. Unsure whether that would give her enough time to get ready, she suggested six-thirty, and while she waited for his response, she wondered whether he was thinking about the *third-date* thing, or whether that was something only women did. A moment later, he agreed to six-thirty with a cheery *See you then!* and she felt the now-familiar flutters in her stomach.

Her afternoon appointments ran late, and by the time she left the office it had begun to rain, making her commute longer than usual. As she pulled into the driveway, she noted that she had less than an hour to get ready.

Inside, Casey and Mitch were on the couch, watching one of the Jurassic Park movies again. "Can we have pizza tonight?" Mitch asked, without looking up.

"What, no 'Hi, Mom! How was your day?'"

"Hi, Mom. How was your day? Can we have pizza tonight?"

"Yes, fine." She nodded, slipping off her wet shoes. "I'm pretty sure I have money in my purse."

Casey glanced at her. "Why don't you just DoorDash it?"

Because, Kaitlyn thought, *I still think first about doing things the old-fashioned way.* "We can do that," she said. "Just remind me before I go."

Rising from the couch, Casey drew near and arched an eyebrow suggestively. "Soooo . . ." she said, drawing out the word, "how're you feeling about the big date, Mom?"

Kaitlyn kept her voice nonchalant. "It's just dinner."

"You're not nervous?"

Yes. "Not at all."

"Can I ask what time you're planning to be home?"

"I'm not sure, but it won't be late," she answered, trying to sound casual.

"Well," Casey said, "just make sure you let me know if anything changes, okay?"

Kaitlyn drew a deep breath, thinking, *I really can't handle this right now.*

IV

WHAT TO WEAR.

That was always the question when going out, wasn't it? Especially since she didn't know where he'd be bringing her. She didn't want to be overdressed if he was planning something casual, but she didn't want to underdress, either, in case he was wearing a blazer. She'd already worn jeans on their previous outings, which made a dress seem like the logical choice, but most of the dresses she owned were either too formal or summery. In the end, she decided on a teal-colored, knee-length dress with cap sleeves, something that Casey would no doubt refer to as a "Mom dress." But whatever—Kaitlyn *was* a mom, and she didn't have many other options. She'd bought it eight years ago for a wedding when Mitch was still a baby and remembered that more than a few people had complimented her on it. The only remaining question was whether it still fit. After removing her clothing, she stepped into the dress and pulled it up, but with no way to zip it herself, she walked to the stairs and called down to Casey.

"You need something?" Casey asked, appearing on the second-floor landing.

"Can you zip me up?"

"Is that what you're going to wear?" She could feel Casey's gaze traveling from head to toe as she continued up the steps.

"As long as it fits," Kaitlyn said, making a point not to look at Casey and her nose, which was probably wrinkled in disdain.

A moment later, she felt the zipper ascending and she automatically tried to suck in her tummy.

"It might be a little tight," Kaitlyn muttered.

"Stop fidgeting," Casey scolded.

Kaitlyn felt as though she was slowly being squeezed into her own casing, until—miraculously—the zipper reached the top.

Wow, she thought. *It fits.*

She stepped in front of the full-length mirror that hung behind the master bedroom door, thinking it was a little snug around the hips, but . . .

She sort of liked the way it looked. It showed just enough of her legs and to her relief seemed to flatter her figure, emphasizing her hourglass shape.

"I don't remember you wearing that dress before. Is it new?" Casey asked.

"No, honey. I've had it for a while."

"It's pretty," she remarked. "But while I'm here, I do have a suggestion."

"What's that?"

"Why don't you let me help you with your hair and makeup."

"What's wrong with the way I usually do it?" Kaitlyn frowned at her in the mirror.

Casey put a hand on her hip. "It's a little *Melrose Place,* don't you think?"

"You mean that old TV show? From like, thirty years ago?"

"That's the one."

"I'm amazed that you've even heard of it."

"I googled old TV shows and thought that employing a pop-culture reference you understood would be a nice way of suggesting that you update your look."

"I've been doing my hair and makeup longer than you've been alive."

"My point exactly," Casey drawled.

"I have no desire to look like a teenager."

"You won't," Casey assured her. "I've watched a lot of tutorials on YouTube. Trust me."

Kaitlyn wasn't sure whether to be offended, but for once Casey's intentions seemed genuine.

"Okay," she agreed. "Let's see what you can do. But first, help me pick a nice pair of shoes."

V

STARING IN THE mirror, Kaitlyn decided that Casey must have been underplaying how many makeup tutorials she'd watched because the final result was subtle enough to be barely noticeable, and the shading on her eyelids was artful.

"I can tell that you like it." Casey smirked. "And you're welcome."

"I do," she said. "It's just . . . unexpected. Thank you."

"There's one more thing."

"What's that?"

"You need to stop being nervous about tonight."

"I'm not nervous," Kaitlyn lied.

"Oh please. I could see it as soon as you got home. But you need to appreciate what you bring to the table. You're smart and successful. You help sick people, you feed the poor, and if your fabulous daughter is any indication, you're obviously a great mom. *And* you're pretty. If anyone is going to be nervous, it should be him."

Kaitlyn felt a lump form in her throat.

"Thank you," she finally said.

"You're welcome." Casey began gathering up the makeup and putting it into her bag. "And by the way, if you need an out, I'll be happy to call you in an hour or so."

"What do you mean?"

"An out? So that you can cut the date short if it's not going well? As in, I'll call you and tell you that Mitch spiked a fever or whatever, and boom, you're out."

"Is this what people do these days?"

"Duh," she responded.

"Okay, yeah. Call me in an hour, then?"

"Will do," Casey said. "But do me a favor, okay?"

"Anything," Kaitlyn said.

"That's exactly what I hoped you'd say," Casey chirped, "be-cause we really need to talk about getting me a car sooner rather than later, especially if you're going to want me to do more of this babysitting thing. I mean, it's the least you can do."

Kaitlyn smiled despite herself. It was reassuring to know that as pleasant as she'd been lately, Casey hadn't changed.

"I'll think about it."

VI

BY THE TIME Kaitlyn had donned a pair of earrings, it was nearly six-thirty. As she descended the stairs, Mitch looked up from his spot on the couch. Casey was beside him, her arm draped over his shoulder. Rain beat steadily against the windows.

"Can we order the pizza now? I'm hungry."

Casey knuckled his head, making him duck and squirm. "You're supposed to tell her that she looks pretty, not that you're hungry."

"But I am hungry. And she always looks pretty. She's the prettiest mom in the whole world."

Kaitlyn smiled, charmed by his conviction. "Let me get my phone. Just cheese, right?"

Mitch nodded and Kaitlyn placed the order just as she saw a flash of headlights through the living room window.

Tanner, she thought. Right on time.

Reminding herself of Casey's words, she drew a breath and pulled her jacket and an umbrella from the closet. Opening the door, she was immediately glad she'd picked the dress she had. Tanner was wearing black slacks and a blazer.

He seemed paralyzed as he stood in the doorway, taking her in.

"You look . . . incredible," he finally said.

"Thank you," she murmured, conscious of the burning intensity of his gaze. As if from far away, she heard another voice. Mitch.

"Is that a limo in the driveway?"

"For real?" Casey exclaimed. "That's awesome!"

Kaitlyn craned to see the driveway over Tanner's shoulder as Casey and Mitch scrambled from the couch.

"Surprise." Tanner grinned.

VII

MITCH AND CASEY clamored to check out the limo, and when Tanner agreed, Mitch raced off to find his jacket and boots. Casey followed her brother to get her boots as well. As she went off in search of footwear, Kaitlyn raised an eyebrow.

"See what you did?"

"I'm really so sorry," Tanner said.

"You didn't need to arrange for a limo," she said with mock reproach.

"My car is still at the shop."

"You have a rental," she protested.

"Have you *seen* my rental?"

She laughed, and once Casey and Mitch were dressed appropriately, they all trooped outside. While Kaitlyn opened the umbrella, the kids simply pulled the hoods of their jackets up. The driver jumped out holding an umbrella and hurried to open the rear door. Mitch peeked inside before turning to her.

"Can I get in, Mom?" he begged.

Kaitlyn glanced at Tanner, who shrugged. "It's fine with me."

Kaitlyn watched as Casey crawled in behind Mitch, both vanishing from view.

"It has lights like a spaceship!" Mitch announced when he finally emerged.

"And champagne on ice," Casey added, following right behind him. Though her daughter was trying to sound casual, Kaitlyn knew she was impressed.

"Now that you both have seen it, can we go?"

"Of course." Casey nodded. To Mitch, she added, "C'mon, Little Bedbug."

"Okay, Bubble Butt," Mitch retorted, sticking out his tongue. "Later, Mom. Love you."

"Love you both," Kaitlyn said, meaning it. She watched them go before turning her attention back to Tanner. He swept an arm toward the car with a flourish.

"Shall we?"

VIII

THE LAST TIME Kaitlyn had been in a limousine was in high school. Her dad had arranged it for her prom, but she realized she couldn't remember the name of the boy with whom she went. She could picture his wavy brown hair and dimples and recalled that he was tall and played basketball, but his name remained a blank space.

"What are you thinking about?"

In the dim lighting of the interior, his face looked shadowy and mysterious. "Nothing important."

He lifted the bottle of champagne out of its ice bucket. "Would you like a glass?"

"I'd love one."

She watched as Tanner removed the foil and loosened the wires before twisting the bottle until she heard the familiar pop. He poured a glass, and when he handed it to her, she caught the earthy scent of his cologne. Rain moved sideways against the glass, making the moment feel even more surreal.

"Can I ask where we're going to dinner?"

"It's a surprise," he hedged. "A little way out of town."

"We have nice restaurants here."

"I know, but after seeing what happened at Our Daily Bread, I wasn't sure that dinner in Asheboro would be a good idea. In case you wanted to keep your private life private."

"Thank you," she said, appreciating his discretion.

He reached for a tin box on the bench seat. "Would you like something sweet to go with the champagne?"

"Chocolate-covered strawberries, perhaps?"

"Even better." He lifted the lid of the box, and it took her a second to comprehend what she was seeing.

"M&M's?"

"Peanut M&M's," he corrected.

"Huh," she said, bemused. "I don't think anyone has ever brought me Halloween candy on a date before."

"They're my favorite."

"And you thought they'd pair well with champagne?"

"Why wouldn't they? There's chocolate *and* peanuts in every bite."

He popped one in his mouth as if to prove his point. She smiled, inexplicably charmed. "How did your search go today?"

"It didn't," he said. "After what you said, I decided I needed a little more time to consider the possible implications. How about you? How was your day? Any new cases of leprosy?"

"No, just the usual." She noticed they were heading north now, through downtown Asheboro. She reached for a peanut M&M, washing it down with a swallow of champagne. "This actually isn't a bad combination," she admitted.

"My grampa used to send me boxes of them whenever I was deployed. The whole it *melts in your mouth, not in your hands* was convenient in the heat of the Middle East, as you can imagine, but it was also a little taste of normal in a place where normal was often in short supply. I think he knew I'd need something like that even more than my grandma did."

"He sounds perceptive."

"He was," Tanner agreed. He twirled the stem of his glass. "But his perceptiveness, unfortunately, came the hard way."

"What do you mean?"

"He was originally from Alabama and—kinda like me, I guess—he never knew his dad. He lived with his mom and a couple of aunts in a tumbledown shack outside of town. His mom used to take him to the textile plant where she worked, starting a few days after she delivered."

"Strong woman." Kaitlyn shook her head in wonder.

"Strong son, too," he said. "My grandfather's mother was black and though he never knew his dad, apparently he was white. And in Alabama, in the late forties and early fifties, that made for a tough upbringing. In town, he wasn't allowed to swim in the community pool, he wasn't allowed to eat in certain places, he had to step aside if someone white was approaching on the sidewalk. He had to attend segregated schools, of course—desegregation didn't happen in Alabama until after he'd graduated—but he wasn't completely accepted at those schools either. He got in lot of fights growing up, and I think that's one of the reasons he ended up joining the army. He wanted to get out of Alabama. Then, sometime in the early sixties, he met my grandma, and it went without saying that her family and friends pretty much cut her off once they fell in love and got married. It was years before they finally started communicating with her again. Meanwhile, he got sent to Vietnam, did his duty, and then returned to the U.S., but even in the seventies, lots of people wouldn't accept a mixed-race couple as next-door neighbors. I think that's why they eventually took the transfer to Italy and ended up staying in Europe for decades. As if that weren't enough, their only daughter died, and they ended up having to raise me."

"Wow," she said in disbelief. "That's hard, what he lived through." She hesitated. "Was he . . ."

"Angry?" Tanner finished for her. He seemed to reflect on it. "I'm sure there must have been some residual anger deep down, but he never betrayed it to me. And though it might be hard to fathom, he loved serving in the army. He would tell me that after leaving Alabama, the army became his family. He was a patriot and believed in the promise of what America could be. That said, he didn't sugarcoat the hardships of his upbringing, reminding me often of how fortunate I was to be born in the era I was, something I didn't appreciate until I was older. And he had his rules, of course—in my grampa's world, there was good and bad, right and wrong, and there was nothing I dreaded more than disappointing him, even though he never raised a hand to me." Tanner stared into his glass, musing. Kaitlyn was silent, waiting for him to go on.

"I had everything I needed growing up, never felt envious of my friends or other kids at school. And he was respectful and loving toward my grandma, but he was quiet. It seemed like the only time he was comfortable talking to me was when we tinkered on engines together. It was only when I became an adult that I began to wonder whether losing his daughter might have had something to do with the distance between us. Like maybe he saw his daughter—and her mistakes—whenever he looked at me. I don't really know."

"Did that ever change?"

"A little, toward the end. They both became more talkative, less tight-lipped about their pasts. But by then, they'd retired in Pensacola, and I saw my grandparents only two or three times a year. Like my grandma, my grampa worried about me, especially since I got deployed so much."

"And your grandma? What was she like?"

Tanner gave a wistful smile. "Warm, but she was as fierce in her beliefs as my grandpa. Stubborn, too, as you can probably imagine, since she defied her family and even threats of violence to marry my granddad. Like him, she had clear ideas about right and wrong, just and unjust." His expression brightened. "She was also kind of eccentric, especially as she got older. She was crazy about canaries. She must have owned six or seven over the years, and whenever one of her birds would start to sing, she'd tell me to hush. 'Listen to him sing his heart out,' she'd marvel, and if I was sitting near her, she'd take my hand and force me to sit there and listen to it. In time, I grew to love those moments."

Kaitlyn glanced toward the rain-splashed window, trying to picture a young Tanner held captive by his strong-willed grandmother. Darkened trees lined the highway, occasionally silhouetted by lights from an isolated farmhouse. Lightning flickered like strobe lights. They were north of Asheboro now, and as she took another sip of champagne, she tried to imagine the horror his grandparents must have felt at losing their only daughter. Kaitlyn knew she'd never be the same if anything happened to Casey or Mitch. Nor could she picture Tanner's grandparents' conflicting emotions as they held her newborn in the aftermath.

Tanner's complicated and fascinating personal history seemed fitting, she thought to herself. In this, too, he was different from any man she'd met before.

"Are you ready to tell me where we're going yet?" she asked, studying him over the rim of her champagne flute.

"We're heading to Sophia," he said.

She tilted her head, puzzled. Sophia was a small town, maybe five or six thousand people. "Is there even a restaurant in Sophia?"

"You'll see. But just so you know, I also have a backup plan. In case you decide you want something different."

"You do realize I have no idea what you're talking about, right?"

He offered a conspiratorial smile without answering and she glanced out the window again. Sipping the champagne, she felt lighter somehow.

Eventually the limousine began to slow before exiting the highway. However, instead of heading toward the town center, the driver made another turn onto a winding country road, the elevation gradually increasing in the low mountains of the Uwharrie. The rain seemed to be falling even harder, and when she saw another flash of lightning in the distance, Kaitlyn felt as though the weather was conspiring with Tanner to make the evening as atmospheric as possible.

There was something bittersweet about the necessarily short-lived nature of their time together, she mused. Tanner would soon be half a world away, but if the last few days had illuminated anything, it was that her life was incomplete, and had been for some time. She realized that she had been missing out on a life of connection—not just romantic or physical connection, but the kind of spontaneity and shared anticipation that came from a broader web of relationships. How long ago did she forget, she wondered, that life was as much about living as it was about re-sponsibility? Or, as Casey had sort of put it, how long ago had she forgotten how to be happy?

Too long, she decided, and she struggled to even recall the last time she had met up with friends. Because most of her friends were part of a couple, she'd told herself that she hadn't wanted to feel like a third wheel. But because she'd stopped accepting others' invitations, the invitations had eventually stopped coming. The net result was—aside from a few crappy dates—the fading of friendships, and the withering of any interests outside of work and parenting.

Studying Tanner's striking profile and long limbs from be-neath lowered lashes, she was glad she'd decided to join him to-night. For the first time in forever, she was throwing caution to the wind, and she couldn't deny the erotic thrill she experienced when she imagined what might happen later between them. Perhaps it was the fact that he was leaving that gave this encounter its forbidden allure. She'd never imagined herself embarking on something like this but found herself uncharacteristically heedless. *Why not?* she asked herself.

Tanner seemed to divine her thoughts, his eyes holding hers as he raised his glass. A moment later, the limo began to slow before turning onto a narrow drive flanked by two low stone columns. There was no sign of a restaurant and Kaitlyn squinted through the front window. Beyond the steadily moving wipers, the drive was growing steeper as it curved. Eventually Tanner's rental car came into view, parked in front of a massive mountain home. It was an imposing structure of wood and stone, with two large wraparound decks that overlooked what she suspected was a canyon. Interior lights spilled through large windows and a wide flagstone staircase led up to what she assumed was the front door.

"A house?" she asked, confused.

"The view is gorgeous," he commented, "but unfortunately, because it's dark, I don't know how much we're going to be able to see. And, at the same time, if you'd rather not spend the evening here, I made official dinner reservations elsewhere. In Greensboro, at a place called the Undercurrent."

She furrowed her brow. "Why wouldn't I want to be here?"

"I didn't want to be presumptuous," he said. "It's not as though you've known me all that long, and it'll be just the two of us."

She thought about it. "The driver will be here, right?"

"He'll be right out front the whole time."

She smiled, impressed by his concern. "I'm okay with it."

Tanner let the driver know they'd be staying, and a moment later, he exited, approaching the rear door with an umbrella. Tanner scooted across the seat, his own umbrella in hand, as she got out.

"Go ahead with Kaitlyn," he called to the driver. "I'll follow."

Sheltered by the wide umbrella, Kaitlyn was guided up the steps to the entrance, Tanner a few steps behind.

He traded places with the driver and once they were alone, he unlocked the door. "After you," he said, following her into the foyer.

Kaitlyn set her purse on the small table just inside the door and slowly took in the house, which was even grander than it appeared from outside. The vaulted ceiling showcased exposed beams and a majestic chandelier designed out of antlers. One wall consisted of floor-to-ceiling windows, while the wall facing the door was dominated by a massive stone fireplace. The floor was wide-plank pine, stained the color of ancient wine barrels, partially covered by a deep-pile white rug; plush couches and chairs framed the roomy seating area, accented by colorful throw pillows. Deco table lamps with delicate glasswork gave off a spar-kly, warm light.

"It's incredible," she gasped. "But how?"

"I got in touch with a local realtor who knew the owner of this place. Ordinarily the minimum rental stay is a month, but I think when she heard that I was planning a special date, she made an exception," he said. "Once I came by, I couldn't resist, and we were able to make a deal." He shrugged. "Okay if I cancel the other dinner reservation and get the fire going?"

"Sounds good."

She listened absently as he made the call before watching him cross the room to the fireplace. The wood was already stacked on the grate, with paper and kindling beneath it, and Kaitlyn wan-dered from the living room toward an open kitchen twice the size of her own, with gleaming appliances built into the cabinets. Off to the side was the formal dining room, with place settings for two and crystal candle holders. Beyond the windows of the dining room, lightning continued to flash, freezing the architectural details of her surroundings in periodic bursts. From across the room, she watched Tanner light the fire.

"Are you going to cook for me?" she asked.

He shook his head as he stood. "No. I'm not much of a cook, so I made arrangements with a chef from the restaurant where I made the backup reservation. It's all in the refrigerator and I just have to reheat it."

"Can I ask what we're having?"

"Crab-stuffed mushrooms as an appetizer, salad, and either beef Wellington or Dijon chicken. I wasn't sure which entrée you'd like, so I had him prepare both."

"No fish option?"

When his face fell, she giggled. "I'm kidding. That sounds heavenly. Is there somewhere I can hang my jacket?"

"Allow me."

Moving behind her, he slid the jacket off, his hand gently brushing the skin of her arm, the sensation electric. As he hung her jacket in the closet near the front door, he called out, "Would you like a glass of wine before dinner? I have red or white."

Why not? she thought again, feeling a hidden thrill. "Let's try the red."

Kaitlyn moved to the living room windows. The sky continued to strobe, briefly revealing the tree-topped mountains beyond the darkened canyon in stark relief. She could see no other houses, no other lights at all, making her feel as if the two of them were the last people on earth. Behind her, she heard Tanner approaching.

"The chef chose the wine," he said, offering her a glass.

He stood beside her, close but not quite close enough to touch. She heard a pop, and from the corner of her eye, she saw sparks rising from the fire. Her first sip of wine left afternotes of cherry and violets. "Mmm. Delicious."

"Would you like me to start reheating dinner? Or would you rather wait a bit?"

"It can wait a few minutes, don't you think? Let's enjoy the fire and the storm for a while."

They sat on the couch, facing the fire, and Tanner pulled his iPhone from his pocket, lazily programming something into an app. A moment later, she heard music drifting through the speakers.

For a while, neither of them said anything. Instead, they savored their wine and absently watched the flickering fire. Beyond the windows, the storm began to increase in intensity, the rain forming little streams on the glass. Behind a flash of lightning, she heard a long and steady roll of thunder. She could feel Tanner surreptitiously watching her, and the sensation made her smile.

"This almost feels like a vacation," she murmured. "My real life doesn't allow for nights like this."

"But you approve?"

"It's a dream," she said, a touch of reverence in her voice. Looking over, she could see the fire reflected in the golden embers of his eyes.

Spellbound, she sensed more than saw Tanner reach for her hand.

From across the room, she heard the distant ring of a cellphone. Tanner frowned at the distraction, and it was only when it rang a second time that she realized it was coming from near the front door, where she'd placed her purse.

Casey.

"I think that's your phone," Tanner said. Kaitlyn feigned confusion as she set her glass of wine on the coffee table and rose from the couch. She quickly strode to the entryway and dug out her phone, trying to regain her composure as she connected the call.

"Soooooo . . . How's it going?" Casey's voice was conspiratorial on the other end. She was clearly enjoying her appointed task.

"Oh, hi, Casey," Kaitlyn said, forcing herself to sound as casual as possible. "What's up?"

She shot Tanner an apologetic smile, certain he'd heard Casey's name.

"Should I tell you Mitch is sick?"

Kaitlyn hesitated, knowing that it was her last chance to hit the brakes before things acquired a momentum of their own; in the same instant, she realized again that she was ready. She wanted to take more risks; she wanted to feel attractive and desirable. Stealing a look at Tanner before the fire, she knew she wanted *him*, and that he wanted her.

"I'm okay," she said.

"You sure?" Casey pressed. "Because you sound like you might be in way over your head."

"Yeah, I'm sure."

Casey was silent for a moment. "Well, okay then. I trust you, but you need to give me a reason for calling. Pretend like I'm making cookies and I need to know where the brown sugar is."

Kaitlyn smiled to herself—leave it to Casey to have it all planned out.

"There should be a bag of brown sugar in the pantry," Kaitlyn announced. "It's on the top shelf, near the rice."

"Uh-huh," Casey said, clearly amused. "He did look pretty good dressed up, don't you think? But anyway, tell me where I can find the recipe."

Kaitlyn closed her eyes, trying to concentrate. "The recipe should be somewhere in the drawer next to the sink. And give Mitch a kiss good night for me, all right?"

"Speaking of *kissing* . . ." Casey began before Kaitlyn hung up on her. Turning, she saw Tanner rise from the couch and stretch, his movements catlike and deliberate.

"Sorry about that," she mumbled. "Kids."

Backlit by the fire, he looked enigmatic as she approached. When she was close, he reached for her hand and gently pulled her against him. She could feel the warmth of his body as their eyes held each other's. Then, as if in slow motion, he tilted his head and brushed his lips against hers, their breaths mingling in tantalizing exploration. When their mouths finally came together, a rush of heat coursed through her, her every nerve ending awakened. When they separated, his slow smile allowed her to feel his desire.

"I'm sorry, but I couldn't resist," he said, still holding her hand, caressing it with teasing languor. "You're so lovely that I couldn't wait any longer."

She smiled, tempted to kiss him again, while another part of her longed to draw out the anticipation of what was to come.

"Would you hate me if I suggested we sit a little while longer?" she said, her voice strangely husky to her ears. "Maybe finish our wine?"

"Of course not," he responded, leading her back to the couch. She reached for her wineglass and Tanner did the same.

Staring at the fire, she took a sip, letting the subtle flavor linger in her mouth. Finally, she cast a sidelong look at him. "Have you ever been in love?" she asked.

Tanner didn't answer right away. "I think so," he finally answered.

"You're not sure?"

"It was a long time ago," he explained. "I was only twenty, and at the time, it felt real enough. Now, though, when I look back on it, I'm not sure I knew what true love really meant. I'm pretty sure we wouldn't have been good for each other in the long run."

"Why do you say that?"

"I don't think I knew who I was back then. I was only a year removed from being a teenager and was living in the U.S. for the first time. I suppose it's possible that we would have grown together, but chances are, we would have grown apart. In retrospect, I can see that we didn't have much in common, other than mutual infatuation."

"And you haven't fallen in love since then?"

"Again, I'm not exactly sure. When I was in my late twenties, I met Janice. Even though we only dated for a few months, I thought she might be the one. I even started eyeing engagement rings. But I was getting deployed every year back then, and when she discovered I was set to be shipped out again, I think she recognized that the life of a military wife wasn't what she wanted. We agreed it was best to take a break and by the time I got back to the States, she was seeing someone else. And if you're curious, the answer is no."

"No what?"

"In case you were wondering whether I've kept in touch with either of them."

Kaitlyn made a face. "I wasn't going to ask you that."

"Fair enough." Tanner laughed. "But sometimes people want to know."

She watched as he finished the last of his wine. "And that's it?"

"After Janice, I dated here and there, but nothing serious. Then came Cameroon, the Ivory Coast, and Haiti, none of which was conducive to long-term relationships. I didn't meet anyone I was really interested in until Hawaii. I met someone there, and we went out for a few months, but I didn't fall in love. In all fairness, she didn't love me either. It was more a Covid thing, something that happened mainly because the world shut down and she conveniently lived just down the street."

"I'm hoping you never said that to her."

"She said it to me, actually," he countered.

She winced. "Ouch."

"It stung at first, but after we split up, I realized she was right."

Kaitlyn searched for signs of regret but failed to see any. Instead, Tanner scooted closer before reaching for her hand again. He brought it to his lips and kissed it, then lowered it, his thumb tracing small circles on her skin. He willed her to meet his eyes.

"Do you know what I'm thinking now?"

"I have no idea."

"I was thinking how glad I am that none of those relationships worked out. If they had, I wouldn't be here with you."

The unguarded quality in his voice made her breath catch, and she watched as Tanner set his empty wineglass on the coffee table. Lifting his hand, he slowly traced a finger down her cheek before leaning closer.

He kissed her softly at first, almost as though asking permission, then with a growing passion that mimicked her own. With his lips on hers, she felt herself giving in to her own desire, and when their tongues finally met, she whimpered, surrendering to the moment. His hand was on her cheek and then tangled in her hair; and as he kissed her even more deeply, she felt all the tension in her body unravel, a sensual release she'd almost forgotten existed.

He nibbled at her lips and tongue before his mouth traveled to her neck. Leaning her head back with a sigh, she reveled in the exquisite sensation.

She allowed him to slowly pull her to her feet; in a trance, she felt him take her glass and set it on the coffee table beside his own. He moved closer then, his arms wrapped around her. When their mouths came together again, she felt his growing hunger;

his hands drifted from her back to her sides and slid over the thin fabric of her dress. Her breasts swelled against his chest, the warmth spreading through her like a wave, her own arms twining around his neck. He kissed the corner of her mouth and then her cheek, the alternating scratch of his stubble and moisture of his tongue as he moved from one tender spot to another unbearably tantalizing.

She closed her eyes as his fingers reached for her zipper; she felt their mutual impatience as he tugged at it, slowly moving it downward. Her dress suddenly loosened and his mouth went back to hers, his intensity and excitement feeding her own.

He slid one sleeve down and then the other before slowly peeling the dress from her body, over her waist and past her hips, until it finally crumpled to the floor. It was her turn then, and her skin felt like it was on fire as she peeled his jacket from his shoulders. They continued to kiss as she unbuttoned his shirt, and they went together then, skin on skin, their heated bodies seared against each other. She heard him moan with pleasure as their hands roved across each other, her breasts freed from her bra as she traced her fingers over his chest and down his stomach. Tanner helped her undo his belt, and she reached for the button on his pants, tugging them down over his hips and helping him shake himself free. Then finally, she felt him reach for her hand and with a gentle tug, he began leading her toward the bedroom.

Though she could see the urgent need in his gaze, he didn't rush. Instead, just inside the doorway, he took her in his arms and buried his face in the hollow of her neck, sending shocks of pleasure cascading through her body. Opening her eyes for a moment, she had the sensation of watching herself from across the room, and took in the scene: the large four-poster bed and chandelier, the wall of rain-lashed windows backlit by a flickering sky; the shelter of his passionate embrace.

She lost any sense of time as they kissed and held each other, but when a clap of thunder echoed overhead, he began tugging at her panties. A moment later, she was naked, as was he, and he finally led her to the bed.

IX

AFTERWARD, THEY LAY beside each other, his arm curled around her. She traced her fingers across his chest and stomach, pausing over scars she hadn't known existed. There were smaller ones on both shoulders, larger ones on his chest and ribs, and a jagged scar on his waist that resembled a lightning bolt. When she asked him about them, he briefly described how he'd come to receive each one. *Lucky shot,* regarding one of his shoulder wounds. *Helicopter crash* for the nasty scar on his waist. Because it was clear he preferred not to talk about them, she didn't press, but it reminded her that as intimate as they'd become, there was much about him that remained a mystery.

After they made love a second time, they lay with their faces close together, Tanner's long lashes nearly brushing her own. Kaitlyn couldn't ever remember feeling so completed by someone, as if her body ended where his began, their limbs tangled and nerve endings thrumming as if they were a single entity.

"Was this part of your plan?" she whispered, studying the shifting green-gold facets of his irises. "And why you rented a house, instead of us going to a restaurant?"

"Well . . ." he said, his suggestive tone making her giggle.

"You know what I want to do now?" she asked.

When he arched an eyebrow, she rolled her eyes. "Not that. We've already done it twice," she said. "I need something to eat."

"How about I start dinner?"

"I was hoping you'd say that. And I'm going to need your help with my zipper."

"You don't have to put your dress back on."

"I'm not going to eat dinner naked," she protested. "That would be weird."

After dressing, Kaitlyn retrieved her purse from the table near the front door and fixed her hair and makeup, not so much for Tanner, but for Casey and Mitch. Or, rather, just Casey. Mitch would likely be asleep by the time she got home, but she had no doubt that Casey would be waiting up, ready to pounce on any telltale details.

By the time she joined Tanner in the kitchen, he was pouring two more glasses of wine. He handed one to her and she glanced around.

"What can I do to help?" she asked.

"I think I've got it covered," he said. "The mushrooms are in the oven and the salads are ready to go."

They were silent as he lit the candles and dimmed the lights in the dining room. Then, back in the kitchen, he donned an oven mitt, pulled out the dish containing the mushrooms, and set it on the counter. From the refrigerator, he pulled out the entrées and popped them into the oven. Together they ferried the mushrooms and salads to the table. After they'd taken their seats, Tanner served the mushrooms. Then he reached for his glass. "I just realized I forgot to offer a toast. I probably should have done it earlier with the champagne."

"I forgive you," she teased. "Now, though, I just want to eat." Cutting into a mushroom, she sampled a first bite.

"Good?" he asked, watching her face.

"Delicious." She ate another mouthful, suddenly ravenous.

He tossed the salad and served them each a generous portion.

"How was Casey today?" he inquired. "I'm hoping she didn't wreck any more cars on her day off?"

Kaitlyn snorted. "If she did, she didn't mention it. She did help me with my hair and makeup, though."

"That was nice of her."

"It was," she said. She speared a tomato on her salad plate. "I think I'm going to have to get her a car."

"So she doesn't move in with her father?"

"That's part of it, but the truth is, she needs one. For when I'm at work or out doing my house calls and she's home with Mitch. If there's an emergency, she's stuck without transportation."

"Have you told her yet?"

"No. Because the moment I do tell her, it's all she'll talk to me about until the car ends up in the driveway."

"And Mitch? How's he doing?"

"He's having pizza for dinner and watching TV with his sister right now. That's pretty much as good as life gets for him."

Tanner smiled, and as the meal continued, they settled into easy conversation. She told Tanner about Casey's college plans and shared more stories about her parents and siblings. While they lingered over their entrées, Kaitlyn listened raptly as Tanner described his far-flung travels and the friends he'd known over the years.

Every now and then, Kaitlyn would find herself picturing more evenings with Tanner, just like this. Catching herself, she gave herself a mental shake and warned herself to keep her feelings in check. A whirlwind fling was one thing, but falling for him was another.

Saying goodbye was going to be hard enough already.

X

Tanner brought the strawberry tarts to the table and set one in front of her. Though she'd eaten almost past the point of comfort, she figured a few bites wouldn't kill her. Hadn't she resolved that life was for living?

"Before I forget," he said, cutting into his own tart, "I should probably tell you the good news."

She looked up from her plate, intrigued. "That came out of nowhere."

"I was distracted earlier," he said with a wink. "The parts for my car are going to take two or three weeks to arrive. In reality, that probably means three or four weeks, so it seems like I'll be sticking around Asheboro longer than I thought."

"What on earth will you do?"

"I'm not sure yet, but who knows? I might just meet someone special."

"Good luck with that," she said, teasing.

"There are also a few more families I want to visit before I head to Cameroon."

"Do they live nearby?"

"They're in Virginia, Pennsylvania, and South Dakota."

"So . . . another road trip, then?"

"I'd love to see Mount Rushmore, maybe do a tour of the Badlands. I've always wanted to see the Black Hills. I hear they're spectacular," he mused, as if he were already mapping out an itinerary.

Kaitlyn was silent. That an alternative existed—he could, for example, instead return sooner to Asheboro to see her—leapt to mind, but she refrained from pointing that out. "How long do you think you'll be gone?" she asked.

He forked a glazed strawberry into his mouth. "I don't know. A few weeks, maybe more? It also depends on their schedules, not just mine."

While that all made sense, she couldn't help feeling a little disappointed that being away from her for three weeks out of the nine or ten he had left in the States didn't seem to give him pause. Still, she reminded herself that his job would take him abroad soon in any case, so less time together now was probably for the best.

"Have you spoken to your friend recently? The one who got you the job with IRC?" She toyed with her fork, making furrows in the gelatin of her tart.

"Vince? Not for a few weeks."

"What projects will IRC be working on in Cameroon? I don't think you told me."

"I know they do a lot of work with refugees and crisis relief, but I don't know the details."

"How can you not know?" Kaitlyn asked.

"I just know I'll be doing security work," he said, polishing off the last of his dessert. He wiped his mouth and pushed his plate away. "I'm sure I'll learn everything once my job starts in September."

She frowned, then hesitated before saying, "I thought you started work in June."

"That's when I fly to Yaoundé, but I won't start work until September."

"Does it take that long to find a place to live?" she asked.

"No. I'll be in temporary housing. Vince promised to set it up."

"I don't understand. Why are you going so early?" Kaitlyn pressed, her confusion growing. "If you don't start work until the fall?"

"I don't have to go early, I guess," Tanner responded with a bemused expression. "But I think I mentioned that I wanted to visit a couple of the national parks, and it would be easiest to do that before I get back to the daily grind. And I think I mentioned, I really enjoyed playing soccer there."

She gave a weak smile, trying to silence the voice in her head that whispered, *He could stay in Asheboro until the end of summer, if he really wanted to.*

"I'll bet it's going to be strange," she remarked, avoiding his eyes. "Going back to work, I mean, after taking so much time off."

"Probably," he admitted. "Vince wanted me to sign a two-year contract, but I told him that I preferred to start with one year and see how it goes."

"What if it doesn't work out?"

"I have no idea," he said, leaning back in his chair and running a hand through his hair. "For all I know, I'll end up retired again. It's not as though I'm going back to work for the paycheck."

She chuckled, but when she saw his matter-of-fact expression it dawned on her that he wasn't kidding.

"What do you mean?" she asked.

"I don't need to work," he said simply. "I could retire now if I wanted."

She stared at him. "How? Did your grandparents leave you a surprise inheritance?"

"Hardly." He chuckled.

"Then army and government work must pay better than I thought."

"I wish," he responded. "I think I mentioned to you that I've done some investing in my past?"

"You did." She nodded. "But it's enough for you to retire on?"

"It is."

"Care to share your investing secrets?" she joked. "Since Casey needs a car and will be heading off to college soon?"

"There's no secret, really. I got lucky, then I was lazy, then I got lucky again."

She fixed him with a level look. "You do know you're being a bit cagey about all this, right?"

"I don't talk about it much," he said. "My grandparents knew, and a couple of my closest friends know, but that's about it." She watched as he reached for his almost-empty wineglass. "After I finished school, my grandparents set me up with a small investment account," he said. "They suggested that once I enlisted, I should set aside part of my paycheck for automatic investment. So that's what I did."

"I do that with my 401(k), too," Kaitlyn rejoined. "But trust me, it hasn't earned enough for me to be able to retire."

"That's because you didn't meet Rodney."

"Who's Rodney?"

"A buddy from the Rangers," he explained. "Back in 2001, he showed up in the barracks with an iPod. I'd never heard of the thing, but he went on and on about how it was the greatest thing ever, and that I should get one, too. I didn't, but a few of the other guys in the barracks did, which got my attention. iPods weren't cheap, and it's not as though any of them were earning very much. I started noticing that a lot of other, regular everyday people were buying them, too, so—despite my grandparents' cautionary warnings—I impulsively moved all the money I had into Apple and set up the account so it would automatically buy more Apple stock with every paycheck."

"You bought Apple stock *back then?*"

"Like I said, I got lucky. And then, because I was lazy, I never bothered to change that investment strategy. Meanwhile, I spent the next ten years either deployed or living in the barracks and my expenses were nil, so my pool of investment capital kept growing and again, month after month, it all went into Apple. Then, in 2007, I got lucky again. The iPhone came out and not long after that, the stock started going through the roof. Factor in all the splits over the years since I first bought it, and . . ."

"You're rich," she said, finishing for him.

He was quiet for a moment. "Yeah," he admitted.

"Like . . . rich rich? Or just rich?"

"I'm not sure what you mean by that, but I have more than I'll ever be able to spend."

She stared at him, finding it difficult to reconcile what he'd just told her with everything she'd come to know about him. She wondered idly if their relationship would have evolved differently had she known this about him from the beginning.

"So . . ." she said slowly, "you could do anything you want, then? Since you don't have to work? You could live anywhere?"

"I guess."

"I see." She found herself unable to say anything else.

Tanner seemed to study her. "Is there a problem?"

As she returned his gaze, she tried to make sense of everything he'd just told her.

He didn't have to work.

He'd rather play soccer with his buddy than see where things might go with her.

He could stay in Asheboro.

She struggled to banish these unwanted thoughts, but it was a losing battle. "I just find it odd," she ventured.

"What part?" Tanner frowned.

She reached for her wineglass, then set it aside again, no longer in the mood for more. "I've been assuming that you had to go back to work for financial reasons. And because of your commitment to the work that IRC is doing in Cameroon. But it doesn't sound like you even know what you'll be doing there."

At her words, he looked equal parts baffled and chagrined. "I'm getting the sense that you're angry with me."

"I'm not angry," she demurred. And she wasn't. *Angry* was too strong of a word to describe what she was feeling. There was disappointment, for sure, maybe even irritation. But her overriding sensation was one of . . . rejection. Maybe even betrayal. Which was irrational, she knew. She'd reminded herself before they even slept together that it was just a fling, but as much as she wished otherwise, she realized that his revelation had changed everything.

If he really wanted to, he could stay and pursue this—whatever this was—with her.

Deep down, she knew that was selfish, and she was jumping the gun in terms of where they were. And yet . . .

If he *could* stay, why wasn't he inclined to? Why do all this—the limo and champagne, the lavish dinner in this mountain house? Just to sleep with her? And more to the point, why wasn't he interested in spending more nights like tonight with her?

"Never mind," she said, looking away. "Can we just forget I brought any of it up? It doesn't matter."

Tanner placed his hands on the table, palms up. When he spoke, his voice was measured. "You're upset with me and I'm not sure what I did."

"It's fine," she said, aware that her tone belied her words.

Meanwhile, the questions continued to nag at her, and all at once, it was hard to stay seated. Rising, she swept some crumbs from the table with her napkin and brought her glass of wine to the kitchen, along with her dessert plate. She dumped the remains down the sink, and uncertain what to do with the leftover tart, she pushed it to the corner of the counter before automatically reaching for the sponge. As if on autopilot, she began wiping down the counters.

Tanner followed her to the kitchen, concerned. "What are you doing?" he asked gently.

"Cleaning up," she said with a shrug.

"I can get that later," he assured her, placing a tentative hand on her waist. "Why don't we go sit by the fire again?"

"It's getting late," she mumbled, moving away.

It was only a few minutes past nine, and they both knew it.

"Talk to me," he pleaded. "Please."

She ran the sponge over the countertop one last time before finally dropping it into the sink.

"Why am I here?" she finally asked, turning to face him.

"What do you mean?" His eyes, a dark green now, searched her face.

"Why did you ask me out in the first place? And why did you keep asking me out?" Kaitlyn's back was pressed against the edge of the sink, her hands on the counter to either side of her.

He looked at her, confused. "Because you're smart and kind and interesting and I wanted to get to know you better."

"For a few weeks, you mean." She crossed her arms.

Tanner took a small step back. For a moment, he said nothing, and she had the sense he was trying to put the pieces together. "Is that it?" he asked slowly. "You're upset because I'm leaving?" When she didn't respond, he went on. "Kaitlyn, don't you think that's a little unfair? I've been open with you all along about my plans."

She stared at him, frustrated.

"Why are you going to Cameroon?"

He frowned, uncertain. "My job——" he began.

"The one you don't need, you mean," she interrupted.

Tanner stared at her, uncomprehending. "I need to do something. I can't just hang out forever. I'd end up going crazy."

"I'm not suggesting you do nothing. I'm just wondering: Why Cameroon?"

"We've talked about this——"

"Yes and no," she said, cutting him off. "You've told me that you think Cameroon is an amazing country. You mentioned a couple of national parks you wanted to visit, and that you enjoyed playing soccer with your friend. You described how fun it was to watch a game in a crowded bar. But you know what you haven't told me about? Or even mentioned in passing? The people you've helped. You never referenced a grateful smile from a hungry person that you fed, or the lives you bettered when you dug a new well or whatever."

"I'm in security. I don't do those things . . ." he protested.

"You're missing my point." She heard the creeping frustration in her tone and took a deep breath, trying to dial it back. "I understand that security work is important. I get that keeping aid workers safe enables them to do their jobs. What I'm asking is why *you're* going back there. Other than giving you something to do, what need does it specifically fill in you? Except enjoyment?"

He opened his mouth to respond before closing it again. Finally: "Not all jobs offer an existential purpose."

"That's my point exactly!" she cried. "I'd understand you going back if you were the only guy in the world who could do what you do, or if you felt compelled to do something good in the world. I'd also understand if you needed the job to pay your bills or were truly motivated to serve others. But when I add up everything you've told me, especially the fact that you barely know what your job will entail . . . I don't get it. But I do think I understand now why your grandmother was so worried about you."

His mouth tightened. "Don't bring her into this."

Kaitlyn's eyes bored into his. "Then tell me why you want to go back to Cameroon."

"I made the decision when my grandma was sick, all right?" Tanner folded his arms across his chest. "She worried that I was drifting and I got to thinking that she might have a point, so when the job came up, I took it."

They said nothing for a fraught moment. When Kaitlyn finally spoke, her voice was muted. "Since you don't have to work at all, you could work anywhere. You could have stayed in Pensacola."

Tanner's expression was challenging. "Or Asheboro, you mean?"

"What's wrong with Asheboro?" she countered, feeling defensive despite herself. "You said yourself that you like small towns. You're the one who said you'd love to be able to run in the Uwharrie every day—"

"You *are* angry," he said, comprehension dawning, even as he shook his head. "I should never have told you—"

She held up her hands to stop him before finally bowing her head. "I guess I'm just trying to say that you're not who I thought you were," she said, her voice subdued. "And that's my fault for not listening to you."

"What's that supposed to mean?"

She lifted her eyes slowly, feeling like a fool. "You did say that if I asked your friends, they'd tell me that you're not wired to settle down."

"That was meant to be a joke."

"Was it?" Her skepticism was plain. "What is it you want from life, Tanner? To stay on the move forever?" When he didn't answer, she went on. "And what about us? You knew you didn't have to leave, but did the thought ever occur to you that we could be more than a fling? That there was even the slightest possibility of something more?"

Again, Tanner said nothing. Kaitlyn glanced away, trying to ignore her feelings of humiliation. "Just so you know, I was okay with the idea of a fling when I came here tonight. I'd reconciled myself to circumstances being what they were. But now I'm not sure what to think." When Tanner remained quiet, she stepped around him, unwilling to meet his eyes. "I think I should proba-bly have the car bring me back home. I've got to work tomorrow."

"Kaitlyn . . . wait . . ."

She hurriedly collected her jacket and purse. At the door, she debated whether to take Tanner's umbrella, but what was the point? Staying dry hardly seemed like a priority now.

Tanner took a step toward her. "Can I at least walk you out?"

"I don't think so," she said.

"Will I see you again?"

A bitter smile came to her lips. *Why bother, when you're only biding time until you can play soccer in the streets of Cameroon?* "My days are pretty full," she said, keeping her tone steady as she opened the front door.

"Kaitlyn . . ."

She turned. "I know I don't have to end things between us," she said with a clarity that surprised even her, "but I can see now that there's no reason to keep it going."

The shock in his eyes gave her a fleeting sense of satisfaction, but it was quickly replaced by the idea that she was better than that. She stepped out onto the porch and let the door fall shut behind her. As she descended the steps, she felt raindrops stream down her face, knowing that they were already blending with her tears.

XI

"YOU'RE HOME ALREADY?" Casey emerged from the kitchen as Kaitlyn stood in the foyer, shaking the rain off her jacket. "I didn't expect you for another hour or two."

Kaitlyn had spent the entire car ride home pulling herself together before she had to face her daughter. The storm of conflicting emotions had subsided a bit, but she knew her feelings were still perilously close to the surface. *Breathe,* she told herself. *Whatever else you may or may not be, you're still a mom.* "I knew I had to get up for work in the morning," she answered, trying her best to sound indifferent. "Where's Mitch?"

"He was falling asleep as soon as the movie was over, so I put him to bed. How did it go?"

There it was, Kaitlyn thought. A loaded question, all things considered. "Fine," she said shortly.

Casey scrutinized her. "Uh-oh. What did he do wrong?"

"He didn't do anything," she said with affected blandness. "We had a lovely dinner."

"But?"

"But what?"

"But you don't think you're going to see him again," Casey surmised. "That's what you're thinking, even if you're not willing to say it out loud. Am I right?"

Kaitlyn was suddenly too exhausted to marvel at Casey's ability to read her. "Yes," she admitted.

Casey pinched her lips together. "Let me make you a cup of hot cocoa."

"I'm not really in the mood to talk, honey," Kaitlyn protested.

"I'm not asking to talk," Casey called over her shoulder as she headed back to the kitchen. "I simply offered to make you some cocoa. It's the drink of choice when guys suddenly become idiots."

Kaitlyn watched as Casey filled a small saucepan with milk and set it on the burner before pulling the cocoa from the cupboard. When the milk was hot, she whisked in the cocoa, dotted it with some mini-marshmallows, and brought Kaitlyn the cup.

"No matter what happened, just remember that I'm on your

side," she said, sounding remarkably like Kaitlyn's mother. "Now turn around and I'll help you with the zipper."

Kaitlyn obediently turned, feeling as Casey tugged at the zipper, loosening the dress. Then, startling her, Casey kissed her on the cheek. "You're going to be okay, Mom."

She walked out of the kitchen, leaving Kaitlyn to reflect that she'd been blessed with the children she had. Well . . . most of the time anyway.

She sipped at the cocoa, finishing half the cup before trudging to her bedroom. Closing the door, she caught sight of herself in the mirror, and her reflection suddenly brought the evening's events back in a rush. She gasped as if she'd been struck in the solar plexus, tears springing to her eyes. She pinched the bridge of her nose, willing them to stop.

I am a grown woman, she told herself.

She forced herself to draw a deep breath. *I knew all along that he'd be leaving.*

Straightening her shoulders, she turned away from the mirror. *Nothing has changed . . .*

Except that it had.

She noticed a tremor in her hands as she slipped off her dress then washed her face. Slowly, she put on her pajamas and crawled into bed. Certain that sleep would answer her bone-deep exhaustion as soon as she turned out the light, she instead found herself staring at the ceiling as memories from the evening continued to flood her mind. The anticipation she'd felt in the limo and the taste of champagne, the smell of Tanner's cologne. The exhilaration and wonder she'd felt when she first walked through the house. The muscled strength of his arms and back as he moved above her in bed, the sound of their voices as they made love . . .

Burying her face in her pillow, she began to cry, knowing that it was over before it ever had a chance to begin.

CHAPTER NINE

I

"WHERE THE HELL *is all the corn?*"
"*Maybe they ate it already.*"
"*That's impossible! We just put it out here last night!*"

From his refuge between the boulders and the ridge, Jasper couldn't hear the Littletons, but he could imagine what they were saying to each other. Melton hadn't come with them, but the brothers were standing directly over the spot where they'd left the bait.

"*Are we in the right place?*"
"*Of course we are.*"

Jasper continued to watch the darkly silhouetted figures while remaining as still as possible, knowing that even in dim light, any movement might be detected. Somehow, he'd been able to grab the corn and the rake and the flashlight; somehow, he'd been able to hobble to the boulders before finally collapsing behind the largest one. But the effort had cost him, and he'd had to bite back a groan as his back began to knot. By the time the spasm had passed, the Littletons had arrived.

Above him, the last of the stars faded away. The old saying *It's always darkest before the dawn* was hogwash; anyone who watched the evening sky knew it was darkest in the middle of the night, halfway between sunset and sunrise, but what did that matter now? Dawn was coming, which meant it would soon be light enough for them to find him if they decided to search. Jasper took hold of Arlo's collar to keep the dog from running into the open.

The Littletons continued to look around, their flashlights moving in sweeping arcs. Jasper again imagined their words.

"Maybe someone took it."

"Who?"

"The wildlife guys, maybe?"

"It wasn't them."

"How do you know?"

"Hold on. I want to check something."

A beam from one of the flashlights swung in his direction and Jasper ducked lower, grimacing in pain. How was he going to get out of here? And what would happen if they found him?

He didn't want to think about that.

Once, decades ago, when he and Audrey had taken the kids camping near Asheville, he'd been awakened by the heavy grunting of a bear right outside his tent. The kids had been young then, sleeping together in their own tent, and Jasper immediately wiggled out of his sleeping bag and rushed to protect his children. But there'd been no bear; aside from the sound of crickets, the forest was quiet. Other tents in the campground were undisturbed, and it was only after Jasper searched the ground for prints that he finally realized he must have been dreaming. Later he wondered what he would have done had there actually been a bear nearby; he had no weapon, hadn't even been wearing a shirt or shoes. There was nothing he could really have done other than wave his arms and scream.

That stew of initial confusion and panic was the same sensation he was experiencing now as he listened for the sound of the Littletons' approach. Hearing nothing, he risked another quick peek over the boulder and realized they were heading toward the fallen tree. Jasper cocked his ear, concentrating, and he was finally able to make out their words.

"That's weird." The voice was Josh's; Jasper would never forget the sound of it.

"What?"

"Do you smell something? I thought I smelled it back there, too, where we dumped the corn last night. Whatever it is, it stinks."

The deer repellent, Jasper thought. And Josh hadn't used the word *stinks;* he'd noted that it *"smells like f——g s——t,"* spewing profanity. Beside Jasper, Arlo yawned, letting out a squeak.

"I don't smell anything."

"Shut up," Josh hissed. "Did you hear something?"

"Like what?"

"Shhhh . . ."

They went silent. Arlo's ears perked up and Jasper held his breath.

"What are we listening for?"

"Would you shut the hell up?"

Jasper closed his fist around Arlo's dog tag so it couldn't clink against his collar. A few seconds passed, then ten. Then twenty.

"I think I smell it, too," Eric said. "What is it?"

"I don't know."

"Do you think it's that deer from the other day? The one you shot?"

"I don't know."

There was a pause. Then: "What do you want to do?"

"What do you mean?"

"Since there's no corn, maybe we should just go home."

"We're not going home."

In the silence that followed, Jasper could feel his fear continue to gnaw at him, almost as though it were a living thing.

II

THE FIRST THING Jasper had done upon leaving the burn center was to have his family's remains exhumed and brought to the property near his cabin. Jasper held his own private service and dug the graves himself, every movement agonizing, and afterward, he moved into the cabin for good. He didn't have the money to rebuild the house, even if he'd wanted to. The insurance money he'd received barely covered his medical bills.

For months, even years, afterward, he simply wanted to die. There were moments when he pulled out his old hunting rifle and loaded it, but he could never summon the courage to use it on himself. Instead, believing that God had chosen to smite him, he set the rifle aside, knowing it was his punishment to simply bear it. *Jasper, you shall suffer day and night,* he imagined God saying to him, and in a twisted sense, Jasper felt that he deserved to suffer. He'd failed to protect his family when they needed him most, when everything was on the line.

Suffering, however, necessitated work, if only to survive. With his injuries, a job in construction was no longer possible, nor was any type of manual labor. Sitting at a desk for more than fifteen minutes at a stretch was excruciating, so working in an office wasn't an option. Because part of his face and scalp had been burned, no one wanted him interacting with customers. In the end, he found a job doing stocking and other work at a local home supply store. It didn't pay much, but then again, Jasper

didn't need much. The owner—a woman named Nell Baker—
had known him and his family for years. He'd supplied the garden center part of her store with Bradford pear trees, and she was
a member of the church that Jasper had once attended; Jasper
assumed she'd hired him out of pity.

Between surgeries, he spent much of his time watering and
fertilizing flowers, herbs, and shrubbery in the garden center. He
swept and mopped and restocked shelves. The job wasn't difficult,
but because many of his sweat glands had been destroyed, he had
to be careful when summer brought higher temperatures. Scar
tissue made it difficult to move without pain. He began wearing
a bandanna over his face. He was careful to keep his distance
from customers; his scars, unhealed skin grafts, and incisions
made him look like Dr. Frankenstein's pet project. At home, he
removed the bathroom mirrors and stored them in the work shed
out back. Other than for work and shopping for basics, he seldom left the cabin.

He stopped reading the Bible and no longer prayed, and slowly,
the years began to pass.

Work. Surgery. Recover. Repeat. Repeat. Repeat. He turned
fifty, and then fifty-five, before God struck again, adding yet
more trials to the Book of Jasper, as though all that had occurred
wasn't quite enough.

A few years after his final surgery and a little more than ten
years after the fire, the skin that had been undamaged began to
itch before giving rise to pink scaly patches that resembled a poi-
son ivy rash. The diagnosis was psoriasis. Doctors speculated that
the fire might have triggered some sort of systemic autoimmune
reaction, but no one could tell him for certain. What he did know
was that the psoriasis continued to spread, eventually taking root
in almost all the places that hadn't been scarred. It itched to the
point of madness, and the doctors tried various medications to

reverse the condition, without success. Eventually, the diagnosis was changed to chronic psoriasis, and he was told he'd have to live with the condition for the rest of his life. In that moment, he knew he was a changed man.

He still had his faith; in his heart, God and Christ were as real as ever. But back at the cabin, he placed his Bible and religious carvings and photographs and albums into boxes he stored in the work shed next to the mirrors, certain that neither God nor Christ had ever really cared about him at all.

III

IN THE FOREST, morning birdcall drifted from the trees, darkness finally giving way to the gray light of dawn. Jasper remained hunkered down behind the boulder with Arlo; the Littleton brothers, meanwhile, had taken up a vigil behind the fallen tree. For the most part, they remained silent. Jasper assumed they had their rifles ready in case the white deer decided to make an appearance. No doubt they hoped it would return in search of more corn, and Jasper was happy that he'd doused the area with repellent and set out those ultrasonic gizmos.

A small rock had begun to dig into Jasper's behind, just enough to be irritating. He wondered if trying to get rid of the rock would cause Arlo to stir, but the dog seemed to be fast asleep. Taking a chance, he shifted, trying to stay as quiet as he could. Arlo's ears twitched but his eyes remained closed, and Jasper was finally able to flick the rock away. It helped, but only a little. Though his back seemed to be improving—albeit slightly—his knee was getting worse. It had swollen to the point that it pressed on the fabric of his pants and he felt a heated throb of pain with every heartbeat.

That was one of many irritations with growing old—injuries were more painful than ever. Worse, they took forever to heal or never fully healed at all. A few years ago, he'd jammed a finger while reaching for the cast-iron frying pan, and even now, the knuckle was larger than the others and ached when it rained. Given the condition of his knee, he figured he'd end up limping for the rest of his life, however long that might be.

Then again, what did he know? A few months back, the doctor had used the phrase "aging with dignity," but as he'd left her office, he wondered if such a thing was possible or even, frankly, what it meant. How did one age with dignity? Did that mean being proud of the fact that you didn't dare drive faster than the speed limit because you couldn't see the road very well? Did it mean holding your head high even if you needed adult diapers? He wasn't judging, mind you, even if he was secretly pleased that at least a few parts of his body still seemed to be working properly.

His thoughts were interrupted again by the sound of voices.

"I don't think any deer are coming," Eric whined.

"Would you keep your damn voice down?"

"I'm just saying. We've been out here for almost an hour already."

"Would you shut up?"

"How long are we going to stay?"

"Why do you care? There's no school today."

At that, the boys went silent again. Jasper shifted, hoping to move the ache from one limb to another. The dog lifted his head at the movement, then closed his eyes again. He looked strangely content, and in that moment, Jasper was reminded of his older son, who'd always looked blissfully untroubled as he slept, especially when he was young.

David had always been the most mature and confident of all their children. Even as a toddler, he'd look people in the eye when they were speaking, and he seldom threw tantrums. Audrey used to describe him as an *old soul.* Even before he'd started kindergarten, he would help Audrey with his younger siblings. He would rock them or feed them and help them get dressed whenever Audrey asked, and he'd clear the table after dinner without complaint. Of all their children, he was the only one who made the bed and kept his room clean through his teenage years.

He was tall from the very beginning, with a cowlick that wasn't tamed until adolescence. He brought his natural maturity with him to school, where he was an excellent student, well-liked by both teachers and other kids. His calm, quiet dignity made him a shoo-in for class president every year of high school.

He didn't laugh much, however. In all the years of his childhood, Jasper had heard that joyful sound only a handful of times, and once he got to college, he seemed to become even more reticent. He didn't seem to feel that taking care of his family and community was enough; the world's problems somehow became his to solve. When he was home over Christmas and during the summer, he spoke little about his classes or the friends he had made. Instead, he worried about the Soviet Union, he fretted about nuclear weapons, he wanted to limit pollution and feed the starving children in Ethiopia. He expressed deep concern about declining rates of church attendance and studied the Bible for hours as though searching for the answers that eluded him. Even after deciding to become a pastor, he confessed to Jasper that he wasn't sure he would be good enough; that if he didn't truly understand God's purpose for him, then how could he help others discover His purpose in their own lives?

Jasper could remember smiling at his son while James 4:10 floated through his mind (*Humble yourselves before the Lord and He will lift you up*).

He said as much before finishing with "I'm proud of you" and holding open his arms. David went into them, clinging like the child he had once been. "I love you, Pop," he'd whispered, "and I thank God every day for you and Mom." The words had filled Jasper's eyes with tears and he held his oldest child for a long time.

Not long after that, David was gone forever.

IV

"WHAT THE HELL is that?" Josh Littleton snarled. He was no longer even attempting to keep his voice down, and Jasper could now hear him easily.

"What?"

"Over there. By that tree. Look."

It must have taken a moment for Eric to see what Josh had pointed out.

"Is that a sprinkler?"

Nope, Jasper thought. *It's a solar-powered ultrasonic gadget to keep the deer away.*

"There are no sprinklers in the forest, you moron. Hold on. I want to check it out."

The clearing went quiet and in his mind's eye, Jasper saw Josh slipping the rifle strap over his shoulder and walking toward the device.

A few minutes later, he heard Josh again, his irritation plain.

"I think it makes sounds that keeps the deer away. Martin's mom used to put things like these in her garden."

"Who's Martin?"

"Just shut up and take a look."

"Who put it here? The wildlife guys?"

"It's not the wildlife guys, you idiot. Whoever took the corn and put these here came after we left last night."

"Then who did it?"

"Take a guess."

It took Eric a moment. "The old burned-up guy who came to the house?"

"Ding, ding, ding!"

"But why?"

"Because he's a . . ."

Jasper tuned out as Josh began cursing him, one foul word after another. "Come on," Josh finally said, his voice thick with disgust and anger. "Let's get the hell out of here."

Things went quiet. Because Jasper was afraid to risk a glance over the boulder, he couldn't be sure they'd left immediately, so he settled in to wait. To his relief, even though his knee continued to swell, the muscles in his back had loosened. Being forced to hide, he thought, had been a blessing in disguise, if only for the chance to recover. Just as he began to think that the coast might be clear, he heard Josh's shout reverberate from a distance, its malice and rage poisoning the morning air.

"I KNOW YOU'RE STILL OUT HERE!"

V

JASPER GAVE IT another hour, just to be safe. Arlo continued to doze. Jasper threaded pebbles between his fingers and watched a pair of squirrels bound along a tree branch. Above him, a hawk was circling in the sky, making bigger and bigger loops, and Jasper followed its flight pattern with fascination, just as he'd often done with Mary.

That girl had always loved animals of every kind. When she was little, her bed had been overrun with stuffed animals— a penguin, an elephant, and a pink horse—but her favorite was a plush arctic fox that she slept with for years and even took along to college. She was one of the reasons Jasper had begun whittling animals—the same kind he now made with the boy. Mary had loved them, and named them all—Wally Woodpecker or Sally Squirrel or Harry Horse—and she would play with them constantly, making up elaborate adventures for them.

It was also because of Mary that they'd owned two dogs (Bert, followed by Ernie); two cats, named Cookie and Cream; a hamster; a gerbil; and even a gecko, until it escaped out the bedroom window. Like Mitch, she loved to visit the North Carolina Zoo, and on weekends Jasper would occasionally bring her to a neighboring farm that had cows and horses as well as Tennessee fainting goats. When the goats were startled, their muscles tightened, causing them to topple over. As a little girl, Mary would clap and watch them fall over, laughing with delight; as she grew older, she felt bad for the goats and tried to make as little noise as possible in their presence. "Making them fall over is mean, Daddy," she admonished. "Look how sweet they are." Sometimes she'd borrow his camera to take pictures, using up entire rolls of film.

For the most part, Mary was a pigtailed tomboy, happier spending time outside than in the confines of her room. She didn't mind getting dirty and could climb trees and hit a ball even better than her brothers. But there was a tender side to her, and not just when it came to animals. In seventh grade, she asked a boy named Michael to attend a Sadie Hawkins dance with her; when he admitted he was hoping that another girl would ask him instead, she spent the rest of the afternoon and evening crying in her room. She cried, too, when it came to studying, for she had to work harder than most to master the material. Sometimes, frustration and anxiety would get the better of her.

She didn't always have an easy time with her younger sister, either, even though Deborah was her best friend in the world. She'd always believed that Deborah was prettier than she was. When she admitted as much to Jasper, he assured her that both were beautiful in their own ways, but his words only made her grimace. "She's taller than I am, her hair is straight and not curly, and boys call the house every night for Deborah, but never for me."

Jasper hadn't known how to respond, and later, he would wonder if his failure in that moment was the reason they never spoke of it again. He pretended not to notice that Mary seldom dated in high school; he pretended not to notice when she announced that she was going to the homecoming dance with a group of girlfriends instead of the boy she had a crush on. It genuinely puzzled Jasper that the boys at her school weren't drawn to her natural beauty and vitality; it was, and still remained, a mystery to him.

Next to animals, and much like they were for Audrey, books were Mary's passion. She loved mysteries and adventures, and often, Jasper would see Mary and Audrey seated next to each other on the couch, each of them transported to another world in the pages of her book, both of them absently twirling thick strands of their hair.

Of all his children, Mary was the most diligent in school, working relentlessly to achieve her hard-won grades. Her study habits served her well in college; at UNC Chapel Hill, she received straight A's every semester and remained focused on her goal of becoming a veterinarian. She also met a young man halfway through her junior year, eventually confiding at one point to Audrey that *he might be the one.* They continued to see each other after graduation, and both enrolled in the veterinary program at NC State. She even invited him to the house over the Christmas holidays, and Jasper noticed him stealing looks at Mary over dinner that seemed to convey the same secret longing Jasper had felt for Audrey as a youth.

It was hard to believe that just half a year after that, only the memory of Mary would remain.

VI

AS THE MORNING sun continued its ascent, Jasper waited, then waited some more. Even Arlo seemed to be getting bored by this point and probably needed water.

He hadn't heard the boys for a long time and when he'd risked a peek over the boulder, he hadn't seen them either. They could, of course, be waiting for him, but he couldn't stay put much longer; if his knee continued to swell, he might not be able to move at all. As it was, he could barely bend his leg.

Deciding to risk it, he scooched closer to the boulder. Gripping it with both hands, he got his good leg into position, and tried to stand. It had been years—*decades!*—since he'd attempted to stand using only one leg and his thigh trembled with the exertion. He strained, trying to keep the momentum going, his thigh shaking and his back beginning to tighten again. The exertion made his vision go black around the edges, and his lungs exploded with a gasp when he was finally upright.

I'll be damned, he thought, trying to catch his breath.

He continued to pant while keeping a tight hold on the boulder, his heart beating out of rhythm. In his pocket were the nitroglycerin tablets, and he leaned against the boulder to open the bottle. He slipped a tablet under his tongue.

Once his breathing and heartbeat stabilized, he studied the

ground. He wondered for a moment if he might use the rake as a crutch or walking stick, but it was too long and lacked a place to grip. Assuming, of course, he could even reach it—or the flashlight—without falling over, which he doubted. As for the bag of corn, in his present condition, it might as well have weighed as much as a ship anchor. He'd have to leave those things behind.

Hesitantly shifting his weight to his bad leg, he tested his knee. It hurt, but the pain wasn't crippling, and he tried again, adding more weight until he began to wince. He wondered if he'd have to get X-rays to make sure he hadn't cracked anything, and he knew the doctor wasn't going to be pleased about any of this. He could already imagine her shaking her head at his recklessness.

All that was in the future, though. For now, he had to get going. He spied another, slightly smaller boulder four or five feet away. He set out for it, limping and hobbling. The bones in his knee felt as though they were rubbing together, but he slowly drew closer. When he finally reached the boulder, he leaned against it, waiting for the pain to subside.

When he was ready, he looked around. There were no more boulders, so this time, he chose a nearby tree, a loblolly pine that stretched toward the sky. He started for it, clenching his teeth at the pain; for a split second he lost his balance and had to windmill his arms to stay upright. *That was close,* he thought. If he fell again, he knew he might not be able to get back up. He gimped forward, finally reaching the trunk. He took another moment to catch his breath.

One tree down, only a gazillion left to go.

And the ridges.

And what if the Littletons found my truck and are waiting for me there?

He forced the question away, figuring he'd cross that bridge when he came to it. Except . . .

He whistled to Arlo, who trotted back to his side. "Don't go wandering off, you hear? I don't want them to take another shot at you."

Arlo stared at him with a dim yet loving expression. Jasper chose the next tree, steeled himself, and started slowly limping forward again. Arlo walked beside him, watching for a moment as though trying to decide if Jasper's jerky movements signaled he was playing a game, before losing interest. Instead, he began nosing at some nearby shrubbery.

A dozen hobble-limps later, Jasper had his hands against the trunk. Again, he rested, waiting for the pain to recede. Then, after focusing, he started for yet another tree.

One at a time, he repeated. *It might take hours or even all day, but I'm going to make it.*

VII

AT SOME POINT in the morning, Jasper lost count of the trees that had served as his way stations. The day continued to warm, and Jasper leaned, exhausted, against the thick trunk of a magnolia. From the treetops, he heard the call of a warbler—like a squeaky wheel turning round and round—mixing with the flute-like melody of a wood thrush. Their chorus made Jasper think of Deborah, whose singing voice was perhaps the most divine sound he had ever heard. He'd always called her *My Little One.* She was born four weeks prematurely, weighing just over four pounds. He could hold her in the palm of his hand, and in the hospital, he wondered how something so tiny could ever grow into a normal-sized human being. Mercifully, she was otherwise healthy, but for the first months of her life, Audrey held Deborah during most of her waking hours and was ready to rush to the pediatrician at the slightest sign of a failure to thrive.

But Deborah grew, just as David and Mary had, albeit at a slower pace. For years, she was in the bottom fifth percentile for her age group in both height and weight, and up until twelve or so, she remained the smallest in her class, a delicate, fine-boned girl always at the far left in the front row of any classroom photo.

Unlike Mary, Deborah didn't have a rough-and-tumble bone in her body. She played with Barbies and loved to have Jasper brush her hair before she crawled into bed. She was always singing along with tunes on the radio, and whenever she sang with the church choir, Jasper was able to pick out Deborah's voice, marveling at her pitch and unusual range. Sometimes when Jasper was whittling on the porch, Deborah would wander outside and ask him to listen to a song she'd just learned. He'd set the pocketknife aside and listen to his daughter's voice, awed by the gift God had given her, which neither Audrey nor he shared.

Deborah was the most talkative of all his children, chattering away at dinners to the point where Audrey sometimes asked her to be quiet so her siblings could speak. She always had a story to tell and loved asking questions, which probably explained her popularity in school. Growing up, Deborah was invited to every classmate's birthday party, and by the time she reached middle school, nearly every weekend was taken up with slumber parties. Jasper remembered making popcorn for her and her friends while they watched movies on television and finally forcing them to turn out the lights and stop giggling.

Her growth spurt arrived when she was a freshman in high school. In the evenings, after finishing her homework, she'd thumb through teen magazines, studying the latest techniques to apply eye shadow or lipstick. Boys began to take particular notice of her. She had a string of boyfriends, most of them lasting a few months, some—like Allen—lasting longer. She went to movies and dances and out for ice cream, and the boy of the moment would call the house almost every evening. At the time, the phone was in the kitchen, but it had a cord long enough for her to stand on the back porch, and she spent hours outside, talking and laughing while waving off the moths attracted by the lights. It all seemed mysterious to Jasper—some of those calls lasted a *long* time. What could they possibly be talking about?

Deborah was especially close to Audrey, and it intuitively made sense that she wanted to become a teacher, just like her mom. Jasper knew she'd become the kind of teacher that children and parents alike would love.

But she never got the chance, for in the space of a single night, she, too, was gone forever.

VIII

JASPER'S WATCH SHOWED he'd been on the move for at least two hours, maybe a little more, and he figured he was halfway back to his truck. He knew the ridges would grow steeper from this point on. Despite the chill, parts of his forehead were starting to perspire, a sign that his body might be beginning to overheat.

Knowing he needed to rest, he spied a downed tree in the distance. He staggered toward it, noting that the hip on his good side had begun to hurt, no doubt due to the strain of supporting most of his weight.

Bad back, bad knee, and now a bad hip.

I'm a living, breathing catastrophe, he thought; *even if I do reach the truck and get back home, then what?*

For all he knew, once he reached the cabin and collapsed in bed, he might not be able to get back up. He might be stuck, unable to even make it to the phone. In time, he'd get hungry and thirsty, and eventually give up the ghost. But the thought of dying wasn't the worst of it. Arlo might go crazy as starvation set in and would probably end up chowing down on Jasper himself. Eventually, when the boy noticed that Jasper hadn't been around the last few Saturdays, officers or deputies would come to the house and they'd probably find Jasper in pieces while Arlo wagged his tail, his belly as round as a Buddha's.

Jasper snorted at his lurid train of thought. *I must be getting loopy,* he mumbled. But allowing his mind to wander made the pain seem more distant, at least for a little while.

By the time he got to the downed tree and sat, he felt as though he'd trekked to California.

Reaching for his bandanna, he dabbed at the perspiration and thought about the last of his children. Paul, he remembered, had been a difficult pregnancy for Audrey. She'd spotted periodically throughout her first trimester; in the last two months, her blood pressure went through the roof, and she was put on bed rest. During her twice-weekly doctor visits, there were multiple discussions about whether to induce Audrey early. Because her symptoms didn't seem to be worsening, the physician recommended that they simply watch and wait. Nonetheless, Jasper brought Audrey's overnight bag to every one of those appointments, just in case she needed to be rushed to the hospital.

To their relief, the pregnancy went almost full term, and Paul weighed more than seven pounds at birth. Audrey, however, was hospitalized for nearly a week due to bleeding complications, and in between hospital visits, Jasper had to care for Paul entirely on his own. It wasn't until he brought Paul home from the hospital that Jasper realized how little he actually knew about caring for infants, despite having three children already. With care for Paul combined with watching over the other children, Jasper staggered around in an exhausted haze, discovering profound and renewed appreciation for all that his wife did. For the six months after Audrey came home, he spent as much time at the house as he could, trying to anticipate her every need. While she was appreciative at first, she eventually suggested that he return to work full-time. She enjoyed her routines, and frankly, Jasper understood, he was getting in her way.

Paul was special to everyone in the family from the very beginning. For Jasper and Audrey, he was the baby; for David, he was the brother he had always wanted. Mary coddled him like a favored pet, while Deborah treated him like one of her dolls, albeit a living one. Jasper remembered that Deborah had once applied Audrey's makeup to Paul's face after squeezing him into one of her old dresses. She must have been five or six at the time. Audrey was so tickled that she took a photograph of the two children. Years later, the photograph vanished from the family album and Jasper knew that Paul was the likely culprit.

Maybe because he was the youngest, Paul was the most sensitive of all the kids. When Bert, their cocker spaniel, had to be put down after getting struck by a car, Paul wept inconsolably for weeks; when his best friend, Jonah, moved away in second grade, Paul fell into a wounded funk, as though he'd never have a best friend again.

Jasper grew concerned when Paul's temperament began to manifest in his teenage years as an unquenchable desire for peer approval. He seemed to try on different identities in phases that often lasted for months: for a while, he mimicked the seriousness of David; other times, he'd insist he wanted to become a veterinarian, just like Mary. He went through a cowboy phase, a sports phase, and a skater phase. In high school—perhaps envious of Deborah's popularity—he began growing his hair longer, as though desperate to fit in with the cool kids the way she did. When he was sixteen, he began wearing jean jackets and Ray-Ban sunglasses, and threatened to get a tattoo as soon as he was old enough to do so.

Though his youngest child seemed to struggle with self-acceptance, Jasper consoled himself with the knowledge that Paul remained an exceptionally kind person. When Mary cried after not being asked to the homecoming dance, Paul cried, too, and spent all weekend writing a poem about how special she was. Mary later told Jasper that it was the nicest thing anyone had ever done for her. When Deborah failed to win a solo in the school Christmas concert—something she desperately wanted—Paul rode his bicycle to the store to get her favorite cookie dough ice cream and asked her to sing the song just for him.

Perhaps as an outlet for the storm of feelings with which he perpetually seemed to grapple, Paul kept journals. He could frequently be seen scribbling furiously while sitting on the porch, or late at night, before bed. Of all the keepsakes of his children that he'd lost in the fire, Jasper regretted the loss of those journals the most. Somehow, he imagined they might have provided the answer to why Paul had chosen to die the way he did.

But then again, Jasper already knew the answer.

His sensitive, emotional child, the one who felt everything deeply and craved the approval of others, simply couldn't live with what he'd done.

IX

JASPER ROSE AND began trekking again, tree after tree, continuing to sweat despite the temperature having begun to fall quickly. A cold front was on the way and he limped, he rested, and limped again, trying to keep a slow but steady pace. Here and there, he was forced to circumvent steep ridges. Having to avoid climbing had probably added at least an extra hour to his trek. Now, between him and the truck rose a ridge too long to skirt. It was fifteen, maybe twenty feet high. He paused to lean against a tree, trying to figure out the best way up. He figured he'd finally be able to spot his truck from the top, but his body felt absolutely wrecked. Even standing in place, he could feel his legs trembling, and his back was on the verge of another spasm.

Arlo, too, was exhausted. His head hung low, his tongue lolled, and he no longer seemed interested in exploring.

"You think we can make it?" Jasper asked. Arlo just looked up at him and wagged his tail once.

Jasper tried to steel himself for the effort, wondering again whether the Littletons might be nearby. They hadn't spotted his truck behind the berm the first time, but that had been at night. He hadn't locked it, so they'd be able to look through the glove compartment. He'd left his wallet there, which would confirm their suspicions that he'd been the one who'd foiled their deer trap.

"If they found the truck, they're probably waiting for me," he muttered to Arlo. "But there's only one way to know for sure."

After eyeballing the ridge a final time, Jasper gritted his teeth and began the climb. He took small, careful steps, and as the angle of the incline increased, he found himself tottering. He planted one foot, rebalanced, inched his other foot forward slightly, and rebalanced again.

He reached the halfway point.

Then, eventually, the three-quarter mark.

Then a bit more, and he could finally see over the top. He kept going, his view becoming clearer. As he readied himself for the final push—*only a few more steps!*—he heard a voice ring out, distant but unmistakable.

"YOU STOLE OUR CORN, DIDN'T YOU?"

Eric.

Jasper felt his heart hammer in his chest, and he swiveled his head, trying to find the source.

"DID YOU SEE HIM?"

This time, it was Josh's voice, closer, but coming from a different direction.

"NO!"

"THEN WHAT THE HELL ARE YOU YELLING ABOUT?"

"I'M BORED! CAN WE PLEASE JUST GO HOME?"

Arlo perked up his ears and before Jasper could stop him, the dog climbed to the top of the ridge. Without tree cover, he was out in the open. Jasper hissed at him to come back, but Arlo either didn't hear him or ignored him.

How soon before the boys spotted him?

With the slow predestination of a nightmare, Arlo wandered farther away. Uncertain where Josh was, Jasper hesitated to raise his voice or whistle. Meanwhile, Arlo continued to meander, now with his nose to the ground. In his mind, Jasper willed the dog to return to the ridge, to no effect.

Arlo, interested in a scent he'd obviously picked up, began veering in the direction of the truck. In that instant, in the distance, Jasper spotted Josh as he stepped from behind a tree. He was facing in the opposite direction, maybe forty yards away, the gun barrel perched on his shoulder. If he turned around, he'd easily spot Jasper and the dog.

There was no way Jasper could reach the truck. His only option was to retreat in the direction he'd just come, back down the ridge. He hoped Arlo would realize that Jasper had turned around and follow. If not, Jasper would risk a low whistle before finding a copse in which to hide.

Jasper knew that going downhill would be more painful than going up. He doubted his knee could handle it, so instead, he decided to move backward, essentially retracing his steps. He took a cautious step; with his second backward step—on the leg with his bad knee—his foot began to slide. He tried to keep his balance; instinctively he rotated his torso, and his lower body followed, his foot coming down lower on the ridge and wedging momentarily between two rocks half-buried in the dirt.

Body weight and momentum did the inevitable. His ankle torqued and Jasper heard an audible crack as he cried out in agony. A moment later, he was tumbling farther down the ridge.

Later, he would vaguely remember landing on his shoulder, his head smashing hard, causing flickers of light. Pain shot through his body like a lengthening crack in a sheet of ice.

He struggled to breathe, fighting to bring the world into focus. Arlo somehow appeared at his side. Above him, he dimly made out a figure standing on the ridge.

Josh.

"You fall, old man? I heard you scream."

Jasper blinked, too disoriented and dizzy to even be frightened.

"Serves you right for what you did. You should have minded your own business."

Jasper's voice was a dry rasp. "Help me."

He wasn't sure, but he thought he could make out a smirk on Josh's face.

"WHAT WAS THAT?" Eric shouted from farther away.

Josh glanced down at Jasper, with a look of calculation. Then he called out, "LET'S GET OUT OF HERE! I'M SICK OF WAITING AROUND!"

A moment later, he was gone.

Jasper closed his eyes, allowing himself to fade away.

X

FROM SOMEWHERE DEEP in his subconscious, Jasper felt a drop of water on his face. It was enough to cause his eyelids to twitch, and when the drop was followed by another, Jasper slowly opened his eyes.

With his head aching, he squinted, watching as tall shadows gradually morphed into the shapes of trees. *The forest*, he remembered, *I'm in the Uwharrie.* Trying to sit up brought a thunderbolt of agony and he cried out, the memory of what had happened returning in a series of fuzzy images.

The white deer. The Littletons. The ridge. Slipping. The crack of his ankle. Tumbling . . .

Gritting his teeth and gasping, he waited for the waves of pain to subside. He didn't need to see his leg to know that his ankle was broken, and he blinked when he felt another drop of water on his face.

Rain.

Above him, the sky was thick with rolling clouds, and he heard a long rumble of thunder in the distance. Slowly moving his head, he looked for Arlo and saw him lying nearby, his tail wagging nervously. The dog had never liked storms.

The thought of even trying to move terrified Jasper. Not with his ankle, not with the bad knee and bad hip and a back that would spasm. Not with a fractured skull or at the very least, a concussion. Once again, he heard thunder, felt another patter of drops, and knew the storm was coming his way.

Drops eventually gave way to a drizzle, followed eventually by steady rain. Water entered his mouth and he coughed, the nerves throughout his body lighting up like a Christmas tree. When the pain finally receded, he slowly turned his head to the side, worried he might otherwise drown. Half his face was resting in mud.

He closed his eyes but sensed the world around him growing darker and colder with the incoming storm. In time, Jasper lost his fight to remain conscious and drifted off again.

XI

WHEN HE WOKE, the world was black. Sheets of rain continued to fall, illuminated by the occasional flicker of lightning.

Evening, he absently noted, and when he shivered it was excruciating. He moaned, then began to weep, his tears blending with the rain. In a fog, he sensed the dog lying beside him, their bodies close together.

Another shiver brought another wave of pain. It happened over and over as the hours slowly crept toward midnight.

Then, finally, the night began inching toward dawn.

CHAPTER TEN

I

TANNER STARED OUT the gigantic picture windows of the mountain house, sipping coffee and trying to take in the sunrise, until he realized it was pointless. Preoccupied as he was, the view wasn't registering, and he wondered again why the evening had turned out the way it had.

He hadn't slept well, tossing and turning and awakening multiple times before finally giving up an hour earlier. Since then, he'd found himself replaying the conversation, and even now, he couldn't sort out how he felt about it. He wasn't upset, exactly, but . . . there'd been a level of presumption on Kaitlyn's part that had rubbed him the wrong way. What was it she'd asked him? Whether he'd ever considered the possibility that she might be anything more than a fling? In that moment, he'd been so busy trying to process why the evening had suddenly turned sour that he hadn't responded. Now, though, if he could go back in time, he would have pointed out that they'd known each other less than a week. What did she expect? A promise ring? A marriage proposal? After only five days?

He drained his cup of coffee, assuring himself again that his ruffled feathers were justified. God knows it was too soon for any kind of deep commitment between them; frankly, it was way too early for her to even pose a question like that. And yet . . .

He'd tossed and turned all night partly because he knew she wasn't wrong in suspecting that even if he'd stayed here until June, the question still might not have occurred to him.

Tanner shook his head, tired of dwelling on it. She'd made it clear that she didn't want to see him again, so that was that. He turned from the window, heading for the kitchen. There, he dumped the remaining food into the garbage and rinsed the dishes before stacking everything on the counter. The chef's assistant was coming to collect the dishes soon, so he had to stay at the house until then.

Tanner showered, gathered his things, and loaded the rental car before settling in to wait. He chose a spot near the windows again, but as before, the view barely registered. Instead, he continued to replay the evening in his mind and despite himself, checked his phone regularly to see if Kaitlyn had texted.

She hadn't. When he finally left the house, he couldn't help feeling a sharp pang of disappointment.

II

As MITCH WAS finishing his cereal in the kitchen, Kaitlyn nibbled on a piece of toast, her stomach still in knots from the night before.

"Will Casey be here when I get home from school?"

It took a moment for Kaitlyn to register that Mitch had spoken. "I'm not sure," she finally answered. "She might have something going on after school, but we'll ask."

"It's okay if she's not," Mitch said, lifting his bowl so he could drink the milk. "I know what to do."

Kaitlyn gave up on the toast and rose from the table to dump the remains into the garbage. "If you're finished with your cereal, bring your bowl to the sink while I track down your sister. We'll meet you at the Suburban in a minute."

"She'll take more than a minute. She always does."

"Yeah, well, just do what I ask, sweetie."

Kaitlyn slid the lunch she'd packed earlier into Mitch's backpack. She held the backpack up as he slipped his arms through the loops. "Can we go to the zoo again on Sunday?" he asked. "And then play Frisbee with Mr. Tanner?"

"I think it's supposed to be cold this weekend," she answered. "Why don't we go to a movie instead?"

"I guess," Mitch said before trudging toward the door. Kaitlyn collected her things and was about to call for Casey when she saw her daughter trotting down the stairs.

"I'm ready," Casey announced.

"You need breakfast," Kaitlyn said. "I'm bringing an apple and a granola bar for you."

"Okay." Casey paused near the front door. "How are you doing?"

"I'm fine." Kaitlyn shrugged, fervently hoping Casey hadn't heard her crying last night.

Casey's gaze was piercing. "If you say so."

III

JASPER OPENED HIS eyes slowly, squinting into the cloudy morning sunlight, his head throbbing with every heartbeat. He was wet and freezing and had lain awake shivering most of the night, the soaked weight of his clothing making it difficult to breathe. And now, when his body began to tremble anew, he let out a moan as the pain coursed through him. From a distance, he thought he heard noises before finally realizing that he was the one making the sounds.

In time, the crashing waves of pain began to diminish, bringing a touch of clarity to his thinking. Somehow, he'd survived the night; somehow, he hadn't drowned in the rain. He noticed his labored breaths coming out in little puffs, dissipating in the cold and gloomy air. His hands were as frigid as fish pulled from the icebox. When he tried to shift so he could make room beneath his jacket for them, the movement of his body was enough to make it feel as though someone had smashed a hammer into his ankle, and he nearly blacked out.

When the dizziness passed, he slowly—carefully—turned his head, looking for Arlo. The dog had wandered off earlier and now was nowhere to be seen. Jasper tried to whistle but didn't have much strength. His mind began to drift, and he wondered whether anyone would ever find him.

IV

ONCE HE WAS back in Asheboro, Tanner went for a longer run than usual, pounding the road for nearly an hour and a half. Despite the chilly temperature, his shirt was soaked with sweat by the time he finally returned to the hotel.

After showering, he had a quick lunch before deciding that more fresh air would do him good. At the park, he zipped his jacket and walked beneath a sky filled with white clouds, his mind no clearer than it had been that morning. On impulse, he called Glen, who answered on the second ring.

"How's it going? Did you find your daddy yet?"

Tanner chuckled, taking a seat on a park bench before asking if he was calling at a good time.

"Your timing is impeccable. The wife and kids are hanging with the neighbors, and I've got the back deck all to myself. What's up?"

Tanner began to talk then, filling him in on his search for his biological father and the accident in the parking lot of Coach's before finally launching into an account of his surprising week with Kaitlyn. Glen made approving noises as Tanner described Kaitlyn and her family, and the immediate, intense connection they'd formed.

"She sounds great, Tan," Glen observed. "When do I get to meet her?"

"Hold up, there's more—"Tanner cautioned. He then went on to tell Glen about the events of the previous night, and the abrupt demise of their relationship. When he finished, Glen cleared his throat, then was silent so long Tanner thought the call had dropped.

"Hello?"Tanner said.

"I'm still here and I get why you called, but frankly, I'm not sure what you want me to say."

"How about you agree with me and confirm that everything she said to me last night was a little crazy?" Tanner responded, only half-joking. "That I probably got off lucky?"

Glen's voice sounded uncharacteristically hesitant. "Listen, Tan, I gotta be honest with you. I don't think she's wrong to ask why you're going back to Cameroon. I told you when you were here that I felt you were taking a step backward. You're one of the few people I know who can do anything he wants, and I'm still not sure why you make some of the decisions you do."

Tanner closed his eyes, wondering how his call to vent to a buddy about a woman had turned into a referendum on his life choices. "Regardless of whether accepting the job in Cameroon was the right decision, she knew all along I was going to be leaving, so why suddenly make it such a big deal?"

"I hear you," Glen said, adopting a more conciliatory tone. "But I also get where she's coming from. Why *not* stay on and see where it leads?"

Tanner was silent. Across the park, he saw a group of children feeding some ducks at the edge of a pond.

Glen went on. "I guess the question you've got to answer for yourself is, What *do* you want, Tan? To stay on the move forever? And what are you going to do when you get bored with Cameroon, which we both know is going to happen?"

It was the same question Kaitlyn had asked, and Tanner found himself wondering how he'd lost control of this conversation as well. Without waiting for an answer, Glen sighed and went on.

"Look, I know you called for reassurance and I'm sorry if I'm letting you down. Would it make you feel better if I said that I have faith you'll figure it out? I have no doubt that you're going to land on your feet and be okay in the long run. But . . ."

"But what?" Tanner asked, uncertain that he wanted to hear the rest.

"You do realize that Kaitlyn is the only woman you've ever called to talk to me about, right?"

"That's not true."

"Yes, it is," Glen said, the words coming out slowly. "You've mentioned some of the others to me in passing, but you've never really talked about them. And the sound of your voice as you described her is different. It's clear she already means something to you."

"She does," Tanner conceded.

"Then why are you talking to me about it and not her?"

"I told you—she doesn't want to see me again."

"So?"

"What do you mean, 'so'?"

"Asheboro's a small town." Glen's voice was patient but firm. "You're going to be there two or three more weeks, maybe more. Chances are, unless you choose to hide out at the hotel, you'll see her again. What you have to figure out first, though, is who you are and what you really want, so you'll know what to say when you do."

After hanging up, Tanner felt weary. Despite himself, he wondered what Kaitlyn was doing at that very moment; he wondered what, if anything, she planned to do with the kids on the weekend. He figured Mitch would spend time whittling with the neighbor, like he always did, and later, they'd have a family dinner. He smiled, recalling his evening at their home, and rose from the bench. He started walking again, and a few minutes later, when he noticed an older couple holding hands, he suddenly realized that as thrilling as it had been to make love to Kaitlyn, part of him wished the night before had never happened, so they could simply start over.

V

AT THE OFFICE, Kaitlyn kept herself as busy as possible. In addition to her regularly scheduled patients there were several unscheduled walk-ins, and Kaitlyn managed to work in almost all of them. She cut her lunch hour short and started seeing her afternoon patients. As midafternoon approached—when Mitch would arrive home from school—Kaitlyn's mental alarm clock went off, and she turned on the ringer on her cellphone. As always, she warned the patient she was seeing in advance that her son would be calling; her patients never minded. Mitch called right on schedule, and after excusing herself, she stepped into the hallway.

"I'm home and school was boring," he said, preempting her questions. "But, Mom? Guess what? Arlo's here."

It took her a second to remember who Arlo was. "You mean Jasper's dog?"

"Uh-huh. He's lying in our yard by the tree. Should I go check on him?"

"No," she said. "Just stay inside for now. If it is Arlo, I'm sure he'll wander back to Jasper's when he's ready."

"What if he doesn't leave?" Mitch sounded worried.

"Then we'll bring him back when I get home from work."

"Okay," he said, not hiding his disappointment.

"And remember that Mrs. Simpson will be by in a little while to check on you, but otherwise keep the door locked."

"I know. You always remind me."

After they'd said their goodbyes, Kaitlyn returned to the exam room. She continued seeing patients while the day wound down, but in quiet moments—while resolutely trying not to think about Tanner—she found herself wondering why Arlo had come to the house. It was odd. As far as she knew, the dog had never done that before, and she wondered whether Jasper realized the dog had wandered off. Toward the end of her workday and knowing that Jasper didn't have a cellular phone, she called his landline.

It rang without answer.

VI

AN EARLY EVENING breeze made the tree branches sway, and Jasper watched them through blurry eyes. While the chill had prevented his clothes from drying, the heat from his body had warmed them and the shivering had finally stopped, which had enabled him to sleep on and off during the day. In his waking moments he'd tried to take stock of how he was holding up, thinking, *Not well at all.* His empty stomach had begun to cramp, and ironically—despite last night's storm—he was thirsty to the point that his throat now felt like gravel. The swelling around his ankle made it resemble a water balloon, and the slightest movement of his leg was torturous. Even worse, the damp clothing had irritated the psoriasis on his back and chest and arms and legs, making his skin sting as though he were lying on a nest of fire ants.

Somehow, he'd survived the day. But where was Arlo?

The dog hadn't come back. He'd be hungry, Jasper reasoned, consoling himself with the idea that the dog had wandered off in search of something to eat. He didn't want to believe the dog had abandoned him, and he hoped Arlo would return soon, if only to share his warmth. Darkness—and colder temperatures—was fast approaching, and he prayed there wouldn't be another storm. At the same time, it wouldn't be unprecedented. After all, he mused, the elements had defined almost everything in his life. There was the story about his grandfather and raining fish, which eventually led to the founding of a church in Asheboro, where Jasper had been born and raised. He thought about the downpour that washed out the surrounding roads, allowing his father to buy the land for the cabin. He remembered the hurricane and rain-flooded river that destroyed his house, and the tornado that ruined his business. He could visualize the sudden gusts of wind that carried flaming embers to the roof of their house on that horrible night, when he'd lost those that he loved.

Now, however, in his weakening state, he found himself recalling the storm he'd experienced as a child, and what his father had said to him in the aftermath.

He'd been eight or nine at the time, and his father had taken him fishing at a lake near Wake Forest. When they'd pushed the canoe from the bank, the sky was blue and cloudless, with air so still it seemed as though the earth had stopped spinning. The flies and mosquitoes swarmed, so both he and his father had dressed in long sleeves, but when they got out on the water, the air cleared, giving way to a perfect summer day. For the next few hours, they fished for crappie with minnow rigs while small bobbers floated on the surface. Neither felt the need to speak, and despite the beauty of the day, Jasper saw no other boats on the water. He could remember thinking that it almost felt as though the two of them were alone in the world.

They'd had good luck. He'd snagged two keepers while his father had pulled in three, promising that they'd eat well that week. As they were storing their rigs, a blast of wind suddenly kicked up from nowhere, hard enough to make Jasper nearly lose his balance. At the horizon, he noticed a huge, angry bank of gray clouds surging toward them.

The wind gusted further, the temperature dropped, and within minutes, swells on the lake began to resemble waves that rolled up on the beaches at the coast. Jasper's father grabbed the paddles with a frown of concern, and the rain began. Jasper tried to paddle in time with his father but wasn't strong enough to keep up. He could see the strain and tension in his father's shoulders and arms through the fabric of his shirt as the swells started lapping over the sides of the canoe. His father paddled like a machine, never seeming to tire, even as water rose halfway up Jasper's shins. Somehow, they made it to shore.

When they pulled the boat onto the bank in the raging downpour, his father stood bent over, drawing heaving breaths, until he finally recovered. Together, they dragged the canoe back to the truck and secured it. In the safety of the truck's cab, his father blew into his hands before finally speaking.

"Psalm 148:8," he whispered.

Back at home, Jasper opened his Bible and read, *Fire and hail; snow and mist; stormy wind, fulfilling His word.*

It didn't mention rain, but nonetheless Jasper thought he understood what his father had been trying to tell him. All that happened in the world, the good and the bad, offers believers the chance to praise God.

But now, broken and helpless in the Uwharrie, Jasper knew that he'd stopped believing in such things long ago.

VII

As soon as Kaitlyn pulled into the driveway, she saw Arlo lying on his side in the grass. Hopping out of the Suburban, she approached him just as Mitch burst from the front door.

"See! I told you it was Arlo!"

"You're right," she said. Squatting down, she stroked the dog's head, noting that he looked as though he'd been rolling in mud. "What are you doing here, old fella? I called Jasper a little bit ago, but he didn't answer. Did you run off while you two were walking?"

At her voice, Arlo's tail began to thump, and he struggled to rise, his rear legs shaking at the effort.

"Can I get him some water before we bring him back?" Mitch asked. "I think he might be thirsty. A little while ago, he was nosing around the hose by the porch."

"Sure," she said. "Grab a Tupperware bowl from—"

"I know where it is," he shouted over his shoulder as he raced back to the house; a minute later he was walking toward her with the bowl the family usually used for popcorn. *One day*, she thought, *I'm hoping my kids actually listen to me*.

Mitch set the bowl of water down and Arlo immediately began to lap at it.

"Can I get him a hot dog, too?" Mitch pleaded. "In case he's hungry?"

"I'm not sure that would be good for him."

"Why not? I eat hot dogs."

And they're not good for you either, she thought. "Yeah. Okay, fine."

Again, Mitch turned and raced into the house, returning a moment later with not one but two hot dogs. He broke one in half and offered it to Arlo, who gulped it down. As Mitch fed him the other half, Kaitlyn saw Camille pull into the drive and come to a stop behind the Suburban. Casey climbed out of the car as Mitch fed Arlo the second hot dog; a moment later, Camille backed out and was on her way.

"Hey, Mom, hey, Mitch," Casey said, crossing the lawn. "What's going on?"

"Arlo came over," Mitch said. By then, Arlo had moved closer to Mitch and was sniffing his pockets as though looking for more. "He was here when I got home from school."

"Why?" Casey looked puzzled.

"I don't know." Kaitlyn shrugged, thinking again how odd it was.

Kaitlyn had initially planned to walk Arlo home, but given how his legs had trembled when he tried to stand, she reconsidered. He still looked as though he was about to topple over.

"I think we should put him in the back of the Suburban and drive him home, but I don't think he'll be able to jump that high."

"We can lift him," Mitch suggested.

Which meant, of course, that Kaitlyn would have to lift him. Assessing his barrel-chested figure, she guessed he might weigh seventy or eighty pounds.

"You're going to need a towel first," Casey commented. "He's gross."

"Okay!" Mitch sprinted to the house for the third time. Kaitlyn barely had time to shout, "Not the nice towels! Use the old ones from the closet!" before Mitch vanished.

"I still don't understand why he's here," Casey said. She was stroking Arlo's head, the dog's eyes nearly closed in pleasure.

Arlo slowly approached the bowl of water again. He drank for a long time, seemingly as thirsty as he'd been when Mitch first placed it in front of him. Meanwhile, Mitch burst out of the front door and ran toward them, carrying the clean white towels from his bathroom. A few seconds later, he was rubbing Arlo with a towel, which quickly became streaked with dirt and mud.

Great, Kaitlyn thought.

"Okay, Mom," Mitch said. "I think he's clean enough to put in the back now."

Not even close, Kaitlyn knew, but she nonetheless walked to the back of the Suburban and opened the lift. She called to Arlo, who slowly ambled toward her. He was moving, she thought, like he was sore.

At the rear of the Suburban, Kaitlyn was trying to figure out the best way to lift the dog into the back when Casey stepped forward and simply scooped him up around the legs and gently placed him in the back. Arlo looked momentarily disconcerted before he wagged his tail. Kaitlyn stared at Casey.

"Cheerleading, Mom," Casey explained with a shrug. "I lift

people at every practice, remember? It's not just about looking cute in the uniform."

"Of course," Kaitlyn said.

Mitch climbed into the second-row seats and Casey got behind the wheel. "I can drive," she said. "And I can help with Arlo getting down."

They made the short trip to Jasper's cabin, but a single glance was enough to let Kaitlyn know that he wasn't home, which explained the unanswered phone call. His truck was gone and the house was dark, but by then, Casey had already climbed out to open the lift and lowered Arlo to the ground. Instead of making for the porch, Arlo stayed in place, tail wagging.

"It doesn't look like he's here," Mitch said, squinting through his glasses.

"I'll check and make sure," Kaitlyn said.

She walked up the steps to the door and knocked, not expecting an answer, and wondered where Jasper could have gone. As far as she knew, he brought Arlo everywhere with him. She debated whether to check if the front door was locked but decided that it was too presumptuous before walking back to the Suburban.

"Not home?" Casey asked.

"I guess not," Kaitlyn answered. "But I'm sure he'll be back soon."

"What about Arlo?" Mitch piped up. "Are we just going to leave him?"

"We can't keep him at our house, sweetie. He's Mr. Jasper's dog."

"What if he gets thirsty again?"

"He'll be okay," Kaitlyn assured him. "C'mon. Let's go home."

As they drove away, Arlo stood in the yard, watching them.

On the short ride back, none of them said anything. Flummoxed, Kaitlyn decided she'd check on Jasper first thing in the morning.

Just in case.

VIII

TANNER SAT AT the bar with a foamy IPA in front of him. It was Friday night, and there was a good-sized crowd already celebrating the beginning of the weekend. Despite the noise, he was able to catch snippets of surrounding conversations, none of which seemed very interesting. Seated a few stools away was a group of three women in their late thirties, dressed for a night on the town. Every now and then he caught one or another glancing in his direction, sometimes offering a smile before looking away, other times trying to hold his gaze. Though he had no way of knowing, they had the look of single women out for a good time, relaxed and open to a low-stakes approach. In a prior life, he would likely have wandered over and struck up a conversation before finally zeroing in on his favorite. They'd chat and flirt and sometime later, he'd suggest that they find someplace quieter, so they could get to know each other better. And after that? The remainder of the evening would take its natural course.

But he wasn't in the mood. It had been a mistake to come here, he thought. Reminders of his evening here with Kaitlyn were everywhere. It seemed inconceivable that it had only been six days since they'd been introduced to each other; he felt as though they'd known each other far longer than that. He could still see the gleam in her eye as she spoke about Casey and Mitch, and even on that first evening together he had sensed a kindness and resilience about her that attracted him in a way he'd seldom experienced before.

That feeling had only grown stronger the more they'd gotten to know each other, and he couldn't help but think that while her life was independent, his nomadic existence, populated by the ghosts of so many lost friends and relationships, felt insubstantial in comparison. Staring into his glass, he wondered if—subconsciously—he'd been drawn to Kaitlyn partly because she presented the opportunity to evolve, but if that was true, it also meant there was part of him endlessly intent on self-sabotage.

He took another drink and from the corner of his eye saw that one of the three women was watching him again. Looking away, he attempted to conjure images of his last stay in Cameroon instead, trying to remind himself of the reasons he'd agreed to go back. While *I liked it the last time* had seemed like a good enough answer, he suspected that both Kaitlyn and Glen had been correct in characterizing it as yet another step in the endless drifting, not something he'd sought out for a particular reason or purpose.

But if he didn't go, then what?

He didn't know. Despite his desire to live a life of meaning, his decisions always seemed to reflect the conviction that his real life was going to be found elsewhere, just beyond the next horizon.

Kaitlyn, he knew, embraced a different philosophy. In words and in actions, she subscribed to the notion that life is less about the *what* and *where* than about the *who*. She'd claim that purpose could be found in caring intimately for those she loved, and for others in need, in a place that felt like home. She had made sense of her life in a way that Tanner never had, and he had a feeling there was something he could still learn from her.

But that wouldn't happen now. Like sand slipping through her fingers, she'd released him, and deep down, he knew his response would be instinctual. He'd leave Asheboro and move on yet again.

IX

NIGHT HAD COME, and Jasper was in agony. He couldn't stop shivering, and every spasm hurt horribly. His skin, his ankle, his knee, his back, and his head, pounding and stabbing every time his body trembled. He cried without tears, for his body was as dry as a mummy's.

He tried to will the pain away by staring at the sky. It radiated an ethereal glow as moonlight dispersed through the clouds. Once, long ago, he and his father had stared at a similar sky, and Jasper imagined that it was how heaven might have looked. God light, his father had called it, and Jasper remembered thinking it was proof that God would always be with him.

But God had turned His back, and when Jasper shivered again, his vision suddenly narrowed. The pain glowed red and hot, like the tip of a fireplace poker. He tried to remind himself that he'd experienced similar pain before, in the aftermath of his burns, but he'd been younger and stronger back then. He was no longer the man he used to be. The next time he shivered, his eyes rolled up in his head and he faded out, his mind as dark as the night itself.

X

LOST IN A dream, Kaitlyn woke to the sensation of someone shaking her. When she opened her eyes, the remnants of the dream dissipated as she focused on her son. Early-morning light was streaming through the windows.

"Mom," she heard him saying. "Are you awake?"

"I am now," she muttered. "What time is it?"

"I don't know," Mitch said. "But you've got to get up."

She rubbed her face before glancing at the clock. It was half past six and she struggled to sit up.

"What's going on? Why are you awake so early on a Saturday?"

"I was worried about Arlo and when I went outside, he was on our porch."

"He's here again?"

Mitch nodded. "Can I bring him some water?"

She swung her legs over the side of the bed and slid her feet into her slippers. "Let's go check on him. And yes, you can get water for him, but you're going to need shoes and a jacket first."

He went off toward his room while she wrapped herself in a robe and staggered down the stairs to the front door. Because the morning sky was just beginning to brighten, she turned on the porch light before opening the door. Sure enough, Arlo was curled in a ball there. When he saw her, he struggled to stand. When she stroked his head, his fur was cold, as if he'd been outside for hours.

Or all night?

By then, Mitch had emerged from the house, carrying the water bowl. She felt a pit of worry in her stomach as he set it down. They watched Arlo begin to drink. "Go ahead and get him some hot dogs."

"Two?"

"Grab four," she said.

When Mitch returned with the hot dogs, he broke them in half and Arlo gobbled them down. Mitch looked up at her. "Why did he come back, Mom?"

"I don't know."

"Is Mr. Jasper okay?"

Again, she felt the pit in her stomach. "I'm sure he's fine, sweetie."

"Can we go check on him?" Mitch fixed her with an anxious look, his eyes enormous in his small face.

"I will in a little bit. It's still early."

"What do we do with Arlo?"

"Can you find the old blankets at the bottom of the linen closet? We'll make a little bed for him on the porch."

"Okay," he answered, scurrying back into the house. When he returned with the blankets, Kaitlyn made up the bed. Arlo curled up in it, looking content.

"I'm going to go shower," she informed Mitch. "If you want, you can sit with him out here."

"Okay."

On her way to her room, Kaitlyn noticed that Casey's door was closed. Peeking in, she was surprised to see Casey's sleeping form under her rumpled bedcovers. Hadn't she said she'd be spending the night at Camille's?

The day was bright and sunny by the time she finished getting ready, and after collecting her keys and her purse, she joined Mitch on the porch.

"Stay here with Arlo," she said. "I'm going to run over to Mr. Jasper's."

Mitch nodded, and Kaitlyn repeated the trip she'd made the night before. Again, she noticed the absence of his truck and the darkened interior of the house; this time, it looked strangely abandoned.

She got out of the SUV and followed the dirt walkway to the porch. She knocked, waited, then knocked again. There was no answer, nor could she hear any sounds coming from within the house. This time she reached for the doorknob, assuming it would be locked, but it turned easily in her hand. Cracking the door open, she poked her head in.

"Jasper?" she called out. "Hello? Are you here? It's me, Dr. Cooper!"

No one answered, and stepping inside, she glanced around, taking in the wood-plank walls and worn but comfortable furniture in the small living room. The air seemed slightly stale, though she caught no odor of decay. That's what she'd been worried about, she suddenly realized—that Jasper had passed away—but her relief was short-lived. None of this felt right to her. She took a few minutes to look around, peeking into both bedrooms and the bathroom before heading to the kitchen. In the sink, she saw a few dirty dishes; they looked as if he'd set them there with the intention of washing them after he returned.

Strange.

As she left the cabin, she was startled by the distant crack of gunfire. She remembered that one of her patients had mentioned he'd be hunting turkeys this weekend with his sons. A moment later, she heard another shot, which seemed closer than the last. She hurried back to the SUV. Over the years, she'd treated a few people who'd been in hunting accidents, and she'd never been a fan of guns; they scared her. It wasn't until she was in the SUV that she let out a breath she hadn't known she'd been holding.

She glanced over her shoulder at the front door one last time. It was one thing for Jasper not to be home this morning—maybe he was having breakfast at a diner, or something—but Arlo's appearance at the house again left her wondering exactly how long he'd been gone.

More than that, she began to wonder what, if anything, she should do.

XI

JASPER HEARD A distant *crack*, but in his delirium, it wasn't until he heard a second one that he was finally able to order his thoughts. His mind felt slow and boggy, and when he opened his eyes the world was blurry around him.

Gunfire, he thought.

He wondered how far away the hunters had been; he wondered whether someone would eventually spot his truck. He wondered if they would linger in the area to investigate and perhaps even find his body. Death, he knew, was coming for him, for despite the blurriness, he could already make out a shadowy figure at the edge of his vision.

He'd seen the shadowy figure once before, a long time ago. Mary was five years old when she woke one morning with a fever, headache, and sore throat. A flu had been going around, and Audrey sat with her the entire day. She wiped Mary's forehead with a cool cloth; she dosed her with Tylenol every few hours, but Mary's fever continued to rise, and she soaked her sheets in sweat. By the following morning, she'd begun to wheeze, and growing fearful, Jasper scooped her into his arms and carried her to his truck while Audrey rushed to the neighbors' house. She asked them to watch the other children while they raced Mary to the emergency room in Greensboro.

Because she was struggling to breathe, Mary was admitted right away. It took little time for the physician to diagnose a severe case of epiglottitis. His face was grim as he told them that Mary was being transferred to the intensive care unit, careful to make no promises.

Jasper held a tearful Audrey before she went home to take care of the other children. He stayed at the hospital the rest of the day and into the evening, either in the ICU or in the waiting room two floors below his daughter. Sometime after midnight, and overwhelmed with a sense of powerlessness, Jasper knelt down and clasped his hands in prayer.

He had been praying for more than an hour when he felt as if his spirit was suddenly lifted from his body. All at once, he was no longer separated from his daughter. He was standing beside her in the ICU and listening to her excruciating wheezes as she fought to breathe. He saw the gray, ghostlike color of her skin, and heard the steady beeping of machines. He could see a blond nurse with a red hair clip tending to an elderly man nearby, and it was then that he became aware of another presence in the room.

In a dark corner, visible as if through a dirty pane of glass, was the faint outline of a figure. Jasper squinted, sensing the dark void within its shape, and when the figure slowly began to move, stretching toward his daughter, Jasper suddenly opened his eyes in the waiting room and scrambled to his feet. He pushed through a set of double doors and started running down the hospital corridor, flying past startled nurses. He heard them calling for him to stop but ignored them. He knew in the depths of his soul that his daughter was in danger.

Somehow, as though God Himself were guiding him, he found the stairs and bounded up them, using the handrails to sling himself upward even faster. He reached the pediatric ICU floor and rushed down the hallway. A moment later, he burst into the ICU. The blond nurse with the red hair clip, who was still at the bedside of the elderly man, turned with a startled scream.

Jasper stared at the blackened shadow now enveloping his daughter and realized that Mary could no longer breathe. Her body was arching, and a moment later, one of the machines began to sound a shrill alarm.

By then, a doctor had reached her room in Jasper's wake and immediately rushed toward Mary. Other nurses followed, and as Jasper backed away, he heard the din of shouted orders. He watched as one of the nurses started CPR; another nurse placed a bag over Mary's face and began to pump. Still another tried to hold Mary down as the physician readied a tube, and a moment later, he watched it being forced down Mary's throat.

Because her throat was so swollen, it took an agonizing length of time to reach its intended position. But when the doctor finally stood upright and drew a long, relieved breath, Jasper realized that the shadow over his daughter had begun to fade. The blackness quickly dissolved to gray before vanishing completely. When the physician turned to look at him, his expression stern, Jasper bowed his head, refusing to meet his eyes. Instead, he left the room without a word and eventually collapsed again in a chair in the waiting room.

He didn't know then that Mary's fever would break in the morning. He didn't know that the breathing tube would be removed soon after that, or that in only four days, Mary would be back in school. All he knew was that his daughter had been in mortal danger and if the doctor and extra nurses had not arrived at the ICU at that exact moment, his daughter would not have survived. Death, in the form of a shadowed figure, had come for her.

And now, as he lay on the ground in the Uwharrie, Jasper stared at the familiar shadowy darkness in the distance. But this time, once it began to move toward him, he knew there would be nothing he could do to stop it.

XII

ON THE WAY home from Jasper's, still preoccupied and uneasy, Kaitlyn swung by the grocery store and bought the makings for lasagna, and some fresh cinnamon rolls, along with a couple of cans of dog food.

At home, she and Mitch ate the rolls for breakfast. Then they brought Arlo inside, gave him a bath, and dried him off. She scooped the dog food into a bowl and watched as Arlo wolfed it down. He was also moving better and when he finished, Mitch asked if he could play with Arlo outside. She nodded after reminding him to put on his jacket.

She wondered again what she should do before finally reaching for the phone. Because it wasn't an emergency, she called the police station and briefly described what was going on before being transferred to a detective. Again, she went through all that she knew and though the detective on the other end was sympathetic, he admitted that aside from swinging by Jasper's house, there was little else he could do.

Kaitlyn expelled a sigh, knowing that wasn't enough. "Have there been any accidents reported?"

She heard the man shuffle some papers on his desk. "That'll take some time to figure out. I'd have to contact the Highway Patrol and . . ."

"Can you please? I'm his physician and he's dealing with some medical conditions. He might be in danger."

By this point she could tell the detective was eager to get off the phone. "I'll get back to you. Is there a number where I can reach you?"

She gave him her number. Forty minutes later, he called back. "Nothing," he reported. "No accidents involving his truck."

She massaged her forehead. "Well . . . what about a Senior Alert or whatever they call it?" she asked, referring to a system similar to AMBER Alert for abducted children, one that would disseminate necessary information to electronic highway signs as well as individual phones.

"Unless we know for sure that he's missing or foul play is involved," the detective explained, "he doesn't meet the criteria. You said yourself that his truck isn't there and the lights in the house aren't on. He probably went to visit someone."

"Jasper wouldn't have left his dog," Kaitlyn insisted. "They go everywhere together."

"Maybe he left the dog with a neighbor and the dog decided to run off. I know it's not what you want to hear, but objectively speaking, it's not even clear that he's missing. And until forty-eight hours have passed, there's not much we can do."

Kaitlyn made a frustrated noise. "If you can't do anything, what should I do?"

"If I were you, I'd start by contacting neighbors, friends, family. Maybe someone will know where he went. And I hate to suggest that something bad did happen to him, but you might consider calling the hospitals, too."

"What if I contacted the sheriff?"

"You're likely going to get the same answer I just gave you. Forty-eight hours. But if he's still missing tomorrow, come in and I'll take a report," he promised. "At the very least, I'll put out an APB on his truck."

It still didn't feel like enough, and after hanging up, Kaitlyn tried to stifle her irritation. At the same time, she was struck by how little she actually knew about Jasper. While she could recite his medical history—and though she knew he'd lost his wife and children years ago—it occurred to her that she had no idea how he generally spent his days. Nor, as far as she could recall, had he mentioned to her any neighbors, friends, or family.

In the end, she took the detective's advice and called all the hospitals in the area, as far away as Winston-Salem and Durham, again without luck. After that, in an effort to distract herself, she spent the next few hours tidying up the house and doing laundry before heading into the kitchen. Casey eventually wandered downstairs, her hair askew and eyes puffy, and popped one of the cinnamon rolls into the microwave.

"I thought you were going to spend the night at Camille's."

Casey leaned against the counter. "She wasn't feeling well, so after the party, I had her drop me off."

"Is she okay?"

"She's fine. She said it was a migraine, but I think she just wanted to call it a night. Steven was being a jerk."

No surprise there, Kaitlyn thought. "How was the party?"

"The usual," Casey said with a shrug. "Drugs, casual sex, booze, stripping, gambling."

"Casey . . ."

"It was freezing," she said. "Like I told you, his parents were there so we mainly hung out in the backyard stomping our feet and wondering whether icicles would form on our noses while everyone pretended to have a great time." She pulled the cinnamon roll from the microwave and glanced out the window. "Wait—is that Arlo again?"

"He was here when we woke up."

"That's so weird," she commented. "Do you think something happened to Mr. Jasper?"

"I don't know, sweetie." Kaitlyn went over the conversation she'd had with the detective.

"So what are you going to do?"

"Mitch is supposed to carve with him later and if he's not back by then, I guess I'll try again to get the police to do something, even though it hasn't been forty-eight hours."

"Like what?"

Kaitlyn said nothing, if only because she wasn't sure what they actually could do, other than put out the APB. Even if she somehow got them to organize volunteers and initiate a search, she doubted the police would know where to begin.

XIII

HIS LEGS STILL sore from the day before, Tanner jogged slowly to the park before stretching and doing push-ups, pull-ups, and sit-ups until his muscles failed. Later at the diner, he had eggs and pancakes while he perused the news on his iPad. He took his time finishing his coffee, but even then, he found himself leaving the diner before eleven with no idea what to do with the rest of his day.

He set off to stroll the downtown streets. When he came across a bench, he stopped and pulled out his phone to call Glen again.

When his friend answered, he said, "I've been thinking a lot about our conversation. I wanted to ask you a question."

"Go ahead."

"How did you know Molly was the one? I mean, you hadn't known her that long before you two eloped, right?"

"Seven weeks," Glen confirmed. "But I think I knew by the second date that I was going to marry her."

"What was it about her that made you so certain?"

"You know her. She's smart and made me laugh and I thought she was beautiful, but I'd met women like that before. With Molly, though, there was something different about the way I felt when I was with her and I just *knew*. I know you're looking for a rational explanation, but sometimes, there isn't any. Sometimes, it's just a gut feeling. But when I'm honest with myself, I also think I got lucky."

"Why do you say that?"

"Because love is more than just an emotion. It's about sharing a life, and it wasn't until after we were married that I truly realized how much we had in common. We have the same values, morals, we're both Catholic. We have the same views about parenting, spending now versus saving for retirement, which set of parents to visit on the holidays, even what we like to do on the weekends. I've come to think that the more you agree about those kinds of things, the more you feel like a team, like you're in it together. And, with all that said, of course, it's never easy. Relationships take work."

"Not for you and Molly."

"Are you kidding?" Glen said with a laugh. "It's a ton of work, on both our parts. We've argued. We've screamed at each other. Slammed doors, slept in separate bedrooms. We've even come close to separating at times."

"Seriously?" Tanner shook his head in disbelief.

"Of course. It never reached the point where one of us left, but that doesn't mean I didn't think about it. And I know for a fact she thought about it, too. All relationships go up and down but, in the end, both of us were committed to making things work, so we did."

Tanner hung up the phone after a few more minutes, his mind churning. Turning back toward his hotel, he found himself thinking through these things in terms of Kaitlyn—at least, what he knew of her from the short time they'd known each other. But more than that, he thought about how he'd felt whenever he was with her. He thought about the fact that she felt . . . right.

XIV

WHEN IT WAS time for Mitch to meet Jasper at the gazebo, Kaitlyn already knew he wouldn't be there. She'd been peeking through the window on and off for the previous twenty minutes hoping to see him but unsurprised that she hadn't. When Mitch asked if they could check the cabin anyway, she nodded. Arlo trailed behind them.

Even from a distance, it was obvious that Jasper still hadn't returned. No truck, no lights, and again, the cabin appeared deserted. Nonetheless she went inside for a quick look around, satisfied that nothing had changed since her earlier visit.

From the vantage point of the porch, she noticed that Arlo had wandered to the edge of the property and was gazing into the Uwharrie.

"What's Arlo doing?"

"I don't know," Mitch answered.

"Go get him so we can bring him back to our place."

As she watched Mitch run off toward the dog, she decided she'd visit the police station and demand that a missing person report be filed immediately, even if the detective didn't agree. As Mitch drew nearer, however, the dog started trotting into the Uwharrie. When Mitch made to follow, Kaitlyn—suddenly remembering the gunfire she'd heard earlier—hurried down the steps. "Mitch! Stop!" she shouted, slightly panicked.

Mitch came to a halt and looked back at her. "But he's running away!"

She strode quickly toward him. "I don't want you going into the forest. It's dangerous, sweetie! There are hunters out there."

"What about Arlo?" Mitch cried.

"I'm sure he goes into the forest all the time," she assured him, wondering if it was true. "He'll be okay. And if he wants to come back, he knows where to find us."

Because Mitch didn't look convinced, they called for the dog for a few minutes, but Arlo ignored them. Afterward, they walked back to the house, where Kaitlyn collected her purse and keys. She ended up spending more than an hour at the police station, filing a report. While it took some persuasion, she also convinced the detective to put out the APB immediately.

Back at home, she was making lasagna when Casey appeared.

"It smells great in here," she said. "When's dinner going to be ready?"

"Not long. Maybe an hour? Are you going out again tonight?"

"Of course," Casey answered. "But not until later. You don't care if I use the Suburban, do you?"

"No, go ahead. I won't need it tonight."

"How did it go with the police?"

Kaitlyn brought Casey up to speed.

"Mitch is really worried about him, Mom. And Arlo. He cried when we were talking."

"I'm worried, too," Kaitlyn admitted.

"Mitch also told me that he thinks Mr. Jasper might be lost in the forest. He thinks that's the reason Arlo went in there. And it explains why Arlo was so dirty."

Kaitlyn stopped layering the cheese in the dish. "Why would Jasper be in the forest?"

"Mitch said he was going to look for mushrooms. He also said he might have been trying to find the white deer."

Kaitlyn recalled Jasper mentioning the white deer to her as well. But . . .

"How does that explain his missing truck?"

"He could have taken his truck into the forest, couldn't he?" Casey speculated.

"Maybe," Kaitlyn said.

"Will the police search for him there? Or the park rangers, or whatever they're called?"

"The police aren't going to do anything until tomorrow at the earliest, and as far as the Uwharrie, I'm guessing whoever's in charge there will say the same thing. Especially since we don't know for sure he's even in the forest."

"Then we should go look for him," Casey said with conviction, crossing her arms.

"It's hunting season," Kaitlyn warned. "I don't want either you or Mitch in the forest."

Casey studied her in silence, a dubious look on her face.

XV

JASPER THOUGHT HE felt something soft and moist pushing at his face. He cracked open an eye, recognizing his dog.

"Arlo," he croaked. "Where've you been?"

In his mind, the words were clear, but he suspected they'd come out as a garbled mess before he faded again into unconsciousness.

When he woke again, Arlo was gone.

XVI

TANNER WENT TO dinner at a local steak house. All around him were couples and friends, the laughter and the low murmur of relaxed conversation. It conjured up images of a family dinner on the other side of town to which he hadn't been invited.

It bothered him more than he'd imagined it would, and he found himself recalling the memory of sneaking out of bed late at night and seeing his grandmother and grandfather dancing in the living room. He was a little kid at the time, but he could remember the way the two of them were looking at each other. There was love there, for sure, but also a familiarity, an unshakable trust that somehow comforted him as he crept back to his bed.

Kaitlyn hadn't gazed at him the way his grandparents had stared at each other that night. While she'd been attracted to him, she hadn't given herself over to him fully, he knew. She'd been holding back since the moment they met, as though she knew in advance that he would eventually hurt her.

And of course, he'd done exactly that, and the realization left him feeling empty in a way he'd never experienced before.

XVII

KAITLYN WAS RINSING the used dinner dishes when she heard Mitch call out to her from the living room.

"Arlo's back!"

"I'm sorry." Kaitlyn turned off the faucet. "What's that?"

"He said 'Arlo's back,'" Casey repeated, heading toward the door. In the time since they'd finished dinner, she'd changed her clothes, put on makeup, and done her hair, looking more like a young adult than a teenager. Kaitlyn dried her hands while Casey opened the door, Mitch crowding beside her.

"Can we let him in?" Mitch pleaded.

"Yes," Kaitlyn said. "I'll get him some food and water."

Arlo followed the kids into the house as though he owned it; meanwhile Kaitlyn opened a can of dog food and scooped it into a bowl. Arlo must have smelled it because he trotted into the kitchen with surprising speed. Casey followed, her expression telegraphing *Now what are we going to do, Mom? You and I both know Jasper is in trouble.*

Kaitlyn stayed silent, casting about for an adequate answer.

XVIII

TANNER HAD JUST paid the bill when his phone vibrated. He frowned as he squinted down at the text, hesitating before answering. A moment later, a second text followed. Tanner slipped on his jacket and started for his rental car.

Turning into the hotel parking lot, he immediately spotted the SUV parked near the entrance and the figure leaning against it, arms crossed. He slowed the rental and pulled into the adjacent space before getting out, curious.

"Hey, Casey," he said cautiously. "Are you okay?"

"I'm fine," she said, standing up straight as he shut the door of his car. "Thanks for agreeing to meet me. My mom doesn't know I'm here by the way, but I think we might need your help."

Tanner's brows knitted together. "What's going on?"

"Our neighbor Jasper is missing. The old man who carves with Mitch." She went on, explaining everything. When she finished, Tanner looked out over the parking lot, processing what she'd told him. After a moment, he turned back to her, his gaze questioning.

"And you're asking me to go look for him in the Uwharrie?"

"Yes," she said simply. "Like I told you, my mom won't let us go look for him because of all the hunters."

Tanner recalled a detail from his Fort Bragg days. "I'm pretty sure hunting's not allowed on Sunday mornings," he said, "so if I'm not mistaken, tomorrow morning should be safe."

"Oh," Casey said. "I didn't know that. I don't think my mom does either." She chewed on that for a moment. "Do you think you'd be willing to look for him anyway? My mom probably still won't let us go and you'd be better at it because of all your army training and stuff."

He considered it. Then: "Is Arlo still at your house?" he asked.

"As far as I know. Why?"

"Can you be up early tomorrow? Around six-thirty? So I can grab Arlo before I go?"

"Yeah, I can be up by then," Casey answered, looking relieved. "And thanks. I know it'll make Mitch feel a lot better." She hesitated. "One more thing—if you do happen to find him, Mr. Jasper looks kinda . . . scary. Especially the first time you see him. He was in a bad fire."

When Tanner nodded, Casey rounded back to the driver's-side door of the SUV and pulled it open before arching an eyebrow at him. "It's really too bad, though."

"What is?"

"That you messed up with my mom. I was just beginning to like you."

Speechless, he took a step back and watched as Casey reversed the SUV before pulling away toward the main road. Once she was gone, he slowly got back into his rental car. Since he'd be heading into the woods—hunters or not—there were a few things he was going to need, and he hoped Walmart was still open.

CHAPTER ELEVEN

I

WHEN TANNER PULLED into the driveway the next morning, he saw Casey standing on the porch in slippers, a thick down jacket over her pajamas. She was prancing from one foot to the other, hugging her arms while Arlo sat patiently beside her. Tanner had already donned the fluorescent orange windbreaker and equally orange baseball cap that he'd purchased at Walmart. Next to a loaded backpack on the front seat was a small electric tag and an orange vest, and he grabbed them before climbing out of the car. Light was just beginning to infiltrate the morning sky.

Casey snorted. "You look like a traffic cone."

"And Arlo will be my twin," he said. "It pays to be cautious."

On the porch, he introduced himself to Arlo before sliding the loop of the vest over the dog's head and securing it. Next, he took out the electronic tag and hooked it to the collar around Arlo's neck.

"What's that?"

"GPS," Tanner answered. "It's linked to an app on my phone."

"Smart." She rubbed her arms, trying to ward off the chill. "Do you think you'll be able to find Mr. Jasper? If he's out there, I mean?"

"There's a lot of ground to cover," he said. "But I'm hoping Arlo will lead the way. What can you tell me about his truck?"

"It's super old and beat-up," she said. "I think it's beige or white, but I can't remember for sure. I think I've only seen it once. Sorry."

"There can't be too many out in the woods matching that description."

She nodded. "You probably need to know where he lives so you have an idea of where Mitch saw Arlo enter the forest. I don't know Mr. Jasper's address, but I can tell you how to find his place. It's close."

While she offered the directions, Tanner hooked a leash to Arlo's collar and Casey walked with him as he led the dog to the car. Opening the rear door, he helped Arlo into the backseat.

"What are you going to tell your mom?" he asked. "When she notices Arlo is gone, I mean."

"The truth," Casey answered with a shrug. She peeked at Arlo before looking at Tanner again. "How long do you think you'll be out there?"

"As long as it takes, I guess."

Tanner opened the driver's-side door and got behind the wheel. He offered a quick wave through the window at Casey and backed out of the driveway. He made the turns Casey had indicated, and a few minutes later, he pulled to a stop at a ramshackle cabin at the end of a short gravel drive.

Staring through the windshield, he thought with a twinge of surprise, *I know this place,* before pushing the thought aside, aware that it wasn't relevant right now. Getting out with the bag, he removed two strips of orange, fluorescent sticky tape and ran them down the sides of his jogging pants, checked the app to

make sure the GPS was working, and flicked the flashlight on
and off to test it. Next, he rechecked the backpack he'd loaded
earlier with a first aid kit, a canteen filled with water, power gels,
and two space blankets, then put it onto his shoulders. Finally,
opening the back door, he let Arlo out and unhooked the leash.

It was clear the dog knew where he was, but he didn't head
toward the house. Instead, he trotted to the edge of the property
before stopping and turning back to gaze at Tanner. A moment
later, the dog vanished into the Uwharrie. Though the sky was
beginning to brighten, Tanner flicked on the flashlight and began
to follow, first at a walk and then a slow jog.

II

JASPER, IN HIS delirium, experienced the world without conscious thought, only physical sensations. Darkness. Light. Exhaustion. Hunger. Thirst. Cold. Pain.

He no longer knew he was in the Uwharrie, no longer knew
what had happened. He continued to shiver, and what once had
been agony now registered only dimly. He felt someone squeeze
his hand, and he knew that Audrey had finally come for him.

"Audrey," he whispered, and for a fleeting instant, Jasper was
able to see her in his mind's eye. But then just as quickly, her
image was gone.

In its place was the shifting shadowy outline of a dark figure,
drawing ever closer.

III

KAITLYN WAS SITTING at the kitchen table, drinking her first cup of coffee, when Casey descended the stairs and padded into the kitchen.

"Good morning," Kaitlyn said, looking at her watch. "You're up awfully early."

"Tell me about it." Casey groaned.

"If you're still tired, go back to bed. It's a cold, gray day, perfect for sleeping in."

"I'm awake," Casey said. She plopped in the seat beside Kaitlyn and explained what she'd done. Kaitlyn could only stare at her over her coffee cup.

"You went to see Tanner last night?" she asked, stunned. "Without asking me first?"

"I assumed you'd tell me not to." Casey shrugged.

"You're right," Kaitlyn snapped, feeling her irritation rise.

"Someone had to go look for Mr. Jasper, Mom." Casey's expression was earnest. "If the police won't, and you won't let us, why not him?"

That might have been true, but . . . Tanner?

IV

TANNER ALTERNATELY WALKED and jogged, trying to stay a consistent distance behind the dog. He didn't want to crowd Arlo, hoping that the dog would lead, but he wasn't convinced Arlo knew where he was going. The old Labrador regularly changed directions, heading right and then left. Twice, he'd even started heading back the way they'd come before finally correcting himself.

Despite the slowly brightening morning, mist hugged the forest floor and Tanner was grateful that he'd thought to put a vest on Arlo. The dog stood out in the gray landscape like a glowing neon sign. Though the woods seemed to be otherwise empty, his senses were on hyperalert, and he continually scanned the ground, searching for tracks. He peered in every direction, looking for an old truck or signs that anyone had been in the area, and halted periodically, listening carefully for anything out of the ordinary.

The terrain undulated, alternating between dense forest and rocky patches. Up ahead, Arlo disappeared over a small ridge. Tanner checked the app on his phone and adjusted his backpack before settling into a jog. Reaching the crest of the ridge, he spotted Arlo between the trees. The dog trotted forward before slowing to a walk, his nose to the ground.

Tanner followed.

V

JASPER HOVERED IN the twilight between consciousness and unconsciousness, his mind a carousel of frozen memories.

His father sitting with a Bible open in his lap.

Audrey hanging sheets to dry on a clothesline.

His children gathered around the dinner table.

But the darkened figure cast a shadow over them all.

VI

FROM THE KITCHEN, Kaitlyn overheard Mitch talking to Casey in the living room.

"Do you think he'll find Mr. Jasper?" Mitch asked. It was midmorning, and Mitch's anxiety had been rising since he awoke to find Arlo gone.

"I do."

"How do you know?"

Casey was quiet for a moment. When she spoke, her voice rang with absolute certainty. "Because I'm pretty sure he's the kind of man who won't stop looking until he does find him. And he knows how important it is to you."

Kaitlyn brought a hand to her mouth, thankful that the kids couldn't see the warring emotions on her face.

VII

THEY'D BEEN IN the forest for more than two hours now, and Arlo was beginning to slow. Tanner kept him in sight, his senses still on high alert. Fortunately, the mist was beginning to burn off, but to that point, he'd yet to see anything that caught his attention.

Despite Arlo's meandering, Tanner knew exactly where he was. His training was invaluable, but Tanner had also been blessed with an internal compass that rarely failed him. The cabin, he estimated, was less than two miles away, even if he and Arlo had probably covered twice that distance.

Now, though, Tanner noticed that Arlo seemed to be walking in a straighter line. Tanner pushed aside a branch, ducked under

more, and hopped over a fallen tree. Arlo, with his nose to the
ground, was moving as though he'd caught a familiar scent.
Again, Arlo disappeared beyond a ridge and Tanner sped up.

Tanner was panting when he reached the top of the ridge. He
spotted Arlo right away, but his gaze was quickly redirected
when he noticed something that didn't belong.

He zeroed in on the rusting bed of an older-model pickup,
light in color, the rest of it partially blocked by a small hill or
berm in the dense forest.

Tanner jogged toward it, quickly closing the distance. When
he glanced over his shoulder, Arlo had vanished again.

VIII

THE PICKUP TRUCK appeared old and battered enough to have
been abandoned in the forest for decades, but as Tanner drew
near he saw that it wasn't covered in decaying leaves or fallen
debris. It had probably only been out here a few days.

Jasper had indeed driven it into the woods, but why?

He looked through the windows before scanning the forest
again. He opened the driver's-side door.

On the passenger seat was a hand-drawn map on the back of
an old receipt; he guessed it traced the roads through the forest,
though he wasn't positive about that. Crawling in the driver's
seat, he unlatched the glove compartment. It was stuffed with
yellowing papers and receipts; on top was a wallet and Tanner
reached for it. Opening it, he pulled out a driver's license. For a
long moment, he studied Jasper's photo and his name and age,
struck by the possible power of coincidence.

He doubted that the old man would have ventured far. So

where was he? Getting out of the truck, Tanner scanned the forest, trying to spot Arlo. Pulling up the app on his phone, he located the dog, wondering if Arlo had led him here because of the truck, or because Jasper was close. He started jogging in Arlo's direction, keeping an eye on the glowing dot in his app. As far as he could tell, the dog was no longer wandering and seemed to have come to a stop.

Tanner sped up to a run, recalling how cold the last few nights had been. His lips compressed in a tight line, he found himself hoping for the best but preparing for the worst.

IX

JASPER TRIED AND failed to summon the image of Audrey again. Where had she gone? he wondered. Wasn't she coming to comfort him?

In his delirium, he saw instead the dark shape of his nightmares. And yet, just when it was almost close enough to touch, the black shape suddenly seemed to resemble Arlo.

X

ACCORDING TO THE app, Tanner was getting close to Arlo, but he still couldn't see the dog. He slowed to a walk and a moment later realized he'd reached the top of a small, steep ridge that had been camouflaged by the rolling topography.

He spotted the dog in the same instant he made out a prone figure on the ground. Scrambling down the ridge, he clawed at the straps of the backpack, his instincts taking over. He'd gone through medical and first aid training multiple times and had treated friends in the field more often than he cared to remember. In a flash he was on his knees by Jasper. He gently nudged Arlo to the side, making room.

"Hey there," he said softly, while simultaneously scanning Jasper for injuries. He cataloged the evidence on hand: the blood on Jasper's skull meant possible brain injury; dry lips and swollen tongue meant probable dehydration. His skin was colorless and pasty. One foot was angled the wrong way, indicating a compound fracture in the lower leg. The knee, too, looked awfully swollen. "Can you hear me, Jasper?" Tanner sang into his ear. "How you doing, buddy? I'm here to help you."

The old man seemed to be mumbling something. Tanner leaned his head closer but made out no words, only a wheezing, croaking moan. He reached for Jasper's wrist to check for a pulse, but the old man's skin was alarmingly cold and the fingers held a bluish tint. The skin at the wrist was scarred with grafts and Tanner felt nothing, so he tried the carotid instead. Here, the skin was pink and scaly; concentrating, Tanner barely detected a weak, thready vibration. Using the flashlight on his phone, he checked for dilation of Jasper's pupils; to his relief, both pupils responded. On his phone, the signal showed only a single bar and he desperately hoped it would suffice for a call.

It did. To the emergency operator, he spoke slowly and clearly, explaining the situation and the extent and severity of Jasper's injuries. He pinned his location and warned them that the ambulance or EMT might not be able to navigate the nearby terrain, necessitating a hand-carried stretcher. He made the operator repeat everything, making sure she had it.

After disconnecting, he turned his attention back to Jasper. He continued to speak to the old man in a soothing voice, assuring him that help was on the way and that he was going to be fine. As he spoke, he rummaged through the backpack, pulling out what he needed. In the first aid kit, there was nothing he could use to splint the ankle, nor would he have risked it in anything but a life-or-death situation. It could wait. Instead, he tried to discern the extent of Jasper's head wound. He didn't want to rotate Jasper's head for fear of further damage, but using the flashlight, he was relieved to see that the wound had clotted and there was less blood than he'd first imagined. It was possible that only the scalp had been injured.

He tore open the space blankets and gently tucked them around Jasper, hoping to raise his body temperature. It seemed clear what had happened—Jasper had stumbled and then fallen, fracturing his ankle and hitting his head. The pain of the fracture was probably too great for him to even attempt to move, so the old man had simply lain here for God knew how many days and nights.

Unscrewing the canteen, Tanner poured some water into the cap and dipped his finger in. He gently moistened Jasper's lips and directed a few drips into Jasper's open mouth. The old man probably needed an IV of fluids pronto, but in the interim he hoped this would help. He did it a few more times before pausing. Too much water too soon might cause Jasper to cough or choke. After a minute, Jasper brought his lips together, his tongue slowly emerging. Tanner continued to moisten Jasper's lips while he waited for help to arrive.

Pulling out his phone again, he decided to text Casey. In the end, he put Kaitlyn on the text as well, then sent a simple message that he'd found Jasper and that he was alive, but that he was severely dehydrated, with a head injury, and had a broken ankle as well. He closed by noting that help was on the way.

He offered Jasper a couple more drops of water, and for the first time, Jasper's eyes fluttered open briefly before closing again.

"Audrey," he whispered. Or at least that's what Tanner thought he said, before Jasper whispered a string of other names. They were barely audible, but again Tanner found himself pausing, marveling again at the mysteries that can sometimes reveal a hidden order.

XI

TANNER FELT HIS heart jump at the sight of Kaitlyn's name on his phone screen a few minutes later.

"Tanner?" she said, as soon as he connected the call. "You're on speakerphone with the kids. You found Jasper?"

"I'm with him now, waiting for the EMTs and an ambulance." He summarized again Jasper's condition before briefing her on what he was doing for Jasper in the meantime.

"Don't give him too much water too quickly," Kaitlyn cautioned. "But he's going to need an IV as soon as he can get one."

"I told them that," he said, "but I'm not sure where the closest road is, and I have no idea how long it will take them to get here."

"Is he conscious?"

"He's mumbling, but I wouldn't call it conscious. He opened his eyes for a second but closed them again."

"Maybe I should head out there with my medical kit. Where are you?"

"I'll pin you my location," Tanner said, pulling his phone away from his ear. "Hold on . . ."

"Got it," Kaitlyn said, businesslike, before disconnecting the call.

XII

TANNER KEPT UP a soothing patter with Jasper and proffered additional drops of water as he waited. He also checked Jasper's pockets, tossing the truck keys into the backpack. As the minutes passed, Tanner took Jasper's hands beneath the space blankets and tried to warm them; finally he called the emergency dispatcher a second time, asking for an update. He was told that someone was on the way.

Half an hour into his vigil at Jasper's side, Tanner heard a siren in the distance. He listened as it slowly grew louder before eventually cutting out completely. He estimated the distance at three-quarters of a mile, maybe more, but in this terrain, it was impossible to tell for sure.

After another fifteen minutes passed, Tanner climbed up to the top of the ridge. He began calling out for help, hoping the paramedics could hear him. When they finally appeared, he waved his arms overhead and shouted, relieved when the two men spotted him and began to hurry toward him. One of them, he noticed, was carrying a foldable stretcher.

Unfortunately, they didn't have much in the way of medical equipment with them, other than a neck collar and the stretcher. Up close, both looked to be in their twenties, and after they gently set the neck collar, Tanner helped them lift Jasper onto the stretcher. Though Jasper wasn't a large man, it would be tough going for two people, considering the terrain and distance, so they willingly accepted Tanner's offer of assistance. Their intent, after getting him into the ambulance, was to transport Jasper to the local hospital in Asheboro, where he would be evaluated before the doctors decided whether to send him on to the larger hospital in Greensboro.

Before setting out, Tanner hoisted his backpack and dashed off a quick text to Kaitlyn and Casey, letting them know they were underway with Jasper and that it might be best to meet the ambulance at the hospital. Then, when everyone was ready, they lifted the stretcher. Tanner called to Arlo, and they were off, Arlo walking beside them.

It was much farther than three-quarters of a mile, Tanner realized, over difficult terrain, and they stopped to rest twice. Finally, Tanner spotted the ambulance on the side of a narrow dirt road, which he recognized as a fire road. They loaded Jasper into the back, one of the EMTs staying with him while the other climbed into the driver's seat. Tanner stayed behind with Arlo.

Soon the ambulance was on its way, siren howling. When it vanished from sight, Tanner turned and headed back to Jasper's truck.

He loaded Arlo into the back and tried to start it, but a loose belt squealed like a banshee and the engine failed to turn over. Tanner tried again and then a third time, gently pumping the gas while trying to avoid flooding the motor. After a few more attempts the engine finally cranked, and he let it idle for a minute before shifting it into gear.

He drove slowly around trees and over fallen branches, bumping over rocks and scrub brush in the general direction of the road he'd just left. When he reached it, he drove in the same direction that the ambulance had gone. He stopped the truck for a moment to try to understand the map Jasper had drawn, but he couldn't make sense of it. He couldn't even tell which way was north or south, so he set it aside.

Fortunately, the dirt road eventually led to a paved one; he took a guess at which way to turn and ended up being correct. After exiting the forest, he drove first to Jasper's, where he left the truck in the driveway, stashing the keys in the glove compartment next to Jasper's wallet.

Loading Arlo into his own car, he swung by a fast-food place for some hamburgers, feeding two to Arlo before driving to Kaitlyn's. The SUV was gone, and when he knocked, no one answered. No doubt they were at the hospital, but because he wasn't comfortable simply leaving Arlo to his own devices, Tanner let Arlo lap some water from the hose before taking a seat on the porch. He leaned back in one of the rockers while Arlo curled into a ball at his feet and fell asleep.

He desperately hoped the old man would make it. He was in bad shape, no question. Given the weather conditions over the last couple of days, it was a wonder Jasper had survived as long as he had.

Pulling out his phone, he began searching the internet. In the silence, he thought about Jasper; he also found his mind turning to thoughts of Kaitlyn, already knowing that coming to Asheboro had changed everything.

CHAPTER TWELVE

I

AFTER THE PHONE call with Tanner, Kaitlyn was mentally composing a list of items and medicines she thought Jasper might need before retrieving her medical bag. The kids insisted on going with her, and once they were in the SUV, Kaitlyn drove to her office, where she quickly grabbed everything. They were already deep in the Uwharrie when Tanner's next text arrived, letting her know that Jasper was being transported out of the forest.

Turning around, she started toward the hospital, wishing she'd asked Tanner for more specifics about Jasper's condition. She'd always found Jasper to be a walking contradiction, both strong and frail at the same time. That he'd still been alive when Tanner found him was something of a miracle, and as she drove, she wondered if he would make it. Two or three days in the forest exposed to the rain and cold was a long time for anyone, let alone someone his age, with his ailments.

She hadn't mentioned her worries to the kids, but she questioned her decision to let them come with her. Too late now.

Casey and Mitch followed her into the emergency room, where she learned the ambulance hadn't yet arrived. While they waited Kaitlyn spoke to Michael Betters, the emergency physician on duty, a man she'd known for years.

She briefed Dr. Betters on what she knew about Jasper's condition as well as his medical history, and they shared their concerns about the possible head injury. Depending on its severity, they agreed to transfer Jasper to the hospital in Greensboro as quickly as they could.

The ambulance arrived almost an hour later, and Kaitlyn walked beside the gurney as Jasper was wheeled in. The ER staff sprang into action—vitals were taken and both a visual and a technical exam commenced, which showed a lower-than-normal body temperature and signs of severe dehydration. Jasper was immediately hooked up to an IV of Ringer's lactate, and within a few minutes, his vitals began to stabilize. A CT scan was ordered, and the results showed a minor subdural hematoma. X-rays of the upper vertebrae and cranium were taken, which to Kaitlyn's relief showed no sign of fracture or cracking. Additional X-rays were taken on his legs, which indicated a severe lateral malleolus fracture, in which the base of his fibula had broken and was poking through the skin, and what appeared to be a sprained knee. Surgery would be required for the ankle, and Kaitlyn reached out to an orthopedist she trusted. Jasper remained unconscious throughout. With his vitals continuing to show improvement, both she and Dr. Betters made the decision to keep him at the local hospital, at least for the next few hours.

When the flurry of medical activity finally slowed, Kaitlyn exhaled and held Jasper's hand for a little while, watching the steady drip of the IV. She knew that when it came to dehydration, fluids often prompted what would otherwise appear to be a miraculous recovery, but Jasper had yet to open his eyes.

When she went to update the kids, they listened quietly, their questions the same as hers. *Would he recover? When would he wake up? How long would he have to stay in the hospital?* When Mitch asked if he could see him, she shook her head.

She was still sitting with them when Dr. Betters surprised her by coming out to find them.

"Believe it or not, he woke a few minutes ago and he's able to talk," he said. "He's a tough old guy."

"Can we go see him now?" Mitch asked again.

"Let me check on him first," Kaitlyn said, brushing a lock of hair out of Mitch's face before following Dr. Betters to Jasper's bedside. Sure enough, his eyes were open, and she smiled.

"Hi . . . Doc," he mumbled, his voice hoarse.

"You gave us quite the scare," she said, taking his hand and giving it a gentle squeeze. "How are you feeling?"

He closed his eyes. "It . . . hurts," he finally croaked out.

"What hurts?"

It took him a long time to answer, and she had to lean close to hear him.

"Every . . . thing," he whispered.

II

KAITLYN BROUGHT MITCH in to see Jasper, though she warned him that Jasper needed rest and they couldn't stay long. Casey tagged along, and Mitch sat next to Jasper, peppering him with questions.

The answers came in fits and starts. Yes, he'd gone to the forest because of the white deer. Yes, he'd slipped and broken his ankle. He'd been in the forest since Thursday morning. Kaitlyn knew there was likely more to the story than Jasper was sharing, but she figured the details would come out in time.

Jasper asked who'd found him, at which point Casey jumped

in, explaining who Tanner was. Listening, Kaitlyn wrestled with her discomfort. Then, witnessing Jasper's exhaustion, she shooed the kids out. Betters promised to keep her updated, although she'd already decided to stop by the hospital again, after she finished her usual house calls.

On the way home, she swung through Bojangles with the kids to pick up a late lunch.

Pulling into the drive at home, she saw Tanner and Arlo waiting for them.

III

CASEY AND MITCH raced onto the porch to talk to Tanner, and after updating him on Jasper's condition, they badgered him for details about how he'd found the old man. He stood as he gave them a quick recap of his search with Arlo, explaining that he hadn't wanted to leave the dog alone.

"I wasn't sure what else to do," he said, meeting Kaitlyn's eyes for the first time. "I hope you don't mind."

"It's all right." Kaitlyn nodded, before handing the bag of food to Casey. "Would you mind bringing these inside for me, and you and Mitch can eat?"

Casey playfully wrapped an arm around Mitch's neck. "C'mon, dopey," she said. "Let's let the grown-ups talk."

Arlo, his nose trailing the bag of food, followed the kids into the house. When the door closed behind them, Kaitlyn crossed her arms, reminding herself to keep her emotions in check. "We all owe you a serious thank-you," she began. "I'm not sure how much longer Jasper would have lasted had you not found him when you did."

"I was glad to help," Tanner said. "Is he going to be okay?"

She told him about Jasper's condition, keeping her demeanor professional, before adding, "And he's going to be in a cast for a while. Whether that means he's going to need crutches or a wheelchair, I'm not sure yet. I've arranged for a first-rate orthopedist to see him."

Tanner was quiet for a moment. "His hands were really cold," he said.

Kaitlyn nodded. "I think it might have something to do with the effects of the fire he survived. I assume you saw the skin grafts."

"I did," Tanner said. "He also has psoriasis."

At her startled look, Tanner explained. "While I was waiting for you, I spent some time on the internet to look up why his skin looks the way it does." He rocked back and forth on his heels for a moment, as if debating his next question. "How much do you know about Jasper?" he asked finally, casting a sidelong glance at her. "Personally, I mean."

"Why are you asking?"

Tanner clasped his hands in front of him. "I saw his license and the registration in the truck," he said. "His last name is Johnson."

At her blank look, he went on: "It turns out, I'd visited his cabin earlier this week, hoping to speak with him, but he wasn't home. He was one of the names I found in the old phone book as well as the new one."

All at once, she recalled Tanner mentioning the name of his biological father and her eyes widened as she processed the implication. "You think he might be your father?"

"No," Tanner said. "His age doesn't fit, and I'm looking for someone named Dave or David."

"But?"

"But he's lived in Asheboro a long time. And he might have relatives."

Thrown by the unexpected direction of their conversation, she slowly lowered herself into a rocker.

"I don't know why I didn't think about his last name in terms of your search. I guess it's because I just think of him as Jasper. I'm sorry about that."

"It's okay," he said. "Would you know if he has relatives? Or if he had sons?"

"I'm pretty sure he was married and had children, but he doesn't really talk about it. I don't know if he had sons. And I don't know if he has other relatives."

"Do you know anyone who might know? Friends or neighbors, for instance?"

Kaitlyn shook her head. "I have the sense he pretty much keeps to himself." She squinted at him. "Have you tried looking online?"

Tanner nodded. "I spent the last hour searching, but I couldn't find anything. The next step would be to try county records, but they're not open until tomorrow." He hesitated. "Do you think Mitch might know something that could help?"

"I'm not sure what all they've talked about. But you can ask him."

Rising from her chair, she went inside, emerging with Mitch a minute later. When Tanner asked if Jasper had relatives or sons, Mitch nodded.

"He had two sons, but I don't know their names."

"Do you know if he has friends in town?"

Mitch wrinkled his nose, thinking about it. "Maybe the sheriff. I think he's mentioned him a couple of times."

When Mitch could add nothing more, Kaitlyn shooed him back into the house. She surreptitiously studied Tanner, who seemed lost in thought before finally offering a quick smile that triggered a raft of memories she preferred not to revisit. As if sensing her discomfort, Tanner took a step off the porch. "Once he's on the mend, do you think it would be possible for me to visit Jasper at the hospital?" he said, turning to gaze up at her, one foot on the stair.

"I'm sure he'd be willing to meet with the man who saved him, but for now, he needs rest. Maybe give it a day or two."

He nodded. "Thanks for your help."

"Thank you. For finding him," she echoed.

Tanner took a few steps toward his car before turning around. "Hey," he said. "There's something else I wanted to say, if it's okay."

Kaitlyn tensed. "Yes?"

"I want to apologize," he said simply. "For not being clear with you from the beginning. About going to Cameroon. And you were right. I hadn't really thought it through, so in addition to the apology, I want to thank you. If you hadn't said what you had . . ." He trailed off, as though grasping for the right words. "I've done some soul-searching over the last couple of days, trying to figure out who I am and who I want to be. I just wanted you to know that you've helped me recognize how important those questions are."

Kaitlyn stared at him, unsure what to say. A second later he turned and left, driving away from the house as she watched him go.

IV

IT DIDN'T TAKE long for Casey to corner her mother in the kitchen.

"What did he say?" she pressed, before Kaitlyn even had a chance to collect herself.

"He wanted to know more about Jasper," she said, pretending to busy herself by cleaning up the remainders of the kids' lunch.

"I know that much, but why?"

Knowing it wasn't her story to tell, Kaitlyn kept it vague. "He just saved his life," she pointed out, storing the leftover chicken in Tupperware. "I think anyone would be curious."

Casey eyed her critically. "What's going on with you? You're acting kinda strange."

"I'm fine," Kaitlyn demurred. "It's just been a crazy day."

"Are you going to see him again?"

Kaitlyn hesitated. "I honestly don't know."

CHAPTER THIRTEEN

I

Tanner returned to the hotel. He stripped and showered, and though he hadn't eaten much, he realized he wasn't hungry. Instead he lay on the bed, his hands clasped behind his head, wondering whether there was some chance Jasper was his grandfather, or an uncle.

He didn't want to leap to conclusions, but if he and Jasper truly were related, the circumstances of their meeting bordered on divine intervention.

As for Kaitlyn . . .

She had been more cordial than he'd expected. He was relieved by that, but as he stared at the ceiling, he wondered: Would she even care that she had inspired a reckoning in him? Would she trust that his reevaluation was sincere? And most important, would she be willing to give him a second chance? All he knew for sure was that meeting her had turned his world upside down.

The uncertainty left him feeling almost adrift. A week ago, he'd known what was coming next for him; a week ago, it felt as though his path was entirely up to him. But something had undeniably shifted inside him. He thought again of what Glen had said . . . I just *knew*, and yet . . .

He forced himself to accept that what happened next was her decision rather than his. It was a situation he was painfully unaccustomed to. Agitated, he lay awake the rest of the night.

II

JASPER HAD BEEN asleep Sunday night when Kaitlyn stopped at the hospital to check on him on the way home after her rounds, so it wasn't until Monday morning that they were able to speak. While still exhausted, he summoned enough energy to tell her more about what had happened to him.

Confessing his worries about the white deer, he described his encounters with the Littleton boys. Kaitlyn frowned at the mention of their names, remembering her instant dislike of Josh. Somehow it didn't surprise her that not only had they been hunting illegally but they had abandoned an elderly man in the forest, perhaps even to die.

After assuring Jasper that she was looking after Arlo, she was about to broach the subject of his sons when Dr. Betters entered the room along with the orthopedic surgeon. Feeling that the conversation about Jasper's family was best saved for a more private moment, Kaitlyn promised to visit again soon.

III

NOT LONG AFTER finishing breakfast, Tanner paid a visit to the sheriff's office. At the counter, he was told that the sheriff was on a call and he was asked whether he'd prefer to meet with someone else. Tanner said he'd wait for the sheriff.

Thirty minutes later, Tanner was finally ushered into the office, where he was greeted with a handshake by a man dressed more like a high school teacher than an officer of the law. After quick introductions, Tanner shared a little of his background and his reason for visiting Asheboro, including the name his grandma had given him. For the moment he refrained from mentioning Jasper.

Charlie Donley leaned back in his chair. "That's quite a story. Why exactly did you ask to see me personally?"

Tanner nodded, leaning forward. "I came here because I've been told that you're acquainted with a man named Jasper Johnson," he said. "He lives in a cabin by the Uwharrie and has a dog named Arlo."

"Jasper?" Charlie looked startled. "Yeah, I know him. What about him?"

Tanner explained what had happened to Jasper over the last few days. When he finished, the sheriff sighed.

"He came into my office last week talking about that albino deer," he said. "He was worried about illegal poaching, and I warned him to be careful. I guess he didn't listen to me." He shook his head in frustration. "You said he's still in the hospital?"

"He is."

"I guess I'll have to pay him a visit."

"He is a friend, then?"

"I suppose I know him as well as anyone does. He's lived in the area his entire life, as have I, but he's not really the social type."

"I was curious if you knew anything about his family," Tanner pressed. "Specifically, I was hoping you could tell me if he had a son or a younger brother who might have been named Dave or David."

It took a few seconds before the sheriff's face registered his shock, but Tanner could see him quickly putting the pieces together. "Dear God," he breathed, before glancing out the window. Drawing a deep breath, he turned back to Tanner.

"I hope you have some time, because Jasper's story is one for the ages."

IV

AFTER LEAVING CHARLIE'S office, Tanner visited the register of deeds at the county office, where he filed a request for a copy of David Johnson's birth certificate. He was told that it would take a few days to be processed.

Though the sheriff couldn't remember David's exact age when he died—early- to mid-twenties was the best he could do—the chronology struck Tanner as close enough to continue working the theory that Jasper might be his grandfather. By his estimate, David would have been roughly the same age as his mother.

He was still wrestling with the question of whether to talk to Jasper. The old man was recovering from a traumatic experience and Tanner didn't want to make things any harder for him than they already were. There was also the possibility that Jasper might not want to meet him, and was it right for Tanner to force the issue? He didn't know . . .

But Kaitlyn might.

Uncertain what else to do, Tanner texted her.

Would you be willing to meet me for coffee after work to discuss Jasper? He had a son named David, whom I believe might be my biological father. I'd be grateful for your advice.

V

KAITLYN WAS IN the office with a patient when she felt her phone vibrate in her pocket. Wondering if it might be the school texting about Casey or Mitch, she took a quick peek at the screen and saw a preview of a text from Tanner on her home screen saying, "Would you be willing to meet me for coffee," before the rest of the message was cut off.

She slipped the phone back into her pocket without opening the actual message to read the whole thing. It was already one of those days in which every appointment had run long. Furthermore, Jasper's situation and Tanner's confusing pronouncement, along with house calls the night before, had left her emotionally and physically drained. She didn't have the time or the energy to deal with Tanner right now, nor did she feel that anything would be accomplished by having coffee with him. What would be the point?

Refusing to dwell on it, she spent the rest of the morning seeing patients, and it wasn't until she'd gone home at lunch to check on Arlo that she remembered he'd texted.

Reading the full message, she found herself reeling. As much as she appreciated what he'd done for Jasper, she didn't want to get any more emotionally entangled with Tanner. But what if he was right about Jasper?

She pondered the options. Jasper was her patient and Tanner was an aborted fling. Her primary allegiance was clear; it would come down to what was best for Jasper. Having settled that, she texted Casey and Mitch, letting them know that she'd be home a little late. Then she responded to Tanner's text, informing him that she would be happy to meet him at half past five, not for coffee, but at her office.

VI

AT THE APPOINTED time, Kaitlyn poked her head into the waiting room. Tanner was the only one seated and she waved him in. In her office, she took a seat behind her desk while Tanner sat in the chair opposite her. He was as handsome as ever, but she steeled herself to ignore it.

"Fill me in," she began, resting her chin on her folded hands, elbows on her desk. Tanner laid out what he'd learned from the sheriff, as well as his reservations about talking to Jasper.

"Well, it sounds like a strong possibility, but who knows?" Kaitlyn commented. "I also agree that the decision about whether to meet should be up to Jasper, especially given his fragile condition. I'm glad we're on the same page."

"What would you suggest?"

"The best proof, of course, would be a DNA test. But I'm sure Jasper is going to want to know the reason for the test before he gives his consent, and to be honest, I have no idea how he'd react to being told."

As Tanner mulled it over, the silence felt weighty. Finally, he looked up, his eyes glittering with golden brown flecks. "What if there's another way to prove he's my grandfather? While still leaving the option of meeting me completely up to him? Without alerting him to my existence, even."

Kaitlyn shot him a quizzical look. "I don't see how that's possible."

"You'd have to be willing to ask him a single question. And after that, you can let me know what he wants to do."

She stared at him. "What are you thinking?"

VII

TANNER DEPARTED SHORTLY afterward. Kaitlyn, meanwhile, remained seated as she reflected on the conversation. Tanner's plan was solid, and she appreciated the fact that he had no intention of adding any stress to the old man's life. God knows, Jasper's life had been hard enough already. Horrible, even. She hadn't known the circumstances of the fire in which he'd been so gravely injured, and as Tanner recounted what the sheriff had told him about the incident—and what Paul had done in the aftermath—she'd felt sick to her stomach. She couldn't imagine how Jasper had managed to keep going.

After a few minutes, she left the office and made the short drive to the hospital. Tanner was already there, seated in the small lobby. He looked up as she passed but said nothing, and after reviewing Jasper's records on the computer she took a deep breath and went to find him.

VIII

AS MUCH AS he knew he needed to stay, Jasper hated being in the hospital. He'd spent too much of his life in hospitals already. He'd said as much to Doc Betters when he'd come by to see him earlier, and he'd repeated it to the orthopedic surgeon, in case Betters hadn't been listening. Betters wouldn't make any promises. Instead, because of Jasper's improving condition, the orthopedic surgeon had made the decision to operate the following morning, which likely meant Jasper would be stuck here for even longer.

The nurses had tried to make him comfortable, of course. They'd adjusted the bed so he could sit up and turn the television on, but the volume was too low for him to make out what was being said. Not that he'd be interested anyway; it was tuned to the Discovery channel and as far as he could tell, the show was about volcanoes. As there were no volcanoes within a thousand miles of Asheboro, he wasn't sure why he should care. What he really wanted to know was whether the white deer was alive. He wondered if the Littleton boys had continued to hunt in the forest after leaving Jasper stranded; he wondered whether they'd gone back on Friday for one last attempt before the hordes of turkey hunters descended. He'd asked the nurses about it, but no one seemed to know anything. Nor did Charlie; the sheriff had dropped by a few hours ago to reproach Jasper for acting like a fool.

He was glad that Dr. Cooper was watching Arlo, though, as she'd told him at her morning visit. That was kind of her, but he should have warned her not to fall for any of Arlo's tricks. The dog wasn't always hungry, even if he acted like he was about to faint from starvation. You couldn't trust Arlo to tell the truth when it came to food.

But he was a good dog. He'd gone to find help, and help had eventually come. If asked beforehand, Jasper would have said the dog wasn't capable of something like that. Oh, he might have wandered out of the forest easy enough. It was pretty much his backyard, but Jasper wouldn't have expected him to be smart enough to make it all the way to Dr. Cooper's. It wasn't as though he'd ever spent a lot of time there, and once the boy had treated him with hot dogs, Jasper figured Arlo would have known a good thing when he saw it and simply stuck around for the duration. *Why look for the old man when I'm eating hot dogs here?* But no. The dog had done his duty.

Miracles never cease, Jasper thought, but the folks at the hospital didn't quite recognize Arlo for the hero he was. When Jasper had asked if the dog could stay with him, he'd been told that pets weren't allowed. He wondered if that applied to service animals, too. Lost in thought, he took a moment to realize Dr. Cooper was standing in the doorway.

"Hi, Jasper," she said. "Do you mind if I come in?"

Jasper fiddled with the sheet, making sure his privates were covered. She might be his doctor, but that didn't mean she needed to see something she wasn't in the mood to see. He waved her inside and she approached with a smile before pulling up a chair.

"You're looking a lot better than you did this morning, I must say," she remarked, "and your numbers are looking good, too. I saw that your surgery is scheduled for tomorrow?"

"The doc said I'm going to need screws to hold my ankle together."

"That's common with a fracture like this," she assured him. "How are you feeling?"

"My skin's itchier than usual, but I'm trying to ignore it."

"Is it working?"

"Nope."

"Are you getting enough food?"

"I told the nurses I don't eat much, but they don't seem to care. One of them fixed me with the evil eye until I finished everything on my tray."

Kaitlyn smiled. "She did the right thing. You need to get your strength back. How's your head?"

"Doc Betters says it's fine. I don't have a headache anymore."

"That's great," she said. "Oh, by the way, Mitch told me to tell you hello. He said he's looking forward to carving with you again, whenever you feel up to it."

Jasper nodded. "I'm thinking of carving him a deer and having him paint it white. Have you heard whether that deer's been spotted again?"

"I haven't, but if I do, I'll let you know. Regardless, I don't think you should venture into the forest for a while."

"Charlie said the same thing to me." He made a sour face.

"Charlie?"

"The sheriff. He came by earlier."

"Is he going to do anything about the Littletons?"

"There isn't much he can do. The forest is federal jurisdiction. And it wasn't as though the boys did anything to me. I just fell."

He watched Kaitlyn's brows form an angry vee. "They could have helped you or called someone for help . . ." she sputtered. "Honestly—"

"It ain't a crime not to do those things," Jasper said with a shrug. "I doubt they knew how bad I was hurt."

"You're being way too reasonable about all this," Kaitlyn protested.

"I've been around longer than you. Some battles you just can't win."

"Well, just so you know, Casey told me she confronted Josh about leaving you in the forest when you were hurt, and he was dumb enough to admit it. Let's just say his popularity has begun to wane, at least at the high school."

Jasper smiled, thinking it wasn't much, but at least it was something. He watched as Kaitlyn drew her chair closer to the bed.

"Jasper? Can I ask you a few questions?"

"That's what you've been doing since you've been here."

She smiled. "I know, but these are different. And I'm not sure quite how to begin. For starters, it's not really any of my business. But it might be yours."

"Just ask what you want."

"Okay, but before I do, I want you to know that I'm on your

side, and I'll do whatever you want me to do." When Jasper nodded, she seemed to gather herself. "I just recently learned about the circumstances of the fire in which you were injured, and what happened to your family. I can't imagine how terrible that must have been for you, and I understand why you never wanted to talk about it. I wouldn't want to talk about it either. And I'm very sorry for what you went through."

Jasper said nothing. He felt her reach for his hand before she went on. "But I'm here because I wanted to ask you something about your son David. If you don't want to answer, that's of course fine."

Jasper nodded, feeling his curiosity grow.

"Do you remember anything about David's teenage years?"

Jasper closed his eyes for a moment. "I remember everything," he whispered, swallowing hard. "It's all I have left."

"Do you know if he ever had a girlfriend or a young woman he cared about?"

"Yes."

"Was her name Monica Hughes?"

At the name, Jasper felt an almost electrical jolt. "How do you know that?" he asked.

"Can you tell me anything about her?"

"David loved her, but she moved away," he said in a shaky voice. "Her father was in the army, and he was posted to somewhere in Europe, I think. David never saw or heard from her again. It broke his heart."

Kaitlyn seemed to be staring at him with infinite tenderness. "If David was anything like you, there's no doubt that Monica loved your son dearly. The reason David never heard from her was because she passed away not too long after she moved."

"She died?"

Kaitlyn's voice was tentative, but gentle. "Did you know she was pregnant when she moved?"

"No," said Jasper.

"She was. I don't know the details, but something went wrong when she was delivering the baby," said Kaitlyn.

It took Jasper a moment to understand what she was telling him.

"She was pregnant, and then she died?"

"Yes. She gave birth to a boy."

"And David was the father?"

"Yes." Kaitlyn nodded.

"You know this for sure?"

"A DNA test will confirm it, but I wouldn't be telling you this unless I was fairly certain."

Jasper's eyes began to fill with tears as comprehension slowly dawned on him. "The boy lived? I have a grandchild?"

"You do," she said, dabbing at her own tears. He listened as she drew a shaky breath before going on. "His name is Tanner Hughes. He's the one who found you in the woods."

It was almost too much for Jasper to process, and he grabbed the bed rail, as if hoping to steady himself. "Tanner Hughes," he repeated.

"Which brings me to another question," Kaitlyn said, squeezing his hand. "Tanner asked me to find out whether you'd like to meet him. If you don't want to meet him, he told me to let you know that he understands, and that he'll never try to contact you again."

Jasper stared at her, the tears beginning to fall. He was silent for at least a minute, as the tears ran down his face.

"Yes," he said finally, trying to steady himself, feeling a sudden sense of wonder. "I'd like very much to meet my family."

EPILOGUE

I

TANNER STOPPED AT a drive-through for three ham biscuits on Friday morning. He was on his way to Jasper's, and he got one for Jasper, one for himself, and one for Arlo. According to Jasper, the dog deserved a reward for doing what he'd done, but Tanner had already figured out that sandwiches were a regular staple of both Jasper's and Arlo's diets.

At the cabin, Tanner let himself in, just as he had the day before. He helped Jasper get dressed and into the wheelchair before rolling him to the kitchen and starting a pot of coffee. When it was ready, Tanner poured two cups and brought them to the table, along with the ham biscuits. Arlo wolfed his down in two rapid gulps before poking his nose at Tanner's pocket, looking for more; Tanner ate his own at a more reasonable pace. Jasper, meanwhile, only finished half of his before setting it aside. Tanner wrapped the remainder and put it in the refrigerator in case Jasper got hungry later, though if the last couple of days were any indication, Jasper wouldn't eat again until Tanner heated up a can of soup or chili for dinner.

After breakfast, he wheeled Jasper out to the front porch with

Arlo on their heels. Because the morning still carried a nip in the air, he'd persuaded Jasper to wear a jacket and hat and also made sure to drape a blanket over his legs. Kaitlyn and Dr. Betters had warned him that Jasper's prolonged exposure to the elements, and the related shock, had likely triggered a severe autoimmune system response; he would have to be monitored closely. The psoriasis on Jasper's neck, chest, and arms remained even more inflamed than usual, and the knuckles of his right hand had swollen suddenly to nearly twice their normal size. Neither Kaitlyn nor Dr. Betters could tell Tanner when, or even if, the inflammation and swelling would subside. Tanner found it hard to believe that Jasper didn't once complain about any of it.

Taking a seat in one of the rockers, Tanner glanced over at Jasper, marveling at what a pleasure it was to spend time with the old man. He hadn't known what to expect—he remembered pausing outside Jasper's hospital room door to prepare himself in case the conversation went sour. But the old man had greeted him with kindness in his eyes, stretching out his hand without a word. Tanner took it in his own and it was clear that Jasper didn't want to let go.

"You found me," Jasper finally rasped.

"Yeah," Tanner said, a smile spreading across his face. "I guess I did. In more ways than one."

Tanner stayed with Jasper for three hours that night. Kaitlyn had arranged for a rapid DNA test, just to be sure, but both Jasper and Tanner seemed to feel they knew, somehow, what it would reveal, beyond any doubt.

Because Jasper was still recovering, Tanner did most of the talking. He traced the chronology of his life, from his upbringing overseas, to his military service, to the security work abroad and the long road trip he made in the aftermath of Covid. He told Jasper about the last few months he'd spent taking care of his grandmother, including her deathbed revelation that had brought him to Asheboro.

Unexpectedly, Tanner even found himself sharing his growing ambivalence about returning to Cameroon. He'd confessed how connected he felt to Casey and Mitch, despite their short acquaintance. When it came to Kaitlyn, he tried to skirt around his feelings for her, but Jasper interrupted.

"You love her," Jasper said. "I can see it in your eyes. You should tell her how you feel."

Tanner was at a loss for words, and that night, he barely slept at all.

Tanner sat in the waiting room while Jasper underwent surgery the next morning and he spent the rest of the afternoon in Jasper's room as he recovered. While Jasper slept, Tanner arranged for the rental of a wheelchair. He also placed orders for lumber, plywood, and tools to be delivered to the cabin the following day.

By the time Jasper was released from the hospital on Wednesday, Tanner had also exchanged his rental car for a larger SUV, and he lifted Jasper into the passenger seat before storing the wheelchair in the back. They picked up Arlo from Kaitlyn's on the way to the cabin. As they pulled up the gravel drive, Tanner saw that the construction supplies had already been delivered.

Tanner spent much of the rest of the afternoon and evening constructing a temporary ramp from the porch to the gravel. While he worked, Jasper told him his story.

Sitting in his wheelchair while Tanner hammered and sawed, he talked of peaches and whittling and Bible verses and a grandfather who'd once witnessed fish falling from the sky. He described the gentle confidence of his father, and the devastation he experienced at his sudden passing. His face glowed with love and wonder while he recounted how Audrey had jumped into his truck. He spoke about hunting for morels, their first kiss, and how hard it had been to say goodbye when she went off to college. Tanner listened closely as Jasper explained his early business success with Bradford pear trees. Mostly, though, Jasper dwelled on the family he and Audrey had raised, sharing stories about each of the four children. And of course, he especially spoke of David—vividly, and in great detail. It made Tanner long for more details of his mother in a way he never had before.

After Tanner had completed all but the railings of the ramp, Jasper directed him to the storage shed and asked him to retrieve the box containing family photos that had been at the cabin, not the house, when the house had burned. Tanner had peered closely at photos of David, stunned by the resemblance. Tanner had his father's nose and chin, and catching Jasper's eye as they bent over the old pictures, he knew that the old man had recognized the resemblance as well. How strange, Tanner reflected, to find comfort in a part of your history you never knew you were missing.

It wasn't until yesterday, however, that Jasper related the rest of his story—the tragic conclusion to his once-blessed life, parts of which Tanner had heard from the sheriff. *The tornado acting like the finger of God, which destroyed his business. The fire. Paul's suicide. Jasper's months in the burn ward and all the surgeries that followed. Chronic psoriasis, proving that God had turned His back on him, once and for all.*

But there were more recent glimpses of joy, he discovered: Carving with Mitch. The sighting of the white deer, which he believed to be a sign from the heavens. And, of course, Tanner's sudden appearance in his life, something he'd never imagined in his wildest dreams.

When Tanner returned to the hotel at night, he lay in bed thinking about the old man's love for his wife and family, which transcended even his incomprehensible losses. It made him think of Kaitlyn and her children, and the home they'd made together. He had a visceral memory of making love to her, the sensations encoded at a cellular level. Mostly, though, he missed the way he felt about himself whenever they'd been together—as if he were connected to a deeper root system, a foundation he'd never known before.

You love her. You should tell her how you feel.

Jasper's words ran through his mind on a constant loop. He'd had his chance already. Kaitlyn had come by the cabin yesterday evening to check Jasper's vitals and examine his swollen knuckles and psoriasis. She was polite with Tanner, but other than informing him that the DNA test had confirmed their relationship, that was it. On her way out, she'd simply reminded Tanner to call her if Jasper's condition worsened. He'd watched her walk away, feeling an ache he hadn't expected, disappointed in himself because he'd disappointed her. And, of course, he'd said nothing.

Now, as he sat with Jasper on the porch, he heard the old man clear his throat.

"Will you bring me to see my family?" Jasper asked.

Tanner carefully wheeled Jasper off the porch, down the ramp. Rolling through the compacted dirt was a little bumpy, but they took their time, finally reaching the small family cemetery. Up close, Tanner could see the names carved on the markers, and he paused to stare down at David's, his hands clasped in front of him. *I wish I'd had the chance to meet you.*

Jasper, his head also bowed as he contemplated the markers, said nothing for a while. In the silence, Tanner put a hand on his grandfather's shoulder, feeling a sense of comfort. He heard Jasper draw a deep breath, and watched as he slowly kneaded the blanket. Off to the side, Arlo was snuffling around the base of a tree.

"For a long time," Jasper confessed, "I wished I'd died with them."

Unable to respond, Tanner gently squeezed Jasper's shoulder. In time, the older man went on.

"Sometimes, I still do. I come out here knowing that everything I once loved is gone and buried, and even after so much time has passed, my heart still feels as though it's been broken into a million pieces. But . . ."

He looked up at Tanner, placing his own gnarled and swollen hand over Tanner's.

"Then I remind myself that my broken heart also means that there was a time when it wasn't broken, when my heart was light and full. Loving Audrey and my kids brought joy and meaning to my life, and I wouldn't have traded that love for anything else in the world."

II

KAITLYN STOPPED BY again on Saturday to examine Jasper in the living room of his cabin. She didn't expect much of a change since Thursday evening, but she hoped that the stronger prescription she'd dropped off last time would bring some relief soon. Though he downplayed his discomfort, she knew he had to be suffering.

Outside, Mitch was waiting for her to finish the examination. Mitch understood that Jasper wouldn't be able to carve with him yet, but he'd insisted on coming along anyway. More surprising was Casey's desire to tag along, but the reason quickly became clear. As soon as she'd buckled herself into the Suburban, she'd casually mentioned that the local Ford dealership had just received four new Broncos, and she'd asked Kaitlyn whether they could swing by on the way home to check them out. "Just to look," Casey quickly promised, and when Mitch chimed in excitedly, Kaitlyn felt outmaneuvered. She knew there wasn't a chance they'd buy one today, but she reluctantly agreed to go.

"The kids really seem to get along with Tanner," Jasper observed.

Following his gaze out the window, she saw Mitch and Casey crowded around Tanner as he explained the ongoing construction of the ramp. Despite the cool temperature, Tanner wore a long-sleeved T-shirt that clung to the tapered shape of his torso. For a split second she flashed on the image of his smooth golden skin as she'd unbuttoned his shirt, but pushing it away, she turned her attention back to Jasper.

"Yeah, they've spent some time together."

"He talks about them quite a bit."

"Who? Tanner, you mean?"

"He thinks you've done a terrific job with your kids."

"I try," she said, wishing Jasper hadn't brought it up. Seeing Tanner at the hospital and at Jasper's hadn't been easy. After returning home, she often had to resist the temptation to drown her regrets in a bottle of wine. She'd thought when she ended things that she'd be able to avoid seeing him until he left town, but it was obvious the universe had other plans.

"He talks about you an awful lot, too," Jasper said, persisting.

"We went out a couple of times." She busied herself packing up her medical bag. "But it didn't work out."

"He mentioned that, too."

Though part of her wanted to know what else Tanner had said, she reverted to professional mode. "I think that's it. I'll come by tomorrow night, before I see my other patients, okay? But you know to call me if anything comes up before then."

"I will," he said. "You're too good to me."

"Can I get you anything while I'm here? A glass of water maybe?"

"I'm not thirsty. But since you're asking, would you mind bringing me my Bible and my readers? They're on the end table."

She retrieved them. "Anything else?"

"Yeah, just one more thing." His expression was earnest.

"What's that?"

"He loves you, even if he hasn't had the courage to tell you yet. I think he's afraid that you might not feel the same way. But I can't help thinking you'd be good for each other."

Kaitlyn felt a sudden heat in her cheeks. "Thank you for telling me that. But what's the point? He's leaving soon."

Jasper nodded, watching the trio outside the window again. When he turned back to her, his gaze was penetrating yet gentle.

"Is he?"

At Jasper's words, Kaitlyn's eyes flicked toward the window a second time. Mitch was holding the drill and concentrating while Tanner held one of the struts to the railing and coached him through the task. She heard the sudden whine as the drill started up; when the sound faded away, Mitch beamed and both Casey and Tanner offered him high fives.

Jasper's comment hung in the air, but when she turned back to him, he was already thumbing through the Bible. Slinging her bag over her shoulder, she stepped out onto the porch.

"Mom!" Mitch called out. "I'm helping to build the railing! Mr. Tanner showed me how to use the drill."

"I saw that," she said. "If you two want to say hi to Jasper, you can go on in now."

Casey, her eyes flitting from Kaitlyn to Tanner, took her brother by the arm. "C'mon, doofus. The sooner we visit, the sooner we can go check out my new car."

"Yeah!" Mitch shouted, skipping up the steps.

Kaitlyn watched as they vanished inside. When she faced Tanner, she saw that the ease she'd witnessed between him and the kids seemed to have vanished.

"Hi," he finally said. He didn't seem to know what to do with the drill, ultimately laying it on the step and shoving his hands in his pockets.

"Hi," she said.

"How's he doing?"

"He's on the road to recovery, but it'll take time."

"Anything in particular I need to watch out for?"

"Same as the other night. Fever, shortness of breath, and let me know if the psoriasis or swelling in his knuckles seems to be getting worse. Of course, make sure he eats and drinks and gets plenty of rest."

"He never eats much."

"Just do your best," she said, beginning to descend the stairs. "He likes you," she said.

"I like him, too." His expression was a mixture of bemusement and pleasure. "It's still hard for me to believe he's my grandfather. I'm not sure it's sunk in completely yet."

"How long do you think you'll be around to take care of him?" she asked. She tried to say it with what she hoped was a nonchalant air.

"As long as it takes, I guess."

She could feel his eyes on her, and she turned to him, serious now. "He's going to be in a cast for another eight weeks. And after that, he'll need physical therapy."

"I know," he interjected.

"What about Cameroon?" She tilted her head, inquisitive.

A slow smile spread across Tanner's face. "He told you, didn't he? That I emailed Vince and let him know I wouldn't be coming?"

She suppressed a smile. A little bubble of happiness surfaced somewhere inside of her, like the pent-up fizz of a soda bottle.

Tanner went on. "Jasper has been telling me something about

what his own family meant to him, and it has had a big effect on me. And once I made the decision not to go, I knew immediately it was the right thing to do."

"Does that mean you're going to stay in Asheboro for a while?"

"That's the plan."

"Do you have any idea how long?"

"Hard to say," he began. "There's Jasper and he's the only family I have left. I'd hate to leave him, especially since we've just started getting to know each other." He caught and held her gaze. "And, of course, there's always the possibility that I could decide to settle down for good."

Kaitlyn felt a slow flush climb up her neck. "Are you going to live at the cabin with Jasper?"

"No. I get the sense he's gotten used to being alone and he'd prefer that."

"Then where are you going to live?"

"I don't know yet," he said. "I was thinking I might see what's available in town."

She arched an eyebrow. "What about work?"

"Didn't I tell you?" He feigned surprise. "I have a bit of a cushion. But, if I do ever end up needing to or wanting to, I have a friend nearby who's willing to let me work with my Delta buddies again."

"Interesting," she said, letting her heavy medical bag slide to the ground.

"I think so."

He moved closer then, reaching for her hand. His eyes, heavy-lidded with promise, traveled over her face.

"I've missed you," he whispered.

"Me, too." She breathed. She placed her other hand on his chest, creating a little space between them. "But I'm going to need some time to process all this. And I don't want to rush into anything." She looked up at him with a determined expression. "We're going to have to start over."

"I understand."

"I'm serious."

"I am, too. I'd be delighted to start over. Did you have anything special in mind? I know a great pub in town."

She raised herself on her toes, trying to stifle the sudden urge to do a pirouette. "How much do you know about cars?"

"I know a bit," he said. "Why?"

"Because Casey wants to go look at some new Broncos today."

"You're going to buy her one?"

"I think it's time. Do you want to come along?"

"What about Jasper?" said Tanner.

She glanced in the direction of the cabin, then leaned closer, conspiratorial. "I think he'll be okay for an hour or so, don't you?"

He leaned in to kiss her then, his lips promising much more. "You're the doctor," he whispered. "I trust you."

III

JASPER WATCHED THEM drive away.

Tanner had promised to return in an hour or so, but Jasper had urged them to take their time. He might be hobbled and a little beat-up, but he'd long since learned how to take care of himself. And frankly, a little privacy would be nice after the last few days.

It had been good to see Mitch again. Casey, too, though he had the sense that she could be a handful when she chose to be. While Mitch had been enthusing about a friend's birthday party he'd be attending later (*Laser tag! And go-karts!*), she'd been peeking out the window at her mom and Tanner while trying to pretend she wasn't spying. He'd acted like he didn't notice, particularly since he wasn't above doing a little *observing* himself. The awkward way they'd interacted in the hospital and at the cabin on Thursday had made it painfully obvious that they were crazy about each other. They just needed a gentle push to finally act on it. He shook his head, thinking, *Young people make things so complicated...*

Alone at last in the cabin, he put on his reading glasses and opened the old Bible, just as he had earlier that morning. He'd had Tanner retrieve it from the box in the work shed, and he thumbed the pages, recalling that Job was the first of the Poetic Books, right before Psalms.

It was a story that had confused him when he was younger; later, it struck too close to home for Jasper to want to revisit. In the Christian version of the story, after all, God marvels to the Devil about Job's faith; the Devil counters that Job is only pious because God has blessed him with wealth, health, and a wonderful family. To prove the integrity of Job's faith, God gives the Devil permission to take it all away. Job loses his crops and flocks, his family is killed, and then Job is afflicted with boils all over his body.

However, as Jasper reread the story, he realized he'd forgotten about the ending. He stared out the window to contemplate it, then startled. Sitting up straight, he whipped off his reading glasses and peered even closer.

"I'll be darned," he said out loud.

There, at the edge of his property where it bordered the Uwharrie, stood the white deer.

From a distance, it resembled a creature of the spirit world, so white it appeared to glow. Jasper blinked once, then blinked again, making sure he wasn't imagining it. *He came to me,* he thought. *He's really here.* He watched, spellbound, as the deer casually turned his head, first in one direction, then the other. The deer, he marveled, was a majestic specimen, a mature buck with heavily muscled haunches and large, symmetrical antlers. Even from a distance, Jasper could sense his intelligence, which had no doubt kept him alive in a world filled with people who wanted nothing more than to kill him, simply because he was beautiful.

Jasper watched as one of the buck's ears twitched; a moment later, he ambled onto Jasper's property. His movements were graceful and unrushed, and he finally stopped when he reached the gravesite under the tree. The white deer turned to stare in Jasper's direction.

Jasper felt his throat tighten as he felt the weight of the family he'd lost, and the joy of the family he'd recently found. If he were counting miracles, the appearance of the white deer was the second one in a week, and he was seized with the sudden certainty that the white deer had presaged Tanner's arrival. And God, he suddenly understood then, had never abandoned him. God brought Tanner into his life, blessing him just as He'd blessed Job with a new family, after so much had been lost. As he pondered that revelation, the deer snorted before turning and walking away, eventually vanishing into the Uwharrie as though it had never been there at all.

Jasper's eyes welled with tears. He let them come, feeling a sense of peace he hadn't known in decades. When the tears finally stopped, he bowed his head to offer the most powerful prayer that he knew.

"Thank you, God," he whispered. "Thank you."

ACKNOWLEDGMENTS

WHILE SOME PEOPLE might find it boring to read the same list of individuals in my acknowledgments year after year, the writing of this list is a ritual I've come to view as a rare blessing. That so many of the key people in my professional and personal life have remained unchanged for almost thirty years is remarkable in a time of deepening cultural polarization and often transient relationships. So let me begin where it all began, back in 1995:

My decades-long literary agent, producing partner, and friend, Theresa Park, has been at my side not only in the creation of every book, but also at almost every milestone in my adult life. I think I can say the same about my presence in her life as well—Theresa, thank you for walking the path of life with me all these years, and for being my partner on this incredible journey.

To the talented, savvy, and consistently forward-looking team at Park & Fine: thank you for maintaining your commitment to excellence when it would be easy to rest on your laurels. Celeste Fine, as the new leader of Park & Fine, your brilliant instincts are already transforming the agency into an ambitious new entity with limitless horizons; Andrea Mai and Emily Sweet, I couldn't ask for more sophisticated, creative, and knowledgeable experts to help guide my work into the hands of the right partners and connect with my fans; Abby Koons and Ben Kaslow-Zieve, you continue to make the publication of my work around the world not only lucrative, but exciting and fascinating—with the help of my many dedicated international publishers and foreign co-agents, who have been tireless and inspired partners. Jen Mecum, you have my deep gratitude and admiration for your legal acumen (and your mentorship skills!). Charlotte Gillies, thank you for acting as the transmitter through which the current of my business and creative life flows, connecting all the dots at Park & Fine and beyond. The agency redefines author representation and I've been the lucky beneficiary of its seamless strategic teamwork for many years.

While I'm a relatively new author at Random House, I already feel as if I've been published there for decades. Much of that is due to my gifted, sensitive, and incredibly hardworking editor and publisher, Jennifer Hershey; despite her exalted position at the publishing house, she is not afraid to roll up her sleeves and do the heavy work of reshaping a complicated novel, and I owe her a huge debt for her work on *Counting Miracles*. Of course, Jennifer could not execute her countless duties as publisher, editor, and manager so effectively without the vision and support of President Kara Welsh and Deputy Publisher Kim Hovey; together they form a triumvirate of outstanding leadership and author care.

All of the teams at Random House bring an unparalleled degree of commitment, experience, and quality to their efforts on every book, including: Jaci Updike and Cynthia Lasky in sales; Quinne Rogers, Taylor Noel, and Megan Whalen in marketing; Jennifer Garza, Karen Fink, Katie Horn, and Chelsea Woodward in publicity; Ellen Folan, Nicole McArdle, Karen Dziekonski, Dan Zitt, and Donna Passannante in audio publishing; and the team of Kelly Chian, Susan Brown, Maggie Hart, Caroline

Cunningham, Kelly Daisley, and David Hammond in production. Of course, the first impression of my book in any store is always defined by the cover, and there I am lucky to find myself in the hands of legendary art director Paolo Pepe, who—with a beautiful assist from my old friend Flag—created the unforgettable look of this one.

I've been extraordinarily fortunate that so many of my novels have found their way into development as films, and now even a Broadway musical(!)—and that is all due to the masterful instincts of Howie Sanders at Anonymous Content, who remains one of my closest friends and confidants. My longtime entertainment lawyer, Scott Schwimer, has been a guardian angel (albeit one with a flaming sword) and protector, always there for me in my hour of need. Also at Anonymous Content, producers David Levine and Garrett Kemble have been visionary collaborators, and I'm particularly grateful to the immensely talented and driven producer Zack Hayden, who has shepherded my newest film projects with such care and focus. At Universal Pictures, Peter Cramer, Donna Langley, Lexi Barta, and Jacqueline Garell continue to impress with their supreme professionalism, artistic guidance, and savvy instincts. Kevin McCollum and Kurt Deutsch, you turned a fanciful dream into a heart-stopping reality— a major Broadway musical based on *The Notebook*! Thank you for this awe-inspiring artistic and professional feat; I am honored and delighted by what you created.

My new publicist, Jill Fritzo, and her colleagues Michael Geiser and Stephen Fertelmes bridge the worlds of publishing and Hollywood with remarkable ease and sophistication, and I'm lucky to be in their capable hands. By this point, LaQuishe Wright ("Q") has become an icon among social-media managers working in the entertainment business, but what makes her truly incomparable is her profound integrity and kindness. Q, thank you for sticking with me all these years. Mollie Smith, you have overseen every iteration of my Web presence, and thus the evolution of my fan outreach for decades, and you remain absolutely essential to me and my work. And to the team who translates all the fruits of my labor into dollars and cents, my accountants Pam Pope and Oscara Stevick, thank you for keeping my livelihood—and that of my family—safe and orderly over the decades.

Tia Scott-Shaver, Jeannie Armentrout, Jerrold, Linda, and Angie deserve my gratitude for their help in keeping my life running smoothly. Andy Sommers and Hannah Mensch keep an eye on big-picture items in my life with skill and aplomb, and for this, I'm grateful. Much love goes to Victoria Vodar.

And, of course, I'd be remiss if I didn't offer a note of appreciation for others as well. Many thanks go to my children—Miles, Ryan, Landon, Lexie, and Savannah—as well as my new granddaughter, Bristol Marie, for providing such joy over the years. To Sarah, Meadowe, and Brad: I love you all.

I'm also blessed to have a number of wonderful friends, including Bill and Pat Mills; David and Morgan Shara; Mike Smith; Christie Bonacci; Jeff and Torrie Van Wie; Jim and Karen Tyler; Todd and Gretchen Lanman; Tony and Shellie Spaedy; Kim and Eric Belcher; Lee and Sandi Minshull; Jonathan and Stephanie Arnold; Austin and Holly Butler; Bill Silva; Jeff Brown; Gray Zuerbregg; James Hickman; and Al Peterson, among others, all of whom have added joy to my life. I'd be remiss if I didn't further mention Paul Du Vair; Chris Matteo; Rick Mench; Kirk Pierce; Pete DeCler; Bob Jacob; Jeannine Kaspar; Joe Westermeyer; Ron Markezich; Shane O'Flaherty; Darryl Gordon; David Wang; Sandy Haddock; Ryan Seeger; Missy Blackerby; Ken Gray; Heather Cope; Dave Simpson; Maureen McDonnell; Joy Lenz; David Geffen; and Anja Schmeltzer as well. My life is blessed because of all of you.

And finally, my love and gratitude to everyone in my extended family. I pray for all of you every single day.

ABOUT THE AUTHOR

NICHOLAS SPARKS is the author of twenty-four books, all of which have been *New York Times* bestsellers. His books have been published across more than fifty languages with over 150 million copies sold worldwide, and eleven have been adapted into films. He is also the founder of the Nicholas Sparks Foundation, a nonprofit committed to improving cultural and international understanding through global education experiences. He lives in North Carolina.

nicholassparks.com

ABOUT THE TYPE

This book was set in Caslon, a typeface first designed in 1722 by William Caslon (1692–1766). Its widespread use by most English printers in the early eighteenth century soon supplanted the Dutch typefaces that had formerly prevailed. The roman is considered a "workhorse" typeface due to its pleasant, open appearance, while the italic is exceedingly decorative.